DO YOU TAKE THIS MAVERICK?

BY
MARIE FERRARELLA

Published in Great Britain 2015
by Mills & Boon, an imprint of Harlequin (UK) Limited,
Eton House, 18-24 Paradise Road, Richmond, Surrey, TW9 1SR

© 2015 Harlequin Books S.A

Special thanks and acknowledgement to Marie Ferrarella for her contribution to the Montana Mavericks: What Happened at the Wedding? series.

ISBN: 978-0-263-25158-6

23-0815

Harlequin (UK) Limited's policy is to use papers that are natural, renewable and recyclable products and made from wood grown in sustainable forests. The logging and manufacturing processes conform to the legal environmental regulations of the country of origin.

Printed and bound in Spain
by CPI, Barcelona

USA TODAY bestselling and RITA® Award-winning author **Marie Ferrarella** has written more than two hundred books for Mills & Boon, some under the name Marie Nicole. Her romances are beloved by fans worldwide. Visit her website, www.marieferrarella.com.

To Gail Chasan,
who is always in my corner.
Thank you.

Prologue

"I don't see what you're so mad about."

Levi Wyatt stared at his wife of two years in absolute confusion. The second he had opened the door and walked into their room, Claire had lit into him, reading him the riot act.

Granted, it was almost dawn and he had never stayed out anywhere *near* this late before, but that was no reason for Claire to be so upset.

This was definitely a side of his wife he had never seen before.

Industrious, ambitious and hardworking, Levi rarely, if ever, took any time off from his job at the furniture store. As the recently promoted store manager, most of the time he even worked on the weekends, but this weekend—the Fourth of July—he'd taken off to escort

Claire to a wedding in Rust Creek Falls. He could have skipped it, personally, but it seemed to be really important to Claire that he attend, too. Her grandparents were putting them up for the weekend at the boarding house that they ran.

The wedding was held in the town's park, and it was a great afternoon. The ceremony was crowded and joyous, the reception even more so. A few of the attendees had decided to get up a little friendly game of poker. Levi wasn't quite sure why, but he was *really* tempted by the game, so he'd joined in.

Since he, Claire and their eight-month-old daughter, Bekka, were all spending the weekend at the boarding house, he felt that Claire wouldn't lack for company while he was gone. Especially since Melba Strickland, Claire's grandma, had graciously offered to babysit so the couple could enjoy the wedding together. This seemed to be the perfect opportunity for him to knock off a little steam.

Besides, he noticed that Claire was busy talking to a woman she knew at the reception when he'd allowed himself to be lured away by the promise of a little harmless diversion.

It was only supposed to be for an hour—two tops.

It had run over.

Way over.

But that still wasn't any reason for Claire to explode this way.

"Oh, you don't, do you?" Claire cried heatedly. Up until this point she had managed to keep her ever-growing discontent under control. She'd never allowed Levi to even catch a glimpse of it, just as she wouldn't dream of letting him see her without her makeup on or with her hair looking anything but perfect. For Claire, it was all about maintaining the illusion of perfection. It always had been.

But tonight, for some reason, she was feeling rather light-headed, although all she'd had to drink at the reception was some of the wedding punch. Despite her petite frame, punch wouldn't affect her like this, she reasoned.

Still, because of her light-headedness, her discontent had slipped out of its usual restraints, and before she knew it, the second Levi had walked into their room at the boarding house, she was giving it to her husband with both barrels.

"No," Levi answered, standing his ground and waiting for Claire to say something that made sense to him, "I don't. I've been working really hard lately, putting in some really long hours. I came to the wedding because *you* wanted to come and when this poker game came up, I didn't see the harm in taking a little time off—"

"Didn't see the harm?" Claire echoed incredulously. Her eyes narrowed into angry, accusing slits. "No, you wouldn't, would you? Well, I'll tell you what the harm is. The harm is that you just walked off and left me— *again*." Not wanting to wake up anyone at the boarding house, she struggled to keep from shouting at him, but it wasn't easy.

"Again? What *again*?" he demanded, stunned. "Claire, what are you talking about? When did I leave you?"

Was he serious? He couldn't possibly be as clueless as he was pretending to be, could he?

"When *didn't* you leave me?" Claire countered, her anger all but running over like a boiling pot of water. "You're always going off out of town to some sales meetings or other. And if it's not a meeting, then it's a *seminar.*" She said the word as if it was a lie that he fed her. "I never get to see you anymore," she complained.

Levi felt his own temper surging, something that almost *never* happened. Ordinarily, he could put up with his wife's fluctuating moods, but right now he felt as if he'd had more than he could stand.

"You're seeing me now." Levi spread his hands wide, as if to highlight his presence. "I'm standing right here," he pointed out.

Was he mocking her? His attitude just kept fueling her anger. "You know what I mean."

"No, I *don't* know what you mean," he told her, feeling more and more bewildered and put upon by the second. "I'm going to those sales meetings and seminars because my job demands it. I'm doing it for you and the baby," Levi stressed.

But Claire saw it differently. "You're doing it to get *away* from me and the baby."

Levi blew out a long breath as he gave up. There was no reasoning with her. "You're tired, you don't know what you're saying," Levi concluded, feeling rather desperate. He just wanted this to stop.

Her big brown eyes—eyes he had fallen in love with

the first time he saw her—were all but shooting daggers at him. "Oh, so now I'm just crazy?"

Where had that come from? "I didn't say that," Levi insisted.

She was twisting everything, he thought helplessly. He felt as if he had stepped into quicksand and was sinking fast, no matter how hard he tried to pull himself free.

"Maybe you didn't *say* it but that's what you implied," Claire retorted haughtily. "And who could blame me if I was crazy—which I'm *not*," Claire underscored. "The only one I get to talk to all day is a colicky, crying baby. Don't get me wrong, Levi, I love Bekka, but you're never around." It was an angry accusation, one she dared him to deny.

"Yes, I am," Levi insisted. "I come home to you every night," Levi told her.

"Sure, you come home," she jeered. "You come home to fall into bed, dead asleep before your head hits the pillow."

"I put in long hours, Claire, and I'm tired," Levi tried to explain.

Claire's back went up as she instantly took offense at what she thought he was implying. "Oh, and I don't and I'm not?"

Levi threw up his hands, thoroughly frustrated. He had stayed longer at the game than he had intended and lost money, to boot. He hadn't meant for any of that to happen. He wasn't really sure *why* it had happened. But he knew that her anger was way out of proportion.

"Look, let's not get into this now," he pleaded. "I'm sorry, okay?"

"No, it's not okay—and you're not sorry," she told him angrily. "But I am. I'm sorry I ever met you. I'm sorry I ever married you!"

Levi was close to being speechless. "Claire, what are you saying?"

Heightened fury was all but etched into her fine features and had colored her cheeks to a bright shade of pink.

"What I'm saying is that it's over," she retorted furiously. "I made a mistake. We *both* made a mistake. We should have never gotten married in the first place."

All this because he stayed out playing poker too long? He couldn't believe what he was hearing. "Claire—"

"Get out!" she cried. Circling him, she put her hands on his back and started pushing him out the door into the hallway. "Get out now!"

"Claire—" It was all Levi could get out of his mouth. He was completely stunned and unable to even understand how they had gotten to this impasse so quickly.

"Now!" she yelled, managing to shove him out all the way only because she had caught him so completely off guard.

The second he was across the threshold and in the hall, Claire pulled off her wedding ring.

"Here, I don't want this anymore, either!" she cried, throwing her wedding ring at him.

The next second she slammed the door shut behind him.

He heard the *click* and knew she'd flipped the lock. Claire had the only key.

Levi stood there in front of the door to their room for several moments, dazed and wondering if he was hallucinating all this for some reason. What had just happened seemed to have come out of nowhere.

This trip was supposed to have picked up Claire's spirits. Instead, he felt that he had just witnessed his marriage falling apart.

What the hell had just happened here? Levi wondered. He hadn't a clue.

As he walked away from the door, Levi heard Bekka beginning to wail from inside the room.

"You and me both, kid," he murmured under his breath. "You and me both."

Chapter One

Almost a month had gone by since the disastrous night of the wedding, and Levi *still* didn't know exactly what had happened. What he did know was that he wanted his wife back.

He missed her.

Missed the baby.

Missed being a married man more than he had ever thought possible.

In one all-too-quick swoop his orderly world had fallen into a state of formless chaos, and he absolutely hated it. He felt directionless. When he and Claire had been together, his life had had purpose, he'd had goals. Now he was just blindly going from one end of the day to the other. He still showed up for work at the furniture store every morning, but he lacked his usual energy, feeling lost and so alone that he literally ached.

Without Claire, absolutely nothing seemed to make any sense to him anymore.

Initially, as he had walked back to his truck right after Claire had thrown him out, his own anger at what he felt was her uncalled-for reaction to his late arrival continued to grow—along with his confusion. Why had she blown a gasket? After all, he'd just been playing poker with some of the guys he'd met at the wedding, not playing around with some little flirt.

He knew lots of men who took any opportunity to cheat on their wives, claiming that marriage hemmed them in, and that they needed something besides the "same old piece of stale cake" to get their adrenaline flowing.

But he wasn't like that. And he certainly didn't feel that way about his marriage.

The moment that he had first laid eyes on Claire in that cute little sundress she'd been wearing the day they met, peering into the show window of the furniture store where he worked, he had fallen for her like the proverbial ton of bricks. He'd even taken the initiative and gone outside the store to tell her that the set she was looking at was on sale. It really wasn't. He'd made that up just to have an excuse to talk to her.

Had she actually wanted to buy that set, he would have had to come up with the difference out of his own pocket, but he was so taken with her, he would have done it and gladly. The way he saw it, it would have been more than worth it to him.

From that day forward, Claire Strickland had always been the only girl for him. He'd loved her so much, he'd been willing to wait until she graduated from college before they got married. In fact, he'd insisted on it. First the degree, then the ring. Because it was best for her, and he didn't want to be the reason she had dropped out of college. From the first moment he met her, it had always been about what was best for her. He felt that she brought out the best in him.

And now he had lost her…and he wasn't even sure *why*.

He could still see that look on her face as she'd pushed him out of the room. She'd been so angry at him, and he hadn't done anything to warrant that degree of fury. One of the men in the game had actually bet and lost the house he was living in. Now *that* was stupid.

What would have been her reaction if he'd done something like *that*?

Trying to be optimistic, Levi had hoped that whatever had gotten her angry to this degree would blow over once they got back home.

But when they *did* get back home—she'd had her grandmother drive her and Bekka home while he'd driven himself—he'd found that his belongings had all been thrown out on the lawn in front of their apartment.

This, in addition to having thrown her wedding ring at him, made the message clear.

It was over.

Except that he didn't want it to be.

Desperate, thinking that maybe she needed a little bit of time to come around, he gave Claire her space. By definition, that required his staying out of her way, so he'd bedded down in the storeroom at the furniture store. He alternated between that and spending the night in his truck. It was August so at least he didn't have to worry about cold weather. But that was small consolation in the face of what was going on in his life.

With each passing day, he kept hoping that Claire would relent and take him back. But she never came to the store, never answered the phone when he called, even though he called her at least three times a day, if not more. For all intents and purposes, Claire was acting as if he didn't exist.

And it was killing him.

Frustrated, Levi decided that enough was enough and went to the apartment where they'd lived for the past two years for a face-to-face confrontation with Claire.

But as he drove up, he saw that there were no lights on in the window to greet him, and he had a very uneasy feeling as he unlocked the front door.

Holding his breath, praying he was wrong, Levi cautiously walked in.

"Claire? Claire, it's me. Levi. Your husband," he added uncertainly. Nothing but silence answered him. "Claire," he called out, "where are you?"

Still nothing. Nothing but the hollow echo of his own voice.

Growing progressively more agitated as well as aggravated, Levi went from room to small room, looking for his wife, for his baby. Finding neither.

"Come on, Claire, this isn't funny anymore. Where *are* you?"

Nervous now, he debated calling Claire's parents. He didn't want to worry them, but then on the other hand, there might be a chance that they knew where their daughter and granddaughter were.

They might even be staying with her parents, for that matter.

He took out his cell phone and was all set to press the appropriate numbers on the keypad, but then he paused, thinking. Maybe calling her parents wasn't such a good idea after all.

Claire's parents, Peter and Donna Strickland, had initially been very hesitant about their daughter getting involved with someone who was several years older than she was and who didn't have a college education. It had taken him a bit of doing to win them over.

But after her parents saw how much he really loved their youngest daughter, how he'd treated her as if she were made out of pure spun gold, they came around and gave their blessings. The older couple, who had been going strong for the past thirty years, had one of those rare, really happy marriages and according to Peter Strickland, they saw no reason why Claire and he couldn't have one, too.

If he called them, asking after Claire, then her parents would realize that they were having marital problems. He had a feeling that Claire *wouldn't* tell her parents what was going on. Because if she did, it was as good as admitting that their initial concerns about her getting married had been right. That he *wasn't* good enough for her. And even though she might actually believe that, he knew Claire well enough to know that she wouldn't readily admit that fact to her parents.

Who did that leave? he thought as he wandered around the empty apartment.

There were her two older sisters, Hadley and Tessa, but they were both professional career women who lived and worked in Bozeman, Montana, too. If Claire called either one of them, asking to be taken in, that would be as good as admitting failure, and she wouldn't do that. There was just the slightest bit of competitiveness among the sisters—at least as far as Claire was concerned.

No, she wouldn't call either one of her sisters, either. She would have rather died than allow her sisters to know that her marriage was in jeopardy.

But she had to call somebody, Levi reasoned. Claire couldn't opt to go it alone. She had the baby to think of.

The answer suddenly came to him. Of course. Claire would have turned to her grandparents for emotional support.

Her grandmother, Melba, was a lively, full-steam-ahead woman who had raised four children, including Claire's father, and had still managed to be a businesswoman. She and her husband, Gene, ran the Strickland Boarding House, where he and Claire had stayed when they'd attended the wedding that had ultimately torn them apart.

Claire admired her grandmother, so it was only natural that she would turn to the older woman. And, as he recalled, the crusty Gene Strickland really doted on his granddaughter and her baby girl, too.

Levi was by nature a private person. He had never gone to anyone with his hat in his hand before, pleading his case, but then, he'd never been in this sort of a situation before, either. He wanted his wife and his daughter back in the worst way. Getting them back meant more to him than his pride, even though the latter was a difficult thing for him to swallow.

But he'd do it. To get Claire back into his life, he'd do whatever was necessary.

Levi slowly looked around the apartment. Claire's clothes were gone. The closets were empty on her side.

He knew that since Claire *was* gone, he could stay here again. The familiar surroundings were infinitely more comfortable than bedding down in the storeroom or utilizing the flatbed of his truck.

But staying here wasn't going to get him any closer to Claire. He needed to go into work every day—taking any more time off was out of the question since the store was introducing a new line of furniture and he was needed to handle whatever problems might come up. That meant that in his off hours, he needed to maintain close proximity to Claire. So he needed to stay somewhere close by to where she was staying.

And that, he concluded, would most likely have to

be at the boarding house. There'd been a couple of vacancies there last month when they were there for that damn wedding.

And even if there hadn't been, her grandfather was the type to find a way to make room for his granddaughter and his great-granddaughter even if it meant that *he* had to go sleep in his car. Gene Strickland would have thought nothing of it if doing so meant helping out Claire.

He needed to go see her grandparents, Levi decided. Her grandmother wasn't exactly a fan of his—the woman had made no bones about telling him that she thought Claire was too young to get married the first time she met him. But he did get along with Gene. If he could win the man over to his side in this, he'd have a fighting chance of winning Claire back, he reasoned.

Taking one last long look around, Levi closed and locked the front door behind him—fervently hoping that it wasn't for the last time.

How had she gone from feeling like a fairy-tale princess to being Cinderella before the fairy godmother had come into the picture in such a short amount of time?

Claire asked herself that question for the umpteenth time since she had come to her grandparents, asking if she could move into the boarding house until she could get on her feet again.

She could remember the way her grandmother had looked at her that day. Melba Strickland had never been what could be called a sentimental woman by any stretch of the imagination. But the woman was fair and she was family, which was what Claire felt she needed at a time like this.

At the time, her grandfather, a somewhat crusty bear of a man, had asked her, "What's wrong with your place?"

That was where she had broken down and cried. "I don't have a place anymore, Grandpa. I've left Levi."

"Left him?" Taking the fussing Bekka into his own arms, Gene cooed a few syllables at the baby, calming her down, and then looked at his granddaughter incredulously. "Don't you just mean that you've had a lovers' spat?"

Claire shook her head, unable to speak for a moment. When she finally could, she showed the two her bare left ring finger and said, "No, not a *lovers' spat*, Grandpa. Levi and I are separated." She took a ragged breath, telling herself that saying the words didn't hurt—but it did. She felt as if a jagged knife had just ripped through her heart. "We're getting divorced."

"Now hold on there, that's a big word, honey," Gene had told her. "Do you know what it means?"

Melba had frowned at her husband, annoyed. "Of course she knows what it means." And then she turned toward her granddaughter. "What happened, Claire? Did he disrespect you?" Her expression suddenly darkened. "He didn't lay a hand on you, did he? Because if he did, your grandfather is going to kill him."

Claire had struggled to keep her sobs from surfacing. "No, he didn't lay a hand on me, Grandmother."

"Then what happened? Why are you divorcing him?" Melba had demanded in her no-nonsense tone.

But Claire just shook her head, waving away the question. She had no intentions of reiterating the incident. She knew she'd break down before she even got to the middle of the story.

"It doesn't matter what happened. We're getting divorced. It's over," she told her grandparents with finality, her voice catching at the end.

For a moment she thought she was going to burst into sobs, but she managed to get herself under control at the last second.

Melba shot her husband a knowing look that all but shouted, "I told you so."

"I *knew* you were too young to get married." Although it was a declaration, there had been no triumph in Melba's voice. "You haven't had a chance to live yet. After graduating college, you're supposed to sample life a little. Travel. Do things, not tie yourself down with a marriage and a baby." She looked at her granddaughter knowingly. "Neither one of you was ready for that, especially not you."

"Melba," Gene warned, giving her a look that told her to keep her piece.

As headstrong and independent as ever, Melba was not about to listen. Hands on her hips, the diminutive woman turned on her husband. "Don't *Melba* me, Gene. She *wasn't* ready."

The steely older woman looked at her granddaughter, then, after a moment, she enfolded the girl in her arms. Melba's intentions were obviously good, but it still made for a rather awkward moment.

"Oh, Claire," Melba said with a sigh, "you wound up setting yourself up. Marriage isn't some magical, happily-ever-after state. At best it's an ongoing work in progress."

"I'll say," Gene chuckled, his chest moving up and down with the deep rumble. It managed to entertain Bekka, who in turn gurgled her approval. "The first hundred years are the hardest, honey," he told his granddaughter with a twinkle in his eye. "After that it gets easier. But you have to invest the time."

Claire had sniffled then, doing her best not to cry. Doing her best to face the rest of her life stoically. "That's all water under the bridge, Grandpa. I threw Levi out." That had been two days ago. "It's over."

Melba's dark eyebrows drew together in a puzzled single line. "If you threw Levi out, what are you doing here?"

Claire shook her head. "Well, it's his apartment. I can't stay there now. Everywhere I look—the kitchen, the closet, our bedroom—I can see him. It's just too hard for me to take."

Gene had glanced over toward his wife as if he knew that Melba was obviously going to say something that would echo the voice of reason—and be utterly practical. But Claire didn't need *practical*. What she needed—rather desperately, if the look in her eyes was any gauge—was understanding.

In order to forestall his wife and whatever it was

that she was going to say, Gene quickly spoke up, trying to stop whatever words were going to come out of Melba's mouth.

"Claire-bear," he said, addressing his granddaughter by the nickname he'd given her when she was about a month old, "You can stay here as long as you like. As it so happens, we've got a couple of vacancies, and it's been a long time since your grandmother and I have heard the sound of little running feet."

"Bekka is only eight months old, Grandpa. She doesn't even walk yet, much less run," Claire reminded her grandfather.

What her daughter did do, almost all night long, was fuss and cry. Another reason that she felt so worn out, hemmed in and trapped, Claire thought, struggling not to be resentful.

Her hostile feelings were redirected toward her husband. If he had been there to share in the responsibility, if he would have taken his turn walking the floor with the baby, then she wouldn't have felt as exhausted and out of sorts as she did.

"But she will," Gene was telling her. "She will and when she does, we'll be there to make sure she doesn't hurt herself, won't we, Mel?" he said, turning toward his wife.

"Sure. And the boarding house will just run itself," Melba commented sarcastically.

Gene shook his head as he looked at his granddaughter. "Don't mind your grandmother. She always sees the downside of things. Me, I see the upside." He winked at Claire. "That's why our marriage works."

"That's why your grandfather is a cockeyed optimist," Melba corrected.

For the sake of peace, Gene ignored his wife's comment. Instead, he said to Claire, "Like I said, you can stay here as long as you like." He turned toward the staircase, still holding Bekka in his arms. "Come on, we'll get you and the princess here settled in."

"I'll pay for the room, Grandmother," Claire had said, looking over her shoulder at Melba.

"You'll do no such thing," Gene informed her. "Family doesn't pay."

"But family pitches in," Melba had interjected. "We'll find something for you to do here at the boarding house, Claire."

"Anything," Claire had offered.

"How's your cooking?" Melba asked her. "I need someone to pick up the slack when Gina is busy," she elaborated, referring to the cook she'd recently hired. "I'm giving having someone else handling the cooking a try. I've already got a lot to keep me busy."

"Anything but that," Claire had amended almost sheepishly. "I'm afraid I still haven't gotten the hang of cooking." And then she brightened. "But I can make beds," she volunteered.

"This is a boarding house, Claire, not a bed-and-breakfast. People here make their own beds," Melba informed her matter-of-factly.

"Don't worry," Gene had said, putting one arm

around his granddaughter's shoulders as he held his great-granddaughter against him with the other, "We'll come up with something for you to do until you find your way."

Claire had sighed then, leaning into him as she had done on so many occasions when she had been a little girl, growing up.

"I hope so, Grandpa," Claire said, doing her best to sound cheerful. "I really hope so."

Chapter Two

Gene Strickland tried to ignore it, but even after all these years of marriage, he hadn't found a way to go about things as if everything was all right when it wasn't. His wife's scowl—which was aimed directly at him and had been an ongoing thing now for the past two weeks—seemed to go clean down to the bone. There was no use pretending that it didn't.

So he didn't even try.

Pushing aside the monthly inventory he was in the process of updating in connection with the boarding house's current supplies, Gene asked, "Okay, woman. Out with it. What's got your panties all in a twist like this?"

Brooding dark brown eyes looked at him accusingly from across the large scarred oak desk they both shared in the corner room that served as an office.

"As if you don't know," she muttered under her breath, but clearly enough for Gene to hear.

"No, I don't know," he'd informed her. "I'd like to think that I'd have the good sense *not* to ask if I knew. I've been with you long enough to know that lots of things set you off and right now, I don't want to risk bringing up any of them."

Melba pursed her lips as her eyes held his. "You're coddling her."

"Her?" Gene echoed innocently.

"Yes, *her*. Claire," she finally said. "Don't play dumb with me," Melba warned. "You know damn well that I'm talking about our granddaughter, Gene."

Unable to properly focus on the inventory while his wife was talking, Gene put down his pen and shook his head. This whole thing with Claire had hit Melba hard, he thought. He had a feeling that his wife blamed herself for not speaking up more to change Claire's mind about marrying so young. Or, at the very least, getting Claire to wait another year or so before leaping into marriage. But they all knew that the young never listened to the old, he thought, resigned.

Melba needed to change her opinion about Claire's marriage as well.

Especially since he was going to have to let her in on a secret he would have rather not had to divulge. However, if Melba found out about this on her own—and she had a knack for doing that—then Claire and Levi's marriage might not be the only one in trouble.

"Claire's going through a really rough patch right now, Mel."

"I know that," the old woman snapped. "And she needs a backbone to get through it, not to be treated as if she was made out of spun glass and could break at any second. She *needs* to toughen up." The very thought of a fragile granddaughter exasperated Melba beyond words. "Her parents were just too soft on her. If it were me, I would have never given my permission for those two to get married two years ago."

"Two years ago she wasn't a minor anymore, Mel," Gene gently reminded her. "Legally, she could make her own decisions," the man pointed out.

Melba threw up her hands. "And look how great that turned out for her," she huffed.

Gene thought of the newest boarder he'd just taken in—without his wife's knowledge, certainly without her permission.

Time to lay some groundwork, he told himself.

"Story's not over yet, Mel. There's a second act coming. I just know it. Just remember," he told her, making eye contact with the woman he had slept beside for five decades, "not everyone has an iron resolve like you." Gene leaned over and kissed his wife's temple.

"Don't try to sweet-talk me into going soft, Gene Strickland," Melba snapped—but with less verve.

It was obvious that even that small a kiss had her lighting up in response. They had a connection, she and Gene. The kind that poets used to celebrate in their works. And spats or not, the warranty on that connection hadn't expired yet.

"I wouldn't dream of it," he told her with a straight face. "As a matter of fact, I'm appealing to the businesswoman in you."

Melba looked at her husband, somewhat confused. Where was all this going? "What's that supposed to mean?" she wanted to know.

"Well, you're a savvy businesswoman, aren't you, Mel?" he asked.

"I like to think so," she said guardedly, watching her husband as if she expected him to pull a rabbit out of a hat or something equally as predictable, yet at bottom, magical. "Okay, out with it. Just where are you going with this?"

He built the blocks up slowly. "Being a good businesswoman means that you like to make money, true?"

"Yes, yes, we already know this," she told her husband impatiently. Everyone knew she loved making money, loved the challenge of running the boarding house efficiently. Having half a dozen adults—or so—in one place presented a great many hurdles to clear. But so far she was managing to run the place very successfully. "Get to the point. Sometime before next Christmas would be nice."

He approached the heart of this matter cautiously, determined to set up a strong foundation first. "A good businesswoman wouldn't allow personal prejudices to get in the way of her making a good-size profit."

Though Gene had argued against it, Levi had insisted

on paying more than the usual going rate for the room. Most likely in an effort to appeal to the entrepreneur in Melba when she learned of his being there.

"A good-size profit," she repeated. "What are you getting us into, Gene?" she wanted to know, eyeing her husband suspiciously. Usually, she could rely on him to ultimately come through at the end of the day, doing nothing to jeopardize their way of life or their income. But he was making her nervous now with his vague innuendos. Just exactly what did the man have up his sleeve?

"Making money in what way?" she asked her husband when he didn't answer her question.

"By renting out the last available room in the boarding house for more than the usual rate," he told her with just a shade too much innocence to satisfy Melba.

"What are you trying to say, Gene? Come on, spit it out," she ordered. "Just who is it that you're renting out this last room to?" she demanded. And then, just before her husband could give her an answer, a look of horrified indignation washed over the older woman's features. "Oh no, you can't mean to tell me—"

Her voice had gone up so high that it completely vanished at its peak.

Wanting to get this out and then, hopefully, put to rest, Gene supplied the name that Melba seemed incapable of uttering.

"Levi. Claire's husband. Yes, I rented it out to him," he told her with an air of finality that let her know that she was not allowed to toss the young man out on his ear under *any* circumstances.

Melba glared at him. "Have you gone and lost your mind, Gene?"

The heated accusation did *not* surprise him. "Not that I know of, no. Last I checked, it was still where it was supposed to be. Right between my ears—same as yours, Mel."

"Then why aren't you using it?" Melba wanted to know. Because the man was certainly acting as if he had lost his mind.

"I thought I was," he told her simply. "Not to mention my heart," he added pointedly.

"Claire came here to get away from that man," Melba reminded her husband. "Or did you somehow forget that little fact?"

"No, I didn't forget that," he replied calmly. "And since when did you condone cowardice?" Gene wanted to know.

The accusation instantly stirred her up. "What are you talking about?" Melba demanded heatedly. "I am most certainly *not* condoning cowardice."

He gave her a skeptical look. "Then what would you call letting her run away from her situation instead of facing up to it and trying to resolve it?"

Melba's scowl deepened, even though it didn't seem physically possible for it to become any deeper than it already was. She debated giving her husband the silent treatment, but the words were burning on her tongue, and she knew she'd have no peace until this was resolved and she said what had been—and still was—on her mind.

"You and I both know that she married too young," she said to Gene.

Gene gave her a knowing look. "As I recall, she was the same age as you were when we got married." Apparently, that little fact had escaped his wife.

"Don't compare us," Melba retorted. "I was years older emotionally."

He tended to agree with her—although there were times when he felt Melba was too young to make competent decisions even at this age. Not that he would ever dare to tell her that.

"Be that as it may," Gene told her, "Levi's a good man, Mel, and he loves her." It was clear that he believed the couple should take another shot at recapturing the magic that had brought them together and had existed in the first months of their marriage.

"Love alone never solved anything," Melba retorted.

Gene gave her a sly, knowing look. "Maybe not, but it sure gave us something to look forward to on those cold, long nights. Remember?"

Melba pressed her lips together and swatted her husband's arm. She could feel her cheeks warming. "Behave yourself, Gene."

Gene chuckled, amused. "You don't really mean that and you know it," he told her.

The impish, sexy look he gave her melted the years away and brought them both back to a time when the only aches they felt involved their hearts and striving to be together over her parents' wishes otherwise.

Rising from his side of the desk, he circled around to where his wife was sitting. Hands bracketing her shoulders, he brought her up to her feet before him. Melba was a small woman. Her bombastic personality made him forget that at times. In reality, Gene all but dwarfed her when he stood beside his wife.

Height difference notwithstanding, Melba filled up his whole world and had from the moment he'd first met her.

"Give him a chance, Mel," he requested. "Give *them both* a chance to work this out."

Melba thought of how hurt Claire had been when she first came to them. How hurt she still seemed to be. "And if she doesn't want to?" she challenged.

"I have a feeling that she does," Gene told her confidently. He saw the skeptical look come over her face and said, "They have a daughter and four years invested in one another, two of them as a married couple. They've simply run into some turbulence just like a lot of other couples, but abandoning ship isn't the answer. If they do, if they don't try to make this work, they'll never forgive each other—or themselves."

Melba frowned, looking at her husband as if for the first time. "Since when did you get to be such a hopeless romantic?" she wanted to know.

That was an easy one to answer. "Since I married the most beautiful girl at the dance," he told her.

Melba huffed and shook her head. Her husband's answer both surprised her and pleased her, but she couldn't let him see that. If she did, she felt that she'd lose the upper hand in their relationship.

"Fine, Levi can stay," she informed him. "But he pays rent like everyone else," she warned. This wasn't a charity mission she was running here, she thought.

Levi had been one step ahead of Melba, Gene now thought. Insisting on paying more than the usual rate had been very smart of him. "I told you, that was already part of the deal."

Melba looked far from pleased. The scowl on her face not only remained, it deepened, too. "One wrong move and he's out of here."

"Understood." Gene paused, allowing her to savor her moment before he decided to bedevil her a little and asked, "Define *wrong move.*"

She was at a disadvantage and not thinking as clearly as she should, Melba realized. Her mind was already on other matters that concerned the boarding house.

She chose the vague way out.

"You'll know it when you see it," she snapped. "Now I have to see if Gina has gotten dinner started," she told him, referring to the boarding-house cook. To that end, Melba shrugged off her husband's large, capable hands from about her shoulders. "One wrong move," she repeated warningly just before she left the room.

"Hard to believe that woman once had what I took to be a soft heart underneath all that," Gene said out loud to the other occupant of the area once his wife had left the room.

Turning around he looked at the young man he knew had been standing in the shadows of the hallway until the matter of his staying at the boarding house had been resolved. He was a little bit afraid of Melba—as were they all.

"But she does," Gene affirmed.

Levi looked off in the direction the woman had gone in. "She doesn't like me very much, does she?"

It wasn't a question so much as an observation on Levi's part.

"She likes you fine, boy," Gene assured him. "What she doesn't like is the situation. She's very protective of the people she loves, kind of like a lioness guarding her cubs. And there is no second-guessing her moves." He looked pointedly at his granddaughter's husband. "Consider yourself warned."

Levi nodded. "Yes, sir. And I appreciate you taking my side in this," he said with genuine gratitude and feeling.

"Not taking sides," Gene corrected the younger man. "Just facilitating things so that they can move ahead if that's what's in the cards. I think that little girl loves you," Gene told the young man who had come to him with his hat in his hand as well as his heart on his sleeve. "The problem is that she just got really overwhelmed by everything.

"People figure that getting married and having babies is no big deal—but it is. It's a *huge* deal, and there's a lot of adjusting to be done by everybody. You impress me as a sensible, hardworking young man, and I can tell that you love Claire—just like I can tell that she loves you. But she expected that life would go on being one great big party, and that's just not so. Marriage takes work and sacrifice. That's the part people forget about. If you find someone you love, there always comes a time when you have to fight for them. And that's a good thing in the long run because nothing that's precious gets that way if it's too easy."

Levi nodded. "I'm willing to fight for Claire until my dying breath."

"Nobody's talking about dying, boy," Gene told him, clapping one hand against Levi's broad shoulders. "Now come with me. I've got some things in the basement I need moved around and brought up to the kitchen. I could use a hand with them."

"Absolutely," Levi responded eagerly, wanting nothing more than to try to pay the man back in some small way for his kindness in allowing him this chance to win back the only woman he had ever loved.

Not a day went by when Claire didn't regret all the hot words that just seemed to fly out of her mouth on their own accord that fateful morning after the wedding reception. Most of all, she regretted throwing Levi out—and throwing her wedding ring at him. But she had been so angry and so hurt that he had preferred a stupid card game to being with her, she'd lost all reason. She'd been so furious, she was almost blinded by it.

At first she'd been so angry, she felt justified in leaving his phone calls unanswered.

But then he'd stopped calling.

Which meant to her that he had stopped caring. Because if Levi cared, he would have upped the number of his calls, not stopped them so abruptly. If he cared about her, truly cared, he would have come looking for her and wouldn't have stopped—not to eat or drink or sleep—until he found her. And then he would have gone on to move heaven and earth to win her back.

Since none of that, heretofore, had happened, nor did it appear to be happening, it just told her that she was right.

Levi *didn't* care anymore.

Well, if he didn't care anymore, then she didn't, either.

Except that she did.

She cared so much, she literally hurt inside. Which just served to make her feel as if she was a fool. Only a fool pined for someone who wasn't worth it, she argued over and over again.

What she needed to do, she told herself at least once a day, was to forget all about Levi and just move on, the way normal people did.

But how could she forget about him when every time she looked down into her daughter's face, she saw traces of Levi?

How could she move on when every morning began with thoughts of Levi? And every night ended that way, as well?

How could she forget about Levi when, in her head, she kept hearing his voice? Seeing his face? Everywhere she turned, she could swear he'd been there, or even *was* there.

She felt haunted, and with each day it was just getting worse, not better.

"Okay, today is the first day of the rest of your life, and you are going to stop this," Claire ordered her reflection in the mirror over the bureau. "You are going to take your adorable baby and march right out that door and into the rest of your life. A life without boundaries and without Levi."

Easier said than done, a little voice said in her head.

Still, she couldn't just live her life standing here in this room, staring at her reflection, too afraid to venture out.

"The hell I am," she declared out loud with enthusiasm.

So resolved, she took her baby daughter into her arms, rested Bekka on her hip and walked out of her room and into the rest of her life, or so she wanted to believe.

Unfortunately, as she all but marched into the hallway, she also walked straight into the person she was trying most to avoid.

She walked straight into Levi.

Chapter Three

Caught completely off guard, Claire shrieked.

Her breath caught in her throat as she felt her heart—an organ she had become painfully aware of in the past month—slam against her rib cage.

Stunned, she blinked, fully expecting Levi to fade away, a mere wistful product of her overactive imagination.

He didn't fade away. Levi remained exactly where he was, standing in front of her, holding on to her shoulders to keep her from falling.

He'd been hoping to run into her, but not quite like this and definitely not so literally.

Reacting automatically, Levi had grabbed his wife by the shoulders to steady her. That turned out to be a good thing, seeing how if he hadn't, Claire would have probably stumbled backward and fallen while still holding Bekka tightly against her.

Holding on to Claire like this did more than just prevent a very unfortunate accident from happening. The exceedingly brief contact once again brought home the fact that he'd missed her. Missed his wife acutely. Missed the sight of her, the *feel* of her. The very first time he'd laid eyes on her, he'd *known*. Known that Claire Strickland was the one for him. Known that there was something very special going on between them.

The chemistry that all but sizzled whenever they were close to one another was just too hard to miss and too intense to ignore. At that moment he'd realized that he would have rather waited forever for Claire than settled for anyone else, no matter how willing she might have been to be in a relationship with him.

Claire was completely shaken. It took everything she had not to visibly tremble. Ever since she had thrown her husband out of her life, her nights had been filled with Levi.

Filled with dreams of him, with memories of him.

Filled with overwhelming longing for him.

In the privacy of the room she and Bekka were living in, she'd allowed herself to cry over a precious relationship that she believed in her heart had died—and it was her fault.

Bumping into Levi like this, in the last place in the world she'd thought that she would see him, her first reaction was a surge of sheer joy, not to mention that every fiber of her being had instantly—physically—

responded to the very sight of him. At that moment she would have thrown her arms around Levi's neck if her arms had been free.

The next moment her sanity, as she chose to view it, returned.

Luckily for her, she realized, her arms were filled with baby, so she couldn't go with her first impulse. That allowed her second impulse to take root and swiftly take over. Her second impulse belonged to the young woman who had felt hurt and abandoned that fateful night a month ago. It belonged to the young woman whose husband was absent a good deal of the time—not to mention that the one time he wasn't absent, he'd turned his back on her, choosing a stupid poker game over her company. That made the whole thing even worse because he'd abandoned her without so much as a second thought, as if she were some inconsequential afterthought in his life.

As that realization had taken root, Claire felt that she had to be worthless and unattractive in his eyes. This despite the fact that she had *always* made sure that she was her most attractive before he laid eyes on her in the morning. Even before she'd said "I do" she was determined not to turn into one of those wives who allowed herself to let her appearance go after the wedding.

To that end, Claire made sure that she was always up before Levi so that she could put on her makeup and be flawlessly beautiful when her husband looked at her first thing in the morning.

It wasn't always easy, but she'd managed. Her

makeup was flawless. The same went for her hair. Not a single strand was out of place, despite the demands of motherhood, made that much more acute by a colicky baby.

Claire's first priority was to make sure that she was just as attractive to her husband on an everyday basis as she had been the first time he'd seen her.

And where had that gotten her? Abandoned for the first night they'd had baby-free in eight months, that's where, she thought angrily.

The honeymoon, Claire thought not for the first time, was definitely over and so was, by default, their marriage.

Claire pressed her lips together, suppressing a sob. She just wished she didn't still want Levi so damn much. Levi was a fantastic, thoughtful lover. She had no need to go through a litany of others to know just how very special he was. Her heart—and her body— told her so.

But even so, she refused to allow herself to be a needy woman in that respect.

Refused to allow Levi to see the advantage he had over her.

Finally finding her voice, she demanded, "What are you doing here?" as she shrugged out of his grasp.

The second he was sure that Claire was steady on her feet, he dropped his hands from her shoulders. Making eye contact with his daughter, he winked at her.

Placing her hand so that she blocked the baby's line

of vision, Claire turned so that Bekka was against her and not between them.

Levi squelched the protest that rose to his lips. The only way he was going to get Claire back was not to antagonize her any further. That entailed walking on eggshells, but, seeing what was at stake, he was up to it. He had to be.

"I'm staying here for a while," he told her.

Claire's eyes widened in disbelief. Levi had never lied to her before—but he had to be lying now. There was no other explanation for what he had just said.

"No, you're not," she cried. Why was he messing with her mind like this? Wasn't it enough that he had ripped her heart right out of her chest?

"Yes, I am," he contradicted. "I convinced your grandfather to rent a room to me."

Claire felt as if someone had just literally yanked a rug out from under her feet and sent her crashing down to the floor.

Her grandfather wouldn't do that to her—would he? As early as this morning, she would have confidently maintained that her grandfather wouldn't rent Levi a room because he knew how much it would upset her—not to mention that allowing Levi to stay at the boarding house would effectively negate the very reason she was staying here instead of in the two-bedroom apartment that she had shared with Levi.

But now, looking at the confident expression on her estranged husband's face, she no longer knew if what he was telling her was a pack of lies—or actually the truth.

The look in her eyes dared him to continue with what she viewed as his fabrication. "Why would my grandfather do that?" she demanded.

It took everything Levi had in him not to just sweep her into his arms and kiss her, baby and all. But he knew he couldn't force this. For now he had to be satisfied with giving her his most sincere look as he pleaded his case, laying it at her feet. "Maybe your grandfather sees how much you mean to me."

Was he still doing this? Still perpetuating the lie he had tried to sell her in the wee hours of the morning when he had come stumbling in after the wedding reception had long been over? She was no more inclined to believe him now than she had been then.

Less, in fact.

There was no way she was going to let Levi think that she bought his story.

"Ha! If I meant anything to you, you'd be around more often, not working at all hours, going out of town for so-called meetings at the drop of a hat and going off to play poker when we were supposed to be spending time together on our first free night in months."

"We *were* spending time together," Levi insisted. "We went to the wedding together."

How gullible did he think she was? "*I* was in a room with a crying baby while *you* were at a poker table surrounded by your friends and playing cards until dawn. Just how is that being *together*?" Claire demanded hotly. Bekka began to fuss, and Claire automatically started to rock the baby to try and soothe her.

"Okay," Levi conceded. "But up to that point, we were together," he reminded her.

Stressed out, Claire began to pat the baby's bottom, trying desperately to calm her down.

"That *was* the whole point," she informed Levi. "After the wedding we were supposed to spend some quality time together," she insisted. "My grandparents were taking care of Bekka. You and I were supposed to spend a nice, romantic evening together."

"How was I to know that? You didn't tell me," Levi pointed out.

Claire stared at him, stunned. He couldn't have been that thickheaded—could he?

"I shouldn't *have* to tell you," she cried. "You're supposed to have *wanted* that on your own, not had me force-feed you your lines or hold up a cue card for you."

The only way he could think to backtrack out of the potential explosion in the making he saw coming was to apologize. So he gave it a shot.

"Look, if I messed up, I'm sorry—"

"If? *If?*" Claire echoed incredulously. "You most certainly *did* mess up, no *if* about it."

She was getting him exasperated again, hitting the ball totally into his yard and then not allowing him to retrieve it or hit it back. He should have expected as much, he thought.

Mentally, Levi counted to ten, telling himself that he had to be calm or he would wind up losing any chance he had to get Claire back.

To get Bekka back.

He missed them both like crazy.

"Claire," he said as evenly as possible, "I'm trying to apologize here."

Her eyes were like small, intense laser beams, trained on his every move. "I'm glad you told me because I wouldn't have known otherwise," she informed him.

"You're making it really hard to be nice to you," he told her, his anger getting the best of him, at least for the moment.

"Then don't bother," Claire snapped coldly. She was forced to raise her voice because Bekka had started to wail again. The increased volume only made the baby cry more. "Because it's not going to get you anywhere. Apologies have to be sincere, and I can see now that every single word out of your mouth is nothing but a fabrication, a lie."

"What are you talking about?" Levi cried, completely confused. "When have I lied to you?"

Claire tossed her head, wanting desperately to get away from him and wanting, just as desperately, to never have gotten to this point in the first place. This wasn't the way she envisioned her life when she'd watched Levi slip the ring on her finger two years ago.

"You said you loved me," she accused.

"How is that a lie?" he wanted to know. "I *do* love you."

"No, you don't!" Claire cried. "If you loved me, you'd be home more often at night and you certainly wouldn't have picked poker over me."

He closed his eyes, searching for strength. How did

he get through to her? "That again," he retorted. "I didn't pick poker over you—"

"Oh, someone put a gun to your head then, telling you to deal or they'd blow your brains out, is that it?"

"It wasn't a choice between you and poker," Levi insisted. How could she possibly think that? "You're not in the same league."

Was that supposed to make her happy? Claire looked at her husband coldly, doing her very best not to allow her mind to drift, to make her think back and relive exciting, intimate moments with him just because of their proximity. "Thanks."

Her icy tone ripped through him, and Levi threw up his hands in total disgust. "I just can't win with you, can I?"

"No, because I see right through you," she informed him, her voice cold enough to freeze a cup of hot coffee. Just then, as if she was aware that she had lapsed into another long, quiet moment, the baby began to cry. "Now look what you've done. You've agitated the baby," she accused.

"Me?" he said, stunned at the way she could shift blame onto someone else's shoulders so easily. "You're the one who's shouting."

Claire made no effort to back down or back off. The baby grew louder with each passing second. "If I'm shouting it's so I can get the words through your thick skull."

He sighed, shaking his head and struggling not to have his temper snap. "You're impossible."

"Right back at you!" she retorted.

Levi strode away before he said something he was going to regret and couldn't take back.

"That's right," she taunted, hurling the words at his back. "Run. That's all you ever do. You're never willing to talk things out, to own your mistakes. It's just easier for you to run away from any confrontation."

Don't say it, don't say it, Levi counseled himself, afraid that if he did open his mouth, he wouldn't be able to control the words that would come flying out. There was no doubt about it. Claire knew how to press all his buttons. Press them until he believed that all the negative thoughts she was spouting and hurling at him were his own, and all the detrimental things that Claire had said against him she actually believed to be the gospel truth.

There was a child to think of, Levi reminded himself. He couldn't just put this all behind him and walk out. Besides, he didn't *want* to. What he wanted was his life back.

Not today, Wyatt. Not after that little run-in, a voice in his head mocked him.

But where did that leave them?

They were at an impasse, he thought. But one of them was going to have to give in if this was ever going to be resolved.

Walking away, Levi paused for a second to look over his shoulder at his wife and daughter. Even as angry as she made him, he couldn't help thinking how much he'd missed having them in his life.

How empty his life seemed with the realization that he didn't have them to come home to anymore.

That had to change.

But how?

He wasn't about to come crawling over to her side. After all, a man did have his pride.

But pride was a cold thing to take to bed with him, Levi thought unhappily.

Besides, there had to be more to this. She couldn't be this angry over a stupid poker game—could she? He needed to get her to do more than just shout at him. He had to get her to come around—and really talk to him about what she was feeling,

Squelching the desire to march back to her, take her into his arms and kiss her until she forgot all about this stupid argument and all the stupid things she was saying to him, Levi forced himself to keep walking.

This was all probably just a ruse on her part anyway. Her so-called accusations were just an excuse she was using to stay away from him because she was disappointed in him.

He'd failed her somehow, and by failing he'd inadvertently shown her that he just wasn't good enough for her. That he couldn't give her the kind of comforts she had grown up with. Even if he tried to approximate the kind of life she'd had before she married him by working his way up the ladder and earning more money, she complained that he was never home. And if he kept the hours that she wanted him to, if he was home earlier, then he couldn't give her any of the things she'd come to expect in her day-to-day life.

Either way, Levi thought glumly, he was doomed.

He had to get his priorities straight. He needed to find a way to fix all this and soon, otherwise, he was going to lose her for good.

Levi didn't know how much longer he could put up with living without his girls. Living without seeing Claire and Bekka every day.

There *had* to be a way to fix all this. There just *had* to be.

"Grandpa, can I see you for a minute?" Claire asked, standing in the doorway of Gene's cubbyhole of an office.

Gene rose to his feet. For the time being, what he was working on was temporarily forgotten.

"You, princess, can see me for a whole hour if you like," he told her cheerfully. Joining them, he asked, "And how are my two best girls this morning?"

Claire thought of her run-in with Levi a few minutes ago. "Stunned and confused," she told him.

Bushy eyebrows drew together, forming a squiggly line worthy of a fat caterpillar.

"Come again?" Gene asked. "Are you stunned and confused, peanut?" he asked Bekka.

Responding to the sound of his deep, resonant voice, the baby cooed at Gene, making him laugh with un-abashed pleasure.

"Grandpa, she can't talk," Claire informed the older man flatly.

"Maybe you can't understand her, but she can talk," he assured Claire with a touch of whimsy. "Look at her expression," he said pointedly. "That little girl is definitely trying to communicate."

"And so am I," Claire said to her grandfather in barely curbed exasperation.

Faced with this situation, Gene sobered slightly. "Go ahead, princess. I'm listening."

Claire's frown deepened. "Levi is staying here at the boarding house."

He had a feeling that Claire knew she wasn't telling him anything that he wasn't already aware of. He didn't bother feigning surprise at her news.

"Yes, I know."

She stared at the older man in disbelief. How could he have betrayed her this way? Unless Levi was lying about this, too. She found herself fervently hoping that he was. Otherwise, this was really going to shake her faith in her grandfather.

"He said you rented him a room." Maybe there was some other explanation for his being here.

The next moment her grandfather dashed that slim hope. He nodded his head. "I did."

Her mouth all but dropped open. "Why?" Claire demanded.

"Well, I couldn't very well not rent it to him," Gene replied seriously. "That would be prejudicial."

Claire's big brown eyes widened. She couldn't believe her ears. "Are you saying you were afraid he'd report you to the sheriff?"

Wide shoulders moved up and down in a vague shrug. He went with the excuse his granddaughter had unknowingly come up with.

"You never know," he told her.

"Grandpa, this is Levi," she reminded him. "He wouldn't do that. Levi *likes* you."

"He also likes you," Gene told her. "A *lot*. And all he wants is a chance to prove it."

Claire couldn't believe her ears. "You're taking his side, Grandpa?" she cried, appalled.

"Like I told your grandmother, I'm not taking any sides, I'm just making sure that both sides get a chance to be heard."

"I don't need to 'hear' anything," his granddaughter informed him. "Besides," she reminded the man, "weren't you the one who once told me that actions speak louder than words?"

"I might have said that," he allowed, then went on to remind her, "I'm also the one who said everyone deserves a second chance."

"If you mean Levi, I *gave* him a second chance." She was working herself up. "I gave him *lots* of second chances, and he blew them all."

"He's been skipping out on you to play poker on a regular basis?" Gene asked innocently.

"No," she admitted reluctantly. As upset as she was about this situation, she wasn't about to lie about it to her grandfather.

Her grandfather looked at her pointedly. "Then what?" he wanted to know.

She was referring to Levi going out of town for meetings and seminars as well as coming home late and falling asleep on the couch before she could get his dinner warmed up. But she had no intentions of going into all that now.

Besides, she had a feeling that her grandfather would be taking Levi's side in that, saying he saw nothing wrong in a man trying to better his family's lot by putting in all those long hours at work.

"I don't want to talk about it," she informed her grandfather and with that, she turned on her heel and hurried away to find her grandmother.

At least her grandmother sided with her, Claire thought.

Or at least she hoped so.

Chapter Four

Holding a fussing Bekka in her arms, Claire went in search of her grandmother. Between feeling betrayed by her grandfather and being subjected to her baby's incessant crying, her nerves felt as if they were stretched as far as they could go. She was beyond stressed out.

"Come on, Bekka. Please stop," she begged.

Bekka went on crying.

At her wit's end, Claire finally found the object of her search in the kitchen. Melba was going over a menu change with the cook. Gina tapped the older woman on the shoulder and pointed behind her.

The moment she realized that her granddaughter was there, Melba paused, telling the cook, "We'll talk later." With that, she waited for Claire to join her.

"Is it true?" Claire asked without any preamble.

"Is *what* true?" Melba wanted to know, peering over the tops of her rimless glasses at her distressed granddaughter. And then she smiled, tickling Bekka under her chin. "Hi, peanut," she cooed.

"I just found out that Grandpa rented out Jordyn Leigh's old room to Levi," Claire complained, referring to the young woman who'd moved out last month after marrying her longtime best friend, Will Clifton, a rancher from Thunder Canyon. They'd apparently tied the knot during the reception of the wedding she and Levi had attended last month.

"Yes, I know," Melba replied matter-of-factly with a dismissive shrug. She wasn't exactly happy at inviting this turmoil onto her home turf, but maybe Gene was right. Maybe Levi should be given another chance to make things right between him and Claire. Her granddaughter certainly wasn't happy with the current state of her marriage.

Claire had come looking for sympathy. That her grandmother had had knowledge of this beforehand— and *hadn't* warned her—all but left her speechless.

It was all she could do not to have her jaw drop open.

"You *know*?" Claire cried, surprised. "Then it's actually all right with you?" She stared at her grandmother, dumbfounded.

Claire made no attempt to hide the fact that she felt deeply wounded by what she viewed as an act of betrayal. It didn't matter that she was having ambivalent feelings about throwing Levi out, that part of her was actually happy about this odd turn of events that was throwing her husband and her together. What mattered was that the rest of her was more than a little upset by the same set of circumstances. Her grandparents were supposed to be on her side; they were supposed to be protecting her, shielding her, not tossing her headfirst into the lion's den.

Levi had hurt her, and she didn't want him thinking that it was no big deal. Nor did she want him to think that all he had to do was turn up on her doorstep and she would forgive him.

The truth of it was that she wasn't sure *what* to feel, but because of what she had told her grandparents—that she'd left Levi because he neglected her and took her for granted—she felt that her grandparents were supposed to be supportive of her. They were supposed to present a united front and most certainly shun Levi because of the thoughtless way he had treated her. Whether or not he was paying them rent didn't change anything. They most certainly shouldn't have allowed Levi to take up residence in the very house where she was staying.

What were they *thinking*?

"I didn't say that," Melba pointed out calmly. "Your grandfather did what he did—renting the room out to Levi—without consulting me."

Claire immediately jumped on what she took to be the rightful implication. "Then you can overrule Grandpa on this, right?" she asked eagerly.

Having Levi here would just heighten her ambivalent feelings, making her go back and forth mentally like some sort of a virtual Ping-Pong ball. It would be for the best to have him leave here. She needed her space so she could make a decision about her future. She couldn't do that with Levi around. Seeing him only reminded her how much she wanted him to hold her, to kiss her, to— He had to go, she thought, agitated. If he didn't, she knew she was liable to do something very stupid.

"You can tell Levi that he's not welcomed here and has to get out," Claire concluded.

Melba gave her a reproving look. "You know I can't very well do that, Claire. According to your grandfather, Levi paid twice the going rate for a month in advance."

"Just give the money back to him," Claire insisted as if it was the simplest thing in the world. "Tell him he has to leave," she pleaded.

Melba gave her granddaughter a long, thoughtful look. "Claire, your grandfather happens to think that Levi deserves a second chance. And I happen to think that your grandfather usually displays good judgment, so he just might be right about your husband."

"Ex-husband," Claire corrected, exasperated. Why was everyone against her? It was hard enough steering clear of Levi. If he was on the same floor as she was, she was doomed.

Melba paused. "You're already divorced?"

Claire flushed as she struggled to quiet her baby. "Well, technically, no," she admitted, "but—"

Melba took the baby from her, patting the baby's bottom and murmuring something soothing into the tiny ear. As if by magic, Bekka began to settle down.

"Then *technically*, you are still married," Melba told

her, "which makes Levi your husband, not your ex-husband."

Claire blew out a breath, surrendering—temporarily. "Technically, yes," she conceded grudgingly, clinging to the word.

Melba studied her for a long moment. Claire was so different from her two older sisters. Those girls took after *her*, Melba thought. They were professionals, focused and driven, unlike Claire. She understood Hadley and Tessa. Claire was harder for her to read.

But she was trying. Lord knew she was trying.

"What are you afraid of, Claire?" Melba gently asked her granddaughter.

"Afraid of?" Claire repeated, somewhat confused by the question. "I'm not afraid of anything."

The more she thought about it, the more convinced Melba was that she was right. Claire was most definitely afraid of something. And she had a sneaky feeling she knew what.

"Oh, yes, you are. You're acting as if you're afraid of being in the same room with Levi. As if, if you remain around Levi, those walls you've built up against him are going to come crumbling down around you, allowing Levi to come back into your life."

Claire waved her grandmother's words away. Indignant and upset at her grandmother's assessment of her, she tossed her head. "You're just imagining things, Grandmother."

Melba's eyes met hers. "I am, am I? Well, if I am,

it doesn't really harm anything to have Levi here now, does it?"

Claire squared her shoulders. "I just don't want him around here," she insisted.

"Why?" The single word seemed to burrow straight into Claire.

She was used to being backed up and getting her way when it came to her family. Losing that crutch left her bewildered and at loose ends, not to mention very unsteady. "Because I don't," Claire stubbornly insisted.

The look Melba gave her made her fidget inside. Furthermore, she looked on with envy at the way her grandmother seemed to be able to quiet Bekka down with no effort at all.

"That's not a reason, Claire."

"It is for me," Claire maintained.

"Well, sadly for you, you don't run Strickland's Boarding House," Melba crisply informed her. "Your grandfather and I do. My advice to you is either make the best of this—or make yourself scarce whenever Levi comes around. By the way, your grandfather is putting that boy's strong back to use while he's here, so you'll be seeing him around a lot during the evening hours."

She couldn't have been on the receiving end of worse news. After a full day of boredom and longing, her resistance to Levi would have the strength of shredded, wet tissue paper.

"I thought you of all people would be on my side," Claire lamented.

"I *am* on your side, Claire," her grandmother informed her in her no-nonsense voice.

Claire knew she was pouting, but she couldn't help herself. "Doesn't feel that way to me."

Melba allowed a small sigh to escape. The girl had a lot of growing up to do, she thought.

"Someday, when you get to be around my age, you'll see that I was right and you'll thank me."

Claire's frown deepened by several degrees. She felt utterly abandoned and at a loss as to what to do and how to proceed. "If you say so," she said without any sort of enthusiasm.

Melba's eyes met her granddaughter's. "I do," the older woman said with conviction. "It's either that," her grandmother went on, "or admit that I was right in the first place."

At this point Claire was utterly confused as to what her grandmother was referring to. "Right about what?" she wanted to know.

"That you were too young and too immature to get married."

Her grandmother certainly didn't pull any punches, Claire thought, dismayed. Well, she wasn't about to admit that the woman was right about that, because she wasn't, Claire thought fiercely. About the only thing she was willing to admit at this point was that Levi had no idea how to treat a wife, how to make her feel loved, rather than inconsequential.

And everything else was beside the point as far as she was concerned.

It felt as if everyone was ganging up on her. There were tears gathering in her eyes, and she had to blink hard to keep them from sliding down her cheeks. She focused on making the tears go away.

Taking a defensive stance, Claire raised her chin pugnaciously. "I was the same age you were when you got married. Grandpa told me so," she added in case her grandmother was going to dispute the fact.

As if to prove that she was a good mother, Claire took the baby from her grandmother and back into her arms. The second she did, Bekka looked discontented. Within moments, she began to fuss again. Claire's heart sank. What *was* it that she was doing wrong?

Meanwhile, Melba looked entirely unaffected by the comparison that her granddaughter had brought up. "Only chronologically."

"Well, yes, chronologically," Claire agreed, clearly puzzled. Her grandmother was trying to confuse her, she thought. "What other way is there?"

"Emotionally," Melba readily answered. "At the time," she recalled, "I was a great deal older than you emotionally—*and* I was fully prepared to take on the responsibility of raising not just one child but eventually four of them—in short order. You can't say the same thing," Melba said with what Claire felt was unnerving certainty. "Raising one child seems to have confounded you."

Inwardly, Claire shuddered at the very mention of four babies. As much as she loved Bekka—and she loved her a great deal—the thought of two children, much less four, had her breaking out in a cold sweat.

She couldn't deny the fact that Bekka was proving to be hard enough for her to deal with. It seemed to her as if, ever since the baby had come into her life, she hadn't had a moment's peace or even a real moment to herself. Every minute of every day seemed to belong to Bekka. Even when the little girl was sleeping, Claire found herself waiting for the next go-round of crying and fussing to begin.

Or, at the very least, the next round of breast-feeding to get underway. Her only function seemed to be to serve the baby.

Claire felt as though she was being held prisoner by an eight-month-old. Even when, in those rare moments Bekka wasn't fussing, it was only a matter of time until she would begin again.

There was no denying that Claire felt as if she was on some giant, endless treadmill that was only moving faster and faster with each passing moment.

And she couldn't keep up.

Bekka was becoming more and more vocal—again. Why couldn't she get the baby to stop crying? Claire wondered with a barely suppressed ragged sigh.

"I guess it's time to go feed her again," she said, resigned.

But as she turned to go, Melba moved suddenly in order to get in front of her, her arms outstretched. "Why don't you let me take care of that?" she suggested then nodded toward the back porch. "Go get yourself some fresh air. Take a walk."

Claire didn't understand what her grandmother was saying. "Are you telling me that you're going to feed Bekka?"

Melba didn't see why her granddaughter looked so befuddled about this. "That's exactly what I'm telling you."

"How?" Claire wanted to know. "I'm breast-feeding her, Grandmother." She would have been willing to bet that it had been a very long time since the other woman had been in her position. "No offense, but you *can't* feed her."

"Yes, I can," Melba contradicted. Resting the baby on her hip, she went toward the refrigerator. Opening the door, she reached toward the shelf that had several bottles all prepared and lined up in a row. Claire could only stare at them. "I'll warm up some formula for the baby."

"Formula?" Claire echoed in surprise. They'd had this discussion earlier, and she had vetoed the idea. Apparently, her grandmother was every bit as headstrong as her grandfather had warned her that she was. "I thought we agreed that Bekka's too young for that."

"*You* agreed, I didn't. Bekka is the *perfect* age for that. What are you going to do?" Melba wanted to know. "Breast-feed that child until she's ready to go off to college?"

"No, of course not," Claire retorted, rolling her eyes at the ludicrous suggestion. "But—"

"No *but*," Melba said firmly, shutting her down. "I raised four children," she said, citing her credentials. "Each of them was on the bottle by the time they were six months old. If you ask me, Bekka's way overdue. You don't want her being socially arrested, now, do you?"

"No," Claire replied in a small voice, confusion reigning all through her. What did one thing have to do with the other? she wondered.

Melba looked at her granddaughter knowingly. "Then stop using the child as an excuse."

Further lost than ever now, Claire could only stare at her grandmother. "What do you mean as an excuse? I'm not using her as an excuse."

Melba saw it different. "Oh, yes, you are." And then she gave Claire an example. "'I know what you're thinking. You feel as though you can't make a move anywhere, can't go out of the house because your baby needs you 24/7." Melba gave her youngest granddaughter a knowing, penetrating look. "The truth is, she doesn't. And you *can* leave her side here and there for a bit. So do it," Melba encouraged. "While it's very true that a baby does shake up your life, there are still parts of that life that belong exclusively to you, so reclaim them. Now go. I've got a great-granddaughter to feed," she told Claire, shooing her granddaughter out of the kitchen with her one free hand.

Claire stopped short just beyond the entrance to the kitchen.

Except for the few hours that she and Levi had at-

tended the wedding, Bekka had either been in her arms
or within arm's reach since the day she was born. The
baby's crib was set up in their bedroom and during her
own waking hours, Claire carried the baby around with
her almost everywhere. If she did set the child down,
she was always close by at all times.

To have her arms empty like this and to have Bekka
out of her line of sight felt very strange.

It also, heaven help her, felt liberating, Claire thought.

So she did as her grandmother had suggested. Leaving the boarding house, she took a walk around the
area, keeping close by—just in case she was needed.
Old habits were hard to break.

It was August, which meant that, for the most part,
the weather was hot and humid—not unlike the summer that she had first met Levi, Claire caught herself
nostalgically remembering.

*No, don't do that. Don't get all sentimental on me
now*, she chided herself. *That's not going to help anything.*

Her head began to hurt.

Admittedly, Claire thought as she walked slowly
around her grandparents' property, she was very confused about her situation. Part of her felt she'd been justified in the way she'd reacted to Levi's absences, and
especially to that night after the reception.

That was the part of her that felt that there was no
turning back from what she'd done, throwing him out
like that. Levi was going to come to his senses, decide
that he could do a lot better than to tie himself down

to a woman who was, for all intents and purposes, a shrew who could only find fault with him rather than to be grateful for the virtues he displayed.

There wasn't a chance in hell that this was going to have the happy ending she was hoping for. Levi was definitely *not* going to want her back after the way she'd treated him.

He was probably here not to try to win her back, but to make her regret what she had done. Regret it and see what she had lost by tossing him out.

That meant that Levi was probably here out for revenge.

Her headache was getting worse.

Not only that, but it felt as if there really was this internal Ping-Pong game going on, and her feelings kept going back and forth like the ball being lobbed over the net.

In all honesty, she didn't know just which side of the net the ball really belonged.

She needed to get back, Claire told herself. The baby had been with her grandmother long enough. She couldn't just pass Bekka along as if she was some sort of a doll. She was a flesh-and-blood child.

Bekka was *her* responsibility, not her grandmother's or her grandfather's.

Holding Bekka in her arms—even when the baby insisted on fussing—was the only time that everything felt even marginally right, Claire thought.

Until she could figure her life out, she was going to hold off on making any major decisions.

She had spent enough time away from her baby, she told herself, quickening her pace.

When she got back into the kitchen, Claire found that neither her grandmother nor her baby were there. She quickly made her way around to the beck of the house and exited through the rear door onto the porch.

Even as she began to push the door open, she heard the sound of voices.

One belonged to her grandmother, and the other voice—Claire cocked her head even as the answer came to her—belonged to Levi.

Moving quickly, Claire's first thought was to retrieve her baby. But even before she could reach Levi and Bekka, she could see that, instead of fussing and crying, the little girl was smiling and cooing.

There was some formula staining her dimples— dimples that the little girl had in common with her daddy, Claire thought ruefully. Despite Bekka's less than pristine appearance, she hadn't seen the baby looking this contented in more than a month—since the last time she had observed Levi and their daughter together.

He had a way with her, Claire admitted grudgingly.

Levi glanced up just as she approached them. He appeared to look just a tad sheepish, but he made no attempt to stop feeding the baby or to get up and surrender their daughter to her.

From out of nowhere, Melba came up directly behind her.

"They look good together, don't they?" her grandmother observed.

Claire fisted her hands at her sides as she turned toward the woman. "I thought you said you were going to feed her."

"I was, but then Levi came over and asked me if I'd mind if he held Bekka for a few minutes. A loving father shouldn't have to ask for permission to hold his own baby daughter," Melba told her, "so I let him take Bekka and feed her." Small brown eyes narrowed as she looked pointedly at her granddaughter. "Do you have a problem with that?"

"No, ma'am, I don't," Claire replied quietly.

"Good, because you shouldn't." She looked from Levi to Claire, making up her mind. "All right, since the two of you are here now, I'll leave my great-granddaughter in your so-called 'capable' hands—try not to argue around her. She might be too young to talk, but she's not too young to hear or to be affected by the sound of raised voices and misbegotten accusations," Melba informed them pointedly.

The next moment the woman turned on her stacked heel and walked away.

Chapter Five

Gently rocking his daughter in his arms as he continued feeding Bekka her bottle, Levi silently watched Melba Strickland walk away.

"Tough lady, your grandmother." There was admiration in his voice.

"Yes," Claire agreed. "Grandmother's been known to be tough as nails."

But Melba only held his attention for a moment. The little beauty in his arms had more than garnered the bulk of it. He could feel his heart swelling as he looked at her. They had been apart for thirty days. How much had he missed out on in thirty days?

He had a feeling that it was a lot. Every moment was precious at this point of his daughter's development. He didn't want to miss any more.

"I can't believe how much she's grown," Levi murmured, more to himself than to the woman standing near him.

Claire's attention had been focused on her grandmother and the fact that the woman was truly acting as if she saw nothing wrong with Levi invading the boarding house like this.

She turned now to look at Levi quizzically. "Grandmother?"

"No," he laughed. Lookswise, Claire's grandmother hadn't changed a hair since he'd first met her four years ago. "Bekka. She looks like she's beginning to really fill out. And there's personality in those eyes of hers. She's going to be a regular heartbreaker when she grows up." As she continued to suck enthusiastically on her bottle, Levi smiled down into his daughter's face. "I've missed you, little darlin'," he told her. "Did you miss me, too?"

More than anything in the world, Claire thought. observing the way he was with Bekka. *And more than you'll ever know.*

With more than a little effort, she blocked and shut down her feelings. She was *not* about to own up to what she was thinking or say the words out loud.

That was all she needed to do, Claire upbraided herself. If Levi had a clue as to what she was thinking, he would just take that to mean that he could move back into their apartment and just like that, it would be business as usual.

Would that be so bad? she questioned herself.

Yes! Yes, it would be that bad. She'd be back to

spending all of her time taking care of the baby and missing Levi while he'd be spending all his free time away from her.

Supposedly securing their future if she was to believe him.

She had to remember how that felt, missing him. Being taken for granted, she silently counseled herself.

But all that—staying angry—required effort. Effort that was hard to maintain when part of her kept longing for the touch of his hand, the feel of his lips on hers.

Seeing him with Bekka certainly didn't help.

Watching Levi with their infant daughter tugged at her heart in a way she'd never anticipated. The feeling sliced through her insecurities and her hurt.

It also did something else she hadn't anticipated.

It made her feel just the slightest bit jealous.

Her baby was responding to Levi the way she didn't to *her*. Bekka was cooing and making a host of other contented noises whereupon when she held Bekka, all the baby did was fuss and cry.

Maybe the baby really *was* picking up on her stress levels, Claire thought. But in that case, it also meant that Levi *wasn't* stressed in the least about their estranged situation.

And that, in turn, meant that he just didn't care about either.

If that was the case, why was she standing here, looking at him like some lovesick simpleton? Didn't she *know* any better by now?

Bekka was finally finished with her bottle. Setting it

aside, he put the baby over his shoulder and patted her back the way he had learned surfing YouTube videos that were meant for new dads.

"You should put something on your shoulder," Claire advised coolly. "She'll spit up on it."

"That's okay," he told her, making small, concentric circles on the baby's small back, intermittently patting it, as well. "The shirt's washable."

His heart swelled just holding his daughter like this. She felt so tiny, so dependent on him. So precious. He'd never thought that he could fall in love so quickly, so completely, and yet this little girl held his heart in the palm of her hand. He'd fallen in love with her even faster than he had fallen for her mother, he thought.

It went without saying that he would do anything for Bekka, anything to keep her safe and warm. And happy. He also didn't want to spend another day without her, much less another month.

There had to be a way.

Searching for a way to initiate "peace talks" with his estranged wife, he glanced up and saw a rather strange expression on Claire's face. One he couldn't really begin to read.

"What?" he asked.

Watching the way Bekka responded to Levi, she was beginning to feel threatened. And left out.

"I'd like my daughter back, please," Claire said primly as she reached for Bekka.

"*Our* daughter," Levi emphasized. "Bekka's *our* daughter."

She wasn't about to be lectured to by this absentee father. Not after all the lonely hours she'd put in, caring for Bekka by herself.

"Oh, so now she's *our* daughter, is she?" Claire demanded hotly.

"What are you talking about?" Levi asked. He could feel another fight brewing. Why did she insist on doing that? On picking fights when all he wanted to do was to make up and go from there? "She's always been our daughter."

She had her hands on Bekka, but Levi was still holding her. "Then why were you never around to help take care of her?"

"It wasn't *never*," he corrected defensively.

"Well, it certainly felt that way. Every time I could have used your help, you weren't there," she accused.

"That's because I was earning money to provide for Bekka *and* for you." Because he was afraid that Bekka could turn into the main component in a tug of war, he relinquished his hold on his daughter, albeit reluctantly. He would have been willing to hold her all day if he could.

Claire rested the baby against her shoulder while she glared at Levi. "Ah, yes. Saint Levi, working all those long hours to bring home a paycheck. Why is it that other fathers seem to be able to keep regular hours while you're gone from dawn to midnight, using any excuse not to come home?"

Now she was just making things up, Levi thought, frustrated. "That's not true and you know it," he told her, struggling not to raise his voice. He didn't want to make Bekka cry. "I got a promotion so I have to put in longer hours. I've got a lot of new responsibilities, as well as my old ones. If I start telling the boss I can't attend those meetings and seminars he keeps sending me to, he'll replace me with someone who can. Tell me, what good will I be doing Bekka or you if I can't pay for a roof over your heads?" he wanted to know.

He thought that would finally be the end of it—but he should have known better.

She narrowed her eyes as she looked at him. "At least we'd both know your face."

"Come on, Claire," he said in disbelief, "that's not fair."

"Fair?" she echoed incredulously. "I'll tell you what's *fair. Fair* is taking your turn walking the floor with a shrieking baby. *Fair* is taking turns changing her diaper, giving her a bath, watching out for her so she doesn't bump her head. *Fair* is giving me someone to talk to once in a while besides a fussing infant."

"Why don't you call your sisters, talk to them?" he suggested.

She could also just as easily have called her mother, but he had a feeling that her pride was keeping her from admitting to her mother that she found motherhood to be far more difficult to deal with than she'd thought— just as her mother had tried to get her to realize that it would be.

Claire was just too stubborn for her own good, he thought.

"What, you mean call them instead of you?" Claire asked in disbelief. "I love my sisters. But I don't have anything in common with them, other than the fact that we all have the same blood running through our veins. They can't understand why I'd want to get married—which in their eyes means tied down, and I can't understand why they'd rather go it alone—at least, I didn't understand why until our marriage fell apart," she amended.

She didn't know what she was talking about, he thought angrily. "It *didn't* fall apart," Levi insisted.

"Oh, no?" What universe did this man live in? "Then what would you call this?" she demanded, waving her hand around to indicate the three of them.

Levi responded without hesitation. "A bump in the road."

"A bump?" she repeated, dumbfounded. "This isn't a *bump*, it's a whole mountain range."

He looked at Bekka. She'd drifted to sleep, but was now beginning to stir again. "Lower your voice," he ordered softly. "Before you make her cry again."

Why was *she* always to blame for everything? Especially when the fault was with him. "Maybe it's *you* that's making her cry again."

Taking a breath, he tried once more, even though he could see failure coming from a mile away. "Look, Claire, I'm trying to apologize here." *Again*, he thought with a mounting feeling of hopelessness threatening to cave in on him.

"Apologize?" she asked incredulously. "Is *that* what you're doing? Well, trust me, you're doing a really terrible job of it. As a matter of fact, this is probably the worst apology in history," Claire informed him haughtily.

With that, she turned on her heel and marched back into the boarding house. She didn't stop walking until she got to their room.

Still holding Bekka in her arms, she locked the door to ensure that Levi couldn't get in. Then she put Bekka down in her crib. Her grandfather had gotten it down from the attic when she'd arrived, announcing that she'd left Levi and was staying with them. She drew some comfort from the fact that, according to her grandmother, the crib had once been her father's. It gave her a sense of continuity.

Once Bekka was lying safely in her crib, Claire threw herself facedown on the bedspread and sobbed her heart out.

She hated this. Hated fighting with the only man she now knew she had ever really loved. Most of all, she hated thinking that there was no saving her marriage.

There had to be. But what if Levi decided that she wasn't worth his changing? What if he had been staying away from her on purpose? Using any excuse he could come up with?.

Her tears flowed faster. And her heart ached more.

"I see it's not going as well as you'd like," Gene Strickland commented as he came up behind his grandson-in-law.

The older man had been privy to the latter half of the

exchange between his granddaughter and Levi, taking care to stay out of sight until it was finally over.

He had a feeling that one of them would need a shoulder to cry on—or at least a sounding board.

He wasn't entirely wrong.

Levi turned around to face the older man. "The way I'd like?" he repeated. "Sir, it's not going well in any manner, shape or form," Levi lamented, trying very hard not to allow despair to swallow him up whole.

"Strickland women are not the easiest people to live with at times," Gene agreed sagely. "They can be stubborn and pigheaded," he admitted. "But they can also be loyal and loving. Just don't give up, boy," Claire's grandfather counseled.

"Oh, I have no intentions of giving up," Levi told the man. "But I'm afraid the problem is that Claire doesn't think I'm good enough for her."

If he knew his granddaughter, the reverse was probably true. She probably worried that Levi thought he was too good for her. The family loyalty he'd mentioned kept him from saying that.

Instead, Gene asked, "Where did you get a fool notion like that?"

The origin of his insecurity in this case wasn't hard to trace. "Well, her parents had their doubts about me because I didn't have a college degree like she has."

"A college degree," Gene repeated, scoffing. "That's just a pretty piece of paper. It's what's in here—" he poked a thick finger in the middle of Levi's chest "—that counts, not some piece of paper with fancy lettering. Give me a man who's graduated from the school of hard knocks instead of one who's graduated from some snobbish 'institution of higher learning' any day. Besides, Claire's folks like you. If they knew what was going on, they'd be right here in your corner, egging you on. Telling her to come to her senses."

Levi looked at the man, stunned. He thought the whole town knew about their situation. Strangers were stopping him in the street to share their advice.

"Wait. Her parents don't know?" Gene shook his head in response. "That makes them practically the only ones who don't know," Levi said. "It feels like everyone in town knows and has an opinion about whether or not Claire and I should get back together. God knows I've heard enough of them."

Gene shrugged his wide, squat shoulders. "It's a small town," Gene told him. "Not much happens here by way of entertainment. Folks get bored. I've seen them make bets on how much snow's gonna fall on the first foot of the front step in front of the general store in a given amount of time."

The word *bets* caught Levi's attention. "Are they making bets on my marriage?"

"Wouldn't surprise me," Gene confessed. And then he waved his hand at the whole enterprise. "Don't pay them no mind," he advised. "What counts is how you and Claire-bear feel about your marriage."

Levi turned the nickname over in his mind. Claire-bear. Right now she seemed to be more "bear" than "Claire."

"How do I get her back, Mr. Strickland?" Levi asked unabashedly.

"Patience," Gene said. "And the name's Gene," he told Levi, offering him a friendly grin. "My advice is just be the best you that you can be and always make her feel loved. That's important to a woman," Gene emphasized.

"What if that's not enough?"

"It will be," Gene promised. "That girl was always falling in and out of love when she went to college," he recalled.

Was that supposed to make him feel better? "Then I'm doomed," Levi lamented.

"No, you're not," Gene contradicted. "Like I said, she was always falling in and out of love, but that summer when she came by and told us about you, she lit up like a Christmas tree. I swear there were stars in her eyes. I knew there and then that you had to be the one—and you were."

He sure didn't feel like *the one* right now—unless it meant "the one who got dumped."

"I don't know about that, Mr. Strickland," Levi said quietly, then amended, "I mean, Gene," when the man looked at him expectantly.

"You ever hear that story about the race between the rabbit and the turtle, boy?" Gene asked sagely.

Who hadn't? "Yes, sir," Levi replied respectfully.

"Then you know that that cocky rabbit was all flashy and confident, telling the turtle he was wasting his time competing and should just pull out and quit right at the start. But that turtle didn't pay any attention to that blowhard rabbit. He just kept doing what he was doing, making his way to the finish line by putting one foot in front of the other and damn, if he didn't make it to the finish line before the rabbit, who was busy taking bows and losing sight of the prize. Be that turtle, boy," he said, daring him to be otherwise. "Don't give up until you cross that finish line. In the meantime, I've got more things I need brought up from the basement. You up for it?" he wanted to know, looking at the young man.

In his opinion, it was the very least he could do for the older man after the latter seemed to have taken a shine to him this way. "Yes, sir."

Gene clapped his hand on his grandson-in-law's back. "That's my boy."

At least her grandfather was on his side, Levi thought. Now if he could only get Claire to feel the same way…

Claire took her meal in her room that night, afraid that if she left it, she would immediately run into Levi, and she just didn't feel as if she was up to that.

The truth of it was, her resolve felt rather shaken, and she was afraid that she would just give up and go back with him. The past four weeks would have all been for nothing.

And everyone would think she had no backbone. She *had* to leave Levi—whether or not, deep down, she really wanted to.

Even her grandmother was giving her her space,

Claire thought, not altogether sure she was happy about that turn of events. What if the woman had just given up on her instead? Then what would she do?

As it turned out, Melba gave her until the following morning to deal with whatever feelings she needed to deal with, then let herself in with her pass key.

Walking in, as big as day, she took Claire completely by surprise.

"You scared me, Grandmother," Claire cried, one hand covering the heart that had almost leaped out of her chest.

"I'm not that bad-looking yet," Melba said, disgruntled.

"I didn't mean that," Claire told her, quick to correct any misunderstanding. "I thought you were Levi."

"Levi's gone," Melba said flatly.

The news completely stunned her. "Gone? You mean he's given up?" The thought that he had devastated her. Didn't he care at all? One try and that was it?

"Why?" Melba asked, peering at her closely. "Would you be upset if he had?" Checking the baby's diaper, she made a quick decision and began to change Bekka right then and there.

"Yes. No," Claire amended quickly. "I just thought that since he was here, he'd try harder. Guess he didn't think I was worth it."

"Don't know what he thought," Melba answered crisply. "Don't have the gift that way," her grandmother told her. "Just know that he had to go to work."

"Work? You mean he left for *work*? Does that mean

he's planning on coming back?" Even she heard the hopeful note in her own voice.

"If he's not, he's gonna run out of clothes pretty quick because his suitcase is still in his room," Melba said matter-of-factly, tossing out the dirty diaper.

"Oh." With the immediate threat over, Claire went back to her ambivalent, confused state.

"What that means is that you can come out of hiding," Melba told her, picking the baby up and cradling her in her arms.

"I wasn't hiding," Claire protested.

"Listen to her, Bekka," Melba said to the baby. "She wasn't *hiding*," Melba repeated the word in an animated voice. "Sure she was, wasn't she?" Melba looked up at her granddaughter, her eyes narrowing. "You've got makeup on, don't you?"

"Yes."

It was only eight in the morning. "You sleep in that stuff?"

"No, of course not," she lied, knowing what her grandmother would say if the woman knew that she actually did wear make up to bed so that Levi would always think she looked pretty. It had gotten to be a habit for her. She just continued doing it automatically. "I put it on this morning," she said.

Melba looked her over with a critical eye. "Who are you getting all dolled up for if you're avoiding that love-sick husband of yours?"

"Nobody," Claire lied. "You really think he's love-sick?"

Melba nodded her head. "Worst case I've ever seen."

But Claire pursed her lips together as she shook her head. "I think you're wrong."

Very thin shoulders rose and fell in quick, dismissive succession. "It's a free country. You can think whatever you want to think, even if you're wrong." And it was obvious that she believed that her granddaughter was wrong.

"If he was so lovesick, then why did he stay after the reception and play poker with his friends instead of coming home to me?" Claire challenged.

Melba frowned, unwilling to go another round with this scenario. "You think on that, honey. When you come up with the answer, you'll be ready to be a real wife. Now let's go. We're going to get you fed and then we're going to put you to work. Aren't we, angel?" she asked Bekka.

Bekka cooed in response.

"Good answer," Melba murmured.

Claire sincerely hoped so.

Chapter Six

Claire looked around at her surroundings, more than a little puzzled when her grandmother had stopped walking and turned around to face her.

"This is the kitchen," Claire said in a quizzical tone of voice.

This didn't make any sense. She'd already had her breakfast in the dining room. Why had her grandmother brought her here?

Melba laughed shortly. "Very good. What was your first clue?"

In the past month she had grown rather accustomed to her grandmother's sarcastic retorts. Claire scarcely took note of the older woman's flippant question. But there was something that she knew did need to be asked.

"I thought you said that after breakfast, you were

going to find some work for me to do." She did want to be able to pull her own weight—and to prove to her grandmother that she was a responsible adult rather than just an overgrown child.

"I did and I am," Melba answered crisply. Taking Bekka from her granddaughter, she told the baby—in a far sweeter, softer voice—"You, peanut, are going to keep your great-grandfather company and out of trouble while I put your mama here to work."

Starting to leave, Melba paused to look over her shoulder at Claire. "Stay here," she ordered. "I'll be right back. Talk to Gina while I'm gone," she suggested, waving a hand toward the cook.

Her voice softened just a touch again as she walked out of the kitchen, talking to the baby as if Bekka understood and was hanging on every word.

Feeling a little awkward, Claire looked around the kitchen and offered a quick, small smile to Gina. The latter short, squat, energetic woman was standing by the industrial sink, washing all the dishes, glasses and cutlery that had just been put to use during breakfast. Because there was nothing else for her to do, Claire picked up a towel and began drying everything that Gina had just washed.

The sound of running water and the clanging of dishes was still not enough to really do away with the silence hovering in the room, so Claire tried making polite conversation with the other woman.

"Have you been working for my grandmother long?" She realized only after the words were out of her mouth that she had failed to include her grandfather in that question. But that was because of the two, it was her grandmother who was the more dynamic of the duo and the one who was always very quick to act. That, consequentially, made the woman stand out. Of the two, her grandfather was the slow and steady one, the one who was always dependable, while her grandmother was the bolt of lightning that lit up the sky and just as easily scrambled the brains of anyone who had the misfortune of getting in that lightning bolt's way.

"About two months, now," Gina answered, raising her voice in order to be heard above the clatter. Working with pots now, the noise grew louder, erasing the need for small talk.

But now that she had started, Claire just continued talking. "She can be a little tough," she conceded, wondering if the other woman was holding back because she was afraid she'd lose her job if she complained about her grandmother's bombastic personality.

Gina looked at her over her shoulder. She appeared to be weighing her words before she said, "She's a lady who knows her mind and knows what she wants."

In Claire's estimation, the vague description could easily cover a multitude of sins and transgressions. Gina was apparently being diplomatic.

Claire nodded her head. "And isn't afraid to go get it," she added.

"Being afraid is a waste of time," Melba said, coming up behind the two younger women.

Startled, Claire jumped. She hadn't expected her

grandmother to be back so soon. For a heavyset woman, she moved rather noiselessly. Claire flashed her a spasmodic smile that vanished as quickly as it had appeared. "I guess you found Grandpa right away."

"No, I left Bekka in the living rooom in the potted plant stand." Her grandmother said the words so calmly, for one terrible second, Claire actually thought that the woman was being serious.

And then she realized her grandmother was merely being sarcastic. "Oh, you're kidding. Wow." Claire blew out a breath, attempting to steady her nerves. "For a second you had me really going there."

Melba paused to stare at her granddaughter, and then she shook her head.

"What goes through that head of yours, girl?" she wanted to know. But the very next moment the woman held up her hand like a police officer directing traffic, except that instead of the flow of cars, her grandmother's intention was to hold back any flow of words that might be coming her way. "No, never mind. Don't tell me. I'd rather not know. If I don't know, it won't depress me. Just in case you're unclear about your daughter's whereabouts, Bekka is with your grandfather. Whatever other faults he might have, your grandfather is an excellent babysitter.

"Now, after you finish helping Gina with the rest of kitchen cleanup, she is going to teach you some of the very basics so that you can start helping her prepare the meals here."

Claire stared at her grandmother, stunned. They'd already had this conversation weeks ago. "Grandmother, I can't cook," she protested with feeling. " We eat a lot of…frozen food," she said lamely, knowing what her grandmother was likely to say about *that*!

About to leave the kitchen, Melba turned and fixed her with a look that seemed to penetrate straight into her bones.

"Can't or won't?" Melba challenged.

"Can't," Claire answered in a very small, helpless voice.

It was obvious by her grandmother's expression that the woman thought otherwise. "When you lose a limb, you *can't* grow it back. It's not possible. That is *not* the case when it comes to cooking. Just because you're currently burning water when you boil it doesn't mean that you're doomed to keep repeating that mistake. You *can* learn how to cook and you *will* learn how to cook," she instructed. "You just need to have someone who is good at it teach you what to do. Gina here," Melba said, gesturing toward the other woman, "is the very best."

Gina smiled, somewhat dazed at the compliment. Everyone knew that it wasn't often that the woman had anything positive to say. This was a very rare moment.

"Thank you, Mrs. Strickland. But I'm not really very good at teaching someone," Gina politely protested.

Melba turned to look at the cook. She had just one word for her.

"Learn."

And with that, Melba left the kitchen. Her very bearing indicated that she expected any miracles that needed to be called into play to be done so, efficiently and quickly.

Gina looked far from happy about the situation, but at the same time she appeared to be stoically resigned to her fate.

"Did you really burn water?" Gina asked her new apprentice.

Claire flushed and stared down at her shoes as she nodded her answer. She took no pride in the fact that the answer to the question was affirmative. She silently nodded her head, thinking that there were really a couple of excuses—one weaker than the next—to be said in her defense.

No one had ever gone out of their way in any manner to attempt to teach her how to cook when she was growing up. Coupled with that was that she had never had the slightest desire to learn. When she was growing up, there was always someone to do the cooking. She ate without giving the meal's preparation a second thought.

When she was finally on her own, away at college, she subsisted on take-out foods and the occasional microwave specials that required from ninety seconds to six minutes of microwave time, no more. The meals were basically satisfactory with no fuss involved.

When she first married Levi, she'd made a couple of halfhearted attempts at cooking before returning to her tried-and-true avenues of provisions: takeouts and microwaveable meals.

Occasionally, Levi would cook or they would go out. Or at least they had gone out before Bekka was born.

Having the baby around changed almost everything, including her eating habits.

Especially when Levi was away on business.

Without giving it much thought, Claire subsisted on sandwiches and microwavable meals.

"So, what *do* you know how to cook?" Gina asked her once the last pot had been washed, dried and put away some twenty minutes later. Her tone of voice indicated that she really didn't believe that the girl standing next to her wasn't able to cook *anything*.

Claire took a deep breath before answering. She did her best not to feel inadequate. "Nothing," she answered honestly.

"O-kay," Gina said, taking the response in stride. It was clear that she was looking for something positive to be gleaned from this. "That means there's nothing to unlearn. Good. We'll start out with a clean slate."

Claire waited a beat longer, holding her breath. Expecting something more derogatory to be said in reference to her lack of any basic culinary skills.

When nothing followed, she released a long sigh of relief. She'd thought that Gina would say something belittling or snide about the fact that she had reached her present age of twenty-four without learning how to even scramble an egg properly—hers came out looking as if they'd been uncovered in a war zone.

A *major* war zone, Claire thought ruefully, remembering her last effort.

"Okay, so this is what we're going to do. We're going to start with the very basics and build up from there,"

Gina told her, giving the impression of mentally rolling up her sleeves. "Do you know how to make mashed potatoes?"

Claire pressed her lips together. She was well aware that she had to be coming across like some sort of an inept idiot. But she didn't know enough to bluff her way through this. She was forced to own up to the truth.

"No," she admitted.

"After today, you will," Gina told her so matter-of-factly that Claire found herself believing the older woman.

It wasn't easy, and he was tired enough to briefly consider just going back to his apartment right here in Bozeman and crashing there after the day he had put in at the store.

A day that required double duty from him in order to be able to leave the store at something approaching regular hours.

But the apartment was as hauntingly empty as ever. He couldn't endure that. It was almost like living with ghosts. After all, they'd had some happy times living in the apartment before things began to go bad.

So, even though he had to push himself, Levi made his mind up and was driving back to Rust Creek Falls. He was doing it in order to at least be sleeping under the same general roof as Claire and the baby.

One baby step at a time in order to get back to where he once was, he told himself.

With one eye watching for any telltale signs of patrol

cars hiding in the shadows, hoping to hand out speeding tickets, Levi wound up making remarkably good time with no mishaps.

Parking his vehicle in the first place he could, he hurried into the boarding house and toward the stairs. He was hoping to be able to at least take one peek into Claire's room to catch a glimpse of her and the baby.

If she let him.

But before he could even reach the staircase, Gene saw him and called him over into the sitting room. The second Levi started to approach, he saw that the older man was not alone.

Levi cut the distance between them quickly.

"Thought you might want to say hi to your best girl here," Gene told him. "Or at least one of them." The man amended his own statement with a wink. Lowering his face so it was next to the baby's, Gene coaxed, "Bekka, say hi to your daddy."

Drained though he was, Levi all but melted at the sight of his daughter. To him she was a ray of sunshine in a disposable diaper. His heart was instantly warm and overflowing with love.

"How's the most beautiful eight-month-old girl in the whole wide world?" Levi asked Bekka.

He picked his daughter up from the very frilly bassinet she was lying in. Gene had gone out and bought the bassinet for her the very first time Claire had brought the baby by for a visit. He'd said he thought it was a very worthwhile investment, even though Bekka would be quick to outgrow it.

"You can always save it for the next baby," Gene had told Claire. He'd had a hopeful gleam in his eye at the time.

In Levi's overjoyed estimation, his daughter looked as if she was excited to see him. Bekka began to wave her tiny fists around while she started to gurgle and coo. A series of tiny, interconnected bubbles were cascading from her lips, formed out of the formula that she'd had earlier.

The resulting mess didn't bother Levi in the slightest. In all honesty, the entire sight pleased him no end.

Taking out his handkerchief, he wiped the drool marks from his daughter's mouth and chin.

"I see your great-grandpa's keeping you fed," he told the baby with a pleased laugh. Mission accomplished, he shoved his handkerchief back into his pocket. "Did you miss your daddy?" He asked the baby the question as seriously as if he was addressing a ten-year-old. "I hate leaving you, baby, but Daddy has to go to work so that you can have all the formula that you want."

Picking Bekka up and holding her close, Levi heard his daughter continue to make a few more noises.

One noise in particular had him suddenly freezing in place.

His lower jaw dropped.

Stunned, he immediately turned toward Gene to see if the other man had heard it, as well, or if his imagination and overwrought state were just playing tricks on him.

"Did you hear that?" he asked in what amounted to

a hushed whisper, afraid that if he voiced the question any louder, the moment would be gone.

"I did, indeed," Gene confirmed, beaming because he was thoroughly pleased with this turn of events. He had always liked his granddaughter's choice of a partner for all eternity.

"She said 'Da,'" Levi cried, utterly thrilled beyond words. And then his eyes shifted back to Gene, his witness in this joyous matter. "She did say 'Da,' right? I mean, you heard her say it. It's not just me, is it?"

Levi's state of ecstasy tickled the older man. He identified with it completely. There was just nothing to compare to the moment that a child suddenly chooses to identify you and bond with that identification. He remembered how it had been with his own boys.

"No, it's not just you and yes, I heard her say it," Gene told him with a laugh.

Another thought suddenly hit Levi. "Is that normal?" he wanted to know. "I mean, do babies her age actually talk?"

Maybe she was some sort of a prodigy, he thought, his mind already racing and making half-formed plans.

"Not so's you can carry on an actual conversation," Gene told him, "but some babies have been known to say a word or two. Or at least make sounds that *sounded* like words." Gene ran his hand lightly over the back of Bekka's exceptionally soft hair. "And this little princess here did say 'Da.' We both heard her. It's a red-letter day. Bekka said her first word."

The moment the impact of the older man's last sentence sank in, the extremely wide grin on Levi's lips faded a degree, replaced by a look of concern. "You can't tell Claire." It was both an instruction and a plea on Levi's part.

Gene didn't quite understand why that was so important to Bekka's dad. "Because you want to be the first one to tell her?" he guessed.

Levi shook his head. "No, no, I don't want to tell her. I don't want *anyone* to tell her. I don't want Claire to know," he insisted.

Gene's shaggy eyebrows drew together over his brow like two hairy spiders. "I don't think I understand."

"When we were still living together in the apartment, Claire spent a lot of her time with the baby while I was working. Her whole life was centered around feeding Bekka, changing Bekka, bathing Bekka—you get the picture," he said, halting the barrage of examples. "For Claire it was almost nothing but Bekka 24/7. After putting in all that time with the baby, to have Bekka's first word be 'Da' instead of 'Mama,' well, it'll just devastate her."

That Levi was so concerned about Claire's feelings was nothing short of touching, Gene thought. "Maybe you're underestimating her."

But Levi apparently didn't think so. "Claire's got feelings, and those feelings can get really hurt," Levi told the older man. "I don't want to take a chance that I'm actually right about this."

"What if Bekka says it in front of Claire? That could happen," Gene pointed out.

"We'll have to take our chances. Maybe she'll say 'Mama,'" Levi said hopefully.

Based on his own children, Gene had his doubts about that. "So you really don't want me to tell her?" Gene questioned. After all, a baby's first word was a really big deal for her parents.

"No," Levi answered. "It's just better if Claire doesn't know."

"What's better if Claire doesn't know?" Claire asked, picking that moment to walk into the room. She had put in close to five hours in the kitchen under Gina's tutelage, and she was utterly exhausted.

But on the outside chance that she might just bump into Levi tonight, she'd hurried to her room to freshen up her makeup and comb her hair into some sort of an attractive style—just in case. She didn't want Levi to *ever* see her looking anything but perfect. She was afraid that he would be disappointed if that ever happened. Her wobbly self-esteem couldn't handle the blow.

Claire looked expectantly now from one man to the other, waiting for an answer.

"I thought it was better if you didn't know that I broke a couple of speed limits getting here from work," Levi told her, improvising on the spot. "I didn't get a ticket, but just the same, I didn't want you getting mad that I broke the law. I guess I was really anxious to get back to you and the baby," he repeated, giving her the most soulful look he could.

"Well, you shouldn't do that," Claire told him. "Speeding tickets are expensive." Then a hint of a smile broke through and she added almost shyly, "But I do understand why you did it."

And it secretly did please her very, very much.

Chapter Seven

Maybe she'd been too hasty, throwing Levi out of their apartment—and her life—the way she had, Claire thought a few days later. She was walking through the quaint streets of Rust Creek Falls, pushing Bekka in the carriage that she and Levi had picked out together a week before Bekka was born.

She remembered the day clearly because she had literally *begged* Levi to let her get out of bed for what had amounted to a rare outing. The latter half of her pregnancy had been exceedingly difficult for her, and the doctor had recommended complete bed rest just to remain on the safe side.

At first, surrounded with books and all the things she'd wanted to catch up on, bed rest had almost been welcomed. It was certainly no big hardship. However, after three months of looking at the same four walls, day in, day out, Claire felt as if she was in danger of going completely crazy.

Since she'd been feeling stronger and by her own assessment, hadn't been feeling violently ill in a long while, she had begged and pleaded with Levi to take her outside of their apartment.

To take her *anywhere* as long as it didn't involve those same four walls.

Eventually, Levi had reluctantly given in and agreed. But rather than allow her to walk outside, her chivalrous cowboy husband had carried her into their flatbed truck. Since he was trying to cheer her up, Levi hinted that he had a specific destination in mind. She'd badgered him, but he had remained steadfast and secretive until they finally got there.

He'd driven them over to a store that dealt exclusively in baby items, from furnishings to clothes to toys. The owner, a friendly man named Jamie Pierce, turned out to be someone Levi had met and struck up a friendship with at one of those seminars he had been required to attend. The upshot of that was that they got a really good deal on the baby carriage.

What she remembered from that day was not the deal, but the fact that Levi had carried her to and from the truck, and that he had surprised her with the baby carriage, one she had seen in a catalog and had wistfully been pining after for the past few months.

The carriage had come unassembled. Levi brought the box into their bedroom so that she could witness the process and offer her suggestions from the sidelines while he stayed up half the night putting all the carriage pieces together. She'd fallen asleep watching him. All she knew was that in the morning, when she woke up, the carriage had been assembled and Levi had already left for work. A simple calculation told her that he had gone to work on—at most—approximately three hours' sleep.

It struck her as truly selfless.

He was a good father, Claire thought now as she crossed the street. And not exactly that shabby a husband, either. Not everyone would have gone out of their way like that to indulge a frustrated, housebound pregnant wife.

What had she been thinking?

The answer was she hadn't been thinking. She'd been too quick to allow her emotions to dictate her actions, she told herself. Before acting on a whim like that, she should have counted to ten—and then ten more. Hardworking, loving men like Levi were hard to find. Tossing him aside like that was crazy.

She just hadn't been herself that July Fourth weekend.

Chewing on her bottom lip, she looked down at Bekka. The baby was still asleep, lulled by the soothing feel of the summer sun warming the area around her, if not her directly.

It was time to start heading back.

But unintentionally, she had just crossed the collective path of a group of Rust Creek Falls' senior citizens, otherwise regarded by some as the town's opinionated, unofficial Greek chorus. They behaved as if they were qualified—and actually obligated—to express their opinions on everything that transpired in the small town.

Today was no exception.

"Heard you gave that no-show husband of yours his walking papers, dearie," Blanche Curtis, an older woman sitting on the extreme left of the bench in front of the One-Stop General Store said to her. The woman had gray hair, more than her share of wrinkles thanks to an unforgiving sun and looked as if she would be perfectly at home playing the wicked witch in a revival of *The Wizard of Oz.* "Good for you," she cried encouragingly. "That'll teach him to take you for granted.

"These men," she continued, casting a critical eye toward her seatmates on the other end of the bench. "They tell you that you're the moon and the stars to them, then they get you pregnant and pretty quick, they lose all interest in you. 'Time to move on to new challenges,'" Blanche said in disgust, shaking her head. "They're all about the hunt and conquest, nothing else."

"I'm sorry," Claire said, unable to get away because the woman was holding on to the side of the carriage with her long, thin fingers, "do I know you?"

"No, but I know you," the woman told her with an air of mystery. "Blanche Curtis," the woman told her, sticking out her hand. "I'm a friend of your grandma's," she added, as if that explained everything.

"If you're such a great friend, why are you trying to

mess with her granddaughter's life and give her advice she doesn't need?" the man sitting on the far side of the bench wanted to know.

"I beg your pardon." Blanche sniffed indignantly. The woman sat up a little straighter, as if that could help her repel any unwanted criticism from the man on the end.

"Don't beg for my pardon, beg for hers," the man said, nodding his head toward Claire. Leaning both hands on the ornate head of his sleek, black cane, he slid forward on the seat just a tad. "Don't pay her any mind, Claire. She's been a bitter old woman since the third grade when Michael Finnegan picked Rachel White to be his square-dance partner instead of her. You put that family of yours together the first chance you get, young lady," the man advised. "A baby deserves to have both a mama and a daddy."

"Billy Joe Ryan, you do an awful lot of talking for a man with no brain," the woman who had introduced herself as Blanche angrily accused.

"Now, Blanche, leave the poor girl alone," a third member of the unofficial town philosophers' group, Homer Gilmore, said. "Can't you see that she's thinking about doing the right thing? Everyone deserves a second chance, even a husband," he said with enthusiastic conviction. And then he turned toward Claire. "You give that man of yours a second chance, Miss Claire," he advised nervously. "You'll be happy you did. You don't like being alone, right?"

Claire stared at the man who she vaguely remembered meeting once before, at the wedding reception. He seemed to be very convinced that she needed to forgive Levi. Why would it matter to him one way or another?

Didn't these people have anything better to do than to sit around, giving out unwanted advice?

"Better alone than being with a man who doesn't care just how much he hurts his wife with his actions," the fourth member on the bench, a woman she'd heard referred to as "Alice" at the reception, proclaimed.

Claire could only take in this unwanted commentary on her life in abject horror. Did *everyone* in this town have an opinion on her marital state and on whether or not she should take Levi back?

The very thought unnerved her and made her want to run for cover. Didn't these people have *lives* of their own?

Upset and protective of her family's right to privacy, Claire asked, "Is that all you people talk about? The state of my marriage?"

"Lately, it's been pretty much of an equal draw between your marriage and the weather," she heard a deep voice behind her saying.

Claire whirled around, startled. Her attention focused on the four people who had just rendered very public their opinions about the very private matter of her home life, Claire hadn't been aware of anyone coming up behind her until just now when he spoke.

When she'd swung around, she was still holding on to the handle of the baby carriage and brought it abruptly around with her. The result was that she came within a hair's breadth of whacking a man's legs with the carriage.

Sucking in her breath, she pulled the carriage to her and away from the man.

"I'm so sorry," Claire apologized then added in her own defense, "but you snuck up on me."

"Wasn't planning it that way. I'm Detective Russ Campbell," he told her. Even as he spoke, all four occupants of the bench seemed to lean forward in unison, obviously intent on hearing what was being said. Campbell was just as intent that they didn't. "Listen, is there anywhere that you and I could go to have a few words?" He left the choice up to her. "I'd like to ask you some questions."

What possible reason would an officer of the law have to question her? Claire couldn't help wondering. Was this because of something that Levi had done, because, to the very best of her knowledge, she certainly wasn't guilty of anything.

Except for cooking, maybe, she silently amended.

"What kind of questions?" Claire wanted to know. Out of the corner of her eye, she saw that the four people on the bench seemed to have moved closer to the side where she and the officer were standing.

"The kind you wouldn't want the people around here to speculate about," Russ wisely replied.

Claire lowered her voice. "You mean it could get worse than this?" she asked incredulously.

The detective laughed at the naive question. "Can it

ever," he said to her. "I believe the old expression that best summarizes this is, 'You ain't seen nothin' yet.'"

That was all she needed, Claire thought, to have the whole town talking and speculating about something in her life.

As if she didn't have enough to deal with.

"Okay, you talked me into it," she told him. And then she remembered. She had obligations now. She didn't want to give her grandmother any reason to think she was behaving irresponsibly. It was a matter of pride. "But will this take long? I have to be getting back to help out with lunch. I'm staying at the Strickland Boarding House," she added.

An easy smile curved the cop's lips. "Yes, I know. I was just getting ready to go over there to see you."

This was beginning to come together for her. "Oh, so I didn't just bump into you."

"Not exactly," he told her.

Claire turned her back to the bench and its occupants, not wanting to give the foursome an opportunity to eavesdrop. "You could come back there with me," she suggested. "We could talk on the way."

Russ glanced over his shoulder and saw four pairs of eyes watching them intently. However, he seemed fairly certain that none of the four would be willing to rise and follow behind them for the sake of satisfying any latent curiosity.

Russ nodded. "Sounds good to me."

Without bothering to say goodbye or anything else to

the foursome, Claire started walking back to the boarding house, pushing Bekka's carriage in front of her.

The detective fell into step beside her.

"What is it you want to know?" she asked.

"On the night of the wedding that you and your husband attended, did you notice anything out of the ordinary going on at the reception?"

She certainly hadn't expected the detective to question her about the harmless wedding reception.

"Out of the ordinary?" Claire repeated, confused. Thinking back to that night, she felt that the goings-on at the reception had all been slightly out of the ordinary. The reception was one big party, and parties were all about people cutting loose. Since it wasn't just a wedding reception but also the Fourth of July, that was to be expected—wasn't it?

"Yes." Russ tried rephrasing his question. "Was anyone behaving suspiciously?"

Claire thought for a moment, but nothing really came to mind. "No, I don't think so."

Russ became more specific. "Did you by any chance notice anyone slipping something into people's drinks, or into the punch bowl?"

That was something she would not have just taken notice of, but mentioned to either Levi or later on to her grandfather. But she hadn't observed anything of the kind.

"No, of course not." Did the man actually think she would have taken that in stride? "I would have said something if I'd seen someone doing that." And then she replayed the detective's question in her mind. "Why? Do you think someone was tampering with people's drinks at the reception?" she asked, horrified by the very thought and what it implied.

Russ didn't answer her directly. Instead, he asked her another question. "Think back to that night. Do you think that anyone had a reason to slip a mickey into your drink?"

Claire blinked. "*My* drink? Why would anyone slip something into my drink?" she wanted to know. There was no reason for the officer to think anything like that. She wasn't a threat to anyone. Nor did she have any enemies or even friendly rivals. "I was planning on going home with my husband when the reception was over."

"But you didn't," Russ pointed out.

"No, I didn't." It took effort to say that without a trace of bitterness. "Levi decided he wanted to join in a poker game some of the guys were getting up."

"Was that usual behavior for him?" Russ asked.

"Usual?" she echoed, not sure what the cop was asking.

Russ rephrased the question. "Does he go off to play poker a lot?"

"No, as a matter of fact, he's *never* done that." *See, even you have to admit that it was unusual for Levi to walk off and leave you like that. Something's just not right here.* "Do you think that someone slipped him something?"

"Do *you* think that?" Russ asked, turning the question back around on her.

"I don't know," she said helplessly. "Levi seemed normal enough. I mean, he wasn't slurring or weaving or anything like that." She got back to the officer's question. "What reason would anyone have to spike his drink?" Claire asked.

Russ tried to make himself clearer. He was still trying to clarify the situation for himself. "I don't think he was targeted specifically. I think that a lot of people might have been affected by the punch being spiked."

"So the punch *was* spiked?" she repeated incredulously. "But why would anyone want to do that?" Claire wanted to know.

That was the giant knot he was attempting to untangle. "That's what I'm trying to find out," Russ told her. "Did anything strike you as being odd that evening?" he asked again. "Anything overall?"

Claire pressed her lips together, thinking. "Well, now that you mention it…*I* felt kind of odd that evening. I mean, I'm small and it doesn't take much to make me feel light-headed, but even I can hold down one drink, or even two, without having the room go spinning around."

Russ stopped walking and looked at her. "And did it?" he asked her. "The room, did it go spinning around for you?"

"Yes," she admitted, recalling the unpleasant sensation. "It did. What does that mean?" she asked him. "I mean, aside from the fact that someone might have tampered with the punch. Why would someone do that? What was there to gain?"

The officer shook his head. "I don't really know. Yet," Russ added. "But I will," he promised. "I will."

Claire couldn't wait for Levi to come back to the boarding house that evening. All through her chores, as she assisted Gina with both lunch and the evening meal, her mind kept going back to the fateful night of the wedding reception.

But nothing enlightening came to her.

The officer had told her that he suspected someone had tampered with the punch, causing everyone who drank it to behave erratically.

But she hadn't.

And Levi hadn't.

Levi hadn't behaved erratically at all. He had just tuned her out and gone off with his friends. That was behaving thoughtlessly, she told herself, not erratically.

Right?

Stop giving the man excuses.

But what if that *had* been Levi's excuse? What if Levi's drink *had* been spiked? That meant that he hadn't been himself that night and couldn't be held accountable for just leaving her like that to go play cards with his friends.

Okay, that was *that* night, but what about all the other nights? The nights that he was out late "working" or away altogether, in another town, at some so-called "furniture" seminar—whatever *that* was.

And what if it hadn't been a seminar? What if Levi

was entertaining an out-of-town guest? A party of one, emphasis on the word *party*?

The very thought that he might be cheating on her, that he had gotten tired of her and maybe struck up a "friendship" with some other younger, prettier, *single* woman began to prey on her mind, making her conjure up a host of terrible scenarios.

By the time Levi returned to the boarding house that evening, it was rather late. Even so, he made it a point to stop at Claire's room and knock on her door. When she didn't answer, he tried again.

There was still no answer.

He knew she wasn't downstairs in the common room because he'd checked there first before coming up.

Had she gone back home? If not that, then what? He'd thought that they were making progress, taking baby steps, but still making progress. But maybe he was wrong.

A feeling of desperation began to mount up within him as he knocked yet a third time. If she didn't answer this time, he was going to go look for her grandfather and—

The door opened. Relief flooded through him, but it was short-lived.

Claire was holding the door ajar, placing her own body in the way like a human doorstop. Levi couldn't get in unless he pushed her out of the way, which he wasn't about to do.

"Detective Campbell wants to talk to you," she told

him coolly. Her body language made it crystal clear that he wasn't setting foot into the room.

"Detective Campbell?" he questioned, trying to put the name to a face. He failed. "About what?"

Claire drew herself up to her full height. "About the night of the reception."

That still really didn't answer his question. "What about it?" he wanted to know.

Claire's eyes met his. "He wants to know if you think you were drugged at the time."

"Drugged? You mean he thinks I took drugs?" Claire wasn't being very clear about this, he thought. "You know I don't do that kind of thing," he told her.

When she didn't immediately respond, telling him that she knew he would never take any sort of unlawful substance, that he was far too responsible to do something like that, Levi was quick to swear an oath. "May I never see my little girl again if I took so much as a larger dosage of aspirin, much less some kind of an illegal drug."

She regarded him for a very long moment, as if she was weighing several things. In the end, she relented. Sort of.

"I believe that *you* don't think you took any kind of an illegal drug, but maybe someone managed to slip you something without your knowledge." Cocking her head, she peered at him, as if a different angle could somehow give her a better perspective. "Would you even know?"

Having had absolutely no experience with any of

that, he shrugged. "I guess that depends on what it was and what the dosage was."

"But offhand? What did you feel that night, after the wedding reception?" Claire pressed, wanting to see what he would say to her.

He thought about it for a long moment, trying to re-create the time frame in his mind. "Maybe I felt a little hyper and somewhat wired." That sounded so lame, he thought, but that was the best he could describe it. "All I know was that I was looking forward to playing poker."

Her eyes narrowed slightly. Well, now she knew. "But not to being with me."

Damn, she was doing it again, Levi thought. She was putting words into his mouth. "I never said that," he protested.

"You didn't have to," she informed him, her hurt galvanizing her again. "Good night!" she cried. Pushing him back, she slammed the door right in his face.

Chapter Eight

She was doing it again, Levi thought glumly. Claire was shutting him out.

He thought that they were finally making progress, and now Claire was giving him the cold shoulder every time they were within a couple feet of each other.

To his overwhelming dismay, this had been going on for a couple of days now, and he was pretty much at his wit's end as to how to win her back or even how to wear her down so that they were back to where they'd been just a few days ago.

He had thought that whatever set Claire off the other evening would have faded away by now. That they would be back to that cautious two-step they were doing, dancing around the issues and the sensitive feelings that were involved while trying to slowly work their way back to where they'd been before this whole wedding reception/Fourth of July fiasco had ever happened.

But they weren't. At least, Claire wasn't.

As for him, he was more than willing to go down on bended knee to ask her forgiveness if that was what it took. He just wanted to get Claire past this hurdle and back on track. Back to being his wife and the mother of his beloved baby girl.

It was getting worse, not better. He missed being with Claire and the baby like crazy. Missed the silent comfort of their ordinary, day-to-day lives.

But each time they'd cross paths, Claire would deliberately and pointedly look away, as if looking at him caused her more distress and annoyance than she could bear.

There had to be something he could do to change that. But what?

The thought that he couldn't think of anything really bothered him as Levi stood near the front door of the furniture store. Knowing that he had a full day of work ahead of him, he managed to plaster a cheerful, albeit very hollow smile on his face.

It was hard for him to keep his mind on business when everything inside him felt as if it was in complete turmoil.

But he knew he had to continue this charade he was presently engaged in. If he didn't—if he allowed the situation to get the better of him and make him fall apart—he'd wind up putting his job in jeopardy, and that was totally unacceptable.

He couldn't dare risk losing his job. Besides having worked long and hard to get to where he was, working here at the furniture store represented the only source of income that he had. Without any income, he knew he was *sure* to lose Claire and Bekka.

The thought struck him as being ironic, since it was initially his job—and the long hours that it required him to keep—that had torn his little family apart in the first place.

There were presently several customers in the store, wandering through the various artfully arranged furnishings that he had personally staged and set up. Levi kept his distance from the potential clients, instinctively knowing that there was nothing that drove customers away faster than a salesperson who hovered, or worse, one who offered a running commentary on whatever piece they might be looking at.

He'd learned early on that customers appreciated being given their space to view and debate before they came to their final decision. If they needed any assistance of any sort, he knew for a fact that they would seek him out.

All he had to do was wait and make himself available to them.

If he was only certain that the same theory was true when it came to Claire. He swore she was like the proverbial wild card that could pop up in a hand at any time. He had absolutely no idea what she was thinking or what she was liable to do. All he knew with certainty was that he had to win her back. As to when and how, well, that was anyone's guess. He certainly didn't have a clue. All he could do was make himself available.

And pray.

His cell phone rang. Pulling it out of his pocket, he answered the phone before it could ring again.

"So how's it going?" the feminine voice on the other end of the line asked.

For just a moment he found the familiarity of his mother's voice comforting. But he wasn't a little boy anymore, and the days that she could make all things right were long gone.

"It's not, Ma," he said honestly. "It's stalled."

There was a long pause on the other end before his mother told him, "It's only stalled if you want it to be."

He refrained from telling his mother that he was attempting to move heaven and earth—and not getting very far doing it. "It's not that simple, Ma."

"It's also not as complicated as you're making it, Levi," Lucy Wyatt told him. "First of all, you have to give yourself permission to be happy. That doesn't mean working yourself to death," she added pointedly.

His mother, he recalled, always worried that he was working too hard. "I'm not, Ma."

Lucy dismissed her son's words. "Oh, if I know you, you are, Levi. And I blame myself for that. I shouldn't have allowed you to turn your back on furthering your education by going out to work right after high school graduation. I know that you did that strictly to help out your brothers, as well as me.

"You're a good boy, Levi," she went on. "Your motives were pure and noble when you took that job. But mine weren't. I should have known better. I shouldn't have accepted the money that you turned over to me." A deep sadness entered her voice as Lucy said, "I sold out your childhood for a paycheck. What kind of a mother does that make me?"

"You are a great mother, and I was hardly a child, Ma," he pointed out.

He could hear the tightness in her throat as she said, "That's right, you hardly were. And that was my fault. When your father walked out on us, leaving me to raise and provide for the three of you, I let you take those part-time jobs, turning a blind eye to what that would eventually mean. I allowed you to put in all those long hours working while your friends were out having fun, being young. You never got that chance."

He didn't want his mother berating herself for what had been his decision. "They were just being kids, Ma," Levi said dismissively.

"Exactly! Something you should have had a right to be, too," she insisted.

He didn't want her to beat herself up for what he felt was one of the better decisions of his life. "I'll do it the second time around."

"The second time?" Lucy repeated, bewildered. "I don't understand."

He laughed. "They say that when people get very old, they regress to their childhood and start behaving like little kids. I'll get to it then," Levi told his mother. "Don't worry about it."

But it was obvious that she did.

However, since it was also obvious that the conversation wasn't going anywhere with this topic, Lucy Wyatt switched back to the topic that had initially prompted her to call her son in the first place.

"So how's the campaign to win back your touchy wife going?"

"Ma—" There was a hint of a warning note in his voice. He and Claire might be having their problems, and he knew that his mother was on his side no matter what, but he couldn't just stand by and allow blame to be heaped on Claire's head this way.

"Sorry," Lucy apologized with little enthusiasm. However, it was clear that she had no intentions of antagonizing her son, either. "How's the campaign to win back your wife going?" she reworded.

Levi refrained from blowing out a long breath. He didn't want to call any undue attention to himself from any of the people currently in the store. "It's not."

Lucy's voice was filled with tenderness as she made her son this offer. "Honey, would you like me to talk to her for you?"

He felt a chill streaking down his back at the very thought of what she was saying. "God forbid. It'll set Claire off. No offense, Ma, but you're not exactly a disinterested party here."

Lucy had never been anything but honest when dealing with her sons. She respected them too much as human beings to indulge in any verbal games.

"No, I'm not. I'm a *very* interested party. You're a

good person and you deserve the best, Levi. I just get upset when I see you being treated with anything but the utmost love and respect," she confessed.

She was putting him up on a pedestal again, Levi thought. She had to stop doing that and get more realistic. "I'm not perfect, Ma."

"Maybe not, but then neither is she," Lucy said loyally. "And besides, there's a baby's happiness at stake here. Bekka needs you in her life." Emotion throbbed in her voice as she told her son, "I won't have Claire painting you as the bad guy."

"She's not, Ma. Really," he told his mother. "Don't take this the wrong way, but please stay out of it." In a moment of weakness and at a very low point, he'd told his mother about their argument and his subsequent—and hopefully temporary—change of address. He more than regretted it now.

It was obvious that his mother wasn't buying his protests, but being his mother, she also didn't want to argue about it since it clearly upset him.

Lucy cast about for another way to help her oldest son. "Maybe if I got together with Claire's mother and father and talked to them... If I made them see that they really needed to talk some sense into their daughter's head—"

That would just make everything that much worse, Levi thought. Didn't his mother see that? She wouldn't have wanted anyone butting into her private affairs. "Ma, promise me you won't interfere." He was all but begging now.

"All right, as long as you promise me you won't give up trying to talk some sense into that girl. I don't want my granddaughter growing up without her father—or her father's mother," Lucy added.

That makes two of us, Ma, Levi thought. "I promise, and Bekka won't, don't worry."

"But I *do* worry," Lucy told her son. "I'm your mother. It's my job to worry. Now promise you'll call me the minute you two get back together."

"Yes, Ma," Levi replied dutifully. "I promise. Look, I've got to go. I'm at the store and I've got a customer who wants to make a purchase—"

"Look at you, making a sale without saying a word," Lucy commented proudly. "I hope your boss knows what a prize you are."

Levi rolled his eyes. He knew if he let her, his mother could go on like that for hours, and he loved her for it. But not right now.

"He does."

"Maybe *he* can talk to your wife, since I can't," Lucy said with a touch of exasperation in her voice.

He knew he had to quit now while he still could. "Bye, Ma. I'm hanging up now," he told her, and then terminated the call.

Although the store did have customers—and one had even looked his way—no one had approached him, indicating that they were ready to talk business. He'd only said that to his mother to get off the phone. He had the uneasy feeling that not only wasn't his mother going to cease and desist, but she was also most likely going to attempt to broker some sort of mediation between himself and Claire.

There would be no way he would even remotely agree to anything his mother had in mind because he was certain that he would be risking having things become even worse than they were at the present moment.

His mother, unfortunately, had that way about her. Besides, what woman wanted to have her mother-in-law butting in to her life?

All he could do, Levi thought as he quietly observed the customers meandering through the various displays in the store, was to make himself as readily available as he could to Claire and hope for the best.

When he finally came back to the boarding house that night, he was just as wiped out as he had been all the previous nights. The drive back to Rust Creek Falls and the boarding house seemed to get longer every evening. But even though he was having trouble putting one foot in front of the other, he still stopped by Claire's room, hoping against hope she would allow him a glimpse of their daughter.

He had even brought flowers with him to smooth the path.

This time, when he knocked on Claire's door, it opened immediately. That it did caught him completely by surprise, especially since Claire had been turning a deaf ear to his knocking—no matter how hard or how long—on the previous last two nights.

When the door opened Levi unconsciously squeezed

the bouquet he was holding a little harder, but made no effort to offer the flowers to her. In actuality, he'd temporarily forgotten that he was clutching them.

Claire was wearing a tank top that didn't quite cover her midriff, and she had on a pair of denim shorts that brought new meaning to the term *cutoffs*. The whimsical fringes that had resulted from the so-called "cut" barely covered what they were intended to cover, flirting outrageously with the eye of the beholder. In addition, the somewhat faded material clung to her curves as if it had been painted on instead of hastily sewn together in some shop.

Levi had to remind himself to breathe. Periodically. And deeply.

And then he looked more closely at the expression on her face. It didn't look like the kind of expression a woman wearing a sexy tank top and pulse-accelerating shorts would have on her face.

Something was definitely up.

"Your mother called."

The three little words swiftly brought down the world he thought he was about to enter in less than three seconds.

"Oh, God," he groaned, afraid to begin to imagine the damage his mother had caused. "I'm sorry, Claire. I told her I didn't want her getting involved or saying anything to you, but my mother has always been a very headstrong woman."

"Nothing wrong with being headstrong," Claire told him then added, "It's probably your mother's best quality." Claire paused for a second before she got to the crux of her statement. "She told me a few things."

"I can just imagine," he said, bracing himself. "Look, whatever she said, I'm sorry. I didn't put her up to anything. As a matter of fact, I told her not to bother you. But she was never very good at listening to what people were saying. Especially if it wasn't exactly what she wanted to hear."

"Why didn't you tell me that you didn't go on to college because you felt you needed to provide for your mother and your two younger brothers?"

He shrugged, fervently wishing that for once in her life, his mother could have just backed off. He knew that she meant well, but he was already having enough trouble with this estranged situation. He didn't want Claire thinking that he'd deliberately had his mother cite something he had done for his family. He'd done it because he wanted to and felt it was the right thing to do. He hadn't done it to come off as some selfless martyr.

"The subject never came up," he answered vaguely.

For just a moment his answer had rendered Claire speechless. And then she found her tongue.

"The hell it didn't," she retorted. "The subject was there every time I came home from college, every time I'd nag you about going to college yourself."

Levi shrugged, uncomfortable with the very nature of the subject.

"I didn't think you'd be interested in hearing the story," he told her.

The real truth was he was afraid that if Claire knew

the whole story, she might look at him with pity because his father had abandoned him, leaving him to struggle and do the best he could for the ones he cared about.

But in his heart, Levi had felt he owed it to his mother and brothers. That if he could make life a little better for them, then he should. It helped him as much as it did them to make life more tolerable for his family.

The same way he now did for Claire and Bekka.

Right now he just wanted to put this whole subject behind him. "Claire, I know it's late, but I was hoping I could look in on Bekka for a couple of minutes. I promise I won't wake her up."

For a second he thought Claire was going to turn him down. And then she laughed softly.

"You won't have to," Claire told him. "Mother Nature beat you to it. Bekka's been wide-awake for hours now." She looked at Levi for a second. "Maybe she was just killing time while she waited to see her daddy."

He looked at Claire. That certainly didn't sound like the sarcastic, flippant woman he had come to know in the past few weeks. He would have said that he was dreaming—except that he knew he wasn't.

He told himself to stop wasting time before Claire realized that she was being kind and rescinded the implied offer.

"You don't mind if I see her?" he asked uncertainly.

"No, I don't mind," Claire answered in the same quiet voice. She gestured toward the baby lying in the portable playpen. "Go on, it's okay. Since Bekka lights up whenever you walk into a room, maybe it might be a good thing for her if you spent a little time with our little girl."

"Thanks," Levi said to her with feeling. Then he slanted another look toward Claire—a longer one as he tried to puzzle things out—and asked, "How do you feel about my spending time with her mother?"

Claire arched one eyebrow as she regarded him. "I wouldn't push it if I were you, Levi," she warned.

He raised his hands in a sign of complete surrender. "Message received. You don't need to say another word, Claire. My question is officially rescinded," he told her. And then, because he prided himself on always being truthful with Claire, he added, "I'm a patient man. I can wait until you decide to change your mind about that."

Because he had really left her no recourse if she was to save face, Claire told him, "I don't think there's enough patience in the whole world for that."

"We'll see," Levi said softly, more to himself than to her. "We'll see."

Claire gave no indication that she had overheard him. But she had.

And something very deep inside her warmed to his words.

Chapter Nine

"Looks like you're going to be flying solo today, kid," Gene said to his granddaughter when she opened the door to his knock a couple of mornings later.

Gene had become his great-granddaughter's official babysitter while Claire was busy in the kitchen, helping Gina prepare meals for the other residents at the boarding house. Melba told her granddaughter that as far as she was concerned, she was killing two birds with one stone. Bekka was well taken care of while Claire was cooking, and Gene had something meaningful to do that "kept him out from underfoot."

Melba herself saw to it that she was everywhere at once, taking care of the myriad details that went into running the boarding house.

"Ah, there's my little playmate," Gene declared

warmly as he walked into the room and crossed directly to Bekka's portable crib. Half a second later, the baby was in his arms and snug against his chest.

Claire still marveled how her usually crusty grandfather transformed into what amounted to a bowl of mush whenever he was around her daughter. It was as if he became an entirely different person if he got within fifteen feet of the baby.

However, this morning it was what he'd said as part of his greeting that had corralled her attention.

"What do you mean by *solo*, Grandpa? I don't understand." Even so, there was a tight feeling of uneasy anticipation in her stomach.

Patting Bekka's bottom in a soothing motion, Gene obligingly spelled it out for his granddaughter. "Gina called in sick this morning, so you're on your own," he explained. "Who's my best girl?" he asked in the next breath, cooing at the baby in his arms.

Bekka gurgled in response, as if she understood her great-grandfather's question.

"Sick?" Claire repeated. That nauseous feeling was beginning to spread. "What do you mean she called in sick?"

Gently swaying to and fro with the baby, Gene looked at his granddaughter as if he didn't understand exactly what she was questioning.

"Just that. I don't know any other languages to use, Claire-bear. Gina said she was sick and she's not going to be coming in today, so you're in charge of making breakfast, lunch and dinner—since the guests have become accustomed to this. Now do you understand?" he asked.

Her knees suddenly weak, Claire sank down on the edge of her bed just in time. A second later her legs completely turned to liquid.

"Oh, God."

"Hey, it's not so bad," he said, attempting to encourage her. "Your grandmother says you're doing terrific."

Claire raised skeptical eyes to the old man's face. "Grandmother doesn't use the word *terrific* to describe *anything*, much less my halting progress in the world of cooking," she pointed out.

"Okay," Gene conceded reluctantly. "So maybe she didn't use that *exact* word, but she meant that one. You know your grandma. If she's not happy with or about something, we *all* know about it. Fast," he underscored.

Claire still looked stricken about the idea of cooking all those meals by herself. It wasn't that the boarding house was teeming with people, but right now *any* people were just too many for her to deal with.

"I don't even know where to start," she confessed to her grandfather.

"In the kitchen would be a good place," Gene told her with only a hint of a smile on his face. "Come on, princess and I will walk you there, Claire-bear," he offered.

Taking in a shaky breath, Claire let it out slowly. Crossing the threshold, she waited for her grandfather to follow, then locked her door, pocketing the key. "I feel like I'm about to walk my last mile to the execution chamber."

"Have a little faith in yourself, Claire-bear," Gene encouraged.

"I do," Claire countered. "Very little."

As they made their way down the hall to the stairs, Levi opened his door. He was dressed in a light gray suit and blue shirt and was obviously about to leave for work. His attention was instantly captured by the minuscule parade and especially by the distressed look on his wife's face.

Rather than extending a typical greeting to Gene, whom he considered a valuable ally, or pausing to say a few loving words of nonsense to his daughter, his attention was completely focused on Claire.

"Anything wrong, Claire?" Levi asked the inane question, even though he knew there *had* to be something wrong. As a rule, Claire did not sport an expression that looked as if she'd just lost her best friend, but she certainly did now.

Denial immediately rose to her lips, but Claire refrained from saying the words out loud. There'd been a time when she and Levi had been not just husband and wife but best friends, as well, and it was to her former best friend that she now spoke.

"Grandpa just told me that I'm supposed to make breakfast, lunch and dinner for the rest of the boarders today."

Gene had already informed him of Claire's new duties in the kitchen, telling him it was Melba's way of making Claire more domestic. "I thought you were doing that already."

Another shaky breath escaped her lips. "Not by myself, I haven't."

"Gina's sick," Gene volunteered.

"Oh, I see." He searched Claire's face, as if it could answer things for him that she couldn't. "But you've been working with Gina for the last couple of weeks, haven't you?"

There was a world of difference between doing something under watchful, supervising eyes and going it alone as she was now expected to do. "Yes, but—"

Levi didn't let her finish. "Was she satisfied with what you were making?"

Claire raised and lowered her shoulder in a vague response to the question. She felt as if she was on very shaky ground here.

"I guess so…"

He wasn't finished yet. "Did what you made get served?"

She didn't have to think; she remembered each occasion. "Yes."

He smiled, lightly patting her shoulder. "Then you'll be fine."

Claire was far from being sold. "I don't know about that."

It looked as if Claire was going to need more support than just a few encouraging words, Levi thought. He weighed his options, although he already knew what he needed to do. "Tell you what. If you want me to, I'll stick around and help you with breakfast."

"Breakfast is from 7:30 to 9:30," Claire pointed out. That was two hours. More if she factored in the prep time.

"I know," Levi replied.

She expected him to offer a barrage of reasons why he couldn't hold her hand in this, not continue to offer to stay and help. "You'll be late for work." Didn't Levi realize that?

Again he surprised Claire by telling her, "I know that, too."

Was this the same man who was never home? Who seemed to be married to his job and chose it over her time and again? "You're actually willing to do that?" she asked in disbelief. "You're willing to be late for work just to help me out?"

He knew he was risking a lot, but at the same time, if he hadn't proven himself at work yet, then he never would, and there was something really important at stake here. He realized that now.

"You're more important to me than work, Claire." Putting his arm around her shoulders, he said, "Come on, let's go downstairs and get started."

Because he was offering to stay, she didn't feel nearly as threatened by his job as she previously had. Her perspective began shifting.

"No, that's okay," Claire said. "I don't need you to hold my hand. Go to work. You've got a long drive ahead of you."

Reaching the bottom of the stairs, Levi made no move to leave. "You're sure you'll be all right?" he wanted to know.

Claire nodded. There was even a small smile on her lips. "Yes, I'm sure. Besides, I've got a feeling that if I start falling behind, Grandmother will be there to pick up the slack. After all, that was what she used to do and she's too much of a type A personality not to try to take over if she thinks I need help."

"Okay," Levi said, scrutinizing her face closely. "Then I guess maybe I'll see you tonight."

"Maybe," she agreed, echoing what was the key word in his sentence.

He had almost reached the front door when she called after him. "Levi?"

One hand on the doorknob, he turned around to face her. Had she changed her mind about accepting his help after all? "Yes?"

"Thank you."

The smile that bloomed on his lips made his face positively irresistible. It took Claire no effort at all to remember the effect he had had on her when they were first dating. She could remember hardly being able to keep her hands off him—and the feeling had been deliciously mutual.

"Don't mention it," he responded. Nodding at Gene, Levi left the house.

He'd held his peace all during the exchanges between his granddaughter and her husband, but now Gene felt he had to speak his mind. "You ask me, Claire-bear, you married a right nice fella."

She couldn't very well sling mud at her husband right now. "I guess he does have his moments."

Gene chuckled. "That he does, Claire-bear. That he does."

She knew where this was going, and she didn't have time for that discussion. Not the time, nor the heart to try to untangle what had gone wrong with a marriage that looked as if it should have been a triumphant success from day one.

Claire squared her shoulders and turned toward the kitchen in the rear of the first floor. "Yes, Grandpa, but it's the hours I'm thinking about, not the moments. See you after breakfast—I hope."

"Like that boy said—" her grandfather paused to kiss the top of her head "—you'll do just fine. It's breakfast. Nothing special."

"Right," Claire murmured under her breath as she took small, measured steps to the kitchen. "Nothing special."

She had been making breakfast every morning now since her grandmother had put her to work in the kitchen. Melba had taken the mystery out of making French toast, blueberry pancakes and Belgian waffles, as well as showing her a number of different ways to prepare and serve eggs.

That should be more than enough to get her through breakfast.

"I can do this," Claire told herself as she finally walked into the kitchen—a kitchen that for some reason felt a lot bigger this morning than it had on previous mornings. "Get a grip, Claire," she instructed herself sternly under her breath. "You haven't poisoned anyone yet."

She tied her apron on, grabbed her whisk and began cracking eggs.

The second the store was locked up for the evening, Levi all but raced to his car. He was behind the wheel and on the road to Rust Creek Falls less than five minutes after he had double-checked that the security alarms had all been set.

There was a huge bouquet of flowers lying on the passenger seat next to him. In order not to waste any time stopping for them on the way home, he had bought the flowers during part of his lunch break. He'd used the rest of his break to work so that he didn't have to stay after hours, attending to myriad details and making sure that everything was taken care of.

Depending on how the day—meaning her cooking debut—had gone for Claire, the flowers were either to celebrate her success or they were to console her if the meals she made hadn't gone as she'd planned.

Either way, he'd gotten her favorites. Pink and white carnations. A whole avalanche of pink and white carnations. If nothing more, he was hoping to bring a smile to her face—and to help make her see that not only was he on her side, but he was also always thinking of her.

Which he was.

He was also always thinking about their separation. It was going on much too long, and it was beginning to really worry him. Levi was becoming really afraid that if he didn't do something about ending it, it would wind up dragging on much too long and could eventually lead to the one thing he couldn't bear to have happen.

A divorce.

He'd already been painfully rejected once in his life when his father had walked out on his family. While he knew that there had been a number of issues between his parents, issues causing them to argue long and loud, he had taken his father's abandonment of the family personally, feeling that if he had just done something right, said something right, he would have been able to change his father's mind and the man would have remained with them. Would have been the father they all needed.

But he hadn't managed to say something right, *do* something right, and his father had taken off for parts unknown—even to this day. His mother would never say as much, never even so much as *hinted* at this, but he acutely felt that his father's walking out on them had somehow been his fault.

And it all came vividly back to him again when Claire had thrown him out and then, within less than a week, had taken off with the baby to live in another town.

If he hadn't come looking for her, she would have most likely remained where she was and they would now be headed for divorce.

What makes you think you're not still headed there? the devil's advocate in him taunted.

But Levi had to believe otherwise, had to believe that with enough effort on his part, he could turn things around. Could make Claire change her mind about leaving him.

However, even with that effort, even desperately *wanting* to turn things around, for his own sanity he was holding a piece of himself back. It was a gesture of self-preservation. He really couldn't bear to put all of him out there and then, very possibly, get rejected.

If that happened, it would, quite simply, just kill him.

He wasn't brave enough to do that. Not right now. Not yet.

Perhaps not ever.

This way, if she *did* reject him, and he hadn't fully connected with her, then she hadn't rejected all of him because she never *had* all of him.

It was contrived, but it was the only way he had of preserving his peace of mind.

As he drove, Levi kept sipping the triple espresso he had in his cup holder, wanting not just to stay awake but to be wired, as well.

When he reached the boarding house in what amounted to record time for him, Levi felt as if he was ready to go ten rounds with whoever wanted to defend the middleweight boxing championship of the world.

On arrival, he parked at the curb some sixty feet away from the boarding house and all but sprinted to the front door—twice. The first time he was about to enter when he realized that he had left the flowers he had bought for Claire on the seat in his car. He hurried back for the bouquet, then swiftly retraced his steps back to the front door.

Walking in, he was greeted by the lingering, tempting scent of recently fried chicken.

He smiled to himself as he inhaled. It appeared that the flowers he'd brought were going to be of the celebratory nature.

Dinner was over, but he knew for a fact that the refrigerator was not off-limits, at least not for him because he was not only a boarder here at Strickland House, he was also family. Even Melba had grudgingly acknowledged that fact after she'd gotten over old Gene's going behind her back.

Levi peeked into the kitchen, not to see if he could sneak a late meal out of the refrigerator, but to see if Claire was still there.

She wasn't.

That meant, more than likely, that she was upstairs in her room. He'd passed by the common room on his way to the kitchen and hadn't seen her. Process of elimination had put her in her room. Unless she'd gone out for the evening, and he didn't want to entertain that thought unless he really had to.

Levi took the back stairs two at a time, humming and hoping for the best.

Chapter Ten

To Levi's surprise, Claire's grandmother opened the door to Claire's room when he knocked on it.

"Yes?" she asked, her small dark brown eyes taking slow, complete measure of him as she deliberately kept him waiting out in the hall. As far as she was concerned, he had hurt Claire—intentionally or not—and she had yet to forgive him.

She stood blocking access to the room and was also blocking any view into it.

Levi managed to keep down his frustration. "I came to see how Claire's big day went."

Melba's expression was quizzical. "Big day?" she repeated.

"She was doing all the cooking by herself."

"Yes?" she asked expectantly.

"She seemed worried about handling the responsibility, and I just wanted to ask her how it went."

"It went," Melba said with a careless shrug. She was proud of Claire, but too much praise might make the girl relax and stop making the progress she was making lately.

She clearly wanted him to leave, but Levi wasn't ready to do that.

"Well?" he prompted. He tried again to peer into the room, but Melba only moved farther forward, pulling the door behind her.

Cutting off any hope for a view.

"Well, what?" she demanded.

That's not the way he'd meant the word. "Did it go *well* for Claire?"

Melba gave him another nonanswer of sorts. "Her grandfather's taking her out to the movies in Kalispell to celebrate," she said, mentioning the town that was some twenty miles away, "so what do you think?"

"The movies?" Levi echoed in surprise. When they were first dating, he and Claire used to go to the movies regularly. At the time he was thrilled to find out that they actually liked the same kind of films: action movies that still maintained a believable premise. But when the baby had come along, that had all stopped. He began picking up extra hours whenever he could.

He'd done the wrong thing for all the right reasons, he thought now.

"That's what I said."

"Have they left yet?" he asked.

"Yes," Melba told him with finality. "They have."

"No, we haven't," the deep voice behind him told Levi. "Claire was just helping me find my string tie—a man likes to spruce up a bit when he's escorting a pretty lady out in public," Gene explained, and then he chuckled. "But then, I don't have to be telling you that, do I?" he asked Levi.

Standing to one side in order to be able to look at both Levi and his granddaughter who was in the hall behind him, Gene quickly put two and two together and he had a suggestion he felt was in everyone's best interests. Although he had a feeling that Melba wasn't going to be crazy about it. But his wife, in this case, wasn't his first concern.

"Listen, honey," he said to Claire. "As much as I'd love to go to the movies with you tonight, I'm an old man and I'm liable to fall asleep right in the middle of all the excitement. You want to go with someone you can talk with about the movie as you're going home."

"That's okay, Grandpa, we don't have to go," Claire demurred, trying not to look disappointed. It had been a while since she'd had an outing, and the moment her grandfather had suggested it, she'd gotten excited.

"No, I insist you go." He looked at the young man his wife had herded into the hall. "Levi, can I get you to make sure my granddaughter has a good time tonight?"

"Eugene," his wife said sharply, her tone of voice taking him to task and silently threatening him with a whole host of things in that single utterance.

"Yes, sir," Levi replied eagerly.

Gene smiled broadly. "Knew I could count on you, boy. All right, then, it's all settled. And of course the movies are still on me," he added, taking out two bills and pressing them into the palm of Levi's hand. "I insist," he added when Levi opened his mouth to protest. "Now go out and have a good time, you two. Have her tell you all about how good the food turned out today," Gene prompted, all but pushing the two of them together and toward the stairs.

"We need to talk, Gene." Melba all but growled out the words.

"Have an especially good time," Gene instructed his granddaughter and her husband. "Hate to think I did this all for no reason," he added quietly.

"What movie were you going to go see?" he asked Claire as they went down the stairs. In the background, they could hear Melba beginning to berate her husband's "damn fool behavior." Levi cringed inwardly.

"Along Came Jones," Claire answered when they reached the bottom of the stairs. She turned toward him. "Listen, we don't have to do this—"

If their relationship had a chance of healing, Levi knew he was going to have to face things rather than hide his head in the sand, hoping things would work themselves out. It was up to *him* to work them out.

"You don't want to go to the movies with me," he guessed.

"No, that's not it," Claire began.

That was all the lead-in he needed. "Great. Then let's go," Levi told her, brightening.

"You *want* to go?" Claire asked, looking at him uncertainly.

"More than you can possibly ever guess," Levi answered then paused by the front door before opening it. "Why would you ask that?"

She'd had the feeling that things were just disintegrating between them. "Well, Grandpa did seem to twist your arm—"

He stopped her there. "Not that I noticed. We used to do this all the time, remember?" he reminded her, referring to all the movies they had gone to see.

A soft, sentimental smile curved her lips. "I remember," she said almost wistfully. "It seems like a million years ago."

"Not quite that long," Levi replied. And, with any luck, the time line would grow shorter. Taking special care not to ignore her feelings, he told her, "If you don't mind going with me, I'd certainly love to go with you."

Claire recalled his actions just that morning. Levi had been willing to be late for work just to help her out if she asked him to. The offer meant the world to her and had left a very positive impression on her.

She smiled broadly. "Then I guess we're going to the movies."

Levi grinned in response. "I guess so," he agreed. And then he realized that he was still holding the bouquet. "Oh, I almost forgot. These are for you."

She smiled as she looked down into the bouquet. "Carnations. My favorite. I have to put them in water," she told him. "Wait right here," she said. "I'll only be a minute." But before she ran to the kitchen, she paused long enough to brush her lips against his cheek. "Thank you."

And then she hurried off to the kitchen.

She was back in less than five minutes. "All ready," she announced.

"Me, too," he told her.

With his hand at the small of her back, he escorted Claire to his truck. Stopping before the passenger door, he appeared to be a bit self-conscious as he said, "Not exactly a royal coach," even though she had ridden countless times in the truck. He opened the door for her and held it, waiting for her to slide in.

"One person's truck is another person's royal coach," she answered, getting in.

He closed the door then rounded the hood to get in on his side.

Claire waited until he buckled up, then asked him the question that had just occurred to her. "Do you know where the movie's playing?"

"In Kalispell," he replied then assured her, "I'll find it. It hasn't been that long since we've gone to the movies."

"More than a year," she told him, "but I think you'll find it faster if I give you directions."

Levi started up the truck. "Fire away."

As she gave him directions, he smiled to himself. For the duration of this isolated interlude, they were a team again.

There was definitely hope for them, he thought.

* * *

Nearly two and a half hours later, they walked out of the theater, the last of the credits scrolling on the screen as the musical score built up to a final crescendo before the movie screen lightened.

Levi had parked the truck three blocks away out of necessity. All the available parking spaces close to the movie theater had been filled.

As they began to cross the street, Claire stumbled over something. Levi managed to catch her by the hand at the last second, keeping her upright rather than having her unceremoniously sprawl out on the ground.

Caught entirely off balance, Claire sucked air in, her heart temporarily launching into double-time.

His free arm went around her, steadying her further, "You okay?" he asked, his eyes searching her face for signs of acute distress. There weren't any. But there definitely was discomfort.

"I just bruised my pride, nothing else," Claire assured him.

"Maybe you should hold on to me until we get to the truck," Levi suggested. Not waiting for an answer, he tucked her hand through his arm.

She knew he meant well, but this rattled her own self-image. "I'm not an invalid, Levi," she protested.

"Nobody said you were, but there're rocks scattered all around here and it's dark. Do it for my sake," he implored. "If I return you with a turned ankle or worse, more than likely your grandmother's going to skin me—and with great pleasure."

Claire laughed at the exaggeration. "Grandpa wouldn't let her."

He didn't see it that way. "Grandpa, in case you haven't noticed, is afraid of her—just like everyone else is."

"I'm not afraid of my grandmother," Claire informed him. Levi said nothing, but merely continued looking at her. "Very much," Claire finally added.

Levi laughed. "Your grandmother does cast a big shadow for such a little person," he observed.

"She lived in a house with five men. She had to do something to keep from being outnumbered and over- whelmed by them."

"Well, if you ask me, I think she definitely suc- ceeded." Pulling out of the parking spot and then the parking lot, Levi turned the truck toward the Strickland Boarding House. "Almost seemed like old times, didn't it?" he asked Claire. He knew he definitely was having more than just one nostalgic moment.

Claire didn't respond immediately. But when she finally did, she had to grudgingly agree that he had a point. "Almost."

Levi decided to nudge her memory just a tad more. "We used to do this every weekend, remember?"

Claire suppressed a sigh. "I remember. I also remem- ber we used to be younger," she added as if that was rea- son enough to put the memory away in a deep, dark box.

"Not *that* much younger," Levi insisted.

She begged to differ. But there was another, more important reason why they really couldn't recapture what once was. "And without a daughter to be responsible for."

"That does change things a bit," he had to agree, although if he had a chance to change things, he knew he wouldn't. He dearly loved that little eight-month-old responsibility.

Silence began to take away bits and pieces of the dusky evening. It grew in width and depth until Levi felt he couldn't tolerate it any longer.

"How did it get to be this complicated?" he wanted to know.

She thought that point had already been made. "We had a baby."

"That was supposed to make it better, not complicated," he told her. "There are lots of people with three, four and even five kids."

"Not many," Claire insisted. In this decade, large families were the exception, not the norm.

He disagreed. "Enough."

She closed her eyes, not wanting to get into an argument and spoil what had been, up to this point, a really nice evening. "I don't know how those women do it."

"It's not just the women," he pointed out.

She turned and looked at him. "Ninety-nine percent of the time, yes, it is. The men, if they're in the picture at all, only get to see what life with a kid is like for a limited amount of time. Unless they're stay-at-home dads—something that there's few and far in between—they have no idea what it's like to spend all your time with a crying kid, day in, day out."

She looked at Levi's profile. He was being quiet. Had he even heard what she'd just said? Or was he simply ignoring her?

"Nothing to say?" she asked him.

"I was just thinking," he told her.

She braced herself. "About what?"

He turned to face her. "That maybe we should trade for a day or so."

She didn't understand what he was talking about. "Trade?"

"Yes." The more he thought about it, the more he felt they should give it a shot. "If I gave you a crash course on what I do and my boss okays it, you could come in and do my job, and I'd stay with Bekka and try to do what you do."

She noticed that he hadn't said he could do it, he'd used the word *try*. Did he mean it or was he just attempting to be polite about the situation? And why did he think she needed a crash course in what he did while he could just walk into her life without any effort?

"You sell furniture," she pointed out. "What's so hard about that?"

"I'm the store manager. That entails more than just selling furniture," he told her. He went over only a few of the things he was required to keep tabs on. "That includes payrolls, dealing with customers' complaints and at times their various requirements, as well. It includes making sure that what the customer asks for, he also needs."

He was making it sound complicated. "What does that mean?"

"Well, for instance, I had a couple who wanted to get a five-piece sofa set—wife just fell in love with the model we had on the floor. But their living room was way too small to adequately accommodate it. Which is what I told them after I'd gone to look it over."

She couldn't remember ever getting that kind of service. "You went to their apartment?"

He nodded then explained, "That was all part of the service that helped put my store over the top in sales. I'm not saying that you can't do it, I'm just saying that you can't walk into my job cold. But I could coach you, get you ready—and then if you find that you're into something that you weren't sure how to handle, you could always call me and I'll talk you through it."

That sounded just like him, she thought. But it also didn't sound fair to him. "Isn't that cheating?"

That didn't make any sense to him. "Why would it be cheating? It's only common sense."

He was being so nice, she was starting to feel guilty not only about the way she'd been treating him but even about the way she'd resented him for being able to leave each morning while she felt stuck, tethered to their apartment while dancing attendance to a colicky, teething baby.

She was being quiet again, Levi noted. That wasn't usually a good sign. Luckily, they were home.

He pulled up into an available spot. "We're here," he announced.

Claire blinked. It took a couple of seconds for his words to sink in. When she looked outside the truck, she saw that they had returned to the boarding house without her even realizing it.

It was intensely dark, with only a couple of lights still on within the house. Beyond that, there was no illumination.

They might as well have been the last two people left alive in the world for all the signs of life she saw outside the car window.

Which was possibly why she did what she did next.

Chapter Eleven

Although Levi had parked his truck and turned off the ignition, neither he nor Claire made any attempt to get out of the vehicle.

It was as if they both knew that the second either one of them opened the door on their side and got out, the evening—and the almost magical time that they had just spent with one another, recapturing "old times"—would dissolve into the night.

And when it did, they would once again be that separated couple contemplating the very real possibility of turning their separation into a permanent state by getting a divorce.

Claire didn't want to face any decisions, didn't want to think of what might be ahead or dwell on just what she had already lost and stood to lose if she went forward with her initial threat.

Quite simply, she wanted to preserve this moment in time, wanted nothing more than to have it go on indefinitely.

Wanted, she realized, Levi to want her as much as she found herself wanting him. If possible, she was more attracted to him now, at this moment, than she had been when she'd first met him.

It was with this on her mind that she leaned into Levi. Not by much, but then, considering the limited space around her, it didn't really take all that much. Even a fraction of an inch brought her into his space, brought her closer to his aura.

Taking a steadying breath, she detected just the slightest hint of the soap that Levi favored.

Something clean and woodsy.

His eyes on hers, Levi matched her, small move for small move. Which was how their lips came to occupy almost the exact same space.

They couldn't avoid having them touch.

Ordinarily, given the circumstances, Claire knew she should have pulled her head back, thereby taking her lips out of range and deliberately avoiding his. She would have, with that one simple movement, evacuated the enticing danger zone.

Except that she wanted very much to be in that danger zone. Wanted very much to be kissed by Levi. Wanted, more than anything, to return that kiss a hundredfold.

More.

Her soul had missed him more than any words could begin to describe.

Her heart pounding, she moved *into* the kiss rather than away from it. And, as she moved into it, she kissed her estranged husband with every fiber of her being. Kissed him as if she had never thrown him and her wedding ring out onto the street.

Kissed him as if she still loved him.

Because she did.

Dazed, Levi felt as though he had just been struck by lightning—but he was definitely *not* complaining. If anything, he would have been celebrating and doing handstands—if he wasn't presently and deliciously otherwise occupied.

Very occupied.

Feeling a huge, electrical-like surge throughout his entire body, he leaned in over the truck's gearshift, taking no note of it as he took Claire into his arms.

Holding on to her because letting her go meant losing his soul.

Levi could feel his body heating up, could feel himself yearning for Claire the way he hadn't thought was humanly possible. A very large part of him felt that he wouldn't be able to breathe if he couldn't have her.

Get a grip, Levi, he sternly upbraided himself.

He didn't want to be guilty of overpowering her. Of making her succumb to the moment if she was only going to regret it later. There was more than just sex involved here, and he didn't want her thinking that *that* was what was foremost in his mind.

As much as his body felt incomplete without being sealed to hers, he didn't want to risk losing her permanently if he let her believe that all he wanted was to make love with her and that he would do anything that was necessary, would move any obstacle that might be in his way, to *get* his way with her.

He loved her too much for that.

And it was that very love that made him vulnerable to her.

Claire felt herself weakening more and more by the second. Within a couple more seconds, she knew she'd be all ready and primed to be taken by him right here, never mind that they were parked in front of her grandparents' boarding house.

There was too much riding on this for her to completely give in to the demands she felt inside. Doing so would only cloud the issue—attaining a better relationship in which they could communicate well enough to be able not to have things blow up between them the way they had since the July Fourth wedding. So she kissed the only man she had ever truly loved once more for the road—a very steamy, rocky road—and then she pulled back, albeit very reluctantly.

Clearing her throat so that she could sound like a human being when she spoke, rather than squeaking, Claire whispered, "I think we'd better be going in."

She was right.

He knew she was right, even as every muscle in his

body loathed to back away. But there was no way, no matter how he felt, that he was about to force himself on her. It didn't matter that she was his wife, that in their brief time together they had made love countless times and with utter, complete abandon.

That was then, this was now.

This time around, she had backed away, indicating, by example, that he had to do the same. He wasn't about to cast a shadow on what they'd had—what he hoped they *would* have again—by pretending not to hear her or just getting it into his head to override her and simply take what was his.

Because that would destroy what they'd had and what he wanted them to have again.

Much as it pained him down to the very bottom of his soul, there were new rules to follow—and Levi was determined that he was going to follow them. This while fervently praying that she would come back to him soon because holding out this way for long was bordering on sainthood.

"Whatever you want, Claire," he replied solemnly.

Whatever I want, Claire thought, repeating his words in her head.

What I want is to rip your clothes off with my teeth and have you do the same to mine.

What I want is to make wild, passionate love with you until neither one of us can breathe.

What I want is for none of this to have ever happened so that we could just go on the way we had once been.

But that wasn't the reality they were faced with,

Claire was forced to admit. She *had* thrown him out, and she *had* pulled up stakes and moved away with Bekka. She couldn't just undo that in the blink of an eye without looking like some kind of a flighty, bird-brained idiot. Why would he want to stay with a flighty, quick-tempered woman, even if her makeup was always perfectly applied and she never had a hair out of place?

The simple answer was that he wouldn't.

Pulling herself together, burying her desire until such time as she could effectively handle it and perhaps even give it a voice in her life, Claire nodded in response and opened the door on her side.

It would have been helpful if a blast of cold air had hit her, making her shiver and focus on trying to keep warm. But this was August, so the only air she detected was on the hot side, and it was more of a waft than a blast.

That was all she needed. The sensation of heat traveling up and down her body— reminding her how she had felt whenever Levi touched her and made her his.

Closing the passenger door behind her, Claire let out a long, shaky breath. And then she squared her shoulders and headed for the boarding house front door. She heard Levi getting out behind her on the driver's side.

"You don't have to walk me to my door," she told him without turning around.

Her very real fear was that if he came in with her, somehow or other, she would wind up pulling him into her room, ruining all her good intentions.

"I'm not," Levi answered. When she turned to look

at him quizzically, as if she had just caught him in a lie, he pointed out, "I live here, too, remember?"

She'd actually forgotten for a second. What was the matter with her? She was too young to be courting senility.

Apparently, Claire decided, her rampant desires were wiping out everything else, including what there was of her thought process.

"Yes," she replied quietly. "I remember."

The hall light was the only lamp lit on the first floor, a clear indication that everyone had either gone to bed—or was making an evening of it somewhere else.

Claire went up the stairs to her room.

She was aware of Levi following her up the stairs. She knew he was just going to his room, which was down the hall from hers, but even so, she was waging a battle within herself, wrestling with the pros and cons of inviting Levi into her room for just a few minutes to see the baby. After all, it was his right.

Claire knew that he and Bekka would both enjoy the interaction. No matter what went down between her and Levi, good and bad, she couldn't deny that he was a fantastic father and that Bekka still lit up like a lighthouse beacon whenever he walked into their daughter's room.

But in her own present state, Claire thought, she lit up, as well.

Maybe even more so, Claire thought in semidespair.

Turning at the top of the stairs, in this position she was eye to eye with Levi. "If Bekka's awake, do you want to stop in for a minute and see her before you go to bed?"

It was *his* turn to light up like that lighthouse beacon.

"If you don't mind," he prefaced. "Sure."

He had to admit, ever since she had thrown him out, he was carrying around a very real fear that even if they got back together, she could easily reject him again. He had to safeguard himself from that.

Because emotionally he just couldn't bear another rejection.

Claire looked at him, puzzled. "Why should I mind? I just asked if you wanted to. If I *minded*, I wouldn't have made the offer."

"No," he agreed, thinking it over. She wouldn't play games where Bekka was concerned. "I guess you wouldn't have. Thanks," he told her with a wide smile.

Levi could always undo her with his smile. "Don't mention it," she murmured, feeling her heart beating in triple time.

The first thing she saw the second she unlocked her door was her grandfather. Gene quickly crossed over and told her in a whisper, "She just dropped off to sleep about ten minutes ago. That means you can get in about two hours of uninterrupted sleep before she's ready to roll again." Her grandfather looked from his granddaughter to the young man who had brought her back. "I suggest you make the most of it," he said just before he slipped out of the room.

It wasn't clear just who Gene was giving that advice to.

Levi took her grandfather's exit to mean that he should be leaving, as well.

"Well, I guess then I'd better—" Levi began, about to back out of Claire's room.

"You can still look at her if you'd like to," Claire told him. "It might even be a little easier to look at her with her asleep. This way she's not bouncing all over the place."

"You might have a point there," Levi said just before he tiptoed over to his daughter's crib. Leaning his arms on the railing, he looked down at the little girl's face. "She looks just like an angel, doesn't she?" he whispered to Claire as he continued gazing at the sleeping, cherubic face.

"God's clever use of deceptive packaging," Claire replied, amusement curving the corners of her generous mouth.

"Bekka will grow out of it and calm down," Levi predicted. "In about five years or so—give or take," he added with a fond laugh. It was obvious that no matter what she did and how old she got, she would always be his little girl, and he'd love her unconditionally.

Which made Bekka, Claire thought, one lucky little girl. And by association, that made her lucky, as well, to have that kind of a loving father for her child.

"Hope you're right," Claire told him. They both stood there, looking down on what amounted to their most precious handiwork, for several moments.

When Levi took her hand in his, her breath caught in her throat. For a second she was afraid to move, afraid of encouraging him—more afraid of doing something to discourage him and chase Levi away.

"Gene said something about her staying asleep for a couple of hours. Does she?" Levi questioned.

Claire nodded. "Bekka's taken to sleeping for two hours at a time. She just started doing that the last couple of weeks. I was stunned," she admitted. "But thrilled at the same time."

"Then I guess you'd better listen to Gene and make the most of it. I should let you get your rest," Levi told her. "I'll see you in the morning," he added, forcing himself to cross to the door.

A sense of urgency washed over her. "Levi—"

When he turned around to look at her and hear whatever last minute words she wanted to send him off with, he found that he didn't have very far to look. Claire was right there, standing right inside his shadow.

"Claire?"

Even the way he said her name excited her.

In the very next heartbeat, she wrapped her arms around his neck, pushed herself up on her toes and then sealed her mouth to his.

Levi resisted.

Or at least he thought he did. That part transpired in far less than a heartbeat, after which time every noble intention he'd gathered together to help him stay strong and rise above his desires was utterly and effectively stripped away from him.

Before he knew what he was doing, Levi kissed her

back. Part of him, a very small part, still struggled to do the right thing and pull back.

When he finally succeeded in creating a small space between them, he'd only been able to draw his head back a couple of inches from hers.

"Claire, are you sure—?"

"Stop talking," she instructed breathlessly.

Claire had no idea if she was strong enough to override the kind of logic he might throw at her. All she knew was that her whole body was burning for him. It felt as if it was vibrating like a freshly struck tuning fork, all because of the very delicious feel of his body pressed against hers.

She had no doubt that come morning, she was going to regret this.

Perhaps a little.

Most likely a lot.

But right now what she would definitely regret was letting him return to his room, leaving her to crawl into her own bed.

Alone.

Heaven help her, she *needed* him.

Chapter Twelve

The ache that came over Levi, instant and acute, reminded him of every single second that he had gone without making love with Claire. But despite the keenly felt desire, a shaky but irrefutable logic still managed to prevail.

For the second time in as many minutes, he drew his lips away from Claire's, leaving her confused and bereft, if the expression on her face was any indication of what she was experiencing.

"The baby," he murmured thickly.

Claire instantly understood what he was referring to, understood the conscientious objection that he was raising.

Moving over to the crib, which was no longer located right next to her bed as it had been when she'd left for the movies—her guess was that her grandfather had had a premonition about the way the evening might wind up going and with that in mind had moved the crib as far away from her bed as possible—she picked up the baby blanket and spread it out so that it covered the entire length of the guard rail.

Spread out this way, the pink blanket would provide the only viewing surface Bekka would be able to look at if the baby should open her eyes while she and Levi were otherwise occupied.

Turning from the now-isolated crib, Claire smiled at the man who had won her heart just a few years ago, her smile clearly indicating that the mission was accomplished.

His concerns about Bekka laid to rest, Levi wasted no time pulling his wife back into his arms. Capturing her lips again, his hands eagerly roamed over all the stirring curves of her body.

Levi worshipped every inch of her and happily celebrated the very thought of their physical reunion to come.

"I've missed this," he breathed against the side of her throat, his breath quickly stirring her to an unimaginable fever pitch. "I've missed *you*, Claire."

Eager for that special form of frenzy that only he could create within her, Claire pushed Levi back against her bed, and quickly began tearing at his shirt, working his belt loose and then urgently tugging at his slacks, drawing them down off his taut hips and hard, muscular thighs.

She had him half-undressed before he had pulled down her tank top and the strapless bra that she wore beneath it.

Her shorts came next, leaving her in what could be rated as the skimpiest of all-but-transparent hot-pink thong panties.

The thong's life expectancy swiftly plummeted down to zero in less than thirty seconds as he slid his fingertips beneath the thin elastic on either side of her hips. And then, in the blink of an eye, the thong and her hips parted company, and she was lying on top of him, completely nude.

Wrapping his arms around her and covering her mouth with his own, Levi reversed their positions and she was suddenly beneath him.

He took great care to balance his weight on the length of his arms and his elbows even as his lips reacquainted themselves with the length and breadth of her skin.

Levi kissed her everywhere, making her head spin, her heart race and her body prime itself for him. The yearning she experienced was almost unbelievably urgent and ever so overwhelming.

She wasn't sure just how she managed to get the remainder of his clothes away from his body, but she finally accomplished that, eager to give as good as she got.

But Levi had always been the master at this game. She had come to him with limited experience, and he had uncovered such mind-blowing pleasures for her that she knew without being told that what she had with Levi was something indescribably precious and wonderful.

Levi kept on kissing her until he had reduced her to a pulsating mass of desire. And then she felt his lips withdrawing from hers only to leave their imprint on her neck, her shoulders, the swell of her breasts and then her newly taut belly.

The muscles quivered beneath his lips and hot, stirring breath. Claire arched into his lips, eager to absorb every nuance, every pass that he made.

Levi went farther down.

Deeper.

Priming her soft, inner core, his tongue wove magic, creating havoc even as it coaxed one climax after another from her.

It was all sweet agony.

Claire chewed on her lip. It was all she could do not to cry out. Only the fact that her cries would wake up the baby held her in check.

Grabbing fistfuls of bedding in her hands as she tried to anchor part of herself to reality, Claire arched higher and higher, eager to experience the full impact of the sensations that Levi was so expertly creating within her.

She fell back, exhausted, only to feel his lips forging a path back up to hers. Claire was sure that there was nothing left within her, nothing to give, nothing to absorb.

She was miles beyond tired.

And then he moved her legs apart with his knee and entered her.

Levi did it slowly, gently, as if he didn't want to take a chance on hurting her even though they had made love this way countless times before, often several times in the space of a few hours.

And yet, she realized, Levi treated her like a virgin bride.

And in so doing, he'd caused her to fall in love with him all over again.

Almost in slow motion, Levi managed to create paradise for her, bringing her closer and closer to the ultimate climax, the ultimate moment that they could both share.

She didn't want slowly.

Claire raced to that wondrous sensation eagerly, knowing that Levi was there to share it with her, to feel everything she was feeling.

That made it twice as special as it had been before.

Clinging to him, Claire climbed up to the very pinnacle of the mountain they were trying to scale.

And then, just like that, they skydived down back to the ground together.

Claire clung to him on the way down, as well, unwilling to give up even a second of the experience or draw into herself before it was time.

She truly wanted to have him there, beside her, guiding her and protecting her. Doing all the things that had made her fall in love with him in the first place.

When the euphoria finally abated, moving back into the shadows, Claire was more than a little reluctant to release her hold on it.

But whether or not she did it, the sensation still receded, vanishing into the ether until there wasn't even a trace of it left.

Claire sighed, burying her face in Levi's shoulder, not wanting to engage with the world just yet.

Levi could feel her turning into him, could feel him wanting her in response. He felt every breath she took and released.

Damn, but she was stirring up things again, making him want her again.

Making him ready to stay the night and pick up all the threads of his life and arrange them the way they had once been.

Closing one arm around his wife to keep her against him, Levi kissed the top of her head. "I have *missed* that," he murmured with great feeling into her hair.

Raising her head ever so slightly so that she could look up at him, Claire said in a hushed whisper, "Me, too."

He wanted to keep on talking, to somehow get her to tell him—no, to promise him—that his period of exile from her life was over. That she was willing to pick up and resume their lives just where they had left them.

To hear that would have meant the world to him, perhaps even put his uneasiness to rest, at least for a while. But he knew that if he said any of this to her, it left him open to the possibility that she could say no, then continue to say that nothing had really changed between them despite this quick visit to happier days.

Because if she said that, it would most likely crush

him, and right now he was far too vulnerable to risk that. He hadn't managed to properly build up his walls, his defenses against the possibility of hearing things that would leave devastating holes in his soul.

So he said nothing and just held her in his arms for as long as he could.

The silence enveloped her.

At first she thought nothing of it. But ever so slowly, it began to make her feel uncomfortable.

Awkward.

Made her feel as if, now that the sexual tension had been addressed and depleted for the time being, they were suddenly being thrown back to the lives they'd been living a few short hours ago.

"Is something wrong?" she heard herself finally asking him.

"No," Levi denied a bit too quickly, belying his thought process. "Why? Do you feel something's wrong?" he asked, throwing the ball back into her court.

"You're not talking."

"Funny, I thought I heard myself talking. I could have sworn that was the sound of my voice just now. Oh, wait, there it goes again," he said, hoping to get his point across to Claire. To make her laugh.

Instead of amused, Claire looked a little frustrated. "You know what I mean."

"No," Levi was forced to admit since he didn't believe in lying. "Not usually."

She propped herself up on her elbow to look at him from a better angle. "We just made love."

"I know," he replied with a solemn expression. "I was there."

"And now you're pulling back," she pointed out.

He balked at the criticism, even though he knew, in his heart, that she was right. "I'm right here," he contradicted.

"Physically," Claire emphasized. Didn't he see the difference? "I'm talking about what you have inside." She jabbed an index finger into his chest.

Levi fell back on logic, the way he always did. "What I have inside is a whole bunch of organs, which still seem to be working at maximum capacity."

She closed her eyes and sighed. Opening them again, she said, "I'm talking about your spirit."

"Spirit," he repeated. "As in ghosts?"

Levi was deliberately baiting her, wanting to see where this was going and just what she truly felt about what had happened. Because he would have liked nothing more than to hear that this meant they were going to get back together. That she missed them being a couple as much as he did.

He was well aware that in each relationship, one person always loved more than the other. It was a given as far as he was concerned. But what he couldn't bear was if it turned out that he was the only one in this relationship. He wouldn't be able to stand it if she was going to turn her back on him and willfully abandon him the way his father had.

He knew he wouldn't be able to live with that or bear up to that.

"No, not as in ghosts," she said, a slight glimmer of anger creasing her brow, tainting her reaction to him and to what had just happened here between them. "As if what we're both carrying within us—what makes us fall in love," she added before he could jump back on that ridiculous analogy about inner organs and whatnot, "doesn't really exist." She drew herself up, holding the sheet against her breasts. "Didn't you *ever* love me?" she wanted to know.

"Of course I did—I do," he amended when he realized that he'd framed his answer using the past tense. All he was doing was following her lead, but he knew if he pointed that out, she'd lash out at him, claiming that he was just being argumentative.

Claire looked unconvinced—but she also looked as if she *wanted* to be convinced.

"If you love me, why did you go off that night to play poker with the guys instead of coming home with me to *play* something else?"

At this point he honestly didn't know, but saying that sounded like a cop-out, so he tried to come up with something that sounded plausible.

"You were busy," he began, thinking of the woman at the wedding that Claire had been talking to.

"I have never been too busy for you—unlike you for me," she said with renewed feeling.

"*When* was I ever too busy for you?" he wanted to know. Was he kidding? "Almost every day—when you don't come home from work," she added, in case he was too obtuse to understand her meaning.

"That's just it. Work. It's *work*, it's not personal—"

She sniffed, showing contempt for his answer, clearly unconvinced. "It certainly felt personal to me. And it would to you, too, if *you* were on the receiving end of what I've had to put up with," she informed him.

It was happening, Levi thought.

He could feel it.

They were slipping back into the quagmire comprised of her grievances about his behavior. If he didn't get up and leave now, she was just going to start going over the entire litany of his faults and shortcomings.

The second she started, any headway that he'd felt being made while they were making love would swiftly become null and void—as if it had never happened, he thought. He would rather leave now and retain a shred of what he felt had transpired between them than to stick around and watch it all come crashing down and burn.

Again.

Sitting up, he swung his legs down on the opposite side of the bed, rose and began picking up his clothing. He began to pull on his slacks and shirt.

Levi was dressed within a couple of minutes.

Claire remained sitting up in bed, watching him. Stunned and speechless. When she finally found her tongue, she demanded, "What do you think you're doing?"

He spared her a fleeting glance. "Putting my clothes on."

She could see that. What she wanted from him was to know *why* he was putting his clothes on.

"Just like that?" she demanded.

"Only way I know how to get dressed," he said, his voice devoid of feeling.

Her eyes narrowed. "That's not what I meant."

He shrugged. "Guess you're just going to have to work on being able to communicate your thoughts better."

He was criticizing her. They'd just made love and she'd thought—she'd thought—

Angry tears filled her eyes,

Damn, nothing had been resolved, she told herself. She was a fool to think that a few loving moments made everything all right.

"Get out," she ordered, pointing at the door. To underscore her command, she threw a pillow at him.

He ducked out of the door and closed it before the pillow could come in contact with him.

Chapter Thirteen

Claire had thrown him out.

Again.

Levi knew in his gut that it was just a matter of time before she would issue a full-scale rejection, banishing him from her life just as she had after that blasted wedding they'd attended.

Except that this time it could very possibly be permanent.

And if that happened, she would be, in essence, abandoning him.

Abandoning him just the way that his father had abandoned him.

Because he wasn't worth loving.

Wasn't worth sticking around for and trying to iron

out the snags that had occurred in the fabric of their relationship.

And he obviously wasn't worth the effort to even *attempt* to set things right.

It was the story of his life, Levi thought glumly as he sat in the dark in his room. He might as well bail rather than stick around and have the point driven home that much more sharply.

Even so, it still hurt, he thought. It hurt like hell.

It was his fault, Levi realized, staring into the darkness. His fault for thinking that he could actually have a woman like Claire in his life. His fault for thinking that a woman like Claire could love him—and that he had an actual shot at building a solid life with her and their daughter.

On some level, he'd known all along that this was liable to happen.

That was why he'd done what he could to consciously hold a piece of himself back when they made love. Because if he held back, then maybe he wouldn't be completely destroyed if she turned her back on him and left him again.

All in all, it was a decent protective, working theory. But in reality, his defense mechanisms weren't nearly as effective as he needed them to be.

He still felt vulnerable and completely stripped down to his skin.

He was just going to have to harden himself, because as long as he remained in the Strickland Boarding House, there was a good chance that he and Claire would run into each other, that their paths would cross no matter how careful he was to keep away from her.

His path, Levi thought, was clear. He was going to have to pack up and leave as soon as he got back from work tomorrow.

But the following evening, when he arrived back at the boarding house, Levi felt far too exhausted to face the prospect of packing, so he put off leaving the boarding house—and Claire—until the following day.

But the evening that followed that one brought with it the same set of circumstances, the same reluctance on his part and consequently, the same results.

So did the day after that.

And the day after that.

Levi made peace with the idea that he wasn't going anywhere for a while, telling himself that it was easier to do nothing and remain in limbo, than to take an inevitable step that would, he felt, irrevocably close a chapter of his life. A chapter, he was sure, he would never be able to open again.

Claire slipped back into her room. Breakfast was finally over. She'd been working on automatic pilot for days now, and she was drained.

Her room was empty and so quiet, the silence all but vibrated around her as well as within her. Her grandfather, bless him, had happily taken over the care and feeding of Bekka, as he did every day while she went off to the kitchen to help feed the masses.

She was very grateful for his help, but as her grandmother had pointed out, he enjoyed caring for Bekka and playing with her, so it wasn't exactly a hardship for him to watch the baby. Besides, it made him feel useful, as well as happy.

Claire had to admit that she envied her grandfather his happiness.

Happiness.

It was something she felt that she would never experience again. Finding out that she'd been right all along in her dealings with Levi didn't make her feel the slightest bit better or vindicated.

This was one time she would have given *anything* to have been wrong. But Levi had proven that she'd been right by his glaring absence from her life.

Ever since she was in her teens, she'd been insecure when it came to her looks. Marriage didn't change anything. It certainly didn't change her thinking. All along she had felt that she wasn't pretty enough to hold on to a man like Levi.

Levi was sharp, clever and so handsome that it almost hurt. What would he want with someone like her? Why would he tie himself down with her? Especially long-term? In a desperate effort to ensure that he would remain in her life, she had gone out of her way to be certain that Levi would never see her without her makeup on, or with her hair uncombed—not even once.

A case in point was the day she had gone into labor. She hadn't called him to take her to the hospital before she had checked her hair and her makeup in the mirror—and touched up her lipstick as well as spraying a fine mist of cologne into her hair. She wanted to look picture-perfect each and every time he looked at her.

So that he wouldn't be tempted to leave her.

Granted, that did make her life that much harder, but she'd wanted to be sure that if he left—as he now indeed had—it wouldn't be because he wanted to find someone more attractive than she was.

But it seemed now that he had grown tired of her anyway.

Even when they had made love that last time, here at the boarding house, she had felt that Levi was definitely holding back, holding a part of himself in check, just out of her reach.

She had wanted to give Levi her all, but after sensing that, she had suddenly shut down and backed away herself.

Two could play the "stranger" game, she thought. If Levi wanted to treat her like someone he barely knew, well, she could do the same with him.

But behaving this way was taking a terrible toll on her, making her usually sunny disposition all but vanish entirely. She managed to sound upbeat when dealing with some of the other residents in the boarding house. And she was fairly certain that she had fooled her grandfather and even her more suspicious grandmother, but it was far from easy.

Which was why she was here in her room, seeking out a little space and trying very hard to rally her spirits which had, over the past few days, plummeted down to a subbasement level.

Thinking of what she'd had and now apparently had lost, Claire couldn't keep the tears from surfacing. However, since she was alone, she let them come, hoping to get all the sadness out of her.

Claire threw herself facedown on her bed, gathered her pillow to her and just cried. She stifled her sobs by burying her head in her pillow.

She wasn't sure just how long she remained like that, crying her heart out. She knew that she'd cried so hard and so long, she was virtually exhausted.

That was when she heard the knock on her door.

Caught off guard, she remained silent, hoping that whoever was on the other side of the door would think she wasn't in and would just go away.

But they didn't go away.

The second round of knocking had her pulling into herself even more, determined to wait it out. The last thing she felt like doing was talking.

To anyone.

Shutting her eyes, she braced herself to wait the person out.

She wasn't prepared for the door to suddenly be opened.

The second it began to move, Claire popped up into a sitting position. She rubbed the heels of her hands against her eyes, trying to clear away as much as she could of the telltale trail of tears.

She was just lucky she wasn't one of those women

who spent a great deal of time on her eye makeup. If she had, she was certain she would have looked like a raccoon right now. Instead, at most, she would be showing some puffiness beneath her eyes, which could mean any one of a number of things, not necessarily a sign of the heartbreak she was experiencing.

The next second, her grandmother walked in, pocketing her pass key.

"Why aren't you answering your door?" Melba Strickland wanted to know.

Scowling, with one hand on her ample hip, the woman looked very formidable despite her short stature.

Claire looked down at the rumpled bedspread on the bed. "Sorry," she mumbled. "I guess I must have fallen asleep and didn't hear you."

The scowl on Melba's face deepened more than just a fraction.

"Okay, then." Melba sniffed, closing the door behind her. Coming into the room, she took her granddaughter's chin in her hand and carefully scrutinized both sides of her face. "And just when, exactly, did you take up lying to your grandmother?" she wanted to know.

Nerves caused adrenaline to go surging through her system. She wasn't any good at this, but since she'd laid the groundwork, she felt she needed to see it through. "I'm not lying. I'm…"

"Experiencing a lapse in good judgment?" Melba supplied.

Feeling very vulnerable in her present position—she

was looking up at her grandmother as if she were down on her knees—Claire got off her bed.

"Is there something I can do for you, Grandmother?" she asked, doing her best to sound calm.

"Yes," the woman answered in a no-nonsense tone of voice. "You can stop feeling sorry for yourself."

Claire's defenses went into high gear. "I'm not feeling sorry for—" Claire stopped. Oh, what was the point of trying to deny it? Her grandmother had this eerie ability to see right through her. "How can you tell?"

Melba snorted. "I'm old and I've seen it all, Claire-bear." Narrowing her eyes, the older woman stared at her granddaughter's face again. "This have anything to do with that exiled husband of yours?" she asked.

Claire waited a couple of beats before asking, "If I said no, would you believe me?"

Melba's eyes held hers. Her face was devoid of any telltale expression. "What do you think?"

She knew her grandmother well enough to give up any attempt at denial. "Then I won't say no."

Melba nodded her head. "Good thinking. And speaking of thinking—or not thinking—just what is going on with you two?" Melba asked. Her tone indicated that she wouldn't put up with any attempts to weasel out of answering her. "A week ago, it looked as if things were getting back on track between you and Levi. Now you're involved in some kind of elaborate game of hide-and-seek—except that neither one of you is seeking." When Claire didn't say anything, Melba ordered, "Out with it."

It was useless to beat around the bush. So she didn't. "He doesn't want me anymore."

"Honey, if that were the case, that man would have been long gone. Nobody's holding a gun to his head, making him stay here—and he *is* still here," her grandmother pointed out.

Sitting down on Claire's bed, the woman looked expectantly at her until Claire followed suit and sat back down on the bed beside her.

"Let me make myself clear," her grandmother began. "Levi Wyatt wouldn't have been my first choice for you—or my second, for that matter. But he does seem to be crazy about Bekka, and any fool can see that man loves you. Ever since you've crawled into that shell of yours, your furniture cowboy seems to have gotten downright mopey. Now, just what makes you think that he doesn't love you anymore?"

Claire took a breath as she looked away. "I'm just not pretty enough," she muttered.

"What?" Melba said sharply.

As if this was easy for her to admit, Claire thought. But she knew that her grandmother would just chip away at her until she had the whole story. Telling her the story right off the bat was just saving her a lot of grief.

"I tried very hard to look perfect for him—I've never let him see me without my makeup. Not even once," Claire said with just a touch of pride. "But that doesn't seem to be enough. I'm just not pretty enough or interesting enough to hold on to him."

Melba stared at her for a moment that grew so long, it became almost intolerable.

And then she spoke. "So what you're telling me is that you married a shallow jerk."

"No!" Claire cried, horrified at the label her grandmother had just slapped on Bekka's father. "He's not a shallow jerk!"

Melba looked far from convinced. "Well, only a shallow jerk is going to stop loving someone because they decided that the woman they married wasn't as *pretty* as they thought she was. Is Levi *that* shallow?" her grandmother wanted to know, her sharp brown eyes pinning Claire down, daring her to defend the indefensible.

"No, he's not," Claire declared loyally. "But I'm still not pretty enough to hang on to him."

Melba sighed, shaking her head. Her granddaughter had *so* much to learn. "Honey, there are a lot of things that go into making and maintaining a good marriage— being pretty doesn't even make the top twenty. Surface beauty doesn't last, and unless it goes beyond being skin-deep, being pretty is not good for anything except maybe making makeup commercials.

"Now, that young man you married is not a rocket scientist, but he's pretty sharp, which means he's got a good head on his shoulders and some decent set of values to guide him." Her grandmother's eyes held hers. "The man doesn't want a picture-perfect wife. He wants a loving wife. One he can talk to and reason with.

"There's no such thing as perfect anyway. Best you can hope for is someone who tries their best to be a good husband—or a good wife," Melba said pointedly, look-ing at her granddaughter. "Now, let me let you in on a little secret. Marriages aren't made in heaven. They're made right here on earth and played out here, as well.

"Nothing good is ever gotten easily. You have to work at it, fight for it, sacrifice for it. That's when you really get to appreciate what you have. Someone hands you something on a silver platter, you might like it and enjoy it for a little while, but that doesn't come close to the way you feel after you've fought the good fight and won something. It also becomes a lot more pre-cious to you. Now, stop hiding in your room and see if you can make that young man want to go on putting up with you."

Claire wished she could, but the sinking feeling in her stomach told her there was no point in even trying. "It's too late."

Melba rose to her feet. Holding her granddaughter's hand, she brought Claire up with her. "It's only too late if one of you is dead, and unless he's expired on his way to work, your man is alive and well and com-ing back here tonight. The only way that man is going to leave you is if you chase him away. So *stop chasing him away.*"

Claire shook her head. "You're wrong. I can feel him holding back—"

"Well, yeah," Melba agreed. "Of course he's hold-ing back. If you thought someone was going to use your heart for flamenco practice, you'd hold back, too.

"Look, you've already declared your marriage

dead—you've got nothing to lose by approaching Levi, and everything to gain." When her granddaughter made no move to leave the room, Melba delivered her ultimate threat. "Just remember, you're not too big for me to take over my knee."

Claire laughed shortly, thinking her grandmother was kidding. "I'm not a kid anymore, Grandmother," she pointed out. "I'm an adult."

"You're an adult," the older woman echoed. Melba's eyes narrowed again as she focused in on her granddaughter. "Fine. Then prove it."

Chapter Fourteen

Claire looked at her grandmother, confused. "I don't understand. What do you mean, *prove it*? What are you telling me to do?"

Melba huffed, exasperated. Shutting the door again, she proceeded to answer her granddaughter's question. "I'm telling you to *act* like an adult. When Levi comes home tonight, go up to him and apologize for your part in this fiasco that's gotten so completely out of hand. Own up to your mistakes—it takes two to have an argument, not just one person."

Frowning, her eyes swept over Claire. "And for heaven's sake, let him see you the way you really are, not like this." She waved her hand to indicate Claire in her entirety. "Not like some girl who's ready to be on the cover of some fashion magazine. If he loves you, then he loves *you*, not your shade of lipstick, or the eye shadow you have on." Melba's gaze was highly disapproving. "Or that powder you use to hide any so-called flaws you think you have.

"The man married *you*, not a makeup case. Give him a little credit," Melba insisted, surprising Claire. She'd been under the impression that her grandmother did *not* approve of Levi. This sounded as if she was in his corner. "Besides," Melba continued, "there's nothing wrong with the way you look. What *is* wrong is your insecurity."

Melba abruptly stopped herself from going on. "Now, despite what you're probably thinking, I'm not here to lecture you. I just want to wake you up to what you stand to lose if you don't get a grip on your behavior." Blowing out a breath, Melba glanced at her wristwatch. "Time for you to stop feeling sorry for yourself and get back to the kitchen, Cinderella. Until she's feeling better, Gina's going to need your help."

Melba opened the door and stepped out into the hallway. Claire was quick to pull herself together and follow her out of the room. "And while you're working," Melba added as a parting shot. "*Think* about what I just said. Think very, very hard."

"Yes, ma'am," Claire murmured.

Heading in a different direction than her granddaughter, Melba spared her one last look and just shook her head without saying another word.

Claire had no idea how to read her grandmother's parting expression, but the woman had certainly given her a great deal to think about. She supposed that her grandmother did have a point. She had married a man, a *real* man, not some prince charming who only existed in fairy tales.

Since he was real, she owed it to Levi to let him see her the way she really looked. He'd earned the right. Levi had followed her here even after she'd thrown him out. That *had* to count for something, she reasoned. Maybe he did really love her and not just the image she had been projecting every day and night since that first day that they met.

It wasn't Levi who had set her on this path of always projecting a picture-perfect image. She had been like this ever since she could remember. She had never allowed herself to appear dirty or messy in public, never left the house unless she passed her own inspection, critically looking herself over in a full-length mirror.

What that amounted to was always being neat, always making sure that her clothes, her makeup and her hair were all impeccable. The idea of looking anything less than exceedingly attractive was just unthinkable to her. She didn't even own a pair of sweatpants or a pair of sneakers.

Her grandmother was right, Claire thought grudgingly. It was time to let her hair down.

In more ways than one.

Claire began to watch the clock, counting the hours and the minutes until Levi came back to the boarding house from the furniture store. Although it had taken a lot of courage, she had made up her mind. She was going to unveil herself, to show Levi the *real* Claire, flaws and all.

And then she was going to pray that he didn't find the real her a turnoff.

Levi stared straight ahead at the dark road in front of him. With little or no traffic before him, the road was numbingly hypnotic. The second he had hit the road tonight, he'd made up his mind.

This was going to be the last time he'd make this run.

It was time to face the facts, pick up his marbles and, in effect, "go home." There was no point in continuing to beat his head against the wall. It wasn't going to change anything, wasn't going to give him the outcome he'd been hoping for.

He and Claire weren't going to get back together again.

For him to pretend otherwise was just another way of prolonging his pain. He'd been stalling these past few days, stubbornly and futilely delaying the inevitable.

He might not be a college graduate, he thought ruefully, but he was certainly bright enough to take a hint and read the signs—especially if Claire was beating him over the head with one of them.

His marriage was over.

The sooner he came to terms with that, the sooner he would…

Would what?

Heal? he asked himself, mocking the very thought. Heal for what reason? So that he could someday fall for someone else and get to go through this all over again? So he could set himself up for another fall? No, living through this brutal experience once was more than enough for him.

Even the most thickheaded of creatures eventually learned their lesson, and it was time for him to learn his. In this case, his lesson was that he was the kind of man who was destined to be abandoned time and again. His father hadn't wanted to stick around. Who knew? Maybe his mother wouldn't have, either, if it wasn't for the fact that she also had two younger sons besides him at home.

Levi pressed his lips together. That wasn't fair, and he knew it. He was just allowing the situation to get the better of him.

He had tried, really honestly *tried*, to be the best husband and father he could be. But without an example to follow, he admittedly was just blindly moving through his days, doing what he *thought* was the right thing without really knowing if he was succeeding.

Levi laughed shortly at himself.

Obviously, he *hadn't* succeeded because if he had, he would have been home in his apartment with Claire and the baby, and all this would have been moot.

And it wasn't.

Levi blinked to clear his vision and focus. He'd been so preoccupied with this new course of action he was plotting for himself that he hadn't realized that he'd driven the entire way back.

The route had gotten to be so automatic for him that

he'd just driven without watching, and he was now parked behind the boarding house.

For a second he just remained where he was, not wanting to move, not wanting to begin implementing what was to be the last leg of his failed union with Claire. And then he shrugged. He supposed he might as well get this over with.

He had to view this the way he viewed removing a Band-Aid from a wound. He had to strike fast and keep it neat. That would help keep the pain at a minimum.

Who the hell was he kidding? The pain wasn't going to be kept at a minimum. The pain was going to be devastating. But it still had to happen.

Opening the front door, Levi glanced in the direction of the dining room and then the kitchen. The pull he experienced to just walk to either one of the rooms in hopes of seeing Claire was strong, but he forced himself to ignore it.

Why prolong his agony? No matter what, it was going to end the same way. He had to do what he had to do and do it like a man, not like a whimpering child.

So instead of going to either room with the hopes of catching a glimpse of Claire, he went straight to the front stairs and headed up to the second floor and his room.

He had things to pack.

Claire frowned as she craned her neck and looked out of the kitchen and down the hall. She could have sworn she'd heard the front door open and then close again. At this hour, that had to be Levi. This was about the time that he'd been coming in the past few weeks.

Then again, maybe he'd stayed at the store longer, she thought. Doing some of that overtime he always talked about.

But would he do that, considering how things were between them right now? she asked herself, playing her own devil's advocate. No, she was fairly sure that he wouldn't.

That meant that perhaps he'd already come home and had just gone up to his room. He could very well be up there at this moment.

Gina looked in her direction and obviously noticed her preoccupation. "Something wrong?" Gina asked.

Claire had noticed that as a rule, Gina did not pry. That the older woman was even asking this question meant that she wasn't masking her feelings very well.

Even so, her first reaction was denial. "No, nothing's wrong." And then Claire paused, rethinking her words. "Well, maybe," she admitted, vacillating.

And then she made up her mind. What was she doing, standing here, talking to Gina, when she could be upstairs, saving her marriage? It was no contest.

"I'll be right back," she told Gina, stripping the apron off and leaving it slung over the back of one of the chairs.

Gina nodded, as if she understood the chaotic thoughts that were bouncing off one another in her head.

"Take your time," Gina advised. "We're almost finished here anyway."

Claire fervently hoped that the statement couldn't also be applied to her own situation with Levi.

Hurrying out of the kitchen, Claire passed her grandfather holding her daughter in his arms just outside the door.

"Look who's here, Bekka. Your mama's rushing to see you—"

"Grandpa, I need a few more minutes," she began, not really sure how to frame the problem she was currently facing.

Fortunately, in her grandfather's eyes, she could do no wrong, and he was more than willing to do anything she wanted him to.

"No problem, Claire-bear. That just means more time for me to spend with the princess here." He cuddled his cheek against the baby's. "Isn't that right, princess?"

Bekka made some sort of a cooing noise, as if she understood the question that had been put to her and was agreeing with her great-grandfather.

Claire breathed a sigh of relief. She needed a few minutes alone with Levi if she was going to convince him that she meant what she was saying.

Patting Gene's arm just before she flew up the stairs, she said, "Thank you, Grandpa. You're the best!"

"Tell your grandmother that," he told her, calling up the stairs after her disappearing form.

"I will," she called back. "I promise."

Mentally, she was already far away from the conversation with her grandfather.

Never superstitious, Claire still crossed her fingers.

Just let this go well, please, she prayed.

Claire stopped just a few steps short of her husband's door. Taking a deep breath, she tried the doorknob.

Expecting to find it open, she turned the knob only to discover that it didn't give. Levi had locked his door. Since when?

A chill zipped up and down her spine, making all of her feel cold.

This was a bad sign, she thought, looking at the door.

Releasing the doorknob, Claire began to turn away. And then, out of nowhere, she heard her grandmother's voice in her head. It was mocking her.

Giving up already? You're no granddaughter of mine if you do.

"Oh, yes, I am," Claire caught herself saying out loud. She had to watch that, she silently upbraided herself. She didn't want anyone thinking she was talking to herself.

The next moment she knocked on Levi's door. "Levi? Are you in there?" She knocked again, more loudly this time. "Levi?"

There was still no answer.

Her pulse quickened. She was making a fool of herself, Claire thought. She was standing out here, knocking on his door, and he probably wasn't in.

And, if he *was* in, then that was even worse because it meant that he was ignoring her.

Well, what did you expect? That he was just going to be standing in the shadows, pining away for you until you gave him the time of day? Give it up.

Her heart ached as she turned away from the door. Claire had taken a total of three steps toward the stairs when she heard the door behind her opening.

Hope suddenly renewed and bursting out inside her, she swung around to see if it was Levi, or if someone else had opened their door to see what all the commotion was about.

It wasn't *someone else*, it was Levi.

A very solemn-looking Levi with flat, unreadable eyes.

This isn't good, a little voice in her head whispered.

All that meant was that she had to make this good, that same voice told her.

The problem was, she wasn't sure if she could anymore.

"Is something wrong with Bekka?" Levi asked, concerned. He couldn't think of any other reason why Claire would come to his door, looking for him.

Levi had given her an excuse to use, and she almost ran with it. But then she stopped herself. The truth. She needed to stick with the truth. That was the only way this was going to work between them.

Levi respected the truth. What he didn't respect, she recalled, were women who played silly games. That was one of the first things he had ever said to her, telling her that he was grateful that she didn't believe in playing games.

"Nothing's wrong with Bekka," she told Levi quietly. And then she took a deep breath and said, almost all in one breath, "There's something wrong with me."

The concern on his face instantly multiplied a dozenfold. Taking her hand in his, Levi asked her, "Are you sick?"

Granted, she felt a little light-headed, but that could have been due to any one of a number of reasons. And right now it would be squandering the moment if she talked about anything else but what she needed to get off her chest.

"May I come in?"

"Sure." Levi stepped back and opened his door. "Sit," he instructed, gesturing toward the bed. One question came swiftly on the heels of another. "Do you want a glass of water? Do you want me to call your grandmother—?"

"No. And no," Claire told him with finality. "I don't need water or my grandmother. What I need is you," she told him slowly, as if she was testing out each word on the tip of her tongue before she said it out loud.

Since he had come to the boarding house and registered for a room just to be near Claire and the baby, he'd allowed his spirits to rise up more than a dozen times, only to have them come crashing down time and again. This time, he kept a tight rein on them.

"I don't understand."

She opened her mouth to explain, then stopped. For the first time Claire looked around the room he'd been living in these past few weeks.

Claire noted that he had both his suitcases on the bed, opened. They were both more than half-filled. Her uneasiness increased.

"Going on a trip?" she asked, doing her best to make her voice sound innocent.

His eyes met hers and held them for a long moment. "Going back," he corrected. "To the apartment."

"You're leaving?" Claire asked numbly, even as something in her head was screaming not to allow that to happen.

"Yeah," he confirmed, shutting the door behind her. "I guess the plus side of that will be that I won't be bothering you anymore."

"What if…" Her voice suddenly evaporated, and she had to concentrate on finding it again. Clearing her throat, Claire tried once more. "What if I said I wanted you to bother me?"

Levi stared at her, wondering what was going on and why she'd say something like that when she couldn't possibly mean it.

"I'd say that nothing would make me happier—but we both know that you're just yanking my chain. I'm not going to hang around here and hope that I wear you down. I don't want you by default. I want you because you want to be with me. Because you love me at least half as much as I love you.

"But I know that I can't make you love me," he continued, his spirit flagging, "and—"

"What about the other night?" she wanted to know, pulling out all the stops. "We made love, and that was pretty special."

"It was more than that."

Pretty special seemed like such a tiny, meaningless

phrase to apply to what had transpired between them. "But it's still not enough," Levi told her. "I want more than just chemistry, Claire. More than just Fourth of July rockets exploding between us. I want—I *need*— the whole package."

He looked at her for a very long moment, framing the last of his summation. "Most of all, I don't want to constantly have to worry that you're going to leave me. That it's just a matter of time before I come home one night to find that you've packed up and left with the baby. Part of me says I should be happy with what I can get, but I can't live that way anymore, Claire. It's just not fair to—"

"You're right," Claire agreed wholeheartedly, jumping the gun and filling in his last word. "It's not fair to you."

That wasn't what he meant. He felt that the way it stood, it was an unfair situation for the both of them, not just him.

"I didn't say that—"

"Well, you should have," she told Levi, cutting him off. And then she had an idea. "Can I use your bathroom for a second?"

The request seemed to come completely out of nowhere and threw him for a second.

But then Levi shrugged and indicated the closed door to the tiny powder room. "Sure. Go ahead. It's right through there. I'll just get back to my packing," he told her, turning away.

She'd almost left then. Seeing the suitcases and

watching him get back to packing, her courage plummeted strongly.

But then she squared her shoulders and silently told herself, *It's now or never. Grandmother had it right. If something was worth having, it was worth fighting for.*

She closed the powder room door behind her.

* * *

Chapter Fifteen

Ordinarily, this would be exactly the time when she would touch up her makeup, make sure that she was, visually, the very best version of herself that she could possibly be. That would involve making sure that her dress—or a skimpy top and abbreviated shorts—showed her off to her best advantage.

She'd also make sure that her hair was combed into a lustrous sheen if she was wearing it down, and if it happened to be up, she would strategically dispense colored-crystal clips discreetly throughout.

That was her total package, and it left no man un-affected.

But tonight, here in Levi's tiny powder room, there were no crystal hairclips, no extra, secret little rituals that helped her create this complete picture of perfection she was usually so desperate to project. Beneath it all, she was certain that she was downright plain.

Claire stared at herself in the framed mirror that took the place of the outside of a medicine cabinet. Then she turned on the faucet and scrubbed her face clean, dried off with a towel and looked back into the mirror.

Well, there she was, Claire thought, just as God had created her. Maybe not entirely a plain Jane, but certainly not a "Jane" who was guaranteed to take a man's breath away.

"Okay," she told the reflection in the mirror. "Time to face the music and show the man what he really wound up getting when he said *I do*."

"Claire?" Levi's voice came through the bathroom door, calling out to her.

Claire froze.

Could he possibly have caught a glimpse of her through a crack in the door?

Turning, she looked at the door that separated them. There was no crack evident. Claire told herself to calm down.

"Yes?" she asked a little hesitantly.

"Who are you talking to?" Levi wanted to know.

"Just myself," she answered. Then so he wouldn't think she was crazy, she added as an explanation, "Working up my courage."

The reply puzzled him more than it answered anything. "Courage for what?"

Putting her hand on the doorknob, Claire slowly turned it. The resulting sound of the tongue leaving the groove, allowing her to open the door, seemed to echo extra loudly in her head, like a final warning sound. She knew that once she stepped out of the powder room and into his bedroom, there would be no turning back.

Her breath seemed to shorten, and the whole procedure felt as if it was taking place in slow motion.

"For this," she told him in a small, hollow voice. Her mouth felt as dry as a desert as she came out and stood before him.

Levi looked at her. He shook his head, not in disapproval but in complete confusion.

"This?" he repeated, completely mystified. "What are you talking about, Claire?"

She couldn't believe that he didn't see it. He had to be pulling her leg. Either that, or the man was so used to her, he wasn't "seeing" her the way she really was, but the way he perceived her in his mind.

"This," she repeated more insistently. She swept her hand up and down in the vicinity of her face. By the look on Levi's face, he still wasn't seeing it. How could he not? "Don't tell me you don't see it," she said incredulously.

He still had no idea what she was talking about. "What I'm seeing is my wife."

"And—?" she asked, trying to lead him to what she believed was the most important part of this soul-searching moment.

"And she looks nice," Levi concluded. But by the exasperated look on Claire's face, that wasn't what she wanted to hear. "Okay, no more games, Claire. What is it you want me to say?"

She threw up her hands, giving up. "I'm not wearing any makeup, Levi. *None,*" she cried. Just how blind *was* he?

He nodded his head, although his expression didn't change. He didn't appear to be a man who had suddenly experienced enlightenment. "I can see that. And I like it better."

That was *not* what she was expecting. "What?"

"I like it better," he repeated. "You look, I don't know, cleaner, fresher." And then he smiled as he said, "Prettier. All that makeup, it always made me feel like I was supposed to be taking you out to some expensive restaurant. It also made me feel that you were just killing time with me until someone better came along, someone who could give you a fancy lifestyle that I couldn't afford—yet," he added, because he fully intended to, someday.

She was having trouble coming to terms with his reaction to her soul-baring experiment. Cocking her head, she tried to read between the lines. Tried to discover if this man was on the level.

"You're actually telling me that you like me *better* this way?"

He didn't want to hurt her feelings or insult her, but the truth was the truth.

"I suppose I am. You look more genuine," he confessed. Since his answer was obviously not making her very happy, he was quick to add, "Not that you're not beautiful with all the stuff on your face, but you just look more…real."

They'd been married nearly two years. Before that, they had been together for two years. And she had never let him see her without her makeup in all that time. "If you felt that way, why didn't you say anything sooner?" she wanted to know.

"Tell you I thought you had on too much makeup?" Levi questioned. "Claire, I might not be the sharpest knife in the drawer, but I'm not a complete idiot, and I don't harbor a death wish. I know better than to tell a beautiful woman she's being heavy-handed with her makeup. Besides, it seemed to make you happy, and I wasn't going to criticize something that made you feel good about yourself."

Claire felt as if she was shell-shocked. She wanted to be sure she absorbed this properly. "So you really, truly *like* me this way?"

"*Like* is a very weak word," Levi pointed out. "I *love* you this way."

Her eyes searched his face to make sure that she'd heard him correctly. And then they strayed to his bed and the opened luggage on it.

"If that's the case, why are the suitcases still out?" she asked.

Since she had let down her hair, so to speak, he felt it was safe to be honest with her the way she was asking him to be. "Because I can't live with the uncertainty anymore."

It was her turn to look confused. Older and more

sophisticated than she was, he had always struck her as the pillar of confidence. This was all news to her. "Uncertainty?"

Levi blew out a breath. This was harder than he imagined. "I was sure that you were going to leave me again the very next time we have an argument."

"You're right," she answered simply.

"Then you *were* going to leave the very next time we had an argument?" Maybe he should be putting that in the present tense, he thought. The pain that caused him hurt his heart.

"No," she corrected, "you're right that you shouldn't have to live this way. Let's just call that our period of adjustment—we were ironing out the kinks of being two married people with a baby. A baby always adds a lot of extra stress until we both learn how to successfully juggle your job, our lives and the baby's needs. And while we're talking about our faults—" She paused for a second, biting her lower lip as she thought about what she was going to say and how to word it.

"I was wrong."

Levi had the distinct feeling that they were waltzing around not one issue but a number of them. "Wrong about what?"

Since she was apologizing, she might as well give it to him with all the trimmings. There was nothing to be gained by being evasive.

"Wrong about getting so upset because you went to play poker and hang out with some of the local guys.

Adults need 'playtime,' too," she told Levi encouragingly.

Levi's mouth dropped open as he stared at his wife. "You're serious?"

She nodded. "Completely. I guess…sometimes it takes me a while to come to my senses. I just felt abandoned every morning when you went off to work, leaving me with the dirty dishes, a crying baby and my ever-depleting feelings of self-worth."

Stunned, he rounded the side of the bed and came closer to Claire, his suitcases and the clothes he was putting into them temporarily forgotten about. They could always be packed later.

She'd caught his attention with an almost throwaway line. The line made absolutely no sense to him. "Why would your feelings of self-worth be depleted?"

There were a lot of answers to that. She gave him the simplest one. "I couldn't even calm down a baby. My grandfather's better at it than I am."

There were reasons for that. "Number one, your grandfather helped raise four boys, and he tells me that the more experience you have with kids, the easier it is to raise them. You were learning how to deal with all that at your own pace," he told her encouragingly. "And I guess I wasn't all that supportive."

He expected her to agree. When she didn't, he began to feel that maybe there was hope for them after all.

"You were trying to make sure that you were earning enough money so that Bekka never needed anything. It couldn't have been easy, pushing yourself like that. Especially when all you had to come home to was a complaining wife."

Feeling a certain lightness had him playfully teasing her. "Hey, don't be so hard on my wife. She had her reasons." He paused, looking at her closely. "So I guess maybe we do have a chance of making this work?" He ended with a question, but there was definitely a hopeful note in his voice.

Her smile was from ear to ear. "I sure hope so. Oh, Levi, I am *so* ready to go home."

He took her into his arms, wrapping them around her as he brought her close to him. "I think we already are home."

She looked at him, puzzled. "Here?" she questioned, looking around the tiny room.

"I'm going to talk to your grandparents, see if maybe we could get one of the larger rooms for the three of us and stay on for a while." He told her his news, news that had all but seemed irrelevant this morning, but now it could very well be the key to straightening out their lives. "The furniture chain is opening up a new branch in Kalispell, which is a lot closer for me so I won't be gone as long as I used to be each day."

She nodded, taking it in. It all sounded like maybe their lives were finally coming together. "And I could go on working here at the boarding house. Grandmother wants me to be the assistant cook. I really didn't think I could manage the job, but it seems to be coming together," she told him proudly. "Cooking is working out pretty well for me. Even my grandmother can't find any-

thing to complain about with my cooking. Or, if Grandmother decides to go back to cooking here herself—she
mentioned that she misses doing it, and Gina and her
husband are considering moving to Bozeman, to be
closer to their kids, so who knows what might happen.
And, if Grandmother does go back to cooking here, I
could get a part-time job at the day care."

He laughed, enjoying his wife's enthusiasm. "Hey,
you can do anything you set your mind to."

She was fixated on her part in this new plan. "I'm
thinking if I had that part-time job, then maybe you
wouldn't have to work as many hours as you do—and
we could spend more time together as a family."

He smiled into her eyes. "Sounds good to me. *Really*
good," he told her, lightly kissing her temple, creating
a delicious warmth within her. "Let's make a deal," he
told her.

"A deal?" She wasn't sure where he was going with
this. She wasn't leery—she loved him—but she tried
to brace herself.

He nodded. "Whatever we do from here on in, we're
going to make our decisions together. As a family. None
of this stoically taking on more than we should and
then expecting that the other person's going to be all
right with it without at least hearing the argument for
it. Does that sound like something you can live with?"
he asked her.

"As long as I can live with you, that's all I care about."
She felt as if a huge, huge boulder had been lifted from

her heart. "And you're sure that you're okay with look-ing at me like this?" she had to ask one last time.

"Perfectly okay," he told her. And then he dead-panned, "I figure if I haven't been turned to stone yet, the odds are pretty good in my favor."

Claire doubled up her fist and punched him in the arm. He laughed, pretending to wince.

"There's my Claire," he announced, delighted. "You haven't done that in a long time."

"I could pummel you to the ground and make up for lost time," she offered.

"I think I'll take a pass on that for now. Besides, if you pummel me to the ground, how am I going to be able to do this?" he asked, kissing first one cheek and then the other.

"Good point," she murmured, feeling the kernel of excitement pop within her inner core and flowering into all the surrounding regions. "Wouldn't want to stifle your creative instincts."

"Speaking of creative instincts, how much longer do you think we can count on your grandfather entertain-ing Bekka and keeping her with him?"

"Indefinitely," she answered. "He usually hangs on to Bekka until I come to his room to collect her."

Levi's expression brightened. "So if we don't show up for a couple of hours to claim her—"

"Grandpa will be, as they like to say, 'in hog heaven.'"

Claire wasn't sure just what was going on. "Why are you asking about Bekka?"

He spared her a long, penetrating look. "Just wanted to be sure that she's not going to suddenly show up at the wrong time."

Claire laughed as she suddenly had a vision of their eight-month-old standing outside their door, plotting to get even for being left with a sitter.

"Not on her own, she wouldn't. She's only a little older than eight months, remember? Babies don't walk at eight months."

"But they do see."

"Yesss." She stretched out the word, waiting to see where he was going with this.

"I think her education should begin a little later, not now."

"You're planning to do something educational with me?" she asked innocently, humor dancing in her eyes.

"Not exactly educational," he allowed. "I think I'd place this in the realm of entertainment instead. Entertainment and pleasure." He smiled. "Think I could interest you in, oh, perhaps getting a sample?"

"I think you could interest me in getting a complete course in the subject."

"I was hoping you'd say that." Just before he kissed her, he framed her face with his hand. "God, but I have missed you."

"I'm right here, Levi. And I'm not going anywhere."

"Amen to that," he murmured just before he lowered his mouth to hers.

"I love you, Claire," he said against her mouth before there wasn't room for any more talk.

At the last possible second, she said, "I love you, too," sending the rest of their marriage off to a wonderfully promising start.

Epilogue

Her eyes still closed, Claire stretched beneath the sheet. Ever so slowly, she shed the confining restraints of sleep from her body.

It took her brain a beat to catch up.

When it did, the fact that her arm didn't come in contact with another body registered. The place beside her in bed was empty.

Her eyes flew open as the significance of that fact sank in.

Levi wasn't next to her.

After making love in his room last night, they had both gotten dressed and gone down together to her grandfather to retrieve Bekka. The old man offered to keep the little girl with him overnight, but they had politely refused. Neither she nor Levi wanted to be that obvious about their reconciliation—yet.

As if she somehow sensed that her parents needed more time together, the baby had fallen right to sleep the moment they laid her down and for once, she didn't wake up crying two or three times during the course of the night. Instead, she'd slept straight through, leaving Levi and her to reexplore the joys of sleeping in the same bed all over again.

Claire couldn't remember when she'd felt as happy as she had when she'd fallen asleep last night.

But this morning was a different story.

She woke up to an empty bed—and an empty crib, she suddenly realized. It was not only Levi who was missing, but it was the baby, too.

Bekka was nowhere to be seen.

Had the baby woken up sick? Had Levi taken her downstairs to her grandmother for help? Or maybe he'd driven Bekka over to the hospital.

Without telling her?

Why wouldn't he wake her up and tell her he was taking the baby to the hospital?

A panic began to set in, stealing her very breath away.

Throwing off the sheet, Claire was about to pull on the first clothes she found when she heard the door opening.

Levi walked in carrying Bekka in one arm while holding a mostly empty baby bottle in the other.

"Oh, look, Bekka, Mommy's up—and she's naked."

Levi then quickly reversed his instructions. "Don't look, Bekka."

Flushing, although more from annoyance than embarrassment, Claire grabbed the robe that was on the floor at the foot of her bed. She assumed it must have slipped off during last night's activities.

"Where were you?" she wanted to know. "You had me really worried."

Levi placed the baby into her crib then joined Claire. He paused to brush his lips against hers.

"Nice to know you worry, but Bekka was fussing and I thought you deserved to sleep in a little bit, especially after that encore performance last night," he added with a wink.

"So you took her downstairs?" Claire asked, surprised.

"Had to eventually. That was where her formula was," Levi explained when she looked at him quizzically.

Claire decided that sounded as plausible as any other explanation. She turned her attention to the baby.

"She's probably soaking wet by now. I'd better change her—"

"Already done," Levi said, stopping her in her tracks.

Claire looked at him in amazement. "Boy, one day on the job and you've gotten better at it than me," she commented.

He was quick to negate her assessment. "That could never happen, not even if I was on the job a hundred years. All I want to do is help," he told her with sincerity.

"You help," Claire assured him. "Just by being here, you help a lot." Tightening the sash at her waist, she proceeded to make her bed. She was going to have to be in the kitchen soon, she thought as she worked her way around the perimeter of the bed.

When she got to Levi's side, she stopped dead. There was a lump under the sheet just beneath his pillow. When she started to smooth it out, she discovered that the lump wasn't caused by a crumpled sheet, it was caused by a black velvet box. She looked at it, and then at Levi. "What's this?"

"Best way to find out is to open it," he told her casually.

Her hands were steady, but she was trembling inside as she slowly drew back the top of the box. Inside the ring box was her wedding ring, gleaming the way it hadn't in two years.

"My ring," she cried. Raising her eyes to his, she asked, "It *is* my wedding ring, right?"

"It is your wedding ring," he confirmed.

"But I looked everywhere for it," she told him, remembering how bitterly unhappy she'd been to lose it. "How did you—?"

"When you threw it at me, it fell onto the floor in the hall, and of course I picked it up so it wouldn't get lost. I held on to it hoping you'd want it—and me—back someday." Taking the box from her, he took the ring out and held it up to her. "Claire Strickland, will you do me the very great honor of becoming my wife—again?"

"Yes!" She threw her arms around him, hugging him tightly. "Oh, yes!"

Levi tugged at her sash and then slipped his arms in beneath her robe.

Claire forgot all about getting ready for work.

They both did.

* * * * *

Something deep and long unused inside him had turned upside down in the face of her grief.

To comfort her became more important than the inhibitions he had imposed upon himself.

He reached out and clasped her hand in his. It was slender and warm but he felt calluses on her palm and fingers. Warrior calluses.

She returned the pressure on his hand, not knowing what a monumental gesture it was for him to reach out to her. For a very long moment his eyes met with hers in a silent connection that shook him. What he felt for her in this moment went way beyond physical attraction.

In the quiet of his kitchen, with the ticking of the clock and the occasional whirring of the fridge the only noise, this one room of many in the vast emptiness of his house suddenly seemed welcoming. Because she was here.

HIRED BY
THE BROODING
BILLIONAIRE

BY
KANDY SHEPHERD

Published in Great Britain 2015
by Mills & Boon, an imprint of Harlequin (UK) Limited,
Eton House, 18-24 Paradise Road, Richmond, Surrey, TW9 1SR

© 2015 Kandy Shepherd

ISBN: 978-0-263-25158-6

23-0815

Harlequin (UK) Limited's policy is to use papers that are natural, renewable and recyclable products and made from wood grown in sustainable forests. The logging and manufacturing processes conform to the legal environmental regulations of the country of origin.

Printed and bound in Spain
by CPI, Barcelona

Kandy Shepherd swapped a career as a magazine editor for a life writing romance. She lives on a small farm in the Blue Mountains near Sydney, Australia, with her husband, daughter and lots of pets. She believes in love at first sight and real-life romance—they worked for her! Kandy loves to hear from her readers. Visit her at www.kandyshepherd.com.

To my daughter Lucy for her invaluable help
in "casting" my characters.

CHAPTER ONE

SHELLEY FAIRHILL HAD walked by the grand old mansion on Bellevue Street at least twenty times before she finally screwed up enough courage to press the old-fashioned buzzer embedded in the sandstone gatepost. Even then, with her hand on the ornate wrought-iron gate, she quailed before pushing it open.

The early twentieth-century house was handsome with peaked roofs and an ornate turret but it was almost overwhelmed by the voracious growth of a once beautiful garden gone wild. It distressed her horticulturalist's heart to see the out-of-control roses, plants stunted and starved of light by rampant vines, and unpruned shrubs grown unchecked into trees.

This was Sydney on a bright winter's afternoon with shafts of sunlight slanting through the undergrowth but there was an element of eeriness to the house, of secrets undisturbed.

In spite of the sunlight, Shelley shivered. *But she had to do this*.

It wasn't just that she was looking for extra work—somehow she had felt compelled by this garden since the day she'd first become aware of it when she'd got lost on her way to the railway station.

The buzzer sounded and the gate clicked a release. She pushed it open with a less than steady hand. Over the last weeks, as she'd walked past the house in the posh inner-eastern suburb of Darling Point, she'd wondered about who lived there. Her imagination had gifted her visions of a broken-hearted old woman who had locked herself away from the world when her fiancé had been killed at war. Or a crabby, Scrooge-like old man cut off from all who loved him.

The reality of the person who opened the door to her was so different her throat tightened and the professional words of greeting she had rehearsed froze unsaid.

Her reaction wasn't just because the man who filled the doorframe with his impressive height and broad shoulders was young—around thirty, she guessed. Not much older than her, in fact. It was because he was so heart-stoppingly good-looking.

A guy this hot, this movie-star handsome, with his black hair, chiselled face and deep blue eyes, hadn't entered into her imaginings for a single second. Yes, he seemed dark and forbidding—but not in the haunted-house way she had expected.

His hair lacked recent acquaintance with a comb, his jaw was two days shy of a razor and his black roll-neck sweater and sweatpants looked as though he'd slept in them. The effect was extraordinarily attractive in a don't-give-a-damn kind of way. His dark scowl was what made him seem intimidating.

She cleared her throat to free her voice but he spoke before she got a chance to open her mouth.

'Where's the parcel?' His voice was deep, his tone abrupt.

'Wh-what parcel?' she stuttered.

He frowned. 'The motherboard.'

She stared blankly at him.

He shook his head impatiently, gestured with his hands. 'Computer parts. The delivery I was expecting.'

Shelley was so shocked at his abrupt tone, she glanced down at her empty hands as if expecting a parcel to materialise. Which was crazy insane.

'You…you think I'm a courier?' she stuttered.

'Obviously,' he said. She didn't like the edge of sarcasm to the word.

But she supposed her uniform of khaki trousers, industrial boots and a shirt embroidered with the logo of the garden design company she worked for could be misconstrued as courier garb.

'I'm not a courier. I—'

'I wouldn't have let you in the gate if I'd known that,' he said. 'Whatever you're selling, I'm not buying.'

Shelley was taken aback by his rudeness. But she refused to let herself get flustered. A cranky old man or eccentric old woman might have given her worse.

'I'm not selling anything. Well, except myself.' *That didn't sound right.* 'I'm a horticulturalist.' She indicated the garden with a wave of her hand. 'You obviously need a gardener. I'm offering my services.'

He frowned again. 'I don't need a gardener. I like the place exactly as it is.'

'But it's a mess. Such a shame. There's a beautiful garden under there somewhere. It's choking itself to death.' She couldn't keep the note of indignation from her voice. To her, plants were living things that deserved love and care.

His dark brows rose. 'And what business is that of yours?'

'It's none of my business. But it…it upsets me to see the garden like that when it could look so different. I… I thought I could help restore it to what it should be. My rates are very reasonable.'

For a long moment her gaze met his and she saw something in his eyes that might have been regret before the shutters went down. He raked both hands through his hair in what seemed to be a well-worn path.

'I don't need help,' he said. 'You've wasted your time.' His tone was dismissive and he turned to go back inside.

Curious, she peered over his shoulder but the room behind him was in darkness. No wonder with all those out-of-control plants blocking out the light.

Her bravado was just about used up. But she pulled out the business card she had tucked into her shirt pocket so it would be easy to retrieve. 'My card. In case you change your mind,' she said. It was her personal card, not for the company she worked for. If she was to achieve her dream of visiting the great gardens of the world, she needed the extra income moonlighting bought her.

He looked at her card without seeming to read it. For a moment she thought he might hand it back to her or tear it up. But he kept it in his hand. The man was rude, but perhaps not rude enough to do that. Most likely he would bin it when he got inside.

Nothing ventured, nothing gained. Her grandmother's words came back to her. At least she'd tried.

'Close the gate behind you when you leave,' the man said, in a voice so cool it was as if he'd thrown a bucket of icy water over her enthusiasm for the garden.

'Sure,' she said through gritted teeth, knowing she would have to fight an impulse to slam it.

As she walked back down the path she snatched the opportunity to look around her to see more of the garden than she'd been able to see over the fence. Up closer it was even more choked by weeds and overgrowth than she'd thought. But it was all she'd ever see of it now.

Strange, strange man, she mused.

Strange, but also strangely attractive. The dark hair, the dark clothes, those brooding blue eyes. He was as compelling as the garden itself. And as mysterious. Maybe he didn't own the house. Maybe he was a movie star or someone who wanted to be incognito. Maybe he was a criminal. Or someone under a witness protection plan. She hadn't lived long enough in Sydney to hear any local gossip about him. But why did it matter? She wouldn't be seeing him again.

She looked like a female warrior. Declan watched the gardener stride down the pathway towards the gate. Her long, thick plait of honey-coloured hair fell to her waist and swayed with barely repressed indignation. She was tall, five ten easily, even in those heavy-duty, elastic-sided work boots. The rolled-up sleeves of the khaki shirt revealed tanned, toned arms; the man-style trousers concealed but hinted at shapely curves and long legs. She looked strong, vigorous, all woman—in spite of the way she dressed. Not what he thought of as a gardener. He glanced down at her card—*Shelley Fairhill.*

The old-fashioned name seemed appropriate for a lover of flowers, all soft focus and spring sunbeams. But the woman behind the name seemed more like the fantasy warrior heroine in the video games that had brought him his first million when he was just eighteen—the assassin Princess Alana, all kick-butt strength, glistening angel wings and exaggerated curves born of his adolescent yearnings. With her deadly bow and arrow Alana had fought many hard-won battles in the fantasy world he had created as a refuge from a miserable childhood.

He could see in this gardener something of the action woman who had kept on making him millions. Billions when he'd sold Alana out. Right now Shelley Fairhill was all tense muscles and compressed angst—seething, he imagined, with unspoken retorts. He could tell by the set of her shoulders the effort she made not to slam the gate off its hinges—he had no doubt with her muscles she could do that with ease. Instead she closed it with exaggerated care. And not for a second did she turn that golden head back to him.

Who would blame her? He'd rejected her pitch for employment in a manner that had stopped just short of rudeness. But Shelley Fairhill should never have breached that gate. He'd only buzzed it open in a moment of distraction. He'd been working for thirty-six hours straight. The gate was kept locked for a reason. He did not want intruders, especially a tall, lithe warrior woman like her, crossing the boundaries of his property. And he liked the garden the way it was—one day the plants might grow over completely and bury the house in darkness like a fortress. *He wanted to be left alone.*

Still, she was undeniably striking—not just in physique but in colouring with her blond hair and warm brown eyes. He couldn't help a moment of regret torn painfully from the barricades he had built up against feeling—barricades like thorn-studded vines that twined ever tighter around his heart stifling all emotion, all hope.

Because when he'd first seen her on his front doorstep for a single, heart-stopping moment he'd forgotten those barriers and the painful reasons they were there. All he'd been aware of was that he was a man and she was a beautiful woman. *He could not allow that boy-meets-girl feeling to exist even for seconds.*

For a long moment he looked at the closed gate, the out-of-control tendrils of some climbing plant waving long, predatory fingers from the arch on top of it, before he turned to slouch back inside.

CHAPTER TWO

DECLAN GRANT. SHELLEY puzzled over the signature on the text that had just pinged into her smartphone.

Contact me immediately re work on garden.

She couldn't place the name. But the abrupt, peremptory tone of the text gave her a clue to his identity.

For two weeks, she had pushed the neglected garden and its bad-mannered—though disturbingly good-looking—owner to the back of her mind. His reaction to her straightforward offer of help had taken the sheen off her delight in imagining how the garden could blossom if restored.

The more she'd thought about him, the more she'd seethed. He hadn't given her even half a chance to explain what she could do. She'd stopped walking that way to the railway station at Edgecliff from the apartment in nearby Double Bay she shared with her sister. And drove the long way around to avoid it when she was in the car. All because of the man she suspected was Declan Grant.

Her immediate thought was to delete the text. She wanted nothing to do with Mr Tall, Dark and Gloomy; couldn't imagine working with him in any kind of harmony. Her finger hovered over the keypad, ready to dispatch his message into the cyber wilderness.

And yet.

She would kill to work on that garden.

Shelley stared at the phone for a long moment. She was at work, planting a hedge to exact specifications in a new apartment complex on the north shore. By the time she crossed the Sydney Harbour Bridge to get back to the east side it would be dark. Ideally she didn't want to meet that man in the shadowy gloom of a July winter nightfall. But she was intrigued. And she didn't want him to change his mind.

She texted back.

This evening, Friday, six p.m.

Then to be sure Declan Grant really was the black-haired guy with the black scowl:

Please confirm address.

The return text confirmed the address on Bellevue Street.

I'll be there, she texted back.

With the winter evening closing in, Shelley walked confidently up the pathway to the house, even though it was shrouded in shadow from the overgrown trees. The first thing she would do if she got this gig would be to recommend a series of solar-powered LED lights that would come on automatically to light a visitor's path to the front door. *Maybe he wanted to discourage visitors by keeping them in the dark.*

She braced herself to deal with Declan Grant. To be polite. Even if he wasn't. *She wanted to work on this garden.* She had to sell herself as the best person for the job, undercut other gardeners' quotes if need be. She practised the words in her head.

But when Declan opened the door, all her rehearsed words froze at the sight of his outstretched hand—and the shock of his unexpected smile.

Okay, so it wasn't a warm, welcoming smile. It was more a polite smile. A professional, employer-greeting-a-candidate smile that didn't quite reach his eyes. Even so, it lifted his face from grouch to gorgeous. *Heavens, the man was handsome.* If his lean face with the high cheekbones and cleft in his chin didn't turn a woman's head his broad shoulders and impressive height surely would.

She stared for a moment too long before she took his proffered hand, his hard warm grip—and was suddenly self-consciously aware of her own work-callused hands. And her inappropriate clothes.

He was attractive—but that didn't mean she was attracted to him. Apart from the fact he was a total stranger and a potential employer, she liked to think she was immune to the appeal of very good-looking men. Her heart-crushing experience with Steve had ensured that. Too-handsome men had it too easy with women—and then found it too easy to destroy their hearts.

No. It was not attraction, just a surge of innate feminine feeling that made her wish she'd taken more care with her appearance for this meeting with Declan Grant.

After work, on a whirlwind visit back to the tiny apartment in Double Bay, she'd quickly showered and changed. Then swapped one set of gardening gear for another— khaki trousers, boots and a plain shirt without any place of employment logo on the pockets. When she'd told her sister she was going to see the potential client in the mysterious overgrown garden in Darling Point, Lynne had been horrified.

'You're not going out to a job interview looking like *that*,' Lynne had said. 'What will any potential employer think of you?'

'I'm a gardener, not a business person,' Shelley had retorted. 'I'm hardly going to dress in a suit and high heels or pile on scads of make-up. These clothes are clean and they're what I wear to work. I hope I look like a serious gardener.'

Now she regretted it. Not the lack of suit and high heels. But jeans and a jacket with smart boots might have been more suitable than the khaki trousers and shirt. This was a very wealthy part of Sydney where appearances were likely to count. Even for a gardener.

She'd got in the habit of dressing down in her male-dominated work world. Gardening was strong, physical work. She'd had to prove herself as good as—better than— her male co-workers. Especially when she had long blond hair and a very female shape that she did not want to draw attention to.

But Declan looked so sophisticated in his fine-knit black sweater and black jeans, clean-shaven, hair brushed back from his forehead, she could only gawk and feel self-conscious. Yes, her clean but old khaki work clothes put her at a definite disadvantage. Not that *he* seemed to notice. In fact she got the impression he was purposely not looking at her.

'Let's discuss the garden,' he said, turning to lead her into the hallway that had seemed so dark behind him in daylight.

She tried to keep her cool, not to gasp at the splendour of the entrance hall. The ornate staircase. The huge chandelier that came down from the floors above to light up the marble-tiled floor. Somehow she'd expected the inside of the house to be as run-down and derelict as the garden.

Not so. It had obviously been restored and with a lot of money thrown at it.

She followed him to a small sitting room that led off the hallway. It was furnished simply and elegantly and she got the impression it was rarely used. Heavy, embroidered curtains were drawn across the windows so she couldn't glimpse the garden through them.

He indicated for her to take a seat on one of the over-stuffed sofas. She perched on its edge, conscious of her gardening trousers on the pristine fabric. He sat opposite, a coffee table between them. The polished surface was just asking for a bowl of fresh flowers from the garden to sit in the centre. That was, if anything was blooming in that jungle outside.

'I apologise for mistaking you for a courier the last time we met,' he said stiffly. 'I work from home and still had my head in my workspace.'

Shelley wondered what he did for work but it was not her place to ask. To live in a place like this, in one of Sydney's most expensive streets, it must be something that earned tons of money. She put aside her fanciful thoughts of him being in witness protection or a criminal on the run. That was when he'd said 'no' to the garden. Now it looked likely he was saying 'yes'.

'That's okay,' she said with a dismissive wave of her hand. 'It was just a misunderstanding.' She wanted to get off on the right foot with him, make polite conversation. 'Did your computer part arrive?'

'Eventually, yes.'

He wasn't a talkative man, that was for sure. There was an awkward pause that she rushed to fill. 'So it seems you've changed your mind about the garden,' she said.

His face contracted into that already familiar scowl. Shelley was glad. She'd been disconcerted by the forced smile. This was the Declan Grant she had been expecting to encounter—that she'd psyched herself up to deal with.

'The damn neighbours and their non-stop complaints. They think my untended garden lowers the tone of the street and therefore their property values. Now I've got the council on my back to clear it. That's why I contacted you.'

Shelley sat forward on the sofa. 'You want the garden cleared? Everything cut down and replaced with minimalist paving and some outsize pots?'

He drew dark brows together. 'No. I want the garden tidied up. Not annihilated.'

She heaved a sigh of relief. 'Good. Because if you want minimalist, I'm not the person for the job. There's a beautiful, traditional garden under all that growth and I want to free it.'

'That…that's what someone else said about it,' he said, tight-lipped, not meeting her eyes.

'I agree with that person one hundred per cent,' she said, not sure what else to say. *Who shared her views on the garden restoration?*

Her first thought was Declan had talked to another gardener. Which, of course, he had every right to do. But the flash of pain that momentarily tightened his face led her to think it might be more personal. Whatever it might be, it was none of her business. She just wanted to work in that garden.

He leaned back in his sofa, though he looked anything but relaxed. He crossed one long, black-jeans-clad leg over the other, then uncrossed it. 'Tell me about your qualifications for the job,' he said.

'I have a degree in horticultural science from Melbourne University. More importantly, I have loads of experience working in both public and private gardens. When I lived in Victoria I was also lucky enough to work with some of the big commercial nurseries. I ran my own one-woman business for a while, too.'

'You're from Melbourne?'

She shook her head. 'No. I lived most of my life in the Blue Mountains area.' Her grandmother had given refuge to her, her sister and her mother in the mountain village of Blackheath, some two hours west of Sydney, when her father had destroyed their family. 'I went down south to Melbourne for university. Then I stayed. They don't call Victoria "The Garden State" for nothing. I loved working there.'

'What brought you back?' He didn't sound as though he was actually interested in her replies. Just going through the motions expected of a prospective employer. *Maybe she already had the job.*

'Family,' she said. It was only half a lie. No need to elaborate on the humiliation dished out to her by Steve that had sent her fleeing to Sydney to live with her sister.

'Do you have references?'

'Glowing references,' she was unable to resist boasting.

'I'll expect to see them.'

'Of course.'

'What's your quote for the work on the garden?'

'A lot depends on what I find in there.'

She'd been peering over the fence for weeks and knew exactly what she'd do in the front of the garden. The back was unknown, but she guessed it was in the same over-grown state. 'I can give you a rough estimate now, but I have to include a twenty per cent variation to cover sur-prises. As well as include an allowance for services like plumbing and stonemasonry.'

'So?'

She quoted him a figure that erred on the low side—but she desperately wanted to work on this garden.

'Sounds reasonable. When can you start?'

'I have a full-time job. But I can work all weekend and—'

The scowl returned, darkening his features and those intense indigo eyes. 'That's not good enough. I want this done quickly so I can get these people off my back.'

'Well, I—'

'Quit your job,' he said. 'I'll double the amount you quoted.'

Shelley was too stunned to speak. That kind of money would make an immense difference to her plans for her future. And the job could be over in around two months.

He must have taken her silence as hesitation. 'I'll triple it,' he said.

She swallowed hard in disbelief. 'I… I didn't mean…' she stuttered.

'That's my final offer. It should more than make up for you leaving your employer.'

'It should. It does. Okay. I accept.' She couldn't stop the excitement from bubbling into her voice.

She wasn't happy with the job at the garden design company. And she was bored. The company seemed to put in variants of the same, ultra-fashionable garden no matter the site. Which was what the clients seemed to want but she found deathly dull. 'I'm on contract but I have to give a week's notice.'

Aren't you being rash? She could hear her sister's voice in her head. *You know nothing about this guy.*

'If you can start earlier, that would be good,' he said. 'Once I've made my mind up to do something I want it done immediately.'

Tell him you'll consider it.

Shelley took a deep, steadying breath. 'I would love to get started on your garden as soon as I can. I'll work seven days a week if needed to get it ready for spring.'

'Good.' He held up his hand. 'Just one thing. I don't want anyone but you working on the garden.'

'I'm not sure what you mean?'

'I value my privacy. I don't want teams of workmen tramping around my place. Just you.'

She nodded. 'I understand.' Though she didn't really. 'I'm strong—'

'I can see that,' he said with narrowed eyes.

Some men made 'strong' into an insult, felt threatened by her physical strength. Was she imagining a note of admiration in Declan's voice? A compliment even?

'But I might need help with some of the bigger jobs,' she said. 'If I have to take out one of those trees, it's not a one-person task. I have to consider my safety. That…that will be an extra cost, too. But I know reliable contractors who won't rip us off.'

Us. She'd said *us.* How stupid. She normally worked in close consultation with a client. Back in Victoria, where she'd worked up until she'd arrived back in New South Wales three months ago, she actually numbered satisfied clients among her friends. But she had a feeling that might not be the case with this particular client.

There would be no *us* in this working relationship. She sensed it would be a strict matter of employer and employee. Him in the house, her outside in the garden.

He paused. 'Point taken. But I want any extra people to be in and out of here as quickly as possible. And never inside the house.'

'Of course.'

Declan got up from the sofa and towered above her. He was at least six foot three, she figured. When she rose to her feet she still had to look up to him, a novel experience for her.

'We're done here,' he said. 'You let me know when you can start. Text me your details, I'll confirm our arrangement. And set up a payment transfer for your bank.' Again came that not-quite-there smile that lifted just one corner of his mouth. Was he out of practice? Or was he just naturally grumpy?

But it did much to soothe her underlying qualms about giving up her job with a reputable company to work for this man. She hadn't even asked about a payment schedule. For him to suggest it was a good sign. A gardener often had to work on trust. After all, she could hardly take back the work she'd done in a garden if the client didn't pay. Though there were methods involving quick-acting herbicides that could be employed for purposes of pay back—not that she had ever gone there.

'Before I go,' she said, 'is there anyone else I need to talk to about the work in the garden? I… I mean, might your…your wife want input into the way things are done?' *Where was Mrs Grant?* She'd learned to assume that a man was married, even if he never admitted to it.

His eyes were bleak, his voice contained when he finally replied. 'I don't have a wife. You will answer only to me.'

She stifled a swear word under her breath. Wished she could breathe back the question. It wasn't bitterness she sensed in his voice. Or evasion. It was grief.

What had she got herself into?

Her grandmother had always told her to think before she spoke. It was advice she didn't always take. With a mumbled thank you as she exited the house, she decided to keep any further conversation with Declan Grant strictly related to gardening.

* * *

Declan hoped he'd made the right decision in hiring the beautiful Shelley to work in his garden. The fact that he found her so beautiful being the number one reason for doubt.

There must be any number of hefty male gardeners readily available. She looked as capable as any of them. But he'd sensed a sensitivity to her, a passion for her work, that had made him hang onto her business card despite that dangerous attraction. If he had to see anyone working in Lisa's garden he wanted it to be her.

Four years ago he and Lisa had moved into this house, her heart full of dreams for the perfect house and the perfect garden, he happy to indulge her. 'House first,' she'd said of the house, untouched for many years. 'Then we'll tackle that garden. I'm sure there's something wonderful under all that growth.'

Instead their dreams had withered and died. Only the garden had flourished; without check it had grown even wilder in the sub-tropical climate of Sydney.

He would have been happy to leave it like that. It was only the neighbours' interference that had forced him to take action. Shelley Fairhill could have a free rein with the garden—so long as it honoured what Lisa would have wanted. And it seemed that was the path Shelley was determined to take.

Not that he would see much of the gorgeous gardener. She had told him she liked to start very early. As an indie producer of computer games, he often worked through the night—in touch with colleagues on different world time zones. They'd rarely be awake at the same time. It would make it easy to avoid face-to-face meetings. That was how he wanted it.

Or so he tried to convince himself. Something about

this blonde warrior woman had awakened in him an instinct that had lain dormant for a long time. Not sexual attraction. He would not *allow* himself to be attracted to her, in spite of that dangerous spark of interest he knew could be fanned into something more if he didn't stomp down hard on it. *He had vowed to have no other woman in his life.* But what he *would* give into was a stirring of creative interest.

He had lost Princess Alana when he'd sold her out for all those millions to a big gaming company. He didn't like the way they'd since changed her—sexualised her. Okay, he'd been guilty of sexualising his teenage creation too. She'd been a fantasy woman in every way—which was why she'd appealed so much to the legions of young men who had bought her games. But he hadn't given Alana what looked like a bad boob job. Or had her fight major battles bare-breasted. Or made her so predatory—sleazy even.

But he hadn't been inspired to replace her. Until now. In the days since he'd met Shelley he'd been imagining a new heroine. Someone strong and fearless, her long golden hair streaming behind her. In a metal breastplate and leather skirt perhaps. No. That had been done before. Wielding a laser sword? That wasn't right either. Princess Alana's wings had been her thing. Warrior Woman Shelley needed something as unique, as identifying. And a different name. Something more powerful, more call to action than the soft and flowery Shelley.

He headed back to his study that took up most of the top floor. Put stylus to electronic pad and started to sketch strong, feminine curves and wild honey-coloured hair.

CHAPTER THREE

DECLAN PACED THE marble floor of his entrance hall. Back and forth, back and forth, feverish for Shelley to arrive for her first day of working on his garden. He'd actually set an alarm to make sure he wouldn't miss her early start—something he hadn't done for a long time. He raked his hands through his hair, looked down at his watch. *Where was she?*

In the ten days since he'd met with Shelley at the house, he had lived with the fantasy warrior-woman character who was slowly evolving in his imagination. Now he was counting down the minutes to when he got to see his inspiration again in the flesh. Not in the actual flesh. Of course not. His musings hadn't got him *that* far.

At eight a.m. on the dot, she buzzed from the street and he released the gate to let her in. Then opened the front door, stepped out onto the porch and watched through narrowed eyes as she strode up the pathway towards him.

He took a deep breath to steady the instant reaction that pulsed through him. She didn't disappoint. Still the same strength, vigour and a fresh kind of beauty that appealed to him. Appealed strictly in a creative way, that was. He had to keep telling himself that; refuse to acknowledge the feelings she aroused that had nothing to do with her as merely a muse. As a woman, the gardener was off-limits.

Any woman was off-limits. He hadn't consciously made

any commitment to celibacy—but after what had happened to Lisa he could not allow himself to get close to another woman. That meant no sex, no relationships, *no love*.

Shelley wore the same ugly khaki clothes—her uniform, it seemed—with a battered, broad-brimmed canvas hat jammed on her head. She swung a large leather tool bag as if it were weightless. It struck him that if the gardener wanted to disguise the fact she was an attractive woman she was going the right way about it. Her attire made him give a thought to her sexual preference. Not that her personal life was any of his concern. Perhaps he could make his prototype warrior of ambivalent sexuality. It could work. He was open to all ideas at this stage.

'Good morning, Mr Grant,' she carolled in a cheerful voice edged with an excitement she couldn't disguise. She looked around her with eager anticipation. 'What a beautiful sunny morning to start on the garden.'

She really wanted to do this—he could have got away with paying her half. Not that he would have haggled on the price. He was scrupulous about paying people fairly—despised people who didn't.

Her words were accompanied by a wide, generous smile that revealed perfect teeth. The smile lingered in her eyes. Eyes that were the colour of nutmeg—in harmony with the honey-gold of her hair. Not that he could see more than a few wisps of that as it was jammed up under her hat. He wished he could see her hair out and flowing around her shoulders. And not just for inspiration.

'Call me Declan,' he said. 'Not Mr Grant. He's my father.' Though these days his father went by the title His Honour as a judge in the Supreme Court of New South Wales.

Besides, Declan didn't do people calling him 'Mister'. Especially a girl who at twenty-eight was only two years younger than himself. Her age had been on the résumé she'd emailed him. Along with an impressive list of references that had checked out as she'd said they would. She appeared to be exactly what she said she was, which was refreshing in itself.

'Sure, Declan,' she said. 'Call me Shelley. But never Michelle. That's my full name and I hate it.'

'Shelley it is,' he said.

She buzzed with barely harnessed energy. 'I'll start clearing some of the overgrowth today—show your nosy neighbours you mean business. But first I really want to have a good look at what we've got here. Can you show me around?' She put down her leather tool bag.

His first thought was to tell her to find her own way around the garden. But that would sound rude. And he wanted to correct the bad first impression he'd made on her. Not only because he was her employer. But also because if he was going to base a character on her, he wanted her to stick around. He had to stomp down again on the feeling that he would enjoy seeing her here simply because she was so lovely. *She was out of bounds.*

'There's not a lot I can tell you about the garden,' he said. 'It was overgrown when I bought it.'

'You can leave the plants to me. But it'll save time if you give me the guided tour rather than have me try to figure out the lay of the garden by myself.'

He shrugged. 'Okay.'

'Is there a shed? Tools? Motor mower?'

'I can show you where the shed is—from memory there are some old tools in there.'

'Good,' she said. 'Let's hope they're in working order, though I do have equipment of my own, of course.'

'I bought this house as a deceased estate,' he said. 'An old lady lived here for many years—'

'So I was half right,' Shelley said, her mouth tilting in amusement.

'What do you mean by that?'

'I imagined an eccentric old lady living here—a Miss Havisham type. You know, from *Great Expectations* by Charles Dickens.'

'I am aware of the book,' he said dryly. He hadn't expected to be discussing literature with the gardener.

'Or a cranky old man.' Her eyes widened and she slapped her hand to her mouth. 'Oh. I didn't mean—'

'So you encountered a cranky younger man instead.'

She flushed, her smooth, lightly tanned skin reddening on her cheekbones.

'I'm sorry, that's not what I—'

'Don't apologise. I do get cranky. Bad mannered. Rude. Whatever you'd like to call it. Usually after I haven't had any sleep. Be forewarned.'

She frowned. 'I'm not sure what you mean.'

'I work from my home office and I'm online until the early hours, sometimes through the night.'

'No wonder you get cranky if you don't get enough sleep.'

He would bet she was an early-to-bed-and-early-to-rise type. *Wholesome.* That was the word for her—and he didn't mean it as an insult.

'I catch up on sleep during the day,' he said.

'Like a vampire,' she said—and clapped her hand over her mouth again. 'I'm sorry, I didn't mean to say that.'

'You don't have to apologise for that either. I actually find the idea amusing.'

'I'm sorry— There I go apologising again. What I meant to say is that I sometimes speak before I think. Not just sometimes, lots of times. I've been told I need to be more…considered in what I say.'

'So far you haven't offended me in any way.' She was so earnest he was finding it difficult not to smile at how flustered she'd become.

'I'll stay out of your way as much as possible, then.'

'That might be an idea,' he said. Then wondered why he didn't like the thought of her avoiding him. He'd been living on his own for a long time and he liked it that way.

Reclusive. Aloof. Intimidating. The labels had been hurled at him often enough. By people who had no idea of the intensity of the pain that had made him lock himself away. People who expected him to get over something he'd never be able to get over. Never be able to stop blaming himself for.

'What do you do that makes you work such unsociable hours?' Shelley asked.

Unsociable. That was the other label.

'I'm an independent producer of computer games.' Then there was his other work he preferred to keep secret.

'Really?' She dismissed his life work with a wave of her hand. 'I don't have time for computer games. I'd rather be outside in the fresh air and sunlight than hunched in front of a computer or glued to a phone.'

He glared at her. More out of habit than intent.

She bit her lower lip and screwed up her face in repentance. 'Oh, dear. I've done it again. Now I've really insulted you.'

'I didn't take it as an insult,' he said through gritted teeth.

'Do you invent games? That could be fun.' Her attempt to feign interest in gaming was transparent and somehow endearing.

'I have done,' he said. 'Have you heard of the Alana series?'

She shook her head and strands of her hair escaped her

hat. They glinted gold in the morning sunlight. 'I played some game with a little purple dragon when I was younger but, as I said, I'd rather be outside.'

'Yet you read?'

'Yes. And these days I listen to audio books if I'm working on a job on my own. I spend a lot of time by myself in this line of work. If I'm in a team it's different, of course.'

'Seems like a good idea,' he said.

'Oh, don't think I don't give one hundred per cent to the job. I do. And your garden is so interesting to me I'll be fully engaged. I dare say I won't get to finish another book until I complete my work here.'

'I wasn't criticising you,' he said. 'If you want to listen to books or music that's fine by me. As long as you get the work done and don't disturb me.'

'Thank you,' she said. She glanced at her watch. 'I'm aching to see the rest of the garden. Tell me, is there a fountain there? I so want there to be a fountain.'

He smiled. Her enthusiasm was contagious. 'There is a fountain. But it doesn't work.'

She fell into step beside him as he headed around the side of the house. Her long strides just about matched his. 'The pump for the fountain is probably broken. Or clogged. Or there could be a leak in the basin,' she said.

'All possibilities just waiting there for you to discover,' he said.

She completely missed the irony of his words. 'Yes. I'm so excited to get it working again. I love water features. They add movement to a garden, for one thing. And attract birds.'

He nodded thoughtfully. 'I hadn't realised that. About water adding movement. But when you think about it, it makes sense.'

'A garden isn't just about plants. There are so many

elements to consider. Of course, being a horticulturalist, plants are my primary interest. But a garden should be an all-round sensory experience, not just visual.'

She stopped, tilted her head back and sniffed. 'Scent is important too. There's a daphne somewhere in this garden. I can smell it. It's a small shrub with a tiny pink flower but the most glorious scent. It blooms in winter.' She closed her eyes and breathed in. 'Oh, yes, that's daphne, all right.' She sighed a sigh of utter bliss. 'Can you smell it?'

Declan was disconcerted by the look of sensual pleasure on Shelley's face, her lips parted as if in anticipation of a kiss, her flawless skin flushed, long dark lashes fanned, a pulse throbbing at the base of her slender neck. *She was beautiful.*

He had to clear his throat before he replied. 'Yes, I can smell it. It's very sweet.'

She opened her eyes and smiled up at him. How had he not noticed her lovely, lush mouth?

'They're notoriously temperamental,' she said. 'Daphne can bloom for years and then just turn up its toes for no reason at all.'

'Is that so?' Ten minutes in Shelley's company and he was learning more about gardening than he ever wanted to know. 'The name of the old lady who owned this house before me was Daphne.'

He thought Shelley was going to clap her hands in delight. 'How wonderful. No wonder there's daphne planted here. It's great to have a plant to echo someone's name. I often give friends a rose that's got the same name as them for a present. A 'Carla' rose for a Carla. A 'Queen Elizabeth' for an Elizabeth.' She paused. 'I don't know if there's a rose called Declan, though. I'll have to check.'

He put up his hand in a halt sign. 'No. Please. I don't want a Declan plant in this garden.'

'Okay. Fair enough. I don't know that Declan is a great name for a rose anyway. Fine for a man. Excellent for a man, in fact…' Her voice dwindled. She looked up at him, pulled a self-deprecating face. 'I'm doing it again, aren't I?'

'Declan is not a good name for a rose, I agree.' She should be annoying him; instead she was amusing him.

'I… I'm nervous around you,' she said. 'Th…that's why I'm putting foot in mouth even more than usual.' She scuffed the weed-lined path with her boot. It was a big boot; there was nothing dainty about this warrior woman.

'Nervous?'

'I… I find you…forbidding.'

Forbidding. Another label to add to the list.

He shifted from one foot to another, uncomfortable with the turn the conversation was taking. 'I can see how you could think that,' he said. What he *wanted* to say was he'd put a force-field around himself and it was difficult to let it down—even to brief a gardener. Especially when the gardener looked as she did—made him react as she did.

She looked up at him, tilted her hat further back off her face. Her brown eyes seemed to search his face. For what? A chink in his forbiddingness?

'You see, I so want to do this job right,' she said. 'There's something about the garden that's had me detouring on my walks to and from the station just to see it. I'm so grateful to your neighbours for forcing you to do something about it and employ me.' She slapped her thigh with a little cry of annoyance. 'No! That's not what I meant. I meant I'm so grateful to you for giving me this chance to spend the next few months working here. I… I don't want to blow it.'

'You haven't blown it,' he said. 'Already you've shown me I made the right decision in hiring you for this job.'

Relief crumpled her features. 'Seriously?'

'Seriously,' he said. If he was the man he used to be, the man for whom 'forbidding' would never have been a label, he might have drawn her into a comforting hug. Instead he started to walk again, heading to the back of the property where the garden stretched to encompass land of a size that had warranted the multimillions he'd paid for it.

She fell in step beside him. 'So tell me about Daphne—the old lady who owned the house before you. I wonder if she planted the garden.'

'I have no idea. It was my…my wife who was…was interested in the garden.'

How he hated having to use the past tense when he talked about Lisa. He would never get used to it.

'Oh,' Shelley said.

He gritted his teeth. 'My wife, Lisa, died two years ago.' Best that Shelley didn't assume he was divorced, which was often the first assumption about a man who no longer lived with his wife.

The stunned silence coming from the voluble Ms Fairhill was almost palpable. He was aware of rustlings in the trees, a car motor starting up out in the street, his own ragged breath. He had stopped without even realising it.

'I… I'm so sorry,' she finally murmured.

Thank God she didn't ask how his wife had died. He hated it when total strangers asked that. As if he wanted to talk about it to them. As if he *ever* wanted to talk about it. But Shelley was going to be here in this garden five days a week. If he told her up front, then she wouldn't be probing at his still-raw wounds. Innocently asking the wrong questions. Wanting to know the details.

'She… Lisa…she died in childbirth,' he choked out.

No matter how many times he said the words, they never got easier. *Died in childbirth.* No one expected that to happen in the twenty-first century. Not in a country with an advanced health-care system. Not to a healthy young couple who could afford the very best medical treatment.

'And…and the baby?' Shelley asked in a voice so low it was nearly a whisper.

'My…my daughter, Alice, died too.'

'I'm so, so sorry. I… I don't know what to say…'

'Say nothing,' he said, his jaw clenched so tightly it hurt. 'Now you know what happened. I won't discuss it further.'

'But…how can you live here after…after that?'

'It was our home. I stay to keep her memory alive.'

And to punish himself.

CHAPTER FOUR

SHELLEY DIDN'T KNOW where to look, what to say. *How could she have got him so wrong?* Declan was a heart-broken widower who had hidden himself away to mourn behind the high walls of his house and the wild growth of his garden. And she had called him Mr Tall, Dark and Grumpy to her sister. She and Lynne had had a good old laugh over that. Now she cringed at the memory of their laughter. Not *grumpy* but *grieving*.

She couldn't begin to imagine the agony of loss the man had endured. Not just his wife but his baby too. No wonder he carried such an aura of darkness when he bore such pain in his soul. And she had told him he was *forbidding*. Why hadn't she recognised the shadow behind his eyes as grief and not bad temper? There'd been a hint of it the night of her interview with him but she'd chosen to ignore it.

Truth was, although she was very good at understanding plants—could diagnose in seconds what was wrong with ailing leaves or flowers—she didn't read people very well. Somehow she didn't seem to pick up cues, both verbal and non-verbal, that other more intuitive folk noticed. No wonder she had believed in and fallen in love with a man as dishonest and deceptive as Steve had been. She just hadn't seen the signs.

'Shelley excels at rushing in where angels fear to tread.' Her grandmother used to say that quite often.

She was going to have to tread very lightly here.

'So it…it was your wife who realised this garden needed to be set free?'

He didn't meet her eyes but looked into the distance and nodded.

'Only she…she wasn't given the time to do it,' she said.

Mentally, Shelley slammed her fist against her forehead. How much more foot in mouth could she get?

Declan went very still and a shadow seemed to pass across his lean, handsome face and dull the deep blue of his eyes. After a moment too long of silence he replied. 'The reason I hired you was because you said much the same as she did about the garden.'

Think before you speak.

'I… I'm glad.' She shifted from foot to foot. 'I'll do my best to…to do what she would have wanted done to the… to her garden.'

'Good,' he said. 'She would have hated to have it all dug up and replaced with something stark and modern.' He took a deep, shuddering breath. 'No need to talk about it again.'

Shelley nodded, not daring to say anything in case it came out wrongly. If she stuck to talk of gardening she surely couldn't go wrong.

He started to walk again and she followed in his wake. She wouldn't let herself admire his broad-shouldered back view. *He was a heartbroken widower.*

Even if he weren't—even if he were the most eligible bachelor in Australia—he was her employer and therefore off-limits.

Then there was the fact she had no desire for a man in her life. Not now, not yet. *Maybe never.*

After the disastrous relationship with Steve that had made her turn tail and run back to Sydney from Melbourne, she'd decided she didn't want the inevitable painful disruption a man brought with him.

She'd learned hard lessons—starting with the father who had abandoned her when she was aged thirteen—that men weren't to be trusted. And that she fell to pieces when it all went wrong. She'd taken it so badly when it had ended with Steve—beaten herself up with recrimination and pain—she'd had to resign from her job, unable to function properly. No way would she be such a trusting fool again.

As she followed her new boss around the side of the house, she kept her eyes down to the cracked pathway where tiny flowers known as erigeron or seaside daisies grew in the gaps. She liked the effect, although some would dismiss them as weeds. Nature sometimes had its own planting schemes that she had learned to accommodate. If there was such a thing as a soft-hearted horticulturalist that was her—others were more ruthless.

She was so busy concentrating on not looking at Declan, that when he paused for her to catch up she almost collided with his broad chest. 'S-sorry,' she spluttered, taking a step back.

How many times had she apologised already today? She had to be more collected, not let his presence fluster her so much—difficult when he was so tall, so self-contained, *so darn handsome*.

'Here it is,' he said with an expansive wave of his hand. Even his hands were attractive: large, well-shaped, with long fingers. 'The garden that is causing my neighbours so much consternation.' He gave the scowl that was already becoming familiar. 'The garden I like because it completely blocks them from my sight.'

'That...that it does.'

There must be neighbours' houses on either side and

maybe at the back but even the tops of their roofs were barely visible through the rampant growth. But, overgrown as it was, the garden was still a splendid sight. The front gave only a hint of the extent of the size of land that lay behind the house.

She stared around her for a long moment before she was able to speak again. 'It's magnificent. Or was magnificent. It could be magnificent again. And…and so much bigger than I thought.'

Declan's dark brows drew together. 'Does that daunt you?'

He must be more competent than she at reading people—because she thought she had hidden that immediate tremor of trepidation.

'A little,' she admitted. 'But I'm more exhilarated by the challenge than worried I might have bitten off more than I can chew.'

'Good. I'm confident you can do it. I wouldn't have hired you if I wasn't,' he said.

Shelley appreciated the unexpected reassurance. She took a deep breath. 'Truly, this is a grand old garden, the kind that rarely gets planted today. A treasure in its own way.'

'And the first thing you see is the fountain,' he said.

'Yes,' she said. 'It's very grand.'

'And very dry,' he said.

The fountain she'd so hoped to see was classical in style, three tiers set in a large, completely dried-out rectangular pond edged by a low sandstone wall. It took quite a stretch of the imagination but she could see water glinting with sunlight flowing into a pond planted with lotus and water iris interspersed by the occasional flash of a surfacing goldfish. *She could hardly wait to start work on it.*

And, beyond her professional pride in her job, she wanted Declan's approval.

Behind the fountain, paved pathways wound their way through a series of planted 'rooms' delineated by old-fashioned stonework walls and littered with piles of leaves that had fallen in autumn. Graceful old-style planters punctuated the corners of the walls. Some of them had been knocked over and lay on their sides, cracked, soil spilling out. The forlorn, broken pots gave the garden a melancholy air. *It was crying out for love.*

And she would be the one to give this beautiful garden the attention it deserved. *It would be magnificent again.*

She turned to Declan. 'Whoever planted this garden knew what they were doing—and had fabulously good taste. Everything is either really overgrown or half choked to death but the design is there even at a quick glance. It will be a challenge, but one I'm definitely up for.'

He nodded his approval. 'It's like anything challenging—take it bit by bit rather than trying to digest it whole. In this case weed by weed.'

She was so surprised by his flash of humour she was momentarily lost for words. But she soon caught up. 'You've got that right. Man, there are some weeds. I've already identified potato vine—it's a hideous thing that strangles and is hard to get rid of. Morning glory is another really invasive vine, though it has beautiful flowers. It's amazing what a difference a lot of Aussie sunshine can do to an imported "garden invader". The morning glory vine is a declared noxious weed here, but they nurture it in greenhouses in England, I believe. And there's oxalis everywhere with its horrible tiny bulbs that make it so difficult to eradicate.'

'Who knew?' he said.

She couldn't tell whether he was being sarcastic or not. Was that a hint of a smile lifting the corners of his mouth and a warming of the glacial blue of his eyes?

Okay, maybe she'd gone on too much about the weeds.

'That's the nasty stuff out of the way.' It was her turn to smile. 'And now to the good stuff.'

'You can see good stuff under all the "garden invaders"?' he said, quirking one dark eyebrow.

'Oh, yes! There's so much happening in this garden—and this is winter. Imagine what it will be like in spring and summer.' She heaved a great sigh of joyous anticipation. *She was going to love this job.*

And it seemed as if Declan Grant might not be as difficult to work with as she had initially feared. That hint of humour was both unexpected and welcome.

She pointed towards the southern border of the garden. 'Look at the size of those camellia bushes shielding you from your neighbours. They must be at least sixty years old. More, perhaps. The flowers are exquisite and the glossy green leaves are beautiful all year round.'

He put up his hand in a halt sign. 'I don't want you getting rid of those. The woman who lives behind there is particularly obnoxious. I want to screen her right out.'

'No way would I get rid of them,' she said, horrified. Then remembered he was the client. 'Uh, unless you wanted me to,' she amended through gritted teeth. 'That particular white flowering camellia—*camellia japonica* "Alba Plena", if you want to be specific—is a classic and one of my favourites.'

'So you're going to baffle me with Latin?' Again that quirk of a dark eyebrow.

'Of course not. I keep to common names with clients who don't know the botanical names.' *Uh-oh.* 'Um, not that I'm talking down to you or anything.'

'Both my parents are lawyers—there was a bit of Latin flying around our house when I was a kid.'

'Oh? So you know Latin?' She understood the Latin-based naming system of plants, but that was as far as it went.

He shook his head. 'I was entirely uninterested in learning a dead language. I was way more interested in learning how computers talked to each other. Much to my parents' horror.'

'They were both lawyers? I guess they wanted you to be a lawyer too.' His mouth clamped into a tight line. 'Or... or not,' she stuttered.

There was another of those awkward silences she was going to have to learn to manage. He was a man of few words and she was a woman of too many. But now that she understood the dark place he was coming from, she didn't feel so uncomfortable around him.

She took a deep breath. 'Back to the camellias. I think we'll find there's a very fine collection here. Did you know Sydney is one of the best places to grow camellias outside of China, where they originate?'

His expression told her he did not.

'Okay. That's way more than you wanted to know and I'm probably boring you.' *When would she learn to edit her words*?

He shook his head. 'No. You're not. I know nothing about gardening so everything you tell me is new.' His eyes met hers for a long moment. 'I guess I'm going to learn whether I want to or not,' he said wryly.

'Good. I mean, I'm glad I'm not boring you. I love what I do so much but I realise not everyone else is the same. So just tell me to button up if I rabbit on too much.'

'I'll take that on board,' he said with another flash of the smile that so disconcerted her.

She looked around her, both to disconnect from that

smile and hungry to discover more of the garden's hidden treasures. 'I want to explore further and think about an action plan. But the first thing I'll do today is prune that rather sick-looking rose that's clambering all over the front of the house. Winter is the right time of year to prune but we're running out of time on that one. It's dropped most of its leaves but in spring it must be so dense it blocks all light from the windows on the second floor.'

'It does,' he said. 'I like it that way.' His jaw set and she realised he could be stubborn.

'Oh. So, do I have permission to prune it—and prune it hard?'

He shrugged. 'I've committed to getting rid of the jungle. I have to tell you to go ahead.'

'You won't regret it. It's a beautiful old rose called "Lamarque". If I prune it and feed it, bring it back to good health, come spring you'll have hundreds of white roses covering the side of the house.'

He went silent again. Then nodded slowly, which she took for assent. 'Lisa would have loved that.'

Shelley swallowed hard against a sudden lump in her throat at the pain that underscored his words. It must be agony for him to stand here talking to her about his late wife when he must long for his Lisa to be here with him. *Not her.*

She forced herself not to rush to fill the silence. No way could she risk a foot-in-mouth comment about his late wife. Instead she mustered up every bit of professional enthusiasm she could.

'When I've finished, the garden will enhance the house and the house the garden. It's going to be breathtaking. Your neighbours should be delighted—this garden will look so good it will be a selling point for them to be near it.'

'I'm sure it will—not that I give a damn about what they

think,' said Declan with a return of the fearsome scowl. He looked pointedly at his watch. 'But I have to go back inside.' He turned on his heel.

Shelley suspected she might have to get used to his abruptness. It was as if he could handle a certain amount of conversation and that was all. And her conversations were twice as long as anyone else's.

Think before you speak.

'Wait,' she said. 'Can you show me the shed first? You know, where there might be garden tools stored.'

He paused, turned to look back to her. A flicker of annoyance rippled over his face and she quailed. He seemed distracted, as if he were already back in his private world inside the house—maybe inside his head.

He was, she supposed, a creative person whereas she was get-her-hands-dirty practical. He made his living designing games. Creative people lived more in their heads. She was very much grounded on solid earth—although she sometimes indulged in crazy flights of the imagination. Like wondering if he was a criminal. Or an incognito movie star—he was certainly handsome enough for it. But she'd been half right about the Miss Havisham-like Daphne.

'The shed is over there at the north end of the garden,' he said.

Without another word he started to stride towards it. Even with her long legs, Shelley had to quicken her pace to keep up.

The substantial shed looked to be of a similar age to the house and was charmingly dilapidated. The door had once been painted blue but was peeling to reveal several different paint colours dating back to heaven knew how long. A rose—she couldn't identify which one immediately—had been trained to grow around the frame of the door.

If the shed were hers, she wouldn't paint that door. Just sand and varnish it and leave the motley colours exactly as they were. It would not only be beautiful but a testament to this place's history.

As if.

She was never likely to own her own house, garden or even a shed. Not with the exorbitant price of Sydney real estate. Worse, she had loaned Steve money that she had no hope of ever getting back. Foolish, yes, she could see that now—but back then she had anticipated them getting engaged.

One day, perhaps, she might aspire to a cottage way out of town somewhere with room for not just a shed but a stable too.

In the meantime, she was grateful to Lynne for letting her share her tiny apartment in return for a reasonable contribution to the rent. All her spare dollars and cents were being stashed away to finance that trip to Europe.

Come to think of it, this shed looked to be bigger than Lynne's entire apartment in nearby Double Bay. *'Double Pay,'* her sister joked.

The door to the shed was barred by a substantial bolt and a big old-fashioned lock. It was rusted over but still intact. Even the strength in Declan's muscled arms wasn't enough to shift it. He gave the door a kick with a black-booted foot but it didn't budge.

He ran his hand through his hair. 'Where the hell is the key? I'll have to go look inside for it.'

He was obviously annoyed she was keeping him from his work but she persevered.

'I'd appreciate that. I'd really like to see what's in there.'

She hoped there would be usable tools inside. While she had a basic collection, she was used to working with equipment supplied by her employer. She didn't want to have to take a hire payment from her fee.

He turned again to head towards the house.

'Sorry,' she said. *There went that darn sorry word again.* 'But one more thing before you go. Is there…well, access to a bathroom? I'll be working here all day and—'

'At the side of the house there's a small self-contained apartment,' he said. 'You can use the bathroom there. I'll get you that key too. A door leads into the house but that's kept locked.'

'Are you sure? I thought maybe there was an outside—'

'You can use the apartment,' he said, in a that's-the-end-of-it tone.

'Thank you,' she said.

'Take a walk around the garden while I go hunt for the keys,' he said. 'I might be a while.'

She watched him as he headed towards the back entrance of the house. Did he always wear black? Or was it his form of mourning? It suited him, with his dark hair and deep blue eyes. The black jeans and fine-knit sweater—cashmere by the look of it—moulded a body that was strong and muscular though not overly bulky. If he spent long hours at a computer, she wondered how he'd developed those impressive muscles.

She realised she'd been staring for a moment too long and turned away. It would be too embarrassing for words if her employer caught her ogling the set of his broad shoulders, the way he filled those butt-hugging jeans. *He was very ogle-worthy.*

She put her disconcerting thoughts about her bereaved boss behind her as—at last—she took the opportunity to explore the garden. Slowly scanning from side to side so she didn't miss any hidden treasures, she walked right around the perimeter of the garden and along the pathways that dissected it. *It was daunting but doable.*

Dew was still on the long grass and her trousers and boots got immediately damp but she didn't care. Sydney winter days were mild—not like the cold in other places she'd lived in inland Victoria and New South Wales where frost and even snow could make early starts problematical and chilblain-inducing. The cold didn't really bother her. Just as well, as she'd set her heart on finding a job in one of the great gardens of the stately homes in England, where winters would be so much more severe than here.

The scent of the daphne haunted each step but she didn't immediately find where it was growing. She would have to search for that particular gem under the undergrowth. There was no rush. She had time to get to know the idiosyncrasies this particular landscape would present to her.

Every garden was different. The same species of plant could vary in its growth from garden to garden depending on its access to sunlight, water and the presence of other vegetation. She suspected there would be surprises aplenty in a garden that had been left to its own devices and was now coming into her care.

A flash of purple caused her to stop and admire a lone pansy blooming at the base of a lichen-splashed stone wall. She marvelled at the sheer will to survive that had seen a tiny seed find its way from its parent plant to a mere thimbleful of hospitable soil and take root there. It didn't really belong there but no way would she move it.

Not only had she learned to expect the unexpected when it came to Mother Nature, she had also learned to embrace it.

Declan Grant was unexpected, unexplained. She batted the thought away from where it hovered around her mind like an insistent butterfly. He was her boss. He was a widower. *He wasn't her type.*

Her experience with men had been of the boring—she'd broken their hearts—and the bad boys—they'd broken hers. She suspected Declan was neither. He was a man who had obviously loved his wife, still revered her memory.

Her thoughts took a bitter twist. He was not the kind of man who cheated and betrayed his wife. Not like Steve, who had pursued her, wooed her, then not until she'd fallen deeply in love with him had she found out he was married.

Steve's wife had confronted her, warned her off, then looked at her with pity mingled with her anger when she had realised Shelley had had no idea that her lover was married.

Shelley still felt nausea rise in her throat when she remembered that day when her life based on a handsome charmer's lies had collapsed around her. She'd felt bad for the wife, too, especially when the poor woman had wearily explained that Shelley hadn't been the first of Steve's infidelities and would most likely not be the last. Even after all that, Steve had thought he could sweet-talk his way back into her affections, had been shocked when she'd both literally and figuratively slammed the door in his face.

The only vaguely comforting thing she'd taken away from the whole sordid episode in her life was that she'd behaved like an honourable 'other woman' when she'd discovered she was a mistress not an about-to-be fiancée. Not like the other type of 'other woman' who had without conscience seduced her father away from his family.

Now she swallowed hard against the remembered pain, took off her hat and lifted her face to the early-morning sun. Then she closed her eyes to listen to the sounds of the garden, the breeze rustling the leaves, the almost imperceptible noise of insects going about their business, the gentle twitter of tiny finches. From high up in the camellias came the raucous chatter of the rainbow lorikeets—the multicoloured parrots she thought of as living jewels.

Out here in the tranquillity of the garden she could forget all that had hurt her so deeply in the past. Banish thoughts of heartbreak and betrayal. Plan for a future far away from here. *'You might have more luck with the English guys.'* She hadn't known whether to laugh at Lynne's words or throw something at her sister.

But she didn't let herself feel down for long—she never did. Her spirits soared at the privilege of working in this wonderful garden—and being paid so generously to do it.

Getting used to working with a too-handsome-for-comfort boss was something she would have to deal with.

CHAPTER FIVE

DECLAN LOCATED THE keys to both the shed and the apartment without too much difficulty. But the tags attached to them were labelled in Lisa's handwriting and it took him a long moment before he could bear to pick them up. He took some comfort that she would be pleased they were at last being put to use.

Before he took the keys out to Shelley, he first detoured by the front porch and grabbed her leather tool bag from where she had left it. He uttered a short, sharp curse it was so heavy. Yet she had carried it as effortlessly as if it were packed with cotton wool. No wonder her arms were so toned.

He lugged it around to the back garden.

No Shelley.

Had she been put off by the magnitude of the task that faced her and taken off? Her old 4x4 was parked on the driveway around the side of the house and he might not have heard it leave. He felt stabbed by a shard of unexpected disappointment at the thought he might not see her again. He would miss her presence in his garden, in his life.

Then he saw sense and realised there was no way she would leave her tool bag behind.

He soon caught sight of her—and exhaled a sigh of relief he hoped she didn't hear.

His warrior-woman gardener had hopped over the wall

and jumped down into the metre-deep empty pond that surrounded the out-of-commission fountain. There she was tramping around it, muttering under her breath, her expression critical and a tad disgusted as though she had encountered something very nasty. Her expression forced from him a reluctant smile. In her own mildly eccentric way, she was very entertaining.

For the first time, Declan felt a twinge of shame that he had let the garden get into such a mess. The previous owner had been ill for a long time but had stubbornly insisted on staying on in her house. Both money and enthusiasm for maintenance had dwindled by the time she had passed away. When he and Lisa had moved in, he had organised to get the lawns mowed regularly. But even he, a total horticultural ignoramus, had known that wasn't enough.

In fact he had mentioned to his wife a few times that maybe they should get cracking on the garden. Her reply had always been she wanted it to be perfect—compromise had never been the answer for Lisa—and she needed to concentrate on the house first.

Her shockingly unexpected death had thrown him into such grief and despair he hadn't cared if the garden had lived or died. *He hadn't cared if* he *had lived or died.* But now, even from the depths of his frozen heart, he knew that Lisa would not have been happy at how he had neglected the garden she had had such plans for.

Grudgingly he conceded that maybe it was a good thing the neighbours had intervened. And a happy chance that Shelley Fairhill had come knocking on his door.

Not that he would ever admit that to anyone.

She looked up as he approached, her face lit by the open sunny smile that seemed to be totally without agenda. Early on in his time as a wealthy widower he had encountered too many smiles of the other kind—greedy, calculating, seductive. It was one of the reasons he had locked himself away in self-imposed exile. He did not want to date, get involved, marry again—and no one could convince him otherwise no matter the enticement.

'Come on in, the water's fine,' Shelley called with her softly chiming laugh.

Declan looked down to see the inch or so of dirty water that had gathered in one corner of the stained and pitted concrete pond. 'I wouldn't go so far as to say that,' he said with a grimace he couldn't hide.

He intended to stand aloof and discuss the state of the pond in a professional employer-employee manner. But, bemused at his own action, he found himself jumping down into the empty pond to join her.

'Watch your nice boots,' she warned. The concrete bottom of the pond was discoloured with black mould and the dark green of long-ago-dried-out algae.

Declan took her advice and moved away from a particularly grungy area. The few steps brought him closer to her. *Too close.* He became disconcertingly aware of her scent—a soft, sweet floral at odds with the masculine way she dressed. He took a rapid step back. Too bad about his designer boots. He would order another pair online from Italy.

If she noticed his retreat from her proximity Shelley didn't show it. She didn't shift from her stance near the sludgy puddle. 'How long has this water been here?' she asked.

'There was rain yesterday,' he said, arms crossed.

Sometimes he would go for days without leaving the temperature-controlled environment of his house, unaware of what the weather might be outside. But yesterday he'd heard rain drumming on the slate tiles of the roof as he'd made his way to his bedroom in the turret some time during the early hours of the morning.

Shelley kicked the nearest corner of the pond with her boot. Her ugly, totally unfeminine boot. 'The reason I ask is I'm trying to gauge the rate of leakage,' she said. 'There are no visible cracks. But there could be other reasons the pond might not be holding water. Subsidence caused by year after year of alternate heating and cooling in the extremes of weather. Maybe even an earth tremor. Or just plain age.'

She looked up to him as if expecting a comment. How in hell would he know the answer?

'You seem to know your stuff,' he said.

'Guesswork really,' she admitted with a shrug of her shoulders, broad for a woman but slender and graceful.

'So what's the verdict?' he asked.

'Bad—but maybe not as bad as it could be if it's still holding water from yesterday. Expensive to fix.'

'How expensive?'

He thought about what she'd said about a fountain bringing movement to a garden. The concept as presented by Shelley appealed to him, when first pleas and then demands from the neighbours to do something about the garden never had.

'I'm not sure,' she said. 'We might have to call in a pool expert. Seems to me it's very old. How old is the house?'

'It was built in 1917.'

Thoughtfully, she nodded her head. 'The fountain is old, but I don't think it's *that* old. I was poking around the garden while you were inside. It has the hallmarks of one designed around the 1930s or 40s. I'd say it was inspired by the designs of Enid Wilson.'

'Never heard of her.'

Gardening had never been on his agenda. Until now. Until this warrior had stormed into his life.

'Enid Wilson is probably Australia's most famous landscape designer. She designed gardens mainly in Victoria starting in the 1920s and worked right up until she died in the1970s. I got to know about her in Melbourne, although she did design gardens in New South Wales, too.'

'Really,' he drawled.

She'd asked him to tell her to button up if she rabbited on. Truth was, he kind of liked her mini lectures. There was something irresistible about her passion for her subject, the way her nutmeg eyes lit with enthusiasm. *She was so vibrant.*

She pulled a self-deprecating face. 'Sorry. That was probably more than you ever wanted to know. About Enid Wilson, I mean. I did a dissertation on her at uni. This garden is definitely based on her style—she had many imitators. Maybe the concrete in the pond dates back to the time it was fashionable to have that style of garden.'

'So what are your thoughts about the pond? Detonate?' he said.

'No way!' she said, alarmed. Then looked into his face. 'You're kidding me, right?'

'I'm kidding you,' he said. His attempts at humour were probably rusty with disuse.

'Don't scare me like that,' she admonished. 'I'm sure the fountain can be restored. It will need a new pump and plumbing. I don't know how to fix the concrete though. Plaster? Resin? A pond liner? Whatever is done, we'd want to preserve the sandstone wall around it.'

He looked at the fountain and its surrounds through narrowed eyes. 'Is it worth repairing?' Could anything so damaged ever come back to life to be as good as new? *Anything as damaged as a heart?*

'I think so,' she said.

'Would it be more cost-effective to replace it with something new?' he asked.

She frowned. 'You mean a reproduction? Maybe. Maybe not. But the fountain is the focal point of the garden. The sandstone edging is the same as the walls in the rest of the garden.'

'So it becomes a visual link,' he said. He was used to thinking in images. He could connect with her on that.

She looked at the faded splendour of the fountain with such longing it moved him. 'It would be such a shame not to try and fix it. I hate to see something old and beautiful go to waste,' she said. 'Something that could still bring pleasure to the eye, to the soul.'

He would not like to be the person who extinguished that light in her eyes. Yet he did not want to get too involved, either. He scuffed his boot on the gravel that surrounded the pond. 'Okay. So we'll aim for restoration.'

'Thank you!' Those nutmeg eyes lit up. For a terrifying moment he thought she would hug him. He kept his arms rigidly by his sides. Took a few steps so the backs of his thighs pressed against the concrete of the pond wall.

He hadn't touched another woman near his own age since that nightmare day he'd lost Lisa. Numb with pain and a raging disbelief, he'd accepted the hugs of the kind nursing staff at the hospital. He'd stood stiffly while his mother had attempted to give comfort—way, way too late in his life for him to accept. The only person he'd willingly hugged was Jeannie—his former nanny, who had been more parent to him than the mother and father he'd been born to. Jeannie had held him while he had sobbed great, racking sobs that had expelled all hope in his life as he'd realised he had lost Lisa and the child he had wanted so much and his life ever after would be irretrievably bleak.

He wasn't about to start hugging now. Especially with this woman who had kick-started his creative fantasies awake from deep dormancy. Whom he found so endearing in spite of his best efforts to stay aloof.

'Don't expect me to be involved. It's up to you,' he said. 'I trust you to get it right.'

'I understand,' she said, her eyes still warm.

Did she? Could she? Declan had spent the last two years in virtual seclusion. He did not welcome the idea of tradespeople intruding on his privacy. *Only her.* And yet if he started something he liked to see it finished. When it was in his control, that was. Not like the deaths he'd been powerless to prevent that had changed his life irrevocably.

'Call in the pool people,' he said gruffly. 'But it's your responsibility to keep them out of my hair. I don't want people tramping all over the place.'

'I'll do my best,' she said. 'Though harnesses and whips might not be welcomed by pool guys. Or other maintenance workers we might have to call in.'

He released another reluctant smile in response to hers. 'I'm sure you'll find a way to charm them into submission.'

As she'd charmed her way into what his mother called Fortress Declan. He realised he had smiled more since he'd met her than he had in a long, long time.

She laughed. 'I'll certainly let them know who's boss,' she said. 'Don't worry, I've had to fight to be taken seriously in this business. If anyone dares crack a blonde joke, they'll be out of here so fast they won't know what hit them.'

He would believe that. A warrior woman. In charge.

He clambered out of the empty pond. Thought about offering Shelley a hand. Thought again. *He did not trust himself to touch her.*

Turned out he wasn't needed. He'd scarcely completed

the thought before agile Shelley effortlessly swung herself out of the pond with all the strength of an athlete. He suspected she wasn't the type of woman who would ever need to lean on a man. Yet at the same time she aroused his protective instincts.

'Are we sorted?' he said brusquely. 'You deal with the pond. I've got work to do.'

He actually didn't have anything that couldn't be put off until the evening. But he didn't want to spend too much time with this woman. Didn't want to find himself looking forward to her visits here. He'd set an alarm clock this morning so he wouldn't miss her. That couldn't happen again.

He pulled out the keys from his pocket. 'I'll open the shed for you. Then I'm disappearing inside.'

To stay locked away from that sweet flowery scent and the laughter in her eyes.

Like much of this property outside the house, the shed was threatening to fall down. Declan found the lock was rusty from disuse and it took a few attempts with the key before he was able to ease the bolt back from the door of the shed.

Unsurprisingly, the shed was a mess. It was lined with benches and shelves and stacked with tools of varying sizes and in various states of repair. Stained old tins and bottles and garden pots that should have been disposed of long ago cluttered the floor. The corners and the edges of the windows were festooned in spider webs and he swore he heard things scuttling into corners as he and Shelley took tentative steps inside.

Typically, she saw beyond the mess. 'Oh, my gosh, it's a real old-fashioned gardener's shed with potting benches and everything,' she exclaimed. 'Who has room for one of these in a suburban garden these days? I love it!'

She took off her hat and squashed it into the pocket of her khaki trousers. That mass of honey-blond hair was twined into plaits and bunched up onto her head; stray wisps feathered down the back of her long, graceful neck. The morning sunlight shafting through the dusty windows made it shine like gold in the dark recesses of the shed.

An errant strand came loose from its constraints and fell across her forehead. Declan jammed both hands firmly in the pockets of his jeans lest he gave into the urge to gently push it back into place.

He ached to see how her hair would look falling to her waist. Would it be considered sexual harassment of an employee if he asked her to let it down so he could sketch its glorious mass? He decided it would. And he did not want to scare her off. She stepped further into the shed, intent on exploration.

'Watch out for spiders,' he warned.

In his experience, most women squealed at even the thought of a spider. Sydney was home to both the deadly funnel web and the vicious redback—he would not be surprised if they had taken up abode in the shed.

Shelley turned to face him. 'I'm not bothered by spiders,' she said.

'Why does that not surprise me?' he muttered.

'I'd never be a gardener if I got freaked out by an itty-bitty spider,' she said in that calm way she had of explaining things.

'What about a great big spider?' There was something about her that made him unable to resist the impulse to tease her. But she didn't take it as teasing.

'I'm still a heck of a lot bigger than the biggest spider,' she said very seriously.

Was it bravado or genuine lack of fear?

'Point taken,' he said. He looked at her big boots that

could no doubt put an aggressive spider well and truly in its place.

'Snakes, now…' she said, her eyes widening, pupils huge in the gloom of the shed. 'They're a different matter. I grew up on a property out near Lithgow, west of the mountains. We'd often see them. I'd be out riding my horse and we'd jump over them.' She shuddered. 'Never got used to them, though.'

'Have you always been so brave and fearless?' he asked.

'Is that how I appear to you?' she asked. 'If so, I'm flattered. Maybe I do a good job of hiding my fears—and snakes are one of them.'

'Not too many snakes in Darling Point,' he said, wondering about her other fears.

'I hope not, it's so close to the city,' she said. 'Though I'll still approach the undergrowth outside with caution. I've been surprised by red-bellied black snakes in north shore gardens.'

Could the fantasy warrior woman forming in his imagination vanquish snakes under foot? Or evil-doers in the guise of snakes? Hordes of alien shape-shifter spiders? No. This new princess warrior would be more defender than attacker. Saving rather than destroying. But would that make the character interesting to the adolescent boys who were his main market?

He realised how much he'd changed since he'd created the assassin Alana with her deadly bow and arrow. Then he'd been angry at the world with all the angst of a boy who'd been told too often that he'd been unplanned, unwanted. His parents had been surprised by his mother's pregnancy. He'd been told so often he'd been 'an accident' but the sting of the words never diminished, never lessened the kick-in-the-gut feeling it gave him. Destruction, death even, had been part of the games he'd created with so much success.

Now he'd suffered the irreversible consequence of death in real life rather than in a fantasy online world where characters could pick themselves up to fight again. He could never again see death as a game.

Shelley reached into her tool bag and pulled out a pair of thick leather gauntlet gloves. 'I dare a spider to sink its fangs through these,' she challenged.

'I hope they don't get close enough for that to happen,' he said.

Gloves. There was something very sensual about gloves. Not the tough utilitarian gardening gloves Shelley was pulling onto her hands. No. Slinky, tight elbow-length gloves that showed off the sleek musculature of strong feminine arms, the elegance of long fingers. He itched to get back to his study and sketch her arms. Not Shelley's arms. Of course not. *He could not go there.* The arms of fictional warrior Princess As Yet Unnamed—he gave himself permission to sketch hers.

'There's a treasure trove in here,' Shelley exclaimed in delight as she poked through corners of the shed that had obviously been left undisturbed for years.

He had to smile at a woman who got excited at a collection of old garden implements. You'd think they were diamond-studded bracelets the way she was reacting. It was refreshing. Shelley was refreshing. He had never met anyone like her.

'Looks like a bunch of rusty old tools to me,' he said.

A motley collection of old garden implements was leaning against the wall. She knocked off the dust and cobwebs from a wooden-handled spade before she picked it up and held it out for him to examine.

'This is vintage,' she said. 'Hand forged and crafted

with skill. Made to last for generations. It's a magnificent piece of craftsmanship. Valuable too. You'd be surprised what you could sell this for. Not that you probably need the money.' She flushed pink on her high cheekbones. 'Sorry. That just slipped out.'

'You're right. I don't need the money.'

He had accumulated more money than he knew how to spend and yet it kept on rolling into his bank accounts. He didn't actually need to work ever again. Did his private work for little recompense. The odd hours his work entailed were something to keep the darkness at bay. Since Lisa and their baby had died he had suffered badly from insomnia. Sleep brought nightmares where he was powerless to save his wife and daughter. Where he tortured himself with endless 'if onlys' repeated on a never-breaking loop.

'What do you plan to do with these tools?' he said.

She brandished the shovel. 'Use them, of course. Though they'll need cleaning and polishing first.' She looked up. 'I'll do that on my own time,' she added.

He liked her honesty. Doubted that Shelley would charge him for five minutes that she wasn't working.

'No need for that,' he said. 'Count restoring these heirloom tools as part of your work here.'

Heirloom? Where did that word come from to describe decrepit garden implements? Was it an attempt to please her?

He so nearly added: *I'll come down and help you with them.* But he drew the words back into his mouth before there was a chance of them being uttered. There would be no cosy sessions down in this shed, cleaning up tools, chatting, getting to know each other.

Shelley was his gardener. And, unwittingly, his muse. That was all she could ever be to him. *No matter how he was beginning to wish otherwise.* That was all any woman, no matter how lovely or how endearing, could be.

Shelley cautiously let herself into the apartment attached to the back of the house with the key Declan had given her. Even though she had his permission, she felt like an intruder. She sucked in a breath of surprise when she got inside. The apartment was more generous in size than she had imagined. Heck, the *shed* here was bigger than the apartment where she lived. This appeared positively palatial by comparison.

The decoration seemed brand-new—stylish in neutral tones with polished wooden floorboards and simple, timeless furnishings in whitewashed timber and natural fabrics. It was posh for staff quarters—which was what she assumed the apartment was.

Had anyone ever lived here since it had been renovated?

She'd taken off her boots at the door. On feet encased in tough woollen work socks, she tiptoed through the rooms: a living room furnished with a stylish, comfortable-looking sofa and a big flat-screen television set; a dining area; a smart, compact kitchen; a bedroom with a large bed and an elegant quilt; a small, immaculate bathroom. It was the most upscale granny flat she'd seen—it wouldn't be out of place on the pages of a design magazine. There was a door at the end of the kitchen she thought might be a pantry. But it was locked and she realised it must be the door into the house. That made sense for staff quarters.

Shelley trailed her hand along the edge of the sofa and wondered about Lisa, Declan's late wife. She must have been a nice person to go to so much trouble to decorate this apartment for a housekeeper. She herself had been in too many grotty staff facilities to know the difference. Her heart contracted inside her at the thought of the tragedy that had played out in this house. Lisa had had her whole life ahead of her, everything to look forward to. And Declan. How could he ever get over it?

She herself had trust issues. Would find it difficult to ever trust a man enough to love again. But loss on this scale was unimaginable. Could Declan ever let himself trust in a future again?

Subdued by the thought, she once again reminded herself how lightly she would have to tread around this man. And that she must not—repeat not—let herself be attracted to him for even a second. She sensed giving into that would lead to heartbreak the like of which she had never even imagined.

CHAPTER SIX

SHELLEY WAS BECOMING Declan's guilty pleasure. From the windows of his office that took up most of the top floor of the house, he could watch her unobserved as she worked in the garden below.

Her energy and output were formidable as she systematically went about getting his garden back into shape. Right now she was on her hands and knees weeding a garden bed in the mid-morning sunshine. They'd had a discussion about the use of herbicides and come to the mutual decision to use an organic-based poison only when needed for the toughest of the garden invaders.

Garden invaders. He was taken by the term, wondered if he could use it for Princess No-Name's game. Not that young male gamers were likely to be interested in gardens—but invaders, yes.

However the pros and cons of spraying weeds were not on his mind as he watched Shelley below in the garden. He admired the way she performed such mundane tasks as weeding or pruning with such strength, grace and rhythm. The play of her muscles, the way she stretched out her arms and long legs and massaged the small of her back after she'd been working in the one place for any length of time all appealed.

Now she was kneeling and he tried to ignore the way her

shapely backside wiggled into his view when she leaned forward to locate and pull weeds.

Dammit—when had gardening ever been sexy?

He pushed the answer to the question he had posed himself to the back of his mind. *Since Shelley had become his gardener.*

She'd been here two weeks and he was more and more impressed by her. Her professionalism. Her knowledge. Her unfailing good humour. And that was on top of her beauty. Was she too good to be true? He kept contact with her to a minimum but he was super aware of her all the time she was on the property.

Too aware.

He had to remind himself he had vowed not to let another woman into his thoughts. Guilt and constant regret dictated that.

Even though he'd been told over and over again he was not responsible for Lisa and his daughter's deaths, he blamed himself. He should have responded quicker when Lisa had told him she was getting rapidly increasing contractions. Not begged for ten minutes to finish the intricate piece of code he'd been writing. Ten minutes that could have made a difference.

His fault.

His own, obsessed workaholic fault.

Selfish, self-centred and single-minded. He and Lisa hadn't quarrelled much—they'd had a happy marriage—but when they had, those were the accusations she had hurled at him. The anger had never lasted more than minutes and she'd laughed and said she hadn't meant a word of it. But he knew there was some truth there.

Because Lisa had told him she wasn't ready to have children. Had wanted to spend a few more years establishing her career in marketing before they started a family.

He'd cajoled, wheedled, begged her to change her mind. Because he'd wanted at least three children to fill up the many empty bedrooms of this house. Children who would grow up knowing how loved and wanted they were.

And look what had happened.

Lisa's death cast a black shadow on his soul. And Alice…he could hardly bear to think about Alice, that tiny baby he'd held so briefly in his arms, whose life had scarcely started before it had ended.

Their deaths were his fault.

He didn't deserve a second chance at happiness.

Down in the garden, Shelley leaned back on her heels and reached into the pocket of her sturdy gardener's trousers and took out her mobile phone. He hadn't heard it ring from where he was but she was obviously taking a call. He was near enough to see her smile.

As she chatted she looked up at the house, the hand that wasn't holding her phone shading her eyes. She couldn't possibly see him from here. He didn't want her to think he was some kind of voyeur. Just in case, he stepped back from the light of the window into the shadows of his office.

The furnishings in his shades-of-grey workspace were dominated by a bank of computer monitors. This was where he lived, his bedroom in the turret above.

Separate from the computers was a large drawing board he had set up to catch the best light from the window. He'd done some preliminary work on Princess No-Name on the computer. Design software could only do so much.

Now he'd gone back to sketching her with charcoal on paper. The old techniques he'd learned from his artist grandmother. Pinned up on a corkboard above the drawing board were sketches of various angles of the princess warrior's head, her arms, the curve of her back. On the sketchpad was a work in progress of her—okay, of Shelley—looking over her shoulder with her hair flowing over her neck.

But the old ways had their limitations too. What fun he could have using motion-capture software to animate his princess warrior character. But to do that he would have to ask Shelley to model for him. To dress her in a tight black spandex suit that revealed every curve. To attach reflective sensors to her limbs and direct her to act out movements from the game.

In the anonymity of a big, professional studio—perhaps.

In the intimacy of his office? *No way.* Much too dangerous.

Further back from the window, though still in the good light, was his easel, where he had started a preliminary painting of the character in acrylic paint. The painting formed the only splash of colour in the monotone room where he spent so much time alone.

The painting was pure indulgence; this kind of image would not be easily scanned for animation. He hadn't painted for years, not since before he was married. But his newly sparked creativity was enjoying the subtle nuances of colour and texture the medium was able to give Princess No-Name.

Shelley's warrior strength and warm blonde beauty had kick-started his imagination but her connection to nature was what was now inspiring him to create his new character. He'd found himself researching the mythical Greek, Roman and Celtic female spirits of nature and fertility. Gaia. Antheia. Flora. The Green Woman. Mother Nature.

He was painting his Shelley-inspired warrior heroine in a skin-tight semi-sheer body stocking patterned with vines and leaves. The gloves that hugged her arms to above her elbows were of the finest, palest green leather. She strode out in sexy, thigh-high suede boots the colour of damp moss. As contrast, he'd painted orange flower buds in various stages of unfurling along the vines.

It would be only too easy to imagine Shelley wearing the exact same outfit. He drew in his breath at the thought of it.

But he could not go there.

Better he reined in his imagination when it came to thinking too closely about Shelley's shape.

He had purposely used Princess Alana's body as a template for Princess No-Name. Shelley's slim, toned arms were there, yes. But he did not want to focus on her breasts, her hips, her thighs to the extent it would take to draw them. That could be misconstrued.

She was his muse—that was all.

His imagination filled in his princess warrior's glorious mane of hair with fine brushstrokes. *If only Shelley would let her hair down for him.*

He modelled his new creation's face on Shelley's strong, vibrant face—with her lovely lush mouth exaggerated into artistic anime proportions. Her eyes were the exact same nutmeg as Shelley's, with added glints of gold and framed by the kind of long, long lashes that owed more to artifice than nature.

His princess was inspired by Shelley, but she was not Shelley—he had to keep telling himself that. His new warrior was a distinct character in the unique style of his bestselling games. She would be a worthy successor to Princess Alana.

A name flashed into his head. *Estella.* He thought the name probably meant star—bright and shining and bold. Yes. It was perfect. Princess Alana. Princess Estella. It fitted. And gave a vague nod to 'Shelley'.

Maybe her weapons could be ninja throwing stars—

sharp and deadly. No. Too obvious, and far too vicious for his Princess Estella.

Wonder Woman had her golden lasso of truth. Maybe Estella could have a magical lariat to incapacitate and capture. *But not kill.* He didn't want Princess Estella taking lives. He kept on painting, working in a fluorescent green lariat looped around her shoulder.

He stepped back, looked at his work with critical, narrowed eyes. Estella was gorgeous; she would make an awesome warrior heroine. But there was something lacking; he needed to add a unique characteristic to make her stand out in the sea of gaming heroines. He hadn't got it right yet.

He needed to spend more time with Shelley.

Purely for inspiration, of course. There must be no doubt it was for any other reason. Other than to oversee the ongoing work in the garden.

So why did the thought of that flood him with excited anticipation that went far beyond the boundaries that restricted employer and employee? Or artist and muse?

Declan had been so engrossed in his work, several hours had gone by without him realising. He glanced down to the garden to see Shelley talking to a man—a tall, well-built man with blond hair. He pulled up abruptly, paintbrush in hand. *Who the hell was he?*

Then he realised the guy wore the same kind of khaki gardening gear as she wore. He must be the horticulturalist she'd asked could she call in to help with getting rid of some large trees she said had no place in the garden.

The man was standing near her. As Declan watched he brought his head close to Shelley and said something that made her laugh. Echoes of her laughter reached him high up in his room.

Declan's grip tightened on the paintbrush. He didn't like seeing her with another man. Was this guy a boyfriend? *A lover?* He realised how very little he knew about his beautiful gardener. *How much he wanted to know.*

He was shocked at the feeling that charged through him, like a car with a dead battery being jump-started after long disuse by a blast of electric current.

Jealousy.

Shelley sensed Declan in the garden before she saw him. The vibrations of his feet on the ground? The distant slam of the door as he'd left the house? Or was it her hyper awareness of him?

She loved working in this garden, in two weeks had achieved so much. But the day seemed...empty if she didn't see him. Even if he came only briefly into the garden to make some quip about her passion for old garden implements. Or to ask if she'd fought off any spiders today. She would update him on her progress and go back to work, not knowing when she'd next see him. *On edge until she did.*

The days he didn't come into the garden at all were days she felt oddly let down and went home feeling dispirited. No. Not just dispirited. Verging on depressed. Which was not like her at all.

Today she had even more cause for concern. Her gardening buddy Mark Brown had just called around to assess what equipment he'd need for the job he was helping her with the next day.

'You mean you don't know who Declan Grant is?' he'd asked.

'He told me he produced computer games,' she'd replied.

'You could say that,' Mark had said. 'The guy is a gaming god, Shelley, a tech wizard. Every guy in the world my age must have grown up with Princess Alana. And she's just one of his incredibly popular games.'

'He might be well known in the gaming world, but I'd never heard of him,' she said, on the defence.

Mark's words had made her feel ignorant until she'd reminded herself that when she was younger gaming had pretty much been a boy thing. *A boring boy thing.* She hadn't known who Declan Grant was. Declan had blanked at the mention of Enid Wilson. Each to his own.

'He used to go by the tag of ArrowLordX—I don't know that he plays with mere mortals these days. He was an indie but sold out to one of the huge companies.' Mark had looked around him and whistled. 'This place must be worth millions—pocket change to him, though, the guy's a billionaire.' He'd narrowed his eyes. 'I hope he's paying you fairly.'

'M-more than fairly,' she'd stuttered. 'He's a generous employer.'

'Yeah. The deal you've got me is good. I'll be back to-morrow to earn it.'

She would have liked to introduce Mark to Declan but she was scrupulous about not disturbing her employer, in-truding on his privacy. If she needed a response from him she texted him. She from the garden, he in his house. The only time she saw him was when he chose to seek her out.

By the time she looked up to see Declan heading to-wards her, Mark had gone.

It was lunchtime and she was sitting near a bank of aza-leas—already budding up for spring—to shelter from the light wind that had sprung up. As her employer approached she put her sandwich back into the chilled lunchbox she brought with her to work and schooled her face into a pro-fessional gardener-greeting-boss expression.

She couldn't let it show how happy she was to see him. How his visits had become the highlights of her day.

Her boss. A grieving widower. Not for her. She had

taken to repeating the phrases like a series of mantras. Now she had to add: *her* billionaire *boss—totally out of her league.*

But when she looked up to see him heading towards her she couldn't help the flutter of awareness deep inside her, the flush that warmed her cheeks. Her knees felt shaky and she stumbled as she got up to greet him.

She'd got used to his abrupt ways, his sly humour that she didn't always get, the way he challenged her to justify her decisions. But she would never get used to the impact of his tall, broad-shouldered body and his extraordinarily handsome face.

This was the first time she'd seen him dressed in anything but black. His jeans were the deepest indigo—only a step away from black really, but it was a step. His sweater was charcoal grey, open at the neck to reveal a hint of rock-solid pecs and pushed up to his elbows to bare strong, muscled forearms.

'Don't get up,' he said. 'I didn't realise I was interrupting your lunch.'

'I haven't actually started eating,' she said. She didn't want to be caught at a disadvantage munching on a cheese and salad sandwich. It would be just her luck to have a shred of lettuce on her tooth when she was trying to be serious and professional around him.

His brow furrowed. 'Do you usually eat outside? Why don't you make use of the kitchen in the apartment?'

'Oh, but I wouldn't… I couldn't. I just dash in there to use the bathroom.'

'Please feel free to use the kitchen too,' he said.

'Thank you,' she said, knowing she wouldn't. She still felt like an intruder every time she went in there.

Declan put his hands behind his back, rocked on his heels. 'You were talking to a man earlier,' he said.

She nodded. 'He's the gardener who's coming to help me tomorrow. His name is Mark Brown. I would have liked to introduce you to him but I didn't think it was worth interrupting you with a text.'

'Is he a friend of yours?'

His question surprised her. But she remembered how concerned Declan was about strangers intruding on his privacy. 'Yes, he is, actually. We were at uni together in Melbourne and both moved to Sydney at about the same time. He's a very good horticulturalist. I could have just hired a tree-removal guy but we need to be careful with some of the surrounding plants. Luckily Mark was available. I can vouch for him one hundred per cent.'

'Lucky indeed,' he said. His eyes were cool, appraising, unreadable. 'Is he your boyfriend?'

Shelley stared at Declan, too flabbergasted at first to speak. 'What? Mark? No!' She'd often got the feeling Mark would like to be more than friends but she didn't see him that way.

'Do you have a boyfriend?' Declan asked.

Those extraordinary blue eyes searched her face. There was something darkly sensual about him that went beyond handsome. Something she should not be registering.

Boss. Widower. Not for her. Frantically she repeated the mantra in her mind. At the same time her body was zinging with awareness.

'No. I don't have a boyfriend. And I… I don't *want* a boyfriend.'

'I see,' he said, nodding, as his speculative gaze took in her drab, serviceable gardening gear—a tad grubby after a morning spent weeding. She was also sporting protective pads made from foam and hard nylon strapped around her knees. *'Nothing could be more unattractive or unappeal-*

ing to a man,' her sister, Lynne, had chortled when she had first seen Shelley decked out in her knee pads.

'No. You don't understand,' she said to Declan. 'I don't want a girlfriend either. I mean, I don't want a girlfriend ever.' *Foot in mouth again.* 'I like men. I'm not gay. I'm happy being single.'

Was that relief that lightened his eyes? Relief she was single? That she wasn't gay? Both?

'No plans for marriage and family?' he asked, which surprised her.

She shook her head. 'Plenty of time for that yet. My career is too important to me right now.'

He didn't reply. Of course, she couldn't resist chattering on to fill the silence that fell between them. 'There... there was a boyfriend in Melbourne. It didn't work out. I'm planning to travel after I finish your job. No point in getting involved with anyone in Sydney if I'm leaving. Men... well, men are more trouble than they're worth.' *And she just said that to a man.* Again she mentally beat her fist against her forehead.

'I get it,' he said and she got the distinct impression he was trying not to smile. There was another long pause, which this time she refused to fill. 'So your *friend* Mark is coming tomorrow?' he said finally.

'Yes,' she said, jumping on the change of subject. 'Let me show you what we'll be doing.'

Declan glanced at his watch. Shelley gritted her teeth. He always seemed to want to be anywhere but in his garden with her. At first she had found it insulting. Now she was beginning to realise it was just his way.

She'd learned now not to ask if she was boring him. Her policy was to take him as she found him. Fact was, though, she liked him way more than she should. She would be very disappointed if he cut short this time with him and headed back indoors.

Not that she would ever let him know that.

'Come let me show you what happens when people misguidedly plant indoor plants out in the garden,' she said.

He frowned. 'I don't get what you mean,' he said.

'You'll see,' she said, thankful that he started to follow her and not to stride off back to the house.

She led him to the area of garden near the eastern border with the house next door. 'These two trees are probably the main points of contention for your neighbours,' she said. 'They're *ficus benjamina*.'

'More Latin,' he said with that quirk of his dark eyebrow she was beginning to find very appealing. 'Translate, please.'

'Otherwise known as weeping fig,' she explained. 'A very popular potted plant. But planted out in the garden in this climate they can grow to thirty metres in height. Their roots are invasive and damaging.' She pointed. 'They've already damaged the fence and probably your neighbour's paving and underground plumbing pipes too. They're a tree suited to a park, not a domestic garden.'

'So a *giant* garden invader?' he said.

'Exactly. They have to go.'

Declan indicated the neighbour's house. 'He's already invoiced me for repairs.'

'Really? A neighbour would do that? Did you pay him?'

He scowled. She would hate to ever see that formidable expression aimed at her. 'I told you, I want these people off my back. I paid him.'

She shrugged. Seemed as if whatever he had paid would be water off a billionaire's back. 'You shouldn't hear any more from them once Mark and I get these darn trees out—and all the potato vine twined around them. There's a big mulberry on the other border fence—we'll get rid of that too.'

'A mulberry tree? I never knew we had one. I like mulberries. My grandmother had a mulberry tree and I'd spend hours up its branches.'

She had a sudden flash of a little black-haired boy with purple mulberry stains all around his mouth and mischief in his blue eyes. He must have been an adorable child.

She diverted her thoughts to the adult Declan. 'The mulberry tree here I want to get rid of is too close to the fence. Don't worry, there's another one planted as a specimen tree in the middle of the lawn that we'll leave. I like mulberries too and it's not causing any trouble there. It's a pity I won't be around when the tree fruits or I'd bake you a mulberry pie.'

Oh, dear heaven, had she actually said that to her boss? She closed her eyes and wished herself far, far away from Declan's garden.

She opened her eyes and he was still there, tall, dark and formidable. He made a sound in response that sounded suspiciously like a strangled laugh. 'You bake pies as well as your other talents?'

'Little Miss Practical, that's me,' she said with a self-effacing laugh. 'My grandmother taught me to cook when we—my mum and my sister—went to live with her after my father booted us out of our home.'

She flushed. 'Sorry, too much information.' She looked around her, frantic to change the subject. 'Whoever designed this garden way back when really *was* paying homage to Enid Wilson. Fruit trees as part of the garden instead of in an orchard. Thyme everywhere as groundcover. Indigenous plants when they weren't really fashionable. I think—'

As she started her next sentence a teasing gust of wind

snatched off her hat. She clutched at her head in vain to see her hat tumbling along the ground.

She went to chase after it, but Declan beat her to it and picked it up. 'I've got it,' he said.

It was such an old, battered hat she felt embarrassed he was touching it. He turned it over in his hand and went to put it back on her head. The movement brought him very close.

His mouth. For the first time she noticed his mouth. His full lips, the top lip slightly narrower than the other. The dark growth of his beard already visible at lunchtime.

Lots of testosterone.

The thought came from nowhere and paralysed her. She stood dead still, wondering what might come next, scarcely able to breathe, her heart thudding too fast.

His eyes looked deep into hers and she couldn't read the expression in their deep blue depths. He tossed the hat aside. Then reached down and around to the back of her head.

She'd got ready in a hurry that morning and had piled her hair out of the way with only the aid of a single claw-grip clip to keep it in place. With one deft movement Declan had it undone. Her heavy mass of hair untwisted and fell around her shoulders and her back, all the way to her waist. *She felt as if he'd undressed her.*

With a hand that wasn't quite steady, she went to push away the long layers that fell across the front of her face but Declan slid it away with his. Slowly, sensuously he pushed his fingers through her hair then ran his hands over her shoulders to come to rest at the small of her back where her hair reached.

'Beautiful,' he murmured in a low, husky voice.

Shelley didn't know whether he meant her or her hair or something else entirely. Shivers of pleasure tingled through her at his touch. She felt dizzy, light-headed and realised she'd been holding her breath. As she let it out in a slow sigh, she swayed towards him, her mouth parting not just for air but for the kiss she felt was surely to follow. His head dipped towards her. She didn't know that she wanted this. Wasn't sure—

Abruptly he dropped his hands from her waist. His expression darkened like the build-up of black cloud before a storm.

'This shouldn't have happened,' he said in a voice that was more a growl torn from the depths of his being.

Shocked, she struggled to find her voice. 'I... I...'

'Don't say it,' he said, his voice brusque and low. 'There's nothing to be said.' He stepped back with savage speed. 'My...my apologies.'

With that he turned on his heel and strode away from her, leaving her grateful for the support of the sturdy trunk of the doomed fig tree.

Still trembling, she watched him, his broad shoulders set taut with some emotion—anger?—as he turned the bend in the sweep of lawn marked by the wall with the tumbledown urn and out of sight. He couldn't wait to get away from her.

What the heck had that been about? And what did it mean for her relationship with her secretive, billionaire boss?

CHAPTER SEVEN

NOTHING, AS IT turned out. The episode meant nothing, she realised in the days that followed. Days where she saw very little of Declan and neither of them mentioned the incident. The longer it went unsaid, the less likely it would ever be aired.

The Rapunzel incident—as she had begun to call it in her mind. Fancifully, she thought of it as: 'Shelley, Shelley, let down your golden hair.' *Let down your hair—and then nothing.* She blushed as she remembered how she had *yearned* for him to take it further.

The moments Declan had spent releasing her hair from its restraint and caressing her had begun to take on the qualities of a distant dream. Making a joke of it—even if only to herself—somehow took the sting out of what had happened.

The way he had avoided her since both puzzled and hurt. But she couldn't—*wouldn't*—let it bother her. Because while she was hurt in one way, she felt relieved in another.

Nothing could come of the incident. He was the billionaire boss, she was the gardener who needed the generous salary he had agreed to pay her. She should be grateful he hadn't taken advantage of that. Be *glad* he hadn't kissed her. She'd worked for men who had made her feel distinctly uncomfortable to be alone with them when she'd been working on their properties. It was one reason she dressed the way she did for work.

Besides, she had another more pressing concern to occupy her thoughts.

Her sister's boyfriend, Keith, had proposed to Lynne. The newly engaged couple wanted to live together as they planned their wedding. And the apartment in Double Bay she shared with Lynne was way, way too small for her to live with them in any privacy.

She had to find somewhere else to live—pronto. Keith wouldn't move in until she moved out. She was happy for her sister; Keith was a really nice guy and just what Lynne needed. Neither of them was pressing her to go, but of course they wanted to start their new life together as soon as they could.

But it was a difficult rental market in Sydney. Apartment hunting meant showing up for an open day and hoping like heck she made a better impression on the letting agent than the other people lined up with her to inspect the same property. There was a one-room apartment open today in nearby Edgecliff and she needed to see it.

In the three weeks she'd been working for Declan she hadn't taken a lunch hour, just grabbed twenty minutes to down the sandwich and coffee in a flask she'd brought from home. She'd wanted to get as much work as possible done in the shorter daylight hours at this time of year.

It was now well into August and the garden was showing definite signs of the early southern hemisphere spring: jonquils scented the air and the nodding pink heads of hellebores gave delight in the cooler, shadier corners of the garden. She had found the elusive daphne, cleared the tough kikuyu grass that was smothering it and made sure it would survive.

But today, four days after the Rapunzel incident, she

needed to take an extended lunch hour. Technically, she should ask Declan's permission for extra time off, but it wasn't really that kind of working relationship. He seemed to take her on trust and she would never take advantage of that. She decided to keep him in the loop anyway.

After a morning's hard work, she was fortunate she had the bathroom in the housekeeper's apartment in which to shower and change. She needed to look smart and responsible, as though she could afford the rent, the deposit and all the other expenses that came with renting an apartment. Expenses that would take a substantial chunk out of her savings.

Lynne and Keith had sprung this on her. As she towelled herself dry she found herself wishing—unreasonably, she knew—that Keith had put off his proposal until she had finished this job and was taking off for Europe.

Six months would be the minimum lease she could sign. She could end up trapped in Sydney for longer than she would choose to be. She wanted to be in Europe by October to see the gardens in autumn. Maybe she should consider a short-term house-share or even house-sitting.

Twenty-eight and still without a home of her own—she couldn't help but be plagued by a sense of failure when she thought about her limited options.

She slipped into the clothes she'd brought with her to change into—the world's most flattering skinny-leg trousers in a deep shade of biscuit teamed with a businesslike crisp white shirt, and topped with a stylish short trench coat in ice-blue with contrasting dark buttons. She finished off with a blue-and-black leopard-print scarf around her neck and short camel boots with a medium stiletto heel.

Lucky for her, Lynne was a fashion buyer for a big retailer and could get her clothes at a sizeable discount. Lynne also had excellent taste in the choices she made for her, which made up for Shelley's own tendency to slide into whatever felt most comfortable.

As she pulled her hair into a high ponytail and slicked on some make-up she thought she scrubbed up rather well.

Still feeling like an intruder in the apartment, she perched on the edge of the sofa and texted Declan.

I need to take a long lunch hour today—will make up the time.

His text came back straight away.

Can I see you before you go? Come to the front door.

Puzzled, Shelley put down her phone. She hadn't been inside the house since the evening of her interview. She hoped she wasn't to be reprimanded for anything. She had a feeling Declan hadn't been too impressed with the way she'd brought Mark in—though arranging for extra help was quite within their terms of agreement.

She flung her fake designer tote bag—a present from a friend, who'd bought it in Thailand—over her shoulder and headed around to the front of the house.

Declan had lost count of the times he had berated himself for giving in to the temptation to free Shelley's glorious hair from its constraints. *For touching her.* It had been out of order. Unprofessional. *Wrong.*

Even if it had only been in the interests of research for Princess Estella.

Or so he'd told himself.

For a moment he had let that self-imposed force field slip—with disastrous consequences. Now she obviously felt uncomfortable around him. And he could not rid his mind of the memory of how it had felt to be so intimately close to her—and her trembling response to his touch.

He felt he owed Shelley an explanation. But he was more fluent in JavaScript than he was at talking about anything personal. How did he explain why he had to keep her at arm's length? That he was not free to pursue another woman?

Technically, yes, he was a widower and able to marry again. But the day Lisa had died he had shut down emotionally. He had imprisoned himself in chains of grief and guilt, shrouded himself in the darkness of self-blame.

Lisa was dead. Their daughter's life snuffed out when it had scarcely begun. How could he expect happiness, love, intimacy for himself? He didn't deserve a second chance.

'Survivor's guilt—a classic case of it,' his mother had said. His top criminal-law-barrister mother, who knew a lot about the darker side of life. She'd given him the contact details of a grief counsellor—details that still sat in the bottom of his desk drawer.

Even she had been devastated by the tragedy. She'd been very fond of Lisa and seen the birth of her first grandchild as a chance to start over. 'To be a better grandmother than I ever was a mother,' she'd said with brutal honesty.

But in these last days, spent mostly in solitude, Declan had decided there was only one honest way to handle the situation with Shelley. He had to get Princess Estella out into the open. Explain to Shelley that she had inspired his new creation. Ask her to model for him.

Not in a body stocking or a skin-tight spandex sensor suit, though his pulse quickened at the thought of it. No. In her gender-neutral gardening gear. But with her long hair let down. Maybe with a fan floating it around her face and behind her like a banner. He would ask her to pose for him so he could get the hair and face right for Estella.

There would be a generous modelling fee, of course. It would all be above board and without any hint of exploitation. He could draw up a contract. Maybe include a share of royalties—he could afford it.

He didn't want dishonesty between them. Outing Estella was the only way to go.

Buoyed by the idea, he had asked Shelley to come to the house so they could discuss it asap.

At the sound of the bell at the front door he took the elevator Lisa had had installed—'*for when we're old and can't make the stairs*'—down from his top-floor office to get to the door more quickly.

He would put things right with Shelley.

But the Shelley who stood on the porch outside was not the Shelley he was expecting. The only thing he recognised about her was her smile—and even that was a subdued version of its usual multi-watt radiance.

His gardener was no longer an amazon but a glamazon.

Gone was the ugly, khaki uniform, replaced by a stylish, elegant outfit that emphasised the feminine shape the uniform concealed. Narrow trousers clung to long, slender legs, the shirt unbuttoned to reveal the delectable swell of her breasts, and the high-heeled boots brought her closer to him in height and gave her hips a sensuous sway.

Subtle dark make-up emphasised the beauty of her eyes, and the lush sensuality of her mouth was deepened by lipstick the colour of ripe raspberries.

For a too-long moment he stared at her, struck dumb with admiration—and an intensely masculine reaction that rocked him.

'You wanted to see me?' she asked, with a puzzled frown.

He could not keep his eyes off her.

He had to clear his throat before he spoke. 'Yes. Come in,' he said as he ushered her through the door.

'I hope there's nothing wrong,' she said with a quiver in her voice.

'Of course not,' he said.

But everything had changed.

He needed time to collect his rapidly racing thoughts.

He led her through the grand entrance hall, her heels clicking on the marble floor, to the small reception room where he'd first interviewed her. Light slanting through the old lead-light windows, original to the house, picked up the gold in her hair. *She brought the sunshine with her.*

Immediately they were in the room she went straight to the window. 'What a beautiful view of the garden,' she said. 'It's starting to take shape. In a few weeks that wisteria arch will be glorious. I've trimmed it but it will need a good prune when it's finished flowering. You have to cut it back well and truly before the buds form for…for the next season's flowering.'

Her words trickled to a halt and she didn't meet his eye. Did she sense his heightened awareness of her as a woman, his ambivalence? She moistened her lovely, raspberry-stained lips with the tip of her tongue. The action fascinated him.

The full impact of his attraction to her hit him like a punch to the gut. He fisted his hands by his sides. He'd been kidding himself from the get go.

This wasn't about Princess Estella.

It was about Shelley.

It had always been about Shelley—warm-hearted, clever, down-to-earth, gorgeous Shelley. Even in the drab uniform with her charmingly eccentric interest in rusty old rakes and broken-down fountains she had delighted him from day one.

He could no longer kid himself that his attraction to Shelley was because she sparked his creative impulse. She sparked male impulses a whole lot more physical and urgent. She was a beautiful woman and he wanted her in a way he had not imagined wanting another woman after his wife had died.

He could not ask her to pose for Estella.

No way could he invite her to spend hours alone with him in his studio while he sketched her. It would be a kind of torture. That idea had to be trashed.

But he found he had to say something else to justify him calling her into the house. 'I wanted to tell you I had a note from the neighbour thanking me for getting rid of the *ficus benjamina*.'

Now that full-beam smile was directed at him.

'It wasn't to…fire me or anything?'

'Of course not.' How could she possibly think that? He realised that under her brightness and bravado lay a deep vein of self-doubt. That although she seemed so strong she was also vulnerable. It unleashed a powerful urge to protect her.

'That's a relief,' she said. 'I was racking my brains to think of what I'd done wrong.'

He had to clear his throat of some deep, choking emotion to speak. 'You've done nothing wrong.'

He ached to take her into his arms and reassure her how invaluable she was, how special. But that was not going to happen. He recognised his attraction to her. That did not mean he intended to act on it.

He now could admit it to himself. Admit the truth that welled out from his subconscious and into his dreams. Now, when he was battling the insomnia that had plagued him since the night his wife had died, in those few hours of broken sleep it wasn't Lisa's face that kept him awake. It was Shelley's.

And that felt like betrayal.

'That's great news about the neighbour,' she said. 'Makes it all worthwhile, doesn't it? And, hey, you spoke Latin. Uh, instead of computer speak. That I don't speak at all. I mean, I can use a computer, of course I can, but I—'

'I get it,' he said. There she went—rabbiting on again. He found it charming. He found *her* charming. And way too appealing in every way.

He realised she was nervous around him. Was he looking particularly *forbidding* today?

She twisted the strap of her handbag in her hands. 'Thank you for telling me that but, if that's all, I have to go. As I said, I need to take a longer lunch hour today.'

'A date?' he blurted out without thinking.

Jealousy speared him again. Who was the lucky guy who would be seeing her dressed up like this?

'Not a date,' she said with a perturbed frown.

Of course she would be perturbed. He had no right to ask about her personal life. She would be quite within her rights to tell him to mind his own business.

He could not deny his relief that she wasn't going out with a man. But if it wasn't a date, why and where was she going?

He forced his voice to sound casual, unconcerned. 'Lunch with a friend? It's quite okay for you to stay as long as you like. I know what hours you've been putting in out there in the garden.'

Her mouth twisted downward. 'Nothing as nice as lunch with a friend, I'm afraid. I have to look for somewhere to live. I share with my sister but she's just got engaged and her fiancé wants to move in.'

'There's no room for you?'

'No. It's a tiny apartment.' She sighed. 'Now I'm heading off to inspect a place in Edgecliff. Along with all the other people desperate to find somewhere with reasonable rent close to the city. I want to stay in this area.' She held up both hands with fingers crossed. 'So wish me luck.'

She turned on her high-heeled boot. 'I'll be back as soon as I can.'

Declan followed her to the door, opened it for her, watched her start down the steps. 'Stop,' he called after her.

She turned. 'I'm sorry, I'll miss the inspection time if I don't leave now. I have to find parking and—'

'Don't go. You don't need to. You can stay here, in the apartment.'

He didn't know what had possessed him to make that offer. It was all kinds of crazy. To have her actually living on the premises would do nothing for his resolve to keep things between them strictly on an employer-employee basis. He should rescind the offer immediately.

'You already have the key,' he said. 'Just move in.'

Shelley was so taken aback she stood with one foot on the bottom of the step, the other on the pathway.

'Are you serious?' she asked.

He shrugged those broad shoulders. 'You need a home. The apartment is empty. It makes sense.'

'But I… I shouldn't… I couldn't—' Excitement fluttered into life only to be vanquished by caution.

'It's there for staff. You're staff.'

'Yes, I am, but…'

How to express her feelings that she was scared of living in such close proximity to him? She found him too attractive to be so near to him twenty-four-seven. Now she could go home, go out, try and forget the Rapunzel incident and how it had made her feel. Living here, knowing he was on the other side of a wall, might not be so easy.

As far as she knew Declan lived alone in the enormous house. A team of cleaners had come in on the last two Tuesdays and stayed half the day. The delivery van of an exclusive grocery store had also swept up the gravel drive several times. But no one else had come, not during the day anyway.

His house would become not just her place of employment, but also her home. Just her and him—the man who sent shivers of awareness through her no matter how she tried to suppress them.

Right now he towered four steps above her, dark, brooding and yet with something in his eyes that made her think he would be hurt if she knocked back his offer of the apartment.

The apartment that would solve her problem of where to live.

A solution that might bring more problems with it than it solved.

He shrugged again. 'Of course, if you'd rather live in a cheap apartment in Edgecliff...'

'No. Of course I wouldn't. I'd love to live in the apartment. It's beautiful. The poshest staff quarters in Sydney, I should imagine. Your lucky housekeeper—she must have been thrilled when she saw how it was decorated.'

He fell silent for a moment too long. 'It was prepared for our nanny,' he said. 'The wonderful woman who used to be my nanny when I was a child. But...but she never moved in.'

'Oh,' she said. *Classic Shelley foot-in-mouth moment.* He looked so bleak that if he had been anyone else, she would have rushed to hug him. But she stayed put on the step.

'I'm sorry,' she said.

The history of her working relationship with Declan would be punctuated by endless repeats of the word *sorry*. 'I need to think before I speak.'

'You weren't to know,' he said. He shifted impatiently from one foot to the other. 'So what's it to be? Yes or no?'

'I want to say yes but I need to know what the rent is first. I... I might not be able to afford it.'

No *might* about it. She almost certainly *wouldn't* be able to afford the rent and the realisation brought with it a fierce regret. She would love to live in that apartment.

'No rent,' he said.

'But—'

'No buts.' The words were accompanied by a dark, Declan scowl.

'But—I mean *not but*. I mean...*if* I don't pay rent I—'

'This is staff accommodation. You're staff. End of story.'

'I have to pay my own way.' She had never been able to accept a gift that might have been tied with invisible strings.

'If you insist on a monetary transaction I will rescind my offer.'

She had no doubt he meant it. 'No! Please don't do that. I'll work on Saturdays. For free. Well, not free. My labour in return for accommodation.'

'There's no need for that. However if you insist—'

'I insist. When can I move in?'

'Whenever you want.'

'Saturday. This Saturday. I'll start the extra work next Saturday.'

'It's a deal,' he said. 'Just remember not to use the door into the house—it's the one in the kitchen.'

'Of course not. I don't have a key, anyway.'

'The key you have operates both doors.'

'I'll respect your privacy,' she said. 'I promise.'

He nodded.

'I don't have a lot of stuff to move in,' she said, bubbling with excitement now that she could accept the reality of the situation. 'Most of my possessions are stored with my grandmother at Blackheath in the mountains. I hope you don't mind if my sister gives me a hand to move in.'

'So long as I don't have to meet her,' he said.

'I'll make sure of that,' she said. 'Thank you, Declan.'

He acknowledged her thanks with another nod.

She looked down at her smart outfit. 'Now I'm all dressed up with nowhere to go,' she said. 'I just might drive on down to Double Bay and treat myself to a café lunch.'

She bit down firmly on words that threatened to spill and invite him to join her for lunch. The fact that he was her boss didn't stop her. There was no law that said work colleagues couldn't share a bite to eat—she did it all the time.

No. She didn't voice the invitation because it would sound perilously close to asking him on a date. *And that was never going to happen.*

She thanked him again and walked down the pathway, happy with the unexpected outcome of her meeting with Declan. She had a beautiful home until her contract here came to an end and she flew away to fulfil her dreams.

For her heart's sake she just had to keep well clear of Declan in the hours that were hers to spend as she pleased.

CHAPTER EIGHT

DECLAN DID NOT want to meet Shelley's sister. Or her sister's fiancé, who was helping with the move. Meeting her family would be a link he did not want to establish. But he felt compelled to watch—perhaps to make it seem real that Shelley was going to be living here from today on.

With typical Shelley efficiency, she'd arrived early in the morning with her crew. Feeling uncomfortably as if he was spying on them, he watched from his office window. A tall, very slender young woman with short brown hair, who must be the sister, and a red-headed guy helped Shelley bring in her stuff.

Just a few boxes and suitcases appeared to constitute her possessions. Shelley herself had a laptop computer slung over her shoulder and some clothes still on their hangers to take in.

It was still a shock to see her out of her gardening gear. Today she wore faded, figure-hugging jeans, a long-sleeved T-shirt and the ugliest running shoes he had ever seen—practical, no doubt, but a shocking contrast to the sexy, stiletto-heeled boots she'd worn earlier in the week. Or Estella's thigh-high boots.

Could the bespoke shoemaker in Italy where he bought his shoes make a pair of moss-green suede boots in Shelley's size?

He pushed the crazy thoughts aside. Both of ordering

the green boots—and of imagining Shelley wearing them, and very little else.

Shelley's helpers were in and out of the apartment within an hour. He wondered if she had so few possessions because she didn't want them or because she couldn't afford them.

He realised he was paying her over the odds for the gardening work. And he didn't begrudge her a cent of it. A horticulturalist was not the highest paid of jobs, which seemed at odds with the incredible depth of knowledge Shelley seemed to have. Again he thanked whatever lucky chance had sent her to him.

His only regret was he could not ask her to pose for him. Princess Estella had stalled on him, still missing that final extra detail that might make her viable as the character on which he could base a new game. But he had to put the thought of Shelley posing for him alone in his eyrie office out of his fantasies. Especially when he spent way too much time thinking about her—as a beautiful woman who attracted him, not as a mere muse.

However, he now had his duties as not only an employer but a landlord to consider. Once she'd had time to settle in, he would go down to the apartment—now *her* apartment—and see if there was anything he could give her a hand with. *That was not making excuses to see her—it was obligation.*

But before he could do so, he saw her heading out—and had to smother a gasp of stunned admiration. She was obviously going horseback riding. Shelley the equestrienne wore tight cream breeches that hugged every curve of her enticing behind, and a black, open-neck shirt that emphasised her slim, toned arms. She wore shiny black leather knee-high riding boots and carried a black velvet riding helmet under her arm, along with a leather riding crop.

Shelley had mentioned she rode horses as a teenager, jumping over snakes in typical warrior manner. Seemed as if she rode them still. But where? Certainly not around here, just minutes away from the heart of the city.

Who knew horseback riding gear could look so hot?

But then Shelley looked good in anything she wore—even the drab khaki. He wouldn't let his mind travel any further along the path that might have him speculating on how she would look in nothing at all.

He watched her as she paused to look at the fountain, now under repair, then continued around the corner of the house to where she parked her so-old-it-was-practically-an-antique 4x4 in the driveway. The multi-car garage was filled with his collection of expensive sports cars that rarely got an airing these days.

But he was not just watching in admiration of how well she wore equestrienne mode. His stalled creativity was also firing back into life.

Now he knew exactly what was needed for Princess Estella.

A horse.

He turned back to his drawing board, his brain firing with so many ideas his hand holding the charcoal could scarcely keep up with his thoughts. As it always did when he was driven by creativity, time seemed to come to a halt as he got lost in the world of his imagination. Hours, days could go past.

He sketched Princess Estella astride a magnificent white horse with a flowing mane and tail that echoed the Warrior Princess's glorious tresses.

But it was still not enough.

He paced up and down, up and down, coming back to the drawing board again and again. It was good but still not right.

Then it hit him. Estella was fantasy. Shelley was earthy, warm, reality.

Shelley rode a horse. But Estella was not bound by human and earthly constrictions.

Princess Estella would ride a unicorn.

Again he went back to his drawing board. It wasn't difficult to transform the horse into a unicorn. He added a silver horn to the centre of its forehead. Made its eyes look less horse, more mythical creature whose gaze gleamed with knowledge and wisdom. Attributes that would help the warrior princess in her epic battles for good.

This time when he finished and stood back to look at his work he was buzzing.

Gorgeous Princess Estella with her long limbs and sensual curves was a young man's fantasy. But it was more than that. He was convinced Estella and her magical unicorn would appeal to female gamers as well. Hadn't even outdoor-orientated Shelley admitted to playing a girly dragon game?

He wished he had someone to share his jubilation with. But he had distanced himself from his friends since his bereavement. Only his mother hadn't given up on him—which never failed to bemuse him as she had scarcely been a presence in his childhood.

His online colleagues these days were working with him on games that had little to do with entertainment and everything to do with education. They would have no interest whatsoever in Princess Estella and her unicorn.

It was with Shelley he wanted to share Estella. To let her know how she had inspired him. But he couldn't. Not now. Not when he had gone this far without letting her in on the secret that she was his muse.

He went back to work, this time on his computer. The creation of a character was only the first step in the long process of producing a new game.

CHAPTER NINE

SHELLEY HAD SPENT both Saturday and Sunday mornings on horseback—the sport she'd loved since she'd been two years old and first begged to be lifted up onto a pony. Horticulture was both her interest and the way she earned her living. Riding a horse was pure pleasure—physical, emotional and spiritual.

A rented horse at a commercial stable could not compare to the joy of riding her own horse. But she was lucky enough to live not too far from Centennial Park, the inner eastern suburbs park that stretched out over four hundred and fifty acres and had extensive horse-riding facilities.

She had a deal with the owner of a beautiful thoroughbred chestnut gelding named Flynn that she rode every weekend. Flynn was loved by his owner, who couldn't exercise him as much as the horse needed, so it worked out well for both of them.

One day she would have that countryside cottage with enough land for a horse. And a dog. In the meantime she made the best of riding Flynn.

She didn't know when she'd get to ride him again on a Saturday now she had committed to working in lieu of paying rent. Most likely she'd saddle up very early before she started work.

It was worth adjusting her working hours to live in this apartment, she thought, looking around her with intense satisfaction. Yesterday she'd finished unpacking her stuff. She had her priorities right—she'd first unpacked the kitchen things. Not that she'd really needed to—the apartment kitchen was completely equipped with every tool and gadget she'd ever need, and more. This afternoon she'd decided to christen the top-of-the-line oven and cooktop.

One of the other things she loved to do in her own time was to bake. On the way back from Centennial Park she'd gone shopping and stocked up on everything she'd needed for a bake-fest.

The oven timer went off and she pulled out the two pies she had baked from scratch. There was something particularly satisfying about making pastry—she got a kick from kneading, crimping edges and forming pastry leaves to put on top. She set the pies to cool on a rack and stood for a long moment critically examining them.

Should she or shouldn't she? She had baked the extra pie with Declan in mind. One for him, the other to share with Lynne and Keith. But she'd assured him she would respect his privacy. Would he consider a text to ask him could she deliver a 'thank you' pie a breach of her promise?

While the pies were cooling she showered and washed her hair to get out the smell of horse—she'd groomed Flynn after their ride. She adored the earthy warm smell of the big animals she loved. She suspected Declan might be rather more fastidious.

Once dressed in pink jeans and a pale pink shirt with a cream sweater slung around her shoulders—all gifts from Lynne, who was always trying to get her to dress in a more feminine manner—she texted Declan.

Can I see you?

His reply took a few minutes to come back.

Sure—come to the back door.

She wrapped the pie with its golden, buttery pastry crust in one of the beautiful French tea towels she'd found in a kitchen drawer.

It was only when she stood at his back door waiting for Declan to open it that she seriously began to question the sanity of baking a pie for her boss.

Declan was surprised to hear from Shelley so late on Sunday afternoon. He was not long awake, having had to catch up on some sleep after the Estella marathon. He'd only just started his workout in the basement gym and normally wouldn't tolerate interruption.

He threw on a sweatshirt over his bare chest. Perhaps it was an emergency in the apartment that needed his attention, he told himself as justification for breaking his no-interruptions rule. As an excuse for the brightening of his spirits when he'd seen her name flash up on his smartphone.

He was even more surprised to see her at his door bearing the most amazing home-made pie. Apple, he guessed, if the enticing aroma was anything to go by.

She held it out to him on both hands like an offering.

'I wanted to thank you for letting me live in the apartment it's fabulous and I can't believe my luck to be living there,' she blurted out.

'You don't have to cook for me,' he said and immediately regretted it when her face fell.

'I wondered if it was…appropriate,' she said, biting her lower lip. 'You mentioned you liked mulberries. Mulberries aren't in season so I couldn't get you mulberries. I'm hoping apple and raspberry might be acceptable. I had to use frozen raspberries because they're not in season either but they're very good and—'

'Shelley,' he said. 'Stop. I'm delighted you made me a pie. It was just…unexpected.' He took it from her hands. It was warm to the touch. 'Thank you.'

'Just out of the oven,' she said. 'An oven that's a very good one, by the way.'

'Come in,' he said.

'Oh, no, I shouldn't, I—'

'Please,' he said. The realisation he had no one to share the creation of Princess Estella with had made him feel… lonely.

He was also surprised to see Shelley all dressed in pink. Pretty, girly pink. She even wore jewellery, a chain holding a silver horseshoe that rested in the dip of her cleavage. *Lucky horseshoe.* He didn't know why he had assumed she would always dress in mannish clothes. Perhaps he'd forced himself to think too much about Shelley as warrior instead of facing up to his attraction to Shelley as woman.

'Okay,' she said and followed him inside.

During the major renovation of the house the back had been opened up and a family room and what the architect had insisted on calling a 'dream kitchen' had been installed.

'Wow,' she said as she unashamedly looked around her. 'This is an amazing space.'

'It's hardly used,' he said.

'Shame,' she said. 'That's truly a dream kitchen for someone who enjoys cooking.'

So the architect had got that one right.

Most of the house wasn't used and was quiet and still with air unbreathed. He couldn't bear to go into the rooms he'd shared with Lisa. They'd been closed off for two years.

He'd never gone into the nursery they'd prepared with such hope. But he wouldn't let anyone clear it. His life in this house was confined to his top-floor workspace, the turret room and the gym with occasional forays into this kitchen.

And now Shelley had brought a shaft of her particular brand of sunshine with her into this too large, too empty, too sad house.

He carried the pie over to the marble countertop and put it down.

'I'm going to have a piece right now while it's warm,' he said. 'You?'

She shook her head. 'I baked another one to share with my sister and her fiancé. I'm having dinner with them tonight.'

Any thought of asking her to join him for dinner—to be delivered from a favourite restaurant he hadn't actually set foot in for two years—was immediately quashed. It was a stupid idea anyway. He reminded himself it was more important than ever to establish boundaries between them now she was living on site, so to speak.

He took out a plate, a knife to cut the pie and a fork with which to eat it, and served himself an enormous slice. Then pulled up a stool at the breakfast bar. Shelley took a seat two stools away.

'So I get to eat this pie all by myself,' he said, circling the plate with his arms in exaggerated possessiveness.

'You could put half in the freezer,' said ever-practical Shelley.

'Believe me, there won't be half left to freeze,' he said.

He bit into his first mouthful, savoured the taste. 'Best pie I ever had,' he said with only mild exaggeration.

She laughed. 'I don't believe that for a minute.'

'Seriously, it's delicious.'

'My grandma's recipe,' she said. 'Trouble with learning to cook from your grandmother is I tend to specialise in old-fashioned treats.'

'This is a treat, all right,' he said. 'It's been a long time since someone baked for me.'

She looked around the room. 'So who uses this kitchen?'

'I do. But only for the most basic meals. I'm useless at anything more complex.' Declan had never needed to learn to cook. He'd moved out of home at age eighteen, already wealthy enough to eat out or hire caterers whenever he wanted.

Shelley leaned her elbows on the countertop. 'Was Lisa a good cook?'

He was so shocked to hear her mention Lisa's name he nearly choked on his pie. But why shouldn't she? It was a perfectly reasonable question. Shelley didn't know of his guilt over the deaths of his wife and daughter and his determination to punish himself for their loss.

'She…she did her best—but we used to laugh at the results more often than not. We ate out a lot. I think she was hoping this kitchen would transform her into a culinary wizard. She used to talk about doing classes but… but she never did.'

'She… Lisa…she sounds lovely.' He could tell Shelley was choosing her words carefully.

'She was. You…you would have liked her and she…she would have liked you.'

He realised it was true. The two women were physically complete opposites; Lisa had been tiny and dark-haired. But there was a common core of…he hesitated to use the bland word 'niceness' but it went some way to articulating what he found almost impossible to articulate.

'I… I'm glad,' Shelley said. He could see sympathy in her eyes. But not pity. He wouldn't tolerate pity.

Even two years later he still found it difficult to talk

about Lisa. It was as if his heart had been torn out of him when she'd died.

But if he were going to talk to anyone it would be Shelley. There was something trustworthy and non-judgemental about her that made him believe he could let his guard down around her. If only in increments.

'Lisa was…vivacious. That was the word people used about her. When I was young I was a quiet kind of guy, awkward around girls. Females ran a mile from me when they learned what a geek I was.'

'I don't believe that for a minute,' Shelley said with an upward tilt to her lovely mouth. 'You're a very good-looking guy. I imagine you would have been beating girls off with a stick.' Was that acknowledgement of a fact or admiration? Whatever it was he liked the feeling her words gave him.

'Not so,' he said, with a self-deprecating shrug. 'I probably spent way too long in front of a screen.'

'But Lisa saw something in you?'

'Lisa grew up with brothers, knew how to handle boys. She took me out of myself. I was an only child of parents too busy to take much notice of me.'

'I'm sorry to hear that,' she murmured.

'They'd decided not to have children. I came as a shock to them.' He tried to make a joke of it but his bitterness filtered through. 'I don't know how many times I heard the words "Declan was our little accident" when I was growing up.'

Her eyes widened. 'Surely they said it with fondness,' she said.

'Perhaps. I didn't see much of my parents anyway. My mother was too busy defending criminals or doing pro bono work for underprivileged people to realise there might be someone at home who needed her time too. Thankfully she shunted me off to her mother for the school vacations.'

'The one with the mulberry tree?'

He nodded. 'The very one. She was an artist and took great delight in passing on her skills to me—to defy my parents, I sometimes think.'

'And your father?'

'Let's just say "typical absentee parent" and be done with it.'

'I… I feel sad for the little boy you were,' she said.

'Don't be. I put that behind me long ago. Who knows, if I'd grown up in a happy household with a boatload of siblings I mightn't have got where I did so fast.'

'That's a thought,' she said, but didn't sound convinced.

'At least they had the sense to hire a wonderful nanny for me. She more than made up for it.'

Until he'd turned twelve and they'd terminated Jeannie's employment, citing that a big boy like him didn't need to be looked after any more. Jeannie had never given up on him, though. She'd stayed an important part of his life.

'Jeannie was going to live in the apartment to…to help you with…?'

He had to change the subject. 'Yes,' he said abruptly. 'What about you? Sounds like your childhood might have been less than ideal.'

'It was very ideal until my father decided he preferred another family to us,' she said. It gutted him to see her face tighten with remembered distress.

'You and your sister?'

She nodded. 'And my mum—none of us saw it coming. He met a younger woman with a little boy. She got her clutches into him and that was the end of it. For us anyway.'

'So why did you have to leave your home?'

'He's a real-estate agent. He said our little farm needed to be sold. Then he pulled some tricky deal and moved right back in with her.'

Declan could think of a few words he'd like to use to describe her father but held his tongue. 'That's terrible.'

'He tried to make it up to Lynne and me. Wanted to keep seeing us. I was allowed to keep my pony, Toby, there. He said it was a good way to make me visit.'

By the tight set of her face Declan doubted the tale would have a happy ending. 'Makes sense,' he said.

'Until the day I got there to find she'd sold my beautiful Toby. And my father had done nothing to stop her.'

This time Declan did let loose with a string of curse words. 'That's cruelty. How old were you?'

'I'd just turned fourteen. It's a long time ago but I still remember how I felt.'

'Did you get your horse back?'

'We tracked down the new owner. But…but…' Tears welled in her beautiful eyes. 'He'd panicked when they were off-loading him from the horse trailer at the other end. My darling boy must have known what was happening to him wasn't right. Apparently he reared and thrashed around and…and broke his leg.' Her voice became almost unintelligible as she fought off tears. 'It wasn't the new owner's fault. They didn't know Toby was…was stolen. But he…he had to be put down.'

'And what about your father?'

'He made me hate him,' she said simply. 'And it never really went away.'

Something deep and long unused inside Declan had turned upside down in the face of her grief. To comfort her became more important than the inhibitions he had imposed upon himself.

He reached out and clasped her hand in his. Her hand was slender and warm but he felt calluses on her palm and fingers. Warrior calluses.

'I'm sorry,' he said. 'Not just about your horse but about

your father too.' He suspected the pain of losing her horse was inextricably tied up with her father's betrayal.

She returned the pressure on his hand, not knowing what a monumental gesture it was for him to reach out to her. For a very long moment his eyes met with hers in a silent connection that shook him. *What he felt for her in this moment went way beyond physical attraction.*

In the quiet of his kitchen, with the ticking of the clock and the occasional whirring of the fridge the only noise, this one room of many in the vast emptiness of his house suddenly seemed welcoming. Because she was there.

'I'm sorry to lose the plot like that,' she said. 'I know that my loss is nothing—absolutely nothing—compared with your loss. I know he was only an animal but—' She sniffed back the tears that obviously still threatened.

'But you loved him.'

There'd been no pets in his childhood household, despite his constant clamouring for a dog. Then Lisa had been allergic to pet hair. One day he might get a dog. It was a new thought and one immediately rejected. He did not want to take the risk of loving anything, *anyone* again.

'Yes,' she said. 'I adored Toby. There's an incredible bond between horse and rider, you know. It's not quite the same as loving a cat or a dog. Two become one, horse and human, when you ride. There's a kind of mutual responsibility. It's very special.'

'Do you still ride?' He couldn't admit how he had observed her heading out of the house dressed in her breeches and boots.

'Fortunately Centennial Park is so close by I can ride each weekend. Riding a hired horse is nothing like riding your own but I'm fortunate enough to ride the same lovely big boy every week. His owner is so grateful to have someone competent to exercise him and groom him, she only charges me a pittance.'

'Sounds like a deal,' he said.

'It's another reason I really wanted to stay in this area rather than moving out further where rents are cheaper. Again, thank you for the apartment. I love it.'

'Thanking me with a pie was a great idea,' he said.

'I make a mean chocolate-fudge cake too,' she said. 'Unless you'd prefer something more savoury.'

'Cake is good,' he said. The strict exercise regime he followed let him eat whatever he wanted.

He realised he was still holding her hand—and he didn't want to let it go. She seemed in no rush to relinquish his grip either.

'Tell me the type of treats you like so I can keep you in mind when I'm baking,' she said with her generous smile, leaning closer, so close he breathed in her sweet, flowery scent. 'If it isn't in my repertoire, I'll find a recipe.'

It was a thoughtful offer. But right now there was only one treat that was tempting him. Before he could rustle up a reason why he shouldn't, he leaned across and kissed her. Her lush, lovely mouth was soft and full under his.

She stilled at first, startled, then relaxed against him, her lips parting for his with a soft murmur as he traced their warm softness with his tongue.

He had not kissed a woman other than Lisa since he was nineteen. The feel of Shelley's mouth under his was both familiar and different at the same time. The thought of Lisa was both poignant and fleeting—then his mind was filled only with Shelley and how much he wanted to keep on kissing her. She tasted of cinnamon and apple with a fresh tang of mint as her tongue tangled with his.

As she kissed him back this kiss became unique, special like nothing he had ever experienced. Shelley. Beautiful Shelley. *It was all about her.*

Her mouth was soft and warm and generous, their hands still linked on the table between them. It started as a gentle, exploratory kiss but very soon escalated into something more passionate as she kissed him back with equal ardour.

They strained towards each other—awkward on bar stools but she didn't seem to care and he certainly didn't—he just wanted to be as close to her as he could possibly be.

But she was the one to break the kiss, her face flushed, her eyes bright.

'That was a surprise, Declan,' she said. He could see a pulse beating rapidly at the base of her throat. 'Of the nice kind. *Very* nice, actually.'

He took a deep breath in an attempt to steady his breathing.

'Much more than nice,' he said.

His thoughts were filled with Shelley. But he felt disloyal that he hadn't given thought to his late wife. Yet from nowhere came the insistent message: *Lisa would approve.* If he had been the first to go, would he have expected her to lead such a desperately lonely life?

But he wasn't ready to move on to someone else—might not ever be ready.

'You know this can't lead to anywhere,' he said, his voice husky. 'I have nothing to give you. Nothing. It…it all drained away when—'

Shelley put her finger on his mouth to silence him.

Her face was flushed, her voice throaty when she finally spoke. 'It was just a kiss. A very nice kiss but just a kiss. Does it have to lead anywhere?'

'I guess not,' he said, somewhat taken aback. Shelley was so different from the predatory women on the hunt for the wealthy widower.

It hadn't entered his head that Shelley might not be interested in him.

'Men are more trouble than they're worth.' Her earlier words echoed through his brain.

Her mouth was pouty and swollen from his kiss—which made him just want to kiss her again.

'I'm aware you might not be ready for…for anything serious.' Her stumble made him realise that perhaps she wasn't as indifferent to him as it might appear. 'And I don't want to risk opening myself to…heartbreak. I've just got over an almighty dose of that.'

He hadn't been planning on *heartbreak*. In fact that was just what he wanted to avoid. Not just for himself but for her too.

'The guy in Melbourne?'

She nodded. 'He was dishonest and he—well, he was a liar and completely untrustworthy and… Never mind, you don't want to hear the details.'

She was right. He didn't want to hear about her with another man. But was he ready to win her for himself?

'It's been two years, Declan. Lisa would not expect you to grieve for ever.' Now it was his mother's words borrowing his brain.

'I have plans,' Shelley continued. 'I don't want heartbreak and angst and all that stuff that seems to come with relationships—or they do for me anyway—to get in the way of achieving my goals.'

'Plans?' he said. *Goals?* He realised he might be guilty of underestimating Shelley. Had he given a thought to her life beyond his garden and her unwitting role as muse?

'Serious goals I've put on the back burner for years—derailed by relationships gone wrong.'

'I'd like to hear those goals.'

'Let me start,' she said. 'I want to visit some of the great gardens in Europe. Gardens that have had such an influence on the way people design gardens even here on the other side of the world. Some say the English perennial border isn't suited to most parts of this country—I'd love to see it at home in England. Then there's Monet's garden at Giverny, near Paris—who doesn't want to see that?'

Declan could think of far more interesting things than a garden to see in France but he was too stunned to interrupt her flow of words.

'And the Gardens of the Alhambra in Spain.' She smiled. 'Lots of fountains.'

He cleared his throat. 'When do you go?'

'As soon as your garden is done. Four more weeks, according to our agreement. Then I'll be flying off to Europe.'

'When will you be back?'

'Who knows? I'm booking an open-return ticket. My father was born in England and I can stay for as long as I like. What I really, really want to do is work as a horticulturalist in the gardens of one of the grand stately homes in England.' Her eyes shone with enthusiasm. 'I apply for every job I see—they advertise through agencies on the internet—and I'm hoping one of them will stick.'

'Sounds exciting,' he said lamely.

He realised that since he had nearly kissed her in his garden when he had unwound her hair, the thought had been quietly ticking away in the back of his mind that one day, if he was ever able to move on, Shelley might be the one. It was a shock to find she had no intention of being here, of giving him time to come to terms with the change her presence in his life might entail.

'So, you see, you're a grieving widower—and I totally understand that, I can't imagine how dreadful it's been for you—and I don't do meaningless flings.'

She leaned across and kissed him lightly on the mouth. Even it had impact, sending want coursing through him.

'So, lovely as that kiss was, I don't think we should do it again.'

Declan was too speechless to respond.

Shelley got up from her stool. 'I have to get going to meet my sister. I can pick up the pie dish when you're done with.'

'Let me see you out,' he said, getting up to follow her.

She put up her hand to halt him. 'No need.'

She strolled out, and suddenly the room seemed very, very empty indeed.

Shelley stood outside the house near the fountain, lit up by the sensor lights that had come on automatically when she had stumbled out of Declan's back door. She hoped the cool evening air would bring her to her senses. She shivered and tugged her cream sweater tightly around her shoulders. Her mouth ached from both the effort of continual smiling and appearing nonchalant—and the unaccustomed dissembling. She wasn't a liar. Yet she had lied and lied and lied to Declan.

'It was just a kiss' was the first lie. She touched her fingers to her mouth, shuddering as she remembered the powerful effect of his lips on hers, his tongue exploring the soft recesses of her mouth, the desire that had ignited and raced through her body. It was so much more than a mere pressing of two mouths together. Of awakened passion.

But the biggest lie of all was that she didn't want him kissing her again. There was nothing she wanted more than to be in his arms and kissing him. *More than kissing him.*

But the lies had been necessary. Because they were overwhelmed by the one big truth. *She didn't want to risk heartbreak.* And everything Declan did, what he said, pointed to massive heartbreak down the line if she let down the guard on her emotions.

Her wounds from Steve were still too raw and painful to risk opening them again. She still hadn't completed that long climb back out of the black pit of distrust that her father's betrayal and rejection of her love had flung her into.

Dating decent—if unexciting—men had set her on the first rungs of finding her way back out until Steve had kicked the ladder out from under her in spectacular fashion. Coming back to Sydney and away from anything that reminded her of Steve had started her recovery.

She had to protect herself from falling down again. Denying that Declan's kiss had affected her was one way to do it.

Although, in doing so, she was actually lying to herself.

CHAPTER TEN

SHELLEY LOOKED LONG and hard at the door in her kitchen that, she now knew, led straight through into Declan's kitchen. The door she had promised never to use. The key was in her hand. All it would take would be to slide it into the lock and—

She put the key—which she had attached to a pewter horseshoe key ring—back down on the countertop with a clatter.

It was five-thirty in the morning. She had been awake since four o'clock. Tossing and turning and unable to get thoughts of Declan from her mind. How it had felt to kiss him. To want so much more than a kiss. More than he could give. *More than it was wise to want.*

She looked at the key again gleaming on the counter-top. *Tempting her.*

At four a.m. it had been way too dark to go out and start work in the garden. She'd tried to read a book—a new one on Enid Wilson she'd ordered from a specialist gardening bookstore—but could not concentrate. Television offerings at that time of morning had not been able to engage her interest either.

So she had baked muffins. Banana and pecan muffins with a maple-syrup glaze. She could have made a pie—she had apples aplenty arranged in a fruit bowl on the table. But both of her pie dishes—enamel ones given to her by her grandma—were not here. One was with Lynne and

Keith. The other was with Declan still, from when she had last seen him three days ago.

Would it be a terribly bad thing to sneak into his kitchen, retrieve the pie dish and leave an offering of some warm banana muffins on the countertop for him?

She wanted that pie dish. She wanted it *now*. She was helping Lynne with the catering for her engagement party on Saturday night. Pie was on the dessert menu. The problem could easily be solved by asking Declan for the pie dish. But she didn't want it to look like a pathetic excuse to see him.

He did not want to see her; that was obvious. But he was here in the house. Last night she had seen the light on in the window high on the second floor she assumed was his office. With that preternatural awareness of his presence she had developed, she knew he was there even without the light as proof.

She picked up the key again. It turned easily in the lock.

Still in her pyjamas, heart in her mouth, she crept into the kitchen of the big house. It was silent, it was creepy, it was almost dark—with only the faint lights on the stove and the computer-controlled fridge to lead her way. She searched for the pie dish in drawers that glided out silently. She found her dish in the third drawer she tried, quite possibly put there by the cleaners.

Mission accomplished.

She eased the plate of muffins down onto the marble countertop so it wouldn't clatter. Then immediately berated herself for such an idiotic move—and blamed it on her lack of sleep. She doubted Declan would notice the absence of the pie dish. But the sudden appearance of a plate of freshly baked muffins? There would be no doubt who had left them there and that she had trespassed.

She picked them up again, and then the pie dish, and

made to tiptoe back to her door and then to her rightful side of it. Then she heard the music. A faint pulsing, driving rhythm coming, it sounded like, from somewhere on this floor.

Curiosity killed the cat—remember that, Shelley.

Another of her grandmother's sayings flashed through her mind. Advice that in this case she really should take. But the house was otherwise dark and deserted. She'd been wondering about Declan's secret life inside this house since the day she'd first met him. She could not resist this particular temptation.

Trying to be as quiet as possible, she tiptoed out of the kitchen and down a very short corridor. She guessed that in the old days this might have led to a scullery or cellar. Just a few silent steps from the kitchen she saw a door with a glass pane at the top—it was only the dim light coming through the glass that let her recognise it.

The music was coming from downstairs. Was Declan there? What would happen if he saw her prowling around where she had no right to prowl?

She could not resist sidling up to the glass panel and looking through.

Not a cellar but a full-size basement gym filled with serious-looking workout equipment.

And Declan was working out.

She nearly dropped her pie dish at the sight of him.

Her breath caught in her throat and her heart started hammering so loudly she could hear it.

Declan, wearing only tight black gym shorts, his upper body completely bare save for a pair of grip gloves. Declan, doing pull-ups on a terrifyingly high multi-step pull-up bar. Declan doing 'salmon pull-ups', so called because they involved not just pulling *himself* up to the bar but pushing the actual bar up with him to the next step, like salmon swimming upstream against the current. It took incredible strength in both upper body and abs to master. Strength and willpower and endurance. And courage. One slip and he'd crash to the ground taking the metal bar with him.

Shelley went to the gym when she could. But she had never seen anyone actually do salmon pull-ups.

She watched in awe as, muscles straining, he pulled both himself and the bar to the very top step without pausing. Then, again without pausing, he hooked his legs over the bar and executed a series of sit-ups punching the air as he jack-knifed his body into a sitting position—upside down.

His cut, defined muscles gleamed with sweat as he grimaced with the effort of the unbelievably tough workout he was forcing his body through.

So that was where the muscles came from.

Mesmerised, she could not tear her eyes away from him, even though she knew she risked discovery. This was a guy who described himself as a *geek*?

Declan working out was the sexiest thing she had ever seen. She was getting turned on just watching. Her whole body was taut with hunger for him. With pure and simple lust. She nearly fainted as he turned in mid-air to show his tight, powerful butt, the straining muscles of his broad back.

'I don't do meaningless flings.'

Her words of three days ago came back to haunt her.

She wanted him more than she had ever imagined she could want a man.

If she could stumble down those stairs and push herself against all that hot, hard muscle she wouldn't be thinking about *meaning*. She had to cross her legs at the thought of it.

The force of her desire for him made her tremble and her knees go suddenly weak. She leaned against the door to support herself just as Declan dropped to the ground from the top of the bar to land with total control on a thick, foam mat. He looked up and her breath stopped but he immediately rolled into a series of alternating one-arm push-ups. *He hadn't seen her.*

But she knew the longer she stayed there, the greater the risk of discovery.

Her heart started an even more furious pounding and she found it difficult to breathe. Not just with her overwhelming longing for him but with terror at the prospect of him catching her spying on him.

With one last look at his incredible body, she turned as quietly and as cautiously as she could and tiptoed back to the door that would send her through to her very short-term leased part of the mansion. The staff *downstairs* to his billionaire *upstairs*.

Once safely back in her kitchen, she stood with her back to the connecting door and braced herself against it, urging her heart to slow down, her breath to steady from short, urgent gasps to a more regular pattern.

How could she ever forget how Declan looked working out in that gym? *How much she wanted him?* Wanted this man who had made it so very clear he had nothing to give her.

Actually, when she thought back, even a meaningless fling was not on offer. He had kissed her. *That was all.* But it had been such a wonderful kiss, of course she had thought further to what that kind of kiss could lead to. *Making love with Declan.* If that one kiss had given her so much pleasure, what would—?

She could not go there. That would be dreaming an impossible dream. Declan was still deeply entrenched in his marriage—even though his wife had passed away two years ago, Declan had not moved on. The only outcome of letting herself fall for him would be heartbreak. And she had had more than enough of that. *She had to keep reminding herself of that.*

The grey light of dawn was starting to filter through the blinds of the apartment. She knew there was zero chance of getting back to sleep now. A quick, very cold shower and then get out into the garden.

She had a big day planned—and a surprise for Declan that he might like, or hate so much she'd never be able to face him again.

Mid-afternoon and Declan was surprised to get a text from Shelley asking him could he come down to the garden as soon as he could.

From his observation point in his office, he'd noticed a lot of activity in the grounds. A delivery of plants. Lots of digging on Shelley's part. And the pool guys were there again.

He heaved himself up from his desk. He was tired and grumpy. He hadn't slept at all the night before. But then what was new about that?

He'd worked right through. Burying himself in work was a better alternative to angsting about Shelley. Thinking about the difference she had made to his life. Not just because of Estella. In fact Estella seemed somehow peripheral now.

He realised now he had used Estella as a block to getting to know the real Shelley, not his imagined version of her. Estella had been self-protection.

There could be no doubt his attraction to Shelley made him see a glimmer of hope in the dark reality of his grief, a thawing of his long-frozen emotions. The kiss had made that very clear.

But the consequences if things went awry were huge—

not just for him but for her. Shelley was an exceptional woman in every way—and he didn't want to hurt her because he'd taken a step towards her too soon.

Perhaps she sensed his ambivalence and that was why she was determined to keep him at a distance, to concentrate on her plans for a career far away from here—and from him.

Before dawn he had gone down to the basement gym and driven his body through a punishing regime. Extended his body to its limits in a gruelling workout so that no thoughts could intrude—just pure physicality.

Even then—on the point of utter exhaustion—he couldn't sleep. After his workout he had showered in the gym bathroom, then made his way up to the kitchen.

Breakfast was the one meal he was expert at preparing. Protein and lots of it was required after such an intense workout. So why in hell had he been hit by a craving for banana muffins? He'd wanted one so badly he had sworn he could smell them fresh out of the oven right there in his kitchen.

He'd been forced to phone through an order to a local bakery and have banana muffins express delivered. They tasted nothing like how he had anticipated—dry and unpalatable. There wasn't a crumb of Shelley's pie left either. He'd bet she'd bake a muffin that would taste a hundred times better than the ones he'd had delivered and that had subsequently landed in the trash.

His unsatisfied craving had made him grumpier than ever. And that was on top of his craving for *her*.

Now Shelley wanted to see him to show him something in the garden. Oddly enough, he was looking forward to it. Seeing the garden emerge from the mess it had been was more satisfying than he could ever have imagined. Shelley had vision; there was no doubt about that.

He texted her: I'll be down in half an hour.

She was waiting for him by the fountain—familiar Shelley in her khaki gardener garb. She coloured high on her cheeks when he greeted her—the previous time they'd met he'd been kissing her.

Inwardly he groaned. He wasn't good at this. The last time he'd dated a woman had been when he'd met Lisa—and there hadn't been many before her in spite of what Shelley might think.

'Notice anything?' she asked cheerfully.

Other than how beautiful you look—even in those awful clothes?

He nodded. 'There's water in the pond.'

'And it's not leaking away. It's been in there for forty-eight hours. I think the pool guys nailed it. Well, not literally nailed it, of course. If they had, it would be leaking more than ever, wouldn't it? I mean…' Her voice trailed away.

In spite of his grumpiness he smiled; Shelley seemed to always make him smile. 'I get what you mean.'

He inspected the pond and its surrounds, now all mellow sandstone free of grime and mould.

'It looks awesome, doesn't it?' she said, eyes wide seeking his approval.

Even if it didn't look awesome, he would say it did just so as not to extinguish that light in her eyes.

'It's awesome, all right. What about the fountain—does it work?'

'That's why I asked you down here,' she said with a flourish of her hand. 'You are formally invited to the grand ceremonial switching on of the fountain.'

She took him around to the back of the far wall of the pond and showed him a small, discreet box housing a switch. 'The pump is behind there and all safely wired up to low-voltage electricity. All you have to do is turn it on.' She paused. 'Go ahead, you do this. It's your fountain.'

'But you're the driving force behind it,' he said. 'The honour should be yours. You've put so much into it.'

Her smile dimmed. 'It's my job, Declan. This is what I do. And when I finish this job there'll be another garden somewhere else.'

He ducked down to turn on the switch, hoping she wouldn't see the sudden pain her words caused him.

Standing beside her—and noting how carefully she kept her distance—he watched as the water started to pump through the fountain, shooting up from the top and cascading down the tiers. The water sparkled as sunlight caught it and refracted off the droplets. Now he knew exactly what she meant about adding movement to the garden. And a different element of beauty. *But Shelley was the most beautiful thing in this garden.*

'It's just wonderful, isn't it?' she said softly. 'I knew it was worth saving. Sometimes the things you have to work hardest to restore become the most valuable.'

'You're right,' he said, his voice suddenly husky.

It was his garden and she a paid employee. But she had put her heart and soul into this restoration.

While he was pleased at how the garden was progressing, he wished he could slow down the progress to give him time to come to terms with what Shelley meant to him. As it was, the days were ticking away until the time she'd pack up her tools and move on.

Unless he stopped her.

Right now he didn't know how that was possible.

A tiny blue wren flew through the spray of the fountain, fluffing his wings as he went. He was immediately followed by his little brown mate.

'Oh, look at that,' Shelley cried in delight.

'The local wildlife seal of approval,' he said.

'I hope everything else in the garden works out as well,' she said slowly.

'I'm sure it will. It's all starting to look very civilised,' he said.

She took a few steps away from him, then turned back to face him.

'There's something else I want to show you,' she said. 'Something I… I didn't discuss with you. I'm hoping it will meet with your approval.'

He was used to her being nervous around his forbidding self. But this was different. She had paled under her light tan and was wringing her hands together. He couldn't imagine why.

'You'd better show me,' he said.

'Just before I do,' she said, 'I want to let you know that I did it with the best of intentions, no matter what you might think.'

His interest roused, he followed her to a prominent bed in an open part of the garden behind the fountain. Looking from the house, he realised it would be in the line of vision from most of the windows of the house.

The stone wall behind the bed had been cleaned and repaired and the two antique planters put back in their place and planted with some spiky-leaved plant.

But that wasn't what Shelley was showing him. The actual garden bed had been completely cleared of weeds and whatever plants had turned up their toes from years of neglect. The earth had been freshly turned over. He realised this was where he'd seen Shelley digging and planting for most of the morning.

He drew his brows together. 'They're plants, I know, but they look to me like a whole lot of brown sticks with a few green shoots here and there.'

'They're roses,' she said. 'This is a perfect aspect for roses and I hope they'll thrive here. I've planted two varieties of roses here. In late spring they'll be glorious.'

'Yes?' he said. What was the big deal here?

She looked up at him, her eyes a little wary. 'At the back I've planted a vibrant orange and pink rose called "Lisa".'

Declan's heart seemed to stop beating and he felt a cold sweat break out on his forehead.

Shelley didn't seem to expect any response from him as she continued. 'The smaller bushes in the front have an exquisite pale pink bloom with a sweet scent. The rose is called "Miss Alice".'

Declan felt as if his throat were swelling to choke any attempt at speech. The grief he'd felt at the loss of his wife and daughter came flooding back. But with that grief came a new emotion of gratitude for the woman who had made this gesture.

'Thank you,' he finally managed to get out. 'It was very…thoughtful of you.'

Shelley expelled a great sigh of relief and he realised the tension she had been holding. 'The "Lisa" rose is probably what you could call a…a vivacious rose. Like Lisa herself, you told me.'

Shelley's eyes were misting with tears. His tears had long run dry.

Her voice was so low he had to lean down to catch it.

'This was Daphne's garden and the daphne she planted remains a memorial for her,' she said. 'Then it was Lisa's garden and I hope the roses will be a beautiful tribute to her and…and to baby Alice.'

Declan was astounded at how thoughtful Shelley had been. It was something his billions could never have bought. But it was almost too much for him to be able to deal with.

'Thank you. What you've done is…extraordinary. I won't forget what you've done for me. And for honouring Lisa and Alice in this way.'

He didn't mean for those words to sound so final but it was the best he could do. His remembered grief was all mixed up with his gratitude for what Shelley had done for him. Something that was so utterly *right*. He honestly couldn't think of anyone else he knew who would have the heart, the compassion and the imagination required.

He started to shake and before he knew it Shelley's arms were around him and he was holding her tight.

Shelley closed her eyes and leaned against Declan's hard strength, loving the feel of those powerful arms around her. During those secret, stolen moments watching him work out this was what she'd been wanting.

Was he hugging her—or in his memory was he hugging Lisa?

This was a man who had genuinely loved his wife. So devastated by grief at her loss he was unable to move on.

She had not believed in such love. Certainly had not experienced it. But now she'd seen it, she wanted it for herself.

She wanted it from him. She couldn't deny that any longer. The lying to herself had to stop.

But was Declan's love all used up?

It would be a tragedy if that was the case. Not just for him but for her.

Because she was falling for him in spite of the very real risk to her heart.

CHAPTER ELEVEN

WAS SHE IN any way envious of her sister and her fiancé's happiness? Dressing for her sister's engagement party, Shelley couldn't help but question herself about love, life and relationships. Her answer? *Maybe.*

Not that she wished she had Keith for herself—he was a very nice man but she wasn't the slightest bit attracted to him. He was perfect for Lynne—they complemented each other's strengths and weaknesses. Above all they were head over heels in love. Keith was a jeweller and had given Lynne a lovely ruby ring he had designed just for her.

It wasn't the engagement ring that Shelley envied. The envy thing happened when she'd witness her sister and her guy planning their wedding, the family they intended to have, their future together. They were so darn committed to that future. So certain of each other.

And her? Teetering on the edge of falling in love with a man who had said point-blank he had *nothing to give her*.

Her sister's joy brought Shelley's own situation into focus. She was twenty-eight. Marriage. Children. They were something she'd always thought would happen in the future. When her career was established. When she'd met the right man. But that man had proved to be elusive.

There'd been one proposal—from a guy she had dated during her final year at university. He'd come from a prominent horse-training family and they'd met through their common love of horses. She'd been very fond of him but she'd known *fond* wasn't enough even though he'd been what her grandmother had called *good marriage material*.

More recently there had been Steve—the married man she hadn't known was married. Afterwards she had beaten herself up for having been so easily deceived. But it had certainly seemed like love at the time. And it had hurt.

And now there was Declan. Not married. But—in a way—still married.

Maybe she needed to have a good long look at herself—did she have a thing for unavailable men? And what could she do about it? Accept steady, nice Mark's long-standing and often repeated invitation to dinner?

She sighed. How could she when she was already in so deep with Declan even though it seemed impossible? How could she give another man a thought? Declan eclipsed anyone she'd ever met. And it wouldn't be fair on Mark or any other man whom she might date.

Her hopes for the future did include marriage and children. But not for the sake of it. No settling for second best, no settling for *fond* because she feared time was running out. Women had children well into their thirties, their forties even. There was no need to panic. But children were definitely on her wish list, which brought to mind another question. Would Declan ever want to have another child?

But she couldn't have Declan and she'd better get used to the thought. Even though every time she closed her eyes she saw him bare-chested down in that gym, his powerful muscles, the look of intense concentration on his face she found so sexy. *She ached for him.*

Lynne was right: she should get out and have some fun.

She viewed herself critically in the mirror, twisting and turning to see the back of her new dress. The cobalt-blue colour alone drew attention but it was the cut of it that had her wondering was it a tad too sexy for an engagement party.

High-necked in the front, it swooped outrageously low in the back, secured by two heavy silver chains that started from the back of her neck and fixed to each side. Thankfully it had a built-in bra, otherwise she'd be too nervous to move in it—let alone dance and party. The stretch jersey fabric was ruched and shaped and *very* figure-hugging.

But Lynne had insisted she wear it to her engagement party, which was to be held at the luxurious harbourside home of one of Keith's school friends. 'There will be lots of single guys there,' her sister had said. 'Wear that sassy dress and get your mind off that reclusive boss of yours.'

Shelley had protested but Lynne had spoken over her. 'Don't try to hide your crush on Devastating Declan from me.'

Shelley had protested that she did not have a crush. And she hadn't been lying. She had way more than a crush on Declan.

For a passing moment, she wished Declan could see her in this dress. It wouldn't hurt for him to see she was more than a down-to-earth gardener in khaki work clothes and an old-fashioned homemaker in an apron who baked pies.

Tonight she didn't want to look in any way like that person. The dress was a start. Now she had to get her hair right. She ended up with a low side ponytail, secured with a glittery holder, that rested over her left shoulder and left her back uncovered.

With such a bold dress, she took more care with her make-up, darkening her eyes, slicking on deep pink glossy lipstick. She usually wore fairly low heels so she didn't tower over many of the men she met. But her sister's engagement party was certainly the occasion to christen the silver stilettos she had bought on a whim but had never worn.

She had promised Lynn she would be early. So she wrapped a light shawl around her bare back and shoulders and picked up a silver evening purse.

Cautiously, in her spiky-heeled shoes, she picked her way over the gravel to where she had parked her car in Declan's driveway. She muttered a curse when she saw there was a car parked behind it, blocking the way out to the street—a new-model luxury coupe that put her ancient 4x4 to shame. Her car was not just second-hand, it was more likely tenth-hand and the other car made it look like every one of its years.

In the weeks she been working in Declan's garden she had never seen a car parked here except when the cleaners came. Who drove this car?

Cranky that the delay was making her late, she teetered on her high heels around to the front door of Declan's house. No time to text. She just wanted him to ask his guest to move that car immediately.

Declan answered the door. She lost all the words that she had prepared to politely ask could his visitor help her out and move the car. It was all she could do not to gawk at him in blatant admiration. Her heartbeat kicked into overdrive and her knees felt distinctly wobbly. How could she have ever imagined she could talk herself out of her attraction to him?

Declan looked hot in his black jeans and cashmere sweaters. He looked especially hot in those gym shorts. But he had never looked more darkly handsome than now in a more formal charcoal wool double-breasted jacket over a black T-shirt and black trousers, clean-shaven and hair brushed back.

She felt a moment of feminine satisfaction that he was

getting to see her in the gorgeous blue dress, looking more womanly than he had ever seen her. Reading other people might not be her greatest skill but she was sure he had noticed.

But who was he so dressed up for—the owner of the coupe? She heard a feminine voice from behind him and her heart fell to the level of her silver stilettos.

A wave of nausea made her want to double over. Declan had a woman there? This man who had said he was closed to any feminine presence in his life? *He had lied to her.* He opened the door wider, stared at her for a long moment before he seemed to find his voice.

'Shelley,' he said, hoarsely, then glanced over his shoulder. Glanced *furtively* over his shoulder, it seemed to Shelley.

She still couldn't see who was there—but his action made it very clear he did not want that woman, whoever she might be, to see *her.*

She gritted her teeth, injected ice into her voice. 'There's a car parked in the driveway that's blocking my car. Could you please ask your guest to move it?'

The voice from behind him called out, 'Who's at the door, Declan?'

A woman came into view behind him. She was older, elegant in a simple wine-coloured dress, with her hair cut in a short grey bob and a expression of curiosity on her face. Declan opened the door further.

He cleared his throat. 'Come in, Shelley. I'd like you to meet my mother. Judith Grant.' He turned to the older woman. 'Mother, can I ask you to please move your car as Shelley can't get her car out?'

His mother! Shelley was so relieved she had to hold on to the doorframe for support. The action made her light shawl slip to her waist. Rather than make a big deal about putting it back on again, she gathered it up and tucked it over her arm. She shivered as the chilly evening air hit her bare back. But was then met by toasty centrally heated air as she took the few steps she needed to take her into the entrance hall.

Declan's mother took in her appearance with interest and frank curiosity.

'Mother, this is Shelley Fairhill, my gardener,' Declan said.

The older woman's eyebrows rose in such a similar way to Declan's, it made Shelley smile. She could see the resemblance between mother and son—the same deep blue eyes and lean face. Though the mother didn't have Declan's very masculine cleft in his chin.

Shelley put out her hand. 'It's nice to meet you, Mrs Grant.'

His mother's handshake was brisk and firm. Again Shelley felt self-conscious about her callused hands—but they were a badge of honour of her job. 'Nice to meet you, Shelley.'

Mrs Grant looked accusingly at Declan. 'You didn't tell me the gardener who is doing such wonderful work at this place was a beautiful young woman.'

Because he doesn't recognise me as such, Shelley thought with a pang.

Maybe because I wanted to keep her to myself, Declan thought. He was finding it difficult to think straight he was so knocked out by the sight of Shelley in a short, tight blue dress that accentuated every curve and showed off her sensational legs. *Legs that went on for ever.*

Shelley turned slightly to better face his mother. Declan gasped in admiration, which he quickly had to disguise as a cough. The dress was backless and revealed all of the toned, smooth perfection of her back before swooping so low it was practically indecent. The fabric was softly shaped and had some kind of central seam in it so it clung intimately to the gorgeous curves of her bottom.

Was she wearing underwear? He had to swallow very hard. And keep his hands fisted by his sides to stop him from reaching out to her and pulling her close to find out.

If his mother weren't here, he might have done just that.

His mother addressed Shelley. 'I'm sorry I blocked your access in the driveway. I had no idea who owned the old workhorse of a 4x4.'

'It is old but it serves me well and I can keep all my equipment safely in it,' Shelley said.

Declan sensed the defensive note in Shelley's voice and in turn felt immediately protective of her—he did not want his mother criticising her in any way.

But his mother was smiling. 'Shelley, of course you need a tough car in your line of work. You're doing an absolutely amazing job on the garden. Who knew that something so superb was hiding under all that mess?'

'Thank you,' Shelley said.

But Declan could sense the anxiety underlying her politeness. Then she glanced up at the big grandfather clock standing beneath the stairs.

'Mother, Shelley has to get going somewhere,' he said. 'I think she needs you to move your car right now.'

Shelley shot him a grateful look. 'I don't mean to be rude, Mrs Grant, but I'm on my way to my sister's engagement party so I can't be late.'

'Skip the Mrs Grant, call me Judith,' his mother said, much to Declan's surprise. 'I'll go get my keys and move the car for you.'

Then his mother paused and her eyes narrowed. She snapped her fingers. 'I've got a better idea,' she said. 'You can't drive a battered old 4x4 wearing that gorgeous dress and looking like you just stepped off a catwalk.'

His mother directed her gaze back to him. 'Declan, let Shelley drive one of your sports cars. Heaven knows, you've got a garage full of them.'

Declan automatically went to say *no*. Why would he let anyone drive one of his valuable European sports cars? But this wasn't just anyone. This was Shelley. And her eyes were lit with a gleam of excitement. Of course she would be the type of woman who would love to get behind the wheel of a performance car.

He took a deep breath. 'Good idea, Mother.'

Shelley did a little jig of excitement in her sky-high heels. 'Really, Declan, you'd let me drive your car?'

He rolled his eyes in a pretence of reluctance. 'There are conditions,' he said. 'The car turns into a pumpkin at midnight. You have to have it home by then.'

Shelley's eyes widened. 'Really?' she said. 'Not about the pumpkin, I mean. Well, of course, I know you're making a joke about that. But about the midnight thing. I mean, it's Lynne's engagement party and I have to stay to the end. She and Keith are party animals so heaven knows what time they—'

Declan smiled. 'Relax. You can bring the car back any time, as long as you drive it carefully—'

'Because it's so valuable?'

'There is that,' he said. 'But it's a very powerful car and I don't want you injured either.' *She was way more valuable than any car.*

She smiled. 'I'm a good driver. I grew up in the country, remember. I was driving around the property when I was twelve, long before I legally got my licence at seventeen. I'll take extra-special care with your car, I promise.'

'I'm sure if you can drive that beast of a 4x4 of yours you can drive anything.'

She nodded in acknowledgement of his words, then turned to his mother. 'Thank you, Judith, for suggesting this. How did you know how much I would love to drive a sports car?'

'A princess can't drive a pumpkin,' said his mother.

Shelley did look like a princess—even more of a princess than Estella—glamorous and enticing. 'I'll go get the car key,' he said.

When he returned it was to find Shelley laughing at something his mother had said—and his mother laughing too. He didn't know how he felt about them getting on so well.

He jangled the keys in front of him. 'I'll take you out to the garage and introduce you to the car,' he said.

'How exciting,' said Shelley, her eyes gleaming. 'I can't wait to see my sister's face when I drive up in it.' She turned to his mother. 'Thank you again, Mrs... I mean, Judith, this is going to be such a treat,' she said.

'It's my absolute pleasure,' said his mother with speculative eyes as she looked from Shelley to Declan and back again. 'And remember, I'll be coming over during the week for a guided tour of the garden. With my son's approval, of course.'

Shelley flung her shawl around her shoulders as he led her through the connecting door to the garage. He was tempted almost beyond endurance to slide it off her. Her back view was sensational and he would have been more than happy to admire it for longer.

He stood back and let Shelley enjoy her first sight of the sleek silver sports car that was to be hers for the evening. She was unable to contain her excitement and made throaty little murmurs of pleasure as she walked around the car admiring it from every angle. She actually stroked the bonnet. *He couldn't be jealous of a car.*

'I can tell you like it,' he said.

'Oh, yes,' she said, her eyes shining, her cheeks flushed.

'The black device opens the garage door,' he said as he handed her the key ring.

She stood close by, her high heels bringing her closer to his eye level. Her sweet scent filled his senses. 'Declan, this is really good of you,' she said. 'I hope you didn't feel pressured into letting me drive the car.'

'I don't get pressured into doing anything I don't want to,' he said hoarsely.

Their eyes met for a long time. 'I wish…' she said wistfully, her voice trailing away.

'You wish what?'

'I wish you could come to the party with me,' she said. 'Of course, you could drive your car if…if you were able to come with me.'

Declan had a sudden, fierce desire to say yes. He sure as hell didn't want her to go to her sister's party alone where she would be a magnet for any red-blooded male in the room—he wondered if she had any idea how outrageously sexy she looked. He had the urge to take off his jacket, fling it over her shoulders and tell her she had to keep it on all evening. *He wanted her for his eyes only.*

'If I could come—and I can't—you would be driving, not me,' he said.

She pulled one of her endearing faces. 'But, of course, you have your mother with you. Who seems very nice, by the way.'

Declan sucked in a quick breath. *Nice* wasn't the word he would ever use to describe his barracuda barrister mother.

'She's okay,' he acknowledged. 'She insists on bringing

her laptop over every few weeks for me to help her with it when I know very well she doesn't need help.'

'No doubt she wants to see if you're okay on your own,' she said. 'My mother checks in with me at least once every few days.'

'Perhaps,' he said. He didn't want to waste time talking about his mother. Not when Shelley's shawl was slipping off her shoulders again. This time he reached over and took it right off, sliding his hands down her bare arms. She trembled—from the cold in the garage or his touch?

'One more thing,' he said.

'About the car?' she asked, eyes wide.

'About this,' he said. He kissed her, hard and hungry and demanding—making sure she went to that party branded by his kisses. With a throaty little murmur of surprise and pleasure, she opened to him and met his tongue with hers, tasting, exploring, pressing her body to his—until want for her ignited through him in a flare of need. He broke away from her mouth, pressing hot kisses down her throat, tasting her, breathing in her sweet, arousing scent, sliding his hands to cup the enticing side swell of her breasts.

She moaned and wrenched herself away from him. 'Declan. No. Stop. If…if it was anything other than Lynne's party I wouldn't go, I'd stay here and we—'

'Don't say it,' he groaned. 'Go. Just go.'

She stared at him for a long moment, her breasts rising and falling as she struggled to control her breath. 'I wish… No. I have to go.' She planted a quick kiss on his mouth and went to step back but he snaked out his arm to tug her back and kiss her again. Only then did he wrest back control of his willpower and release her.

'Whatever time you get home, let me know,' he said, fighting to regain his breath in great, tearing gasps.

'Even if it's three in the morning?' Her lipstick was

smeared from his kisses, the pupils of her eyes so dilated he could scarcely see the colour, a pink beard rash around her chin. Good. Those other guys at the party would know she'd been thoroughly kissed and be warned off his woman.

His woman. When had he allowed himself to think of her as that?

'I'll be awake and waiting for you,' he said.

She slid behind the wheel of his car, as if she drove a high-performance sports vehicle every day, her dress sliding tantalisingly high up on her thighs. She laughed in exhilaration as the car started with a low, throaty roar.

'I am so going to enjoy this,' she called out to him.

He watched as she drove his favourite car, which no one else but he had ever driven, out of the garage and into the night, then he slammed his fist on the wall of the garage. He wanted to be with her. But here he was, surrounded by expensive cars in the garage of his multimillion-dollar mansion but cold and alone.

Only then came the full realisation of the prison he had created for himself.

Declan knew the second he got back in the house, his mother would grill him. She did not disappoint.

'Who is Shelley Fairhill and where did you find her?' she demanded, getting up from the sofa in the formal living room that was only used on her visits.

Declan shrugged. 'She found me,' he said. 'She knocked on the door and asked could she help me with the garden.'

'And you didn't glower and send her on the way?'

'Yes, I did,' he said, tight-lipped. 'But she persevered.' He added *glowering* to the list of words people used to describe him. *Forbidding* was still his favourite.

'I would have liked to have been a fly on the wall for that encounter. Did she—?'

'Long story.'

'And one I'm unlikely to hear the details of,' said his shrewd mother. 'She's beautiful, Declan. And obviously very talented at what she does.'

He nodded. What he felt about Shelley was his own business—he did not want to discuss it with anyone, certainly not his mother.

'Have you even *noticed* how beautiful Shelley is?' She put up her hand. 'Don't answer that. I saw the way you were looking at her—and the way she was looking at you.'

'What do you mean, the way she was looking at me?'

His mother laughed. 'I'm sure I don't have to tell you that. I haven't seen you smile so much for…for a long time.'

'You're imagining things,' he said stiffly.

'No, I'm not,' she said. 'I didn't get to be where I am without being able to read people. By the way, why was her car parked in your driveway?'

Reluctantly he replied. 'Because she's living in the apartment.'

'Oh,' said his mother with raised eyebrows.

'Nothing like that,' he said too hastily. 'She just needed somewhere to stay.'

His mother sighed. 'I believe you. But for your sake I wish it were otherwise. She's lovely, Declan—warm, open and she has kind eyes. I had a really good feeling about her.'

Declan gritted his teeth. 'She's all that and more,' he said. 'But what is it to you?'

His mother stilled. 'Despite what you think, I'm desperately concerned about you. Lisa was the best thing that ever happened to you, to the family. But she's gone, Declan. You're young. You can't let yourself just shrivel up and die inside because we lost Lisa. She would never have wanted you to lock yourself away like this.'

Declan gritted his teeth so hard his jaw ached. 'You know I—'

'You blame yourself. But it wasn't your fault. Lisa died of a sudden embolism. Nothing could have predicted it or prevented it. And baby Alice? That precious little girl was just born too soon. You mustn't let the tragedy of their loss cut you off from happiness in your future.'

Declan shifted from foot to foot. 'It's not like that.' He had convinced Lisa to get pregnant when she'd wanted to wait and she'd died in childbirth. *His fault.*

'Isn't it?' His mother persevered, much as she must do in court. 'I know I didn't love you enough when you were that fiercely intelligent, questioning little boy who had his own agenda from the word go. I didn't know how to be a mother. I'm doing my best to make up for it. You need love more *now* than you did when you were that little boy.'

He shook his head. 'I don't want to talk about this.'

'But you must,' she said. 'Don't close yourself off from the possibility of love. I saw how you looked at Shelley. I saw how she looked at you. You deserve love, no matter what you might think.'

Her voice caught in a tremor and he realised how difficult it was for his mother to be talking to him like this. He also saw how sincere she was.

'I'll take that on board,' he said, relenting.

'Whatever you might have thought in the past, whatever mistakes I've made, I'm on your side and I always will be. But I don't want to grow into one of those old women protecting her sad, middle-aged son who never got over his wife's loss. There's a beautiful young woman there who might help you move on. Shelley won't wait for ever, you know. Not a girl who looks like she does.'

'It's not just the way she looks,' he muttered. 'She's kind, honest, good. So much more than just beautiful.'

He decided to tell his mother about the new bed of roses Shelley had planted in honour of Lisa and Alice.

'What an incredibly sensitive and inspired thing to do.' His mother's voice was choked and she paused to wipe tears from her eyes. 'The tragedy of it comes rushing back. I wish they were both still with us. I loved Lisa like a daughter. But this Shelley, she's a rare one, Declan. Don't let her go. Trust me, it will be like another little death for you if you do.'

Declan thought about what she'd said long after his mother left to go home. All through the long, lonely evening as he worked on the background of the Estella portrait and waited for the sound of his car bringing Shelley back home.

CHAPTER TWELVE

SHELLEY RECKONED SHE could have gone home from Lynne's party with the phone numbers of at least three good-looking, single—or so they said—eligible men. And that wasn't counting the television producer—she'd actually given him her number after ascertaining he was the real deal.

There was something to be said about a backless dress. Or maybe it was the reckless confidence that came from being so thoroughly kissed by the man she wanted before she'd sashayed on to the party. The power of pulling up to a party in a sports car probably did something to enhance her desirability to the male population, too.

But she didn't collect any phone numbers. There was only one man who interested her and she was on her way home to him. Well, not technically home to him. He lived in the mansion, she lived in the housekeeper's apartment and she'd be wise to remember that.

It was well past midnight when she pulled into the garage—the party was still in full swing but she'd only stayed as late as she did for Lynne's sake. Before she could think about texting Declan that she was back, the connecting door from the main house opened and he was there. He still wore the same jacket, but his hair was dishevelled as though he had been pushing through it with his fingers as she'd noticed he tended to do. Dark shadows under his eyes indicated he hadn't slept. His face wore an expression of strained expectancy. *Was that for her?*

A surge of desire for him swept through her so powerfully she had to remain seated in the driver's seat and grip the steering wheel so tightly her knuckles went white and press her knees together hard. Not just sexual desire—although there was certainly that in spades—but an intense yearning to be with him, to help ease his pain, to feel his arms around her, for him to be *hers*. Her heart seemed to physically turn over in her chest with longing for this darkly handsome man who had become so important, so quickly.

She took her time to gather her evening purse and shawl, slide out of the car, lock the door, to give herself a chance to collect her feelings before she faced him. Right now, a cheerful recounting of the assets of his superb car did not seem possible.

But words did not seem to be required as he strode towards her and opened his arms. 'You're home,' he said. She went into them with a great, choking sigh of relief and shut her eyes in bliss as they closed around her and enveloped her in his strength and warmth.

He held her tight, his chin resting on the top of her head. She could feel the rise and fall of his chest, the thud of his heartbeat, strong, steady, reassuring and she let herself relax against him.

For a long, enchanted moment she stood there like that, unaware of her surroundings, the concrete walls and floor of the garage, the other cars shrouded in grey covers, the intermittent *ping-ping-ping* sounds the sports car made as its engine cooled down. She was aware only of Declan— and the joy that flooded her heart at being so close to him, the certainty that this was where she was meant to be. *That everything that had come before in her life had led to this.*

'Declan,' she finally murmured, loving the sound of his name in her voice.

He pulled her even closer. She could feel the strength of his thighs, rock hard with muscle. 'I spent all evening wishing you were with me,' she murmured, then pulled back in his arms, needing to see his face.

His arms dropped from around her, leaving her bereft. Then he cupped her face in his large hands, hands she noticed were stained with traces of paint—blue, green, white all mixed in together—and smelled vaguely of turpentine. He caressed the little hollows in front of her ears—such a simple gesture yet it sent shivers of pleasure to her deepest core.

'I spent all evening regretting I wasn't,' he said hoarsely.

She met his gaze. 'I'm glad. I mean, I'm glad I'm not imagining this...this thing between us. These...these feelings.'

Declan groaned and her heart gave a painful lurch. *He was going to fight it all the way.* 'I...don't know what to do about...about you. I wasn't expecting, didn't—'

'Didn't *want...*' she supplied the words for him.

'That's right. I didn't want the life I'd made for myself disturbed. Then you burst into it, flooding light into the shadows in which I existed.'

She swallowed hard against a sudden lump of tension in her throat. *She didn't know how to reply.*

He looked deeper into her face. 'But eyes that have become accustomed to the dark can...can be dazzled by too much light too quickly. They blink and wonder what hit them.'

'Like a bat,' she said.

Shelley stilled, mortified. *Where had that idiotic comment come from?*

Declan stilled too. His eyes widened as he stared at her.

And then she realised he was shaking with laughter he was fighting a losing battle to suppress.

'I… I'm sorry,' she stuttered. 'I can't believe I just said that.'

'First a vampire, now a bat. You really do see me as a creature of darkness, don't you?'

He let go his laughter and she couldn't help but laugh alongside him though it felt forced. But when the laughter spluttered to a halt, stopped, she berated herself. 'Why do I say things like that? Why don't I think before I speak? I've been told often enough.'

'Because you're *you*, delightful and unique and I wouldn't have you any other way.'

She sniffed back threatening tears. 'Really?' A niggling voice deep down inside her prodded her—was that ill-timed comment her way of deflecting emotional confrontations she wasn't at all sure she was equipped to handle?

'Yes,' he said. 'Really. I've laughed more since I've known you than I have since…since heaven knows when.' He sobered. 'Don't change—promise me?'

She nodded. 'I… I promise.'

'Now how about we go inside out of this chilly garage?' he said.

'Yes,' she said. She went to add: *It's hardly the most romantic place on earth* but bit down on the words. There had been no mention of *romance* between them.

He put his arm around her shoulder and steered her towards the door. 'You can think of some other dark creatures to compare me to. Maybe something that lives under a rock.'

Of course she took him literally and started to think of actual creatures that lived under rocks before she realised that was not what was required. 'Not for one second will I compare you to a centipede or a slug.'

'And I so appreciate that,' he said. 'Vampires and bats have a certain black glamour that slugs definitely do not.'

They laughed again as he walked her, with his arm still around her shoulders, into the house. Lights switched on automatically ahead of them but she immediately felt oppressed by the stillness, the vague mustiness of unlived-in rooms. She wanted to extend her time with him this evening but not here, not in this place so marked by tragedy and loss and dreams unfulfilled.

'Did you…are you going to bed now?' she asked, immediately wishing she'd said *sleep* and not *bed* with all its unspoken connotations.

'No. You?' He tightened his grip on her shoulder.

She shook her head. 'I'm still way too wired up from the party. Can I…can I interest you in a herbal tea or coffee— I don't drink coffee at night but you might want coffee— and perhaps a muffin? I baked banana muffins the other day and have them in the freezer. I just have to heat—'

Those dark brows drew together. 'Did you say banana muffins?'

She nodded, wishing now she hadn't brought up the subject. Not when she never wanted to admit how she had snuck into his house in her pyjamas and spied on him as he'd worked out.

'Strange, that,' he said. 'I thought I could smell banana muffins in my kitchen. That inter-connecting door is meant to be odour, sound and light-proof.'

She froze. 'Maybe…maybe you'd better get the door checked—the seals might need attention,' she finally managed to get out.

'I will,' he said.

'Let's go through,' she said.

'I don't have a key. The apartment is your private place.'

She'd wondered if he'd maintained access to the apartment, was glad that he hadn't.

'I... I have the key on the key ring in my purse,' she said.

The apartment seemed a sanctuary but somehow smaller with Declan's tall, broad-shouldered presence taking up so much room. She stood near him in the living room, suddenly very conscious that they were alone in complete privacy.

A meaningless fling. The words echoed through her head and her body tingled in all sorts of places at the thought of what that might entail. He hadn't offered one, why shouldn't she?

Not *meaningless* but *without commitment*—commitment she very much doubted Declan was prepared to make, despite the kind words he'd said about her lighting his darkness. *She wanted him so much.*

She turned to face him, thrilled to the desire for her she saw smouldering in his eyes. Her shawl was long gone and she knew from all the compliments she'd fielded at the party that she quite possibly looked the best she ever had in the blue dress.

But she'd been the one to deny the possibility of a fling. She would have to be the one to suggest it. She took the few steps needed to close the distance between them. She wound her arms around his neck, drew his face close and kissed him, her lips parted in a sensual invitation he accepted with a hard, hungry possession.

Pleasure and anticipation throbbed through her as she welcomed his mouth, his tongue, his passion. His hands slid around to her back, hard and exciting on her bare skin. She slid her hands from his neck so she could push off his jacket, tug his T-shirt from his belt with impatient fingers, splay her hands flat against the warm, solid muscle of his chest, feel the rapid thudding of his heart.

Her breath was coming in short, ragged gasps echoed by his. She wanted him so badly it was an ache. Every physical instinct she had screamed at her to proceed. To let Declan caress her—and her caress him back. To rid themselves of their clothes. To stagger into the bedroom locked in each other's arms and fall together on the bed. To bring each other's body to the peaks of ultimate pleasure.

But her instincts for common sense, for self-preservation, overrode them and begged her to stop this before it went any further. It was too soon—not just for her but for him.

She'd never been one for sex without emotion, without love. And she sensed that would never develop if the physical took over while the emotional lagged so far behind. Oh, but she wanted him so much she burned with it.

But as his hand grazed the side of her breasts, as her nipples tightened to hard points and hunger for him throbbed through her body she knew she couldn't go through with a fling of any kind. That way lay certain heartbreak and she should have realised it before it got this far.

Meaningless would never be for her, no matter how you masked it.

She broke away from the kiss, panting. It was an effort to speak. 'Declan. No. I mean… I mean… I mean stop.' *That sounded like such a cliché.* 'I don't want you to think I'm a…a tease but I can't go further than this. I thought I could. I want you. Want you more than I could ever have imagined but—'

He pulled away immediately, his breathing ragged and harsh. 'But you're not ready.'

She struggled for the right words. 'Are you? I would make love with you in a heartbeat but I don't think either of us is ready for that…that complication. Not now. Not yet. Some time I hope if you…when we…' She did not want him to think she was assuming they would work towards being a couple—though there was nothing she wanted more.

He paced the width of the room and she could see it was an effort for him to restore his equilibrium. 'You're right. It's too soon. I'm only just getting used to the thought of another woman—you—in my life. I don't want to hurt you.'

He took the few strides necessary to bring him back to her. Then groaned in a wrenching anguish of frustration that called to her too and planted a hard, hungry kiss on her mouth. 'But be in no doubt how much I want you. How difficult it is for me to stop.'

This was a man who knew how to love. She was prepared to wait until he felt able to love again. No matter how long that took.

She stepped back before her resolve broke and she flung herself at him and begged him for anything he was prepared to give. Another deep breath restored the beating of her heart to something less erratic.

'How…how about that muffin?' she asked, desperate to change the subject.

'Satisfy a different kind of hunger, you mean,' he said with a wry twist of that mouth she wanted so much to kiss and kiss and kiss again.

'That's one way of putting it,' she said.

Declan watched Shelley move around the small kitchen with the same efficiency of movement she gave to her work. A warrior who could cook—and cook well. She'd put the frozen muffin in the microwave and a delicious—and familiar—aroma was wafting its way to his nose. He was hungry. All his appetites had diminished in the intensity of his grief after Lisa died. But Shelley had awoken them and they came raging back. Especially his hunger for her.

She'd kicked off her shoes before she went into the kitchen. But she still wore that tantalising blue dress. He had to stop fantasising about stripping it off her, of releasing those chains that were all that held it together. She was wearing panties under the dress, he'd ascertained that in his first explorations. But no bra. Unhook that chain and the dress would fall to the floor leaving her in just panties and her silver stilettos—and then not even them.

He forced himself to think thoughts other than of undressing Shelley and carrying her into the bedroom. He leaned against the countertop.

'Tell me about the party,' he said, though he had no real interest in it. She'd come home to him and that was all that counted.

'I met a television producer. A friend of a friend of Keith's. He was really nice.'

Jealousy speared him. 'I'll bet he was.' What male wouldn't be nice to Shelley in that dress?

'Not in that way,' she said, shaking her head. 'He was there with his wife, and she was really interesting too. He produces a lifestyle show for one of the cable channels. As soon as he heard what I did he asked me would I be interested in being their gardening presenter. They want gardening to be seen as younger and…and sexier.'

Declan couldn't help his growl of possessive jealousy. 'What do you mean "sexier"?'

'Not me. Well, yes, maybe me, in that I'm young and female compared to the older guy they already have who is retiring, but they want to appeal to younger viewers who might think of gardening as something for their grandparents. He said he was excited about me because I was… well…attractive but also authoritative and knew my stuff.'

The growl subsided. 'Fair enough.'

'I was really flattered that he was interested in me.'

'Of course he'd be interested in you. Why wouldn't he? He must have thought all his Christmases had come at once. What did you say to him?'

'I told him about my plans to go visit the gardens in Europe.'

'So you'd put those plans on hold if you were to take him up on the offer?' Which would give him more time with her.

'I'd have to audition first before there would even be an offer,' she said.

'You'd be a natural for it,' he said.

'That's what he said,' she said with a delighted smile. 'He also said they could work around my travel plans if need be, that I can pre-record a series of segments filmed at those famous gardens. It would be like bringing them into the viewers' homes.'

'You obviously like the idea,' he said, knowing he sounded stilted but unable to do anything about it. She would leave here no matter what he did and he couldn't stop her. Not until he had something to offer her.

'I do,' she said. 'Gardening is really hard physical work. I don't know that I could do it for ever. This could be a really wonderful opportunity to still do what I love but in a different way.'

'It's certainly worth considering,' he said. Anything that might delay her departure would be worth considering.

He helped her to carry the chamomile tea and plate of muffins to the coffee table. Then sat down beside her. She kept a polite distance away from him but he pulled her close and she snuggled in next to him with a contented little sigh that pleased him inordinately.

'Aren't you going to have a muffin?' he asked as she sipped her tea. 'Mine is absolutely delicious.'

She shook her head. 'Too tired to eat,' she said. 'The

muffins are for you and I'm glad you like them. I thought you might.'

The muffins were everything he'd hoped his ill-fated muffin delivery would have been, and more.

She put down the pretty old-fashioned teacup that he doubted was part of the apartment's inventory. 'I'm even too tired to drink the tea—which is fine as it's meant to help you sleep and I don't think I need any help. I was digging and moving shrubs all day and it's way past my bedtime. It's suddenly hit me.' She stifled a yawn with her hand.

He pulled her closer and she snuggled her head against his shoulder. He could not resist dropping a kiss on her hair, inhaling the fresh, sweet scent of her. It was intoxicating.

'Tell me more about what the television producer said,' he asked.

'Well, the studio is in Sydney but they shoot at gardens all around the country. The producer was really interested when he heard how familiar I was with Victoria. There are some really beautiful gardens in Victoria, South Australia too. I reckon some of my former clients would love to have their gardens showcased. Or just used as a location for me to demonstrate gardening techniques.' She yawned again and her body relaxed against his. 'People don't know... don't know...about pruning and...and stuff,' she murmured and her voice trailed into nothing. Her breathing became deep and even and he realised she had fallen asleep.

He held her there for a long time until he started to get sleepy too—blessedly sleepy. Carefully he shifted on the sofa, planning to slide off and help her lie down. 'No. Don't want you to go. Stay with me,' she whispered. He wasn't sure she was even awake. But he didn't want to leave her either.

Declan tried to get comfortable but both he and Shelley were tall and the sofa wasn't long enough. His leg started to cramp.

There was only one thing to do. He got up from the sofa, despite her sleepy protests, then swung her effortlessly into his arms and carried her through to the bedroom. He pulled back the quilt and laid her on the bed, her honey-blond hair spilling out over the pillow. She shifted and opened her eyes, though they were unfocused and again he wasn't really sure she was awake. She held out her arms. 'Stay with me. Please.'

He would stay just until she fell into a deep sleep—a luxury that had been denied him for too long.

Cautiously, he took off his shoes and lay down next to her. She immediately burrowed close, pressing the length of her body against his.

I'm sorry, Lisa, he said in his mind, feeling as if he was betraying her memory, but immediately had the feeling that she wouldn't mind at all, that Lisa was giving him her blessing.

He held Shelley close as he in turn drifted off to sleep.

Declan awoke to morning sunshine filtering through the blinds to find Shelley spooning into his back, one arm wrapped around his waist, the other resting above her head on her pillow.

He was aroused. How could he not be with her breasts pressing into his back, her long, slender legs entwined with his, her sweet womanly scent heady and exciting? He placed his hand on her bare shoulder and she murmured throatily in her sleep as she pressed herself even closer. But it would not be right to stroke her into arousal to wake her by—

He rolled onto his back, gently disengaging her arm. The sunlight picked up glints of gold in her hair and her make-up was smeared dark around her eyes. Her lips were slightly parted as she breathed deeply and steadily. He had never seen her look more beautiful.

It was the first deep, refreshing sleep he had enjoyed for two years. He felt deeply content and…he sought to describe the feeling that overwhelmed him as he lay there so intimately close to Shelley, but could only come up with *happy*.

CHAPTER THIRTEEN

SHELLEY LOVED EVERYTHING about Declan's garden and was immensely proud of the restoration work she had done. Spring was taking over—the crab apple tree in a froth of delicate pink blossom, daffodils that had naturalised over many years coming up in golden drifts in the lawn, the scent of daphne replaced by that of old-fashioned white freesias.

The restored dry stonewalls and hedges delineated the concept of separate garden 'rooms' that made the space such a delight. She had even uncovered a small kitchen garden with an espaliered lemon tree growing flat against a wall, a rosemary hedge and herbs, including sage, tarragon plus three different varieties of thyme. She would plant annual herbs like basil and coriander if she thought anyone would use them in their one season of growth. Declan? He'd told her he rarely cooked but he might have use for fresh herbs. She must ask him.

In the front of the garden, the climbing rose 'Lamarque' was covered in hundreds of white buds ready to burst into glorious bloom—as she had promised Declan it would. Those higher rooms in his house must now be flooded with light and soon the delicate scent of the roses. *But would she be here to see it?*

The more she worked on the garden, the more she appreciated its design, and the work of the gardeners who had come before her. The original design certainly paid homage to Enid Wilson, which was perhaps one of the reasons she'd been so drawn to it.

But on Sunday morning—the day after Lynne's party— even though she wasn't officially working, she decided to spend the morning sorting out the shed.

It was a late start. She'd awoken to the surprise of finding Declan in her bed. Well, technically *on* her bed and fully clothed—as she was too. She'd only vaguely remembered him carrying her into the bedroom the night before. He'd stayed while she'd cooked him breakfast then he'd gone back to his part of the house.

But before he'd gone he'd kissed her and said he would catch up with her later in the day. She'd been itching to ask *when* but had resisted. Declan was coming from a dark place—if anything important was going to develop between them, it wouldn't be overnight. Hope, like the spring garden, had blossomed in her heart.

She'd rebelled at wearing her gardening uniform on a Sunday. After all, it was officially her day off and she was going to fit in a ride with Flynn if she could. And, yes, if she *was* going to catch up with Declan she'd rather be seen in something other than khaki.

She didn't want to look too eager, either, so compromised with slim-legged blue jeans and a shirt with fine stripes of blue and lavender. Eye make-up and lipstick for working in the shed? Why not? With her hair in a long plait down her back instead of jammed up under a hat. And her favourite French rose perfume liberally sprayed on her pulse spots.

Over the last weeks she'd managed to get some semblance of order into the shed and turned it into a useful workshop. She'd sorted out many of the wonderful old tools and garden implements. Having a wide, clear workbench made it easier to strike cuttings, plant seeds in trays, change the soil and trim the roots of potted plants and was especially useful in wet weather. But there was a large, weatherproof metal chest she hadn't yet tackled.

Wearing her sturdy gloves, she'd brushed off the dust and cobwebs from the chest and was just about to force open the rusted lid when she heard the door opening. She turned and her heart leapt in delight to see Declan. He came over and dropped a kiss on her mouth. 'I've come down to give you a hand,' he said.

Shelley was stunned. Never had she expected that Declan would help her in the garden, the billionaire descending from his tower. 'Thank you,' she said. She hadn't expected the kiss either; casual as it had been, it was a real turning point.

He was wearing jeans and a faded grey T-shirt with sleeves that rolled up to his biceps and showed off his impressive pecs and broad shoulders. She wondered if he had left her after breakfast to do one of his gruelling workouts. He had not shaved and she decided she liked the dark stubble on his jaw, the graze of it on her skin.

'What can I do to help?' he asked.

'I'll think of something,' she said.

Shelley could think of a number of things she would like to direct Declan to do. None of them had anything to do with gardening. Just looking at him brought a flush of desire.

But she hadn't changed her mind since the previous night. When she'd woken up next to Declan, she had been relieved they hadn't made love. It took the pressure off getting to know each other, to take small steps instead of leaping in head first. To be certain.

'What's in the chest?' he asked. It still bemused her that he owned this wonderful garden and yet knew so very little—and cared even less—about the treasures it contained.

'I have no idea,' she said. 'If I can get the lid off we'll find out.'

'Let me do that,' he said. With one firm wrench he had the lid up.

They were met with the musty scent of old paper. She peered into the depths of the chest. There was a number of what looked like old diaries and a bundle of papers wrapped in oilskin and tied firmly with sturdy string.

She didn't need Declan's warning to watch out for spiders. Tentatively she reached into the chest and pulled out two of the diaries, flipped through their pages. 'They're garden diaries,' she said, unable to keep the excitement from her voice. 'Can you get the rest, please?'

Declan pulled out all the diaries and put them on the desk. It only took him a few minutes to stack them in chronological order. 'They date right back to pre-World War Two,' he said.

She picked one up randomly and flicked through the pages. Then another. And another. 'This is gardener's gold,' she said. 'Daphne and before that her mother, Lily, kept meticulous dairies about their work in the garden. What they planted, what worked, what didn't. When the first tomatoes ripened. When they sprayed for bugs. How they dealt with water restrictions in times of drought.'

She turned to Declan. 'It's the history of your garden. One of the grand old gardens of Sydney. A hidden gem.'

'That's quite a find,' he said.

'Aren't you just the littlest bit excited?' she asked.

'Why would I be?' he said. 'But I'm glad you're excited.'

'Of course I'm thrilled,' she said. 'I can't wait to read through them all.'

'Remember, it was Lisa's garden not…not mine. She… she would have been excited.'

Shelley gripped the edge of the diary in her hand. *Lisa.* Lucky Lisa in one way as she had had Declan's love, yet so very tragic that she had died so young in such sad circumstances. Yes, Lisa probably would have been excited to find the diaries. If things had been different she and Lisa might have been working together on the restoration of this garden with doting husband Declan occasionally dropping by to check on the progress of his wife's project. Vivacious Lisa, remembered now in the garden with a planting of roses that would every year in late spring be a blaze of vibrant colour.

But Lisa was gone and, no matter how he grieved, Declan could not bring her back. Shelley as a gardener knew only too well about the cycle of death and renewal of life. The shrivelled autumn leaves making way for the fresh green shoots of spring. The perennial plants that died right down in winter only to shoot gloriously to life when the days got longer. The caterpillars she let chew holes on some of the leaves so they survived to transform into butterflies. All around her in this garden she was witnessing that everyday miracle.

From what she had heard about Lisa, she doubted she would have wanted her husband to spend the rest of his years alone, to live a shadowy half life with a shrivelled husk of a heart.

Shelley made a silent vow to the dead woman: if she had the chance she would rescue Declan from his blighted life, make him happy and— She fought against using the word *love*. Not now. Not yet. She had jumped too soon into *love* before and suffered heartbreak. But if she were granted a future with Declan, she would allow herself to love him and cherish him. *He'll be in good hands, Lisa.*

But if she and Declan had any chance of that future together she had to ask. 'Declan, why do you blame yourself for Lisa's death?'

The colour drained from his face, leaving it as grey as his T-shirt. 'Because I should have got her to the hospital quicker. The doctors said it wouldn't have made any difference but I've asked myself over and over if those ten minutes I took to complete my work might have made a difference. I let my work come before her.'

'Wh… What exactly happened? I know you said she… she died in childbirth but…how exactly?'

She had never seen him look so bleak and drawn. 'The baby was premature but that apparently wasn't what caused it.'

He paused and she waited to let him gather his thoughts, stomping down on her usual urge to fill a blank silence.

'Tiny Alice had to be put on a ventilator—her lungs weren't properly developed. I went with the doctors to see what was happening. But while I was in the neonatal intensive care unit with her one of the other doctors came to find me. Lisa had complained of feeling faint. They were concerned. By the time I got back to her bed she… she'd slipped away.'

Shelley closed her eyes. She wished she hadn't asked. Could scarcely comprehend his anguish and pain. But she had to know.

'How? Why?'

'An embolism. A blood clot. It lodged in her heart. There was nothing the doctors could do. There was no warning.'

She put her hand on his arm. 'Declan, I am so, so sorry. Thank you for telling me. It…it helps me to understand you better.'

'I wish I could understand it better myself,' he said savagely, his mouth a bitter twist.

She had to tread lightly. 'But seems to me that there can be absolutely no blame attached to you.'

'So they told me. But I *should* have been able to stop it.'

'How? If a team of highly trained doctors couldn't have saved her and your baby, how could you have?'

'I know all that,' he said. 'But I... I... Lisa wanted to wait a few more years. If I hadn't cajoled her into starting a family earlier it...it wouldn't have happened.'

'How can you say that? Something else might have taken her. An accident. Disease. Anything. It was out of your hands.'

In response he made some inarticulate sound that speared her heart.

A millionaire at age eighteen. A billionaire in his twenties. Here was a brilliant man used to making things happen his way. Yet he had not been able to save his little family. And had turned it all back on himself.

Was Declan really ready to move forward? Would he *ever* be ready? And did she have the strength to be the one to help him? To keep on shining her light—as he put it—into the shadowy recesses of his soul?

She would darn well try.

She put her arms around him and was mightily relieved he didn't push her away.

'It's dusty in here,' she said. 'Let's go outside. Maybe I can make you a coffee.'

His face was set like granite. 'I don't need to be babied, Shelley. I've been living with this for two years. I can deal with it.'

Yes—if locking yourself away from the rest of the world meant dealing with it.

'If you're sure you're not letting misplaced guilt—'

'Maybe I am.' He looked deep into her face. To her relief there was a softening of his features, a dawning warmth in his eyes. 'But...but for the first time I'm beginning to believe I can forgive myself. You. My mother. You're helping.'

'And you're letting yourself be helped. That's the first step.'

'But I have to do it at my pace. I don't want to talk about it any more. Not now. Not ever.'

Shelley shook her head so vehemently her plait flew around to the front. 'There you go, being so black and white about it. You *can* talk about it. You *should* talk about it. And when you're ready I'm here to listen.'

She held out her arms to him and he came to her, holding her close against the solid wall of muscle that was his chest. She felt him take a deep, shuddering breath. 'Thank you, Shelley. I'm glad you're here,' he said simply.

Her heart soared at this first recognition of her place in his life. 'I'm happy to be here for you.'

They stood like that for a long time until Shelley pulled away. She looked up at him. 'I'm not going to talk about bats or vampires, I promise.'

He smiled. 'I don't mind them. It's the slugs I don't like being compared to.'

'And rightly so,' she said. 'It's plants I'm thinking about—plants that thrive in the shade. If you dig them up and plunk them straight away into the bright sunlight they shrivel up and die. Moving them from the shadow to sun is a gradual process. It might be the same with you—too much light too soon might mean—'

He tilted her chin so she looked straight up into his face 'If you're the light, Shelley, I don't think I could have too much of you,' he said.

She met his gaze for a long moment as the import of

his words ticked through her. 'That…that's good,' she stuttered. 'You don't mind being compared to a plant? I'm talking plants that can live indoors like *hosta* and *spathiphyllum* and—'

There she went, deflecting anything emotional when it came to her. *Why did she do this?*

'Baffling me with Latin again,' he said.

'You might know a *spathiphyllum* as a peace lily. At least I'm not comparing you to mushrooms,' she said. 'They love living in the dark and they feed on sh— Well, they feed on manure.'

Declan laughed and she loved the sound of his rare laughter. 'I'll add mushroom to the list of my attributes,' he said in a voice choked with mirth. Then he sobered. 'You really are adorable, Shelley. Don't change.'

She looked up at him. 'Just be honest with me, Declan, that's all I ask. I… I so want to be the light in your life.'

He pulled her to him and kissed her. For a long time they kissed in the filtered sunlight coming through the dusty windows of the old shed. Kissing, touching, exploring.

The pile of papers wrapped in oilskin would have to wait.

Nothing was more important than this.

CHAPTER FOURTEEN

A WEEK LATER, Shelley stood in the spring sunshine in front of the fountain, tapping her foot impatiently. She could hardly wait to tell Declan the news that was consuming her but he was taking his time coming downstairs to the garden.

Deep breaths, Shelley, deep breaths, she told herself. She concentrated on the soothing splash of the water falling down the three tiers of the fountain, admired her plantings of purple and yellow Louisiana iris unfurling into bloom. The goldfish had doubled in size since she'd set them free into the waters of the pond, adding welcome flashes of gold as they flitted in and out of the plants. There were plenty of places for them to hide from interested kookaburras and other fisher birds.

She was struck by a sudden flash of déjà vu. Hadn't she stood at the site of the derelict fountain and imagined just this scene—right down to the goldfish?

Back then she couldn't have predicted how important this place would become to her. Most of all she could never have imagined how close she would become to Declan. Then Mr Tall, Dark and Grumpy, now...well, now he was everything she could ever want in a man.

The last week had been an accelerated getting-to-know-you process. She'd gone from teetering on the edge of falling in love with Declan to preparing to dive on in head first.

He got her. He accepted her for the way she was, didn't just put up with her foibles but actually seemed to like them. She could relax and be herself around him as she'd never been able to before. It was an exhilarating feeling.

She was ready to take the next step. Tonight she was cooking him dinner at the apartment. Sex would change the dynamic between them but it was getting more and more difficult to stop at kisses—for both of them. But she judged she was ready for that change—and she suspected he felt the same.

Then she saw him, heading towards her with the smile that seemed to have replaced his perpetual scowl. *Because of her*. She had made the difference—she made him smile with her encouragement, her support, her not-going-to-call-it-that-yet love. Oh, and the gaffes and blunders she still made in spite of her best efforts. But they made him laugh.

'You in a pink dress, the fountain, the flowers—I wish I had my camera on me,' he said. 'You make a beautiful picture.'

She was still getting used to this Declan, still surprised at the man who was revealing himself by gradually peeling off layer by protective layer. 'Thank you,' she said.

He swooped her into his arms and spun her around. 'So what's the big excitement that couldn't wait?'

Declan wished he could pause that moment of Shelley standing in front of the fountain with a look of anticipation on her face as she'd lifted her head from something she was examining in the fountain to see him. Not just anticipation. Affection too. *For him*. She was giving him the second chance he'd thought he hadn't deserved.

He wanted to paint her like this. Not Estella. *Shelley*. Not a mythical warrior woman created from his own imagination but the real woman whose warm heart and generosity of spirit were slowly thawing his own frozen emotions.

He swooped her, laughing, back to earth, set her on her feet and waited for her reply.

Her eyes were wide and sparkling. 'First I went to see the television producer and he's very interested in progressing the presenter role with me.'

'That *is* good news,' he said. 'Well done.' He hoped she would get the job. And that it would keep her here in Sydney.

She pulled out a large envelope from her tote bag. 'But the mind-blowing news is this,' she said. 'Though of course you might not find it as mind-blowing as I did. After all, I know you—'

'Get on with it,' he said with a smile that he knew she would see as indulgent. The day Shelley didn't rabbit on was the day he'd be concerned.

'Do you remember when we opened the old chest in the shed last week and found the diaries?'

'Of course.' How could he forget that time with her in that darned shed she liked so much? Although it was memories of her in his arms that came to mind rather than the set of old notebooks that had caused her such pleasure.

'I went back into the shed the next day to look at that bundle of papers that were wrapped in the oilskin.'

'I remember them,' he said. He'd been thankful she'd forgotten them and he could keep on kissing her. If there'd been somewhere more comfortable in that shed than a wooden work bench there might have been a whole lot more than kissing going on in there.

Shelley tapped the envelope. 'These are those papers.' Reverently, she pulled out a sheaf of the old documents, yellowed and faded around the edges, and pointed to the hand-drawn illustrations. 'These are original plans by Enid

Wilson for this garden. Look, there's the fountain, the walls, everything. Can you believe it?'

Declan took the plans from her hands, held them up to the light, looked at them critically. 'The plans certainly look like this garden. They're beautifully rendered in watercolour.' His grandmother's favourite medium had been watercolour. 'These are good. Very good,' he said, judging them as paintings rather than horticultural plans.

'Of course they are. Enid Wilson was an artist. Her plans were works of art and so were her gardens.' Her voice rose with her excitement. 'Your garden wasn't just inspired by her designs, it was actually designed by her.'

She waved her hand to encompass the garden. 'This is an undiscovered Enid Wilson garden.'

She seemed disappointed that he didn't pick up on her excitement. He'd told her often enough he had no real interest in gardening—the interest for him in this garden was her. 'Well, that's great,' he said, forcing interest into his voice for her sake.

She smiled. 'I get that you don't see what I see in these amazing plans.'

'Tell me what you see,' he said, prepared to stand back and listen to her enthusiastic explanation.

'As I uncovered the garden I had my suspicions. It seemed such a fabulously good imitation of a Wilson garden. There are later additions, of course, like those dreaded *ficus benjamina*. But more and more I came to think it had all the hallmarks of her designs.'

Declan frowned. 'Why is it such a big deal?'

'Most of Enid Wilson's gardens were in Victoria. She designed some gardens in this state but to my knowledge they were all rural. I didn't know if there were any city gardens in Sydney. That's one reason I didn't take my hunch too seriously. It seemed unlikely and there was no proof.' She flourished the plans. 'These are proof. It's the most amazing discovery. *My* discovery.' Her eyes shone.

He frowned. 'How can you be sure? Couldn't the plans be imitations too?'

'That's what I thought. That's why I didn't tell you until I could get an expert to look at them for me and confirm their authenticity. I scanned the plans and sent them to one of my professors in Melbourne.'

'You *what*?'

'Yes, wasn't it fortunate he was available? He's validated them as genuine. He's excited too. I hope he can get up here and see the garden for himself. I didn't say anything to the television producer, of course, but wouldn't it be the most amazing story? To reveal this hidden masterpiece?'

She kept on and on and didn't seem to realise that his enthusiasm had dwindled to zero. In fact he was furious.

'No,' he said.

She pulled up, stared at him, obviously shocked at his abrupt tone.

'What do you mean "no"?'

'There will be no visiting professors. Or any other experts. And certainly no television people.'

He felt as if he were under attack. And she—the woman he had grown to trust—was the one who'd punched a hole in the barricades to allow access to the invaders of his privacy. For so long this house had been his refuge and his haven. He would not tolerate people tramping around the place, investigating, reporting, no doubt expecting interaction from him. He wouldn't allow it. He *couldn't* allow it. *How did Shelley not get that?*

'But, Declan, this is such a find. People will be so excited about this discovery. Personally, it's so important to me, important to my career.'

He kept hold of the papers. 'These plans belong to me. You had no right to take them out of this house. To show them to other people. To invite so-called experts onto my property without my permission.'

He hated the way her face crumpled at the harshness of his words. 'I didn't realise. I honestly thought you'd be pleased,' she said.

Her mouth twisted in a cynical way he hadn't seen before and certainly didn't like. 'Your neighbours will be pleased. A heritage garden like this will add value to the street.'

'I don't give a damn about my neighbours. You should know that by now.'

Her eyes flashed. 'What do you give a damn about, Declan? Certainly not me. You won't even consider what this could mean to my career.'

'Give me the rest of the papers,' he said, reaching out for the envelope. Reluctantly, she handed them to him.

One part of him wanted to climb down. To compromise. To say she could be recognised as having discovered the lost garden. To possibly invite her professor for a private visit just the one time.

But that would be opening the floodgates. And he wasn't ready for that. Not by a long shot.

'Don't discuss this with me again,' he said over his shoulder as he strode back to the house.

Still shaking from Declan's abrupt change of mood, Shelley walked around the garden to calm herself down, to let the tranquillity of this beautiful place soothe her and work the kind of magic only nature could.

He was right; she'd overstepped the mark. How could she have let her enthusiasm for her discovery override her caution in dealing with Declan?

When it came to emerging from the shadows of his isolation she'd decided he needed to walk before he could run. So she'd darn well dug in the spurs and tried to force him to gallop.

He was still too damaged to face public scrutiny of any kind—especially on his own turf. Why hadn't she seen how far from ready he was to let down his guard and face the world? Instead she had just gone blundering in there, as was her way.

She sighed out loud, knowing there was no one to hear her. *Was Declan too much for her to manage?*

Her walk around the garden brought her back to the fountain. She thought about how hopeless a project it had seemed at the beginning, all damaged and dirty, unable to fulfil its function as a garden ornament, let alone a working water feature. Even she had quailed at the difficulty of restoring it. Had considered just pulling it down and filling in the pond. But she'd persevered—helped, of course, by Declan's generous budget—and look at it now.

Declan was still broken. But she was prepared to work with him. These last weeks she'd been given glimpses of the extraordinary man he had been—could be again. *And beyond all reason she wanted him.*

No matter how angry he was with her, she intended to hang around. It would take time, more time than she might have imagined. But she could postpone her trip to Europe. When this garden was complete, she could find another job in Sydney. Her old employer had said he would welcome her back. And then there was the television opportunity. Declan might be convinced to let her remain in the apartment. She would be there for him. For however long it took.

He was worth it.

Her gaze went automatically up to the top-storey window where he worked. She could text him now and ask him to come down to her again. So she could apologise. Explain. State her case. *Let him know how much she cared.*

But no.

She had her key that opened the door into the kitchen of his house. She would not give him a chance to think up excuses to put up his barriers against her again.

She would brave him in his house. Surprise him. Tell him exactly how she felt. Even if the thought terrified her.

CHAPTER FIFTEEN

SHELLEY'S HEART WAS pounding so hard she imagined Declan could hear it—even from two floors above her. She tiptoed down his hallway in stockinged feet, holding in one hand the metallic pumps she'd worn with her pink dress to the interview with the television producer.

She paused before the elevator, decided against it. Too uncertain. What if she got trapped in it? It would have to be the stairs.

Cautiously she made her way up the flight of marble stairs with its ornate iron balustrades, past the silent floor of doors closed on what she assumed were bedrooms and bathrooms. Sad, unlived-in rooms.

She paused at the next landing to look out of the leadlight window at the view of the garden laid out below. All the structures perfectly matched the plan. The design was classic Enid Wilson—how could she have ever doubted it? But her discovery would remain private—she had to respect Declan's wishes on that. Much as she wanted—deserved—the recognition.

The top floor had another smaller flight of stairs she assumed led to the turret. The rest of the floor might have been servants' quarters in the days when a grand house like this would have employed them.

Now dividing walls had been pulled down and it had been modernised into a sophisticated living space furnished in tones of grey and black leather. Declan's domain. Beyond the living room was a door she could only assume was his office and others led to a small kitchen and a bathroom. Framed black-and-white photos of an attractive young woman with a cap of dark hair, a small, sharp face and a huge smile lined the walls. *Lisa.*

As she knocked on the door to Declan's office Shelley realised her hands were trembling. He had been so angry, so dark—as black in his mood as the storm clouds that gathered over Sydney before a violent summer storm.

Yes, she was a little afraid. Afraid of the man she was falling in love with. Afraid of the man she had planned to seduce this evening. No. Not *afraid.* Not in a million years would Declan hurt her. She was *nervous.* Nervous of his reaction when he realised she had broken her promise to him and invaded his sacrosanct, private space.

There was no reply to her knock. But she was convinced he was in there. An earlier quick glance through the window to his basement gym had shown it to be empty.

She turned the handle of the door and pushed it open.

Declan sat intently in front of an enormous computer screen, a black headset over his head covered his ears. He wore large black-framed glasses. They were hot—made him appear even more attractive to her. But they also made him look like a stranger.

This was a bad, bad idea.

She turned to leave, to scurry back down those stairs as fast as she could. But her movement must have caught Declan's eye. He turned. For a long moment their eyes met—his dark and shuttered, hers no doubt wide with terror.

'Shelley, what the hell?'

He took off his headset and his glasses. But even then he looked dark and forbidding.

'I'm sorry. I didn't mean to intrude on you in your... your bat cave.'

He frowned. 'My bat cave?'

She looked around her at the banks of computers and high-tech equipment. 'It does look like a bat cave—a movie–super-hero bat cave, not a real bat cave. If it was a real bat cave it would be dirty and smelly and...' Her words dwindled to a halt. She turned again. 'I'm sorry. I'm going.'

Declan leapt up from his chair. 'Shelley. Don't go. Don't apologise. I'm the one who should be apologising for the way I behaved down there. I—'

When he said 'down there' her eyes went automatically to the window, which looked over the fountain and the sweep of the back garden. There was a large artist's easel standing there, poised to catch the light, and a drawing board with a series of charcoal drawings clipped to it.

She took a step further towards the windows and she dropped her shoes with a clatter. Her hand went to her mouth but that didn't stop her gasp. 'What's this?' she said. 'Who is this?' Her heart thumped even harder and her mouth went dry.

'It's—'

She stepped closer. 'It's *me*. Paintings of me. Drawings of me. What does this mean?'

In the large canvas on the easel she rode bareback astride a white unicorn. She wore something so skin-tight it was practically nothing, and long green boots with her hair flying behind her like a banner against a background of a forest. The painting was magnificent. Breathtaking. But she felt...violated.

She turned to the drawing board. The sketches were of her too. Declan was talented; she recognised that through her shock. Just a few lines and some shading brought to life the curve of her jaw, the sweep of her hair and an action series where she was lassoing something outside the image.

'It's not you, Shelley,' he said. 'It's…it's Estella.'

'Estella? Who the heck is Estella? The only Estella I know is the character in *Great Expectations*. Is that the link? Miss Havisham. This creepy house.'

'Princess Estella is a character for a computer game.'

'*Princess* Estella? So where do I come in?'

'You're…you're my muse. My inspiration for a beautiful, kick-ass warrior princess.' He closed his eyes, shook his head from side to side in a gesture of deep regret. When he opened his eyes again it was to look deep into her face. 'I should have told you. Wanted to tell you.'

She looked to the screen where an animated character—who didn't look as much like her as the painting did—was on her unicorn and fighting an army of some kind of mutant creatures.

She turned on Declan. 'You were *using* me. So that's why you…you made friends with me. Why you…why you let me think we could be more than friends?'

She had to swallow down hard on a sickening sense of betrayal that made her want to double over. *Thank heaven she hadn't slept with him.* Having shared the intimacies of love with him would only have intensified his treachery.

He took her arm but she shook him off, unable to bear the touch of this man who was suddenly again a stranger. She had trusted him to be honest and straightforward with her but he'd thrown her back deep into that dark pit of distrust as brutally as the other men who had hurt her.

'Not true, Shelley,' he said. 'I couldn't let myself near you—though I realise now I wanted you from the get go. Maybe…maybe that's why I created Princess Estella. As a device to keep you at a distance.'

Bitterness and disappointment made it difficult for her

to speak and she had to choke out the words. 'You mean so you could make even more millions.'

His face contorted in anguish. 'No. You can't believe that.'

She didn't care if her words hurt him. 'Why not? Was this why you hired me? To…to use my image behind my back? Not for the garden at all.'

Now she began to doubt the veracity of everything he'd told her. He had lied and misrepresented himself the way Steve had told her he was single, the way her father had denied his mistress was anything more than a work colleague. She had thought Declan was different. *She had believed in him*.

'Was there really a complaining neighbour? Or did you invent all that to observe me for that…for *her*?' She pointed at the painting with a finger that wavered and trembled despite her best efforts to make a dramatic gesture.

'No,' Declan exploded. 'The neighbours' complaints were only too real. I needed you to do the garden. But unwittingly you unlocked my creativity. *Just by being you*. Your strength, your beauty, like a modern-day warrior. You inspired me like nothing or no one ever had.'

His blue eyes blazed with sincerity. She wanted to believe him. If she wasn't feeling so angry and betrayed she might even have felt flattered. But he should have told her all that long before this. Before her blundering into his bat cave had forced the issue. Had he ever intended to tell her? Or to just wave goodbye when the garden was finished?

'And yet you didn't say a word to me,' she said.

'You have to believe me, Shelley. I wanted to but…but I couldn't. I hadn't invented a game since…since…'

He didn't have to say the words. *Since two years ago.*

Would it always come back to that—the tragedy he could never put behind him?

Her shoulders sagged as she felt overwhelmed by the inevitability that she was fighting a battle she could never win—even if she were to be mounted on a unicorn and armed with a magic lasso.

He deserved a second chance at love and she yearned to give it to him. But she was ill-equipped to bring down the barriers he'd built around his heart to punish himself for the loss of his wife and baby.

She couldn't risk losing *her* heart in a futile battle for *his*.

She took in a deep breath and forced herself to speak normally—or as normally as could be expected under such circumstances. 'So if you haven't been inventing games, what's all this for? Why do you spend so much time up here all by yourself?' She spread out her arms to indicate the banks of equipment in the room.

It was obviously an effort for Declan to get his words out too. 'I haven't worked on commercial games until Estella. Instead I've worked on non-profit educational games to help train surgeons, to help save lives. There's also work for government defence departments on games that simulate terrorist attacks to help train the military.'

'Th… That's very noble of you.' She hadn't been expecting that. He was a good person—had proved himself to be kind and generous to her. Why couldn't he be good to himself?

'Not noble,' he said with that wry twist of his mouth. 'Trying to give back. To make amends.'

'To assuage the guilt you heaped upon yourself.' *For something that was not his fault.*

'Yes,' he said. 'But also because I have more money than I need and I want to contribute not just with dollars but also with my skills.'

'So what happens to Princess Estella?'

'She could be the next commercial big thing for me. Estella has a strong environmental focus, which is timely.'

Shelley shook her head. 'I don't get all this, though I like her green message and…and her green boots. But what I *do* get is I thought we had something special happening between us. I don't mind arriving second in your life after Lisa—she was your first love and I respect that. But I won't be *second best* for you. And I certainly won't compete with…with *her*—a cartoon character.' She couldn't help her voice from rising.

He looked as grim as she had seen him. 'I should have told you about Estella.'

'You're darn right you should have. I would have posed for you, you know. Not in that…that body stocking. But it could have been fun.' Her voice diminished to barely a whisper. 'Something for us to share.'

Those impossible hopes of a life with him had started to feel possible but now they slipped away like the water draining from the cracks in the old fountain.

'You still could,' he said, his voice low and urgent. 'We could develop Estella together.'

She shook her head. Her voice still came out as a half-choked whisper. 'Too late. Too late for you and me, Declan. I could never trust you again—and trust is vital to me. You were dishonest with me—from the word go, it appears.'

He groaned. 'Shelley, I—'

She spoke across him. 'I don't just mean about Estella. I guess she's the way you earn a buck—or two or a billion. You probably couldn't help yourself from…from using me.'

'You've got it so wrong,' he said through clenched teeth.

'I don't think so,' she said. 'What's worse is that you've been dishonest with yourself. You're not ready for me or for any other woman. You're lying to yourself if you think you are.' *And she couldn't deal with it.*

'That's not true,' he said, his face dark and contorted with anguish. 'I care for you, Shelley.' He took a step towards her, went to take her in his arms but she quickly sidestepped him. How could she bear to be close to him when she knew it would be for the last time? *She had to guard her heart.*

Slowly she shook her head. 'But not enough. Not enough to truly step out into the sunshine with me. You seem to need the shadows. I can't exist without the light.'

Her heart ached as though it were being torn in two, broken and bleeding. She took a final look around the grey room where this man she had come to care for so much had locked himself away and didn't seem to be able to free himself—despite her best efforts.

The warrior princess Estella would probably never give up on the battlefield. But she, Shelley Fairhill, humble gardener and heartbroken woman, conceded defeat.

She'd thought she could slash through the overgrown forest and scale the fortress Declan had erected around his heart but she'd scarcely breached the outer walls. To keep on fighting would be futile and only lead to further devastation.

With willpower she dragged from some deep, inner resource she refused to let tears fall, forced her voice to be firm. 'I'm going, Declan.'

He took a step towards her but she put up her hand in a wavering halt sign. 'Don't follow me. Please.'

She picked up her shoes. Somehow she stumbled down the two flights of stairs, holding on to the railings for support, and did not break down until she got to the privacy of the apartment.

Declan had a tormented, sleepless night high up in his solitary bedroom in the turret. Looking back at the way he had behaved since Shelley had come into his life, he realised he had made mistake upon mistake.

Especially the Estella thing. No wonder Shelley had found what had seemed like gross deception impossible to forgive.

In the grey light of early morning, he stumbled down the stairs to his studio and stood in front of the painting that had caused so much trouble. He picked up a palette knife intending to slash the canvas to shreds. But he couldn't do it. Estella had too much of Shelley in her. He could not hurt even her image. *Had never wanted to hurt her.*

How bitterly he regretted all the hours he'd spent up here creating Estella instead of spending more time with Shelley. His creation had become a barrier between him and the real woman he was falling for. Had the memory of Lisa become a barrier, too, long after he should have let his memories rest?

He hated to admit it, but his mother had been right. If he was to survive, it was time for him to move on. He would never forget Lisa or their baby. But Shelley had to come first now if he wanted a future with her. When she had told him he made her feel *second best* it was as if he'd been kicked in the gut. How could he have hurt her like that?

He could not lose her from his life.

He paced the floor of the studio, back and forth, back and forth, raking his hair with his fingers, working through possible solutions. Shelley was right. He didn't know how to get out from under the shadow that was blighting his life.

Professional help. It was an avenue he hadn't tried. He burrowed in his desk drawer for the card with the name of the counsellor his mother had suggested he see after Lisa's death. He hated the idea of revealing himself to a stranger.

But if he wanted Shelley it would have to be done. *And he would have to finally leave this house to find that help.*

He had to make amends to Shelley. Tell her what she'd come to mean to him. Seek her out in her apartment. Admit she was right, he couldn't climb out of the shadows on his own. Ask her to wait for him.

But when he got downstairs it was to the shock of finding her key to the apartment on his kitchen countertop. And a note in her bold handwriting. He picked it up, dreading what it might contain.

Don't try to find me, Declan, because I don't want to be found. There are a few boxes of my possessions in the shed that I couldn't fit into the 4x4. Could you please give access to Lynne when she comes around to collect them for me?

I've arranged for Mark Brown to finish the last work on the garden—it's nearly done. I suggest you hire him for ongoing maintenance. It would be a tragedy to let the garden go again.

I could have loved you, Declan. I hope your heart can heal enough for you to find love again one day.
Shelley

He stared at the words in utter disbelief, then crumpled up the piece of paper and threw it on the floor with a massive roar of pain that echoed through his empty, lonely house. For a long time he stood, focusing on the forlorn piece of paper, white against the dark-stained wood of his floor, that had destroyed his hope of making amends to Shelley.

Finally with a great shudder of agony and grief he picked it up and smoothed it out again. There were echoes of her sweet scent on the paper—he shut his eyes and breathed it in. Then he folded her note and put it into his pocket, next to his heart.

His mother's words came back to him. *Don't let her go. Trust me, it will be like another little death for you if you do.*

Why did his mother have to be so damn right?

But Shelley hadn't died. This didn't have to be final. The grief he felt at her loss wasn't the hopeless kind of grief he had endured before. He had it within his power to find his beautiful warrior and win her back.

No matter what it took.

CHAPTER SIXTEEN

Two months later

SHELLEY KNELT AT the edge of the perfectly maintained lawn of one of the most famous gardens in England as she precisely planted bulbs that would flower next spring—paperwhite jonquils and blue hyacinths. She couldn't help but wonder where she would be when they bloomed.

She was glad she'd packed her knee pads with her when she'd left Australia. Autumn was well and truly under way in Kent and, although there had been crisp, sunny days, today the ground was wet and cold. The head gardener was exacting and she was determined to do the best job she could. She considered it a privilege to work in a garden planted by Vita Sackville-West, one of the most famous garden designers of her time and a contemporary—and idol—of Enid Wilson.

At first, it had felt disconcerting to leave Declan's spring garden and arrive in autumn for her tour of the European gardens she had longed to see but she had loved every second of it. No books or videos could give the experience of actually being in a garden like this one.

This was what she wanted—to see gardens that had influenced designs all over the world, even in climates as inhospitable to an English-style garden as Australia could be. To actually work as a horticulturalist in one was the icing on the cake.

But she was lonely and there wasn't a day that went by she didn't think about Declan. In protecting her heart she feared she'd doomed herself to a lifetime of her heart crying out for him.

She'd met a nice guy in the village where she was living—a farmer who had invited her out to ride horses on his property. Now he was pressing for a proper date. But she still longed for Declan like a physical ache. He was an impossible act for any everyday kind of man to follow.

She paused, trowel in her hand. Thinking about Declan was making her imagine things because suddenly she had that preternatural feeling she used to get in Sydney when he was nearby.

Slowly she turned around to face the lawn. A tall, broad-shouldered man with black hair and wearing an immaculately cut black coat was walking towards her. Was she hallucinating? Had she wanted him so badly she'd somehow conjured him up out of nowhere? Or was it like the other times during the previous months in England, France, and Spain when her heart would skip a beat at the glimpse of a man she thought was him only for it to be a stranger?

She blinked. Took off her glove to scrub at her eyes. But when she looked up again he was there, looming over her, a quizzical expression in his deep blue eyes. *Declan.*

She stumbled to her feet and he caught her elbow to steady her. Of all the words of greeting she could have chosen, words to let him know of her longing and regret, all she could blurt out was: 'How did you find me?'

'Mark Brown. He took some convincing to give me your contact details. But he eventually caved.'

Shelley took off her other glove to give herself time

to think. 'So why are you in Kent? In town for a gaming convention? Or a gathering of billionaires doing billionaire things? There's certainly enough wealthy people living around here for you to be in fine company.'

He smiled that familiar, indulgent smile he gave her when she was talking nonsense. 'None of those.'

'Actually, *how* are you here when I thought you could never leave that house?' she asked.

He stood very close. 'I'm here to tell you I love you, Shelley.'

She nearly fell over backwards on the slippery ground. 'Wh… What?' She managed to right herself—but her thoughts remained topsy-turvy.

Her first impulse was to blurt out *I love you too* but she suppressed it. In the two months since she'd last seen him she'd gone through too much heartache and pain to dive back in so easily.

'I love you,' he said again, slowly. 'I don't know how you feel about me, but I hope you might feel in some measure the same.' His eyes searched her face, seeking her answer.

'I might do…' she said slowly. 'Well, I did back then, now I'm not so sure. It…it's been so long.' She had told him not to seek her out, but somewhere deep inside her she had hoped he would—and been disappointed when he hadn't.

Now he was here.

'Two months I needed to sort myself out, to…to heal. You were right. I wasn't ready for you. I needed help and I went out and found it.'

'What kind of help?' she asked, amazed that he would unbend enough to admit it.

He shifted from foot to foot. 'It's difficult for a guy like me to say I saw a counsellor but that's exactly what I did.'

She frowned. 'You mean you didn't see a professional after Lisa and the baby died?'

'I did not.'

She shook her head. 'You should have. No wonder you were such a mess back then.' She slammed her hand to her mouth. 'I'm sorry,' she said. 'There I go again.'

He smiled. 'I've missed that.'

'You mean my foot-in-mouth blunders?'

'Your plain speaking and telling the truth as you see it,' he said.

'That's one way of putting it,' she said, smiling in spite of herself.

He placed his hands on her shoulders. Even through the bulk of her down jacket she could feel their warmth. 'You were right,' he said. 'I wasn't ready to give or receive love and I'm sorry you were collateral damage along the way.'

She looked up at him into those remarkable blue eyes that were now free of the shadows that had haunted them, the handsome lean face that had lost the lines of tension around his mouth that had always been there. *His mouth.* That looked as kissable as ever. 'But…' She couldn't remember what she was going to say next, too distracted by the thought of claiming his mouth for herself again.

Declan continued. 'I had to come to terms with grief and loss and guilt and to stop blaming myself for what was out of my control.'

'All…those things I couldn't help you with. And…and I had my own trust issues to deal with.' She'd had a very long talk with her mother before she'd flown out of Sydney that had helped immensely.

'Maybe neither of us was ready then,' he said. He slid his hands from her shoulders, down her arms, and pulled her closer.

'But now?' she breathed.

'I'm ready to love you like you deserve to be loved, Shelley Fairhill.'

This time she didn't hesitate. 'I love you too, Declan. So much.'

Shelley pressed her mouth to his. His lips were cold but didn't stay that way for long. She put all her hope and longing and love into the kiss. Until they were rudely interrupted by a loud wolf whistle from one of the other gardeners.

She pulled away, flushed. 'Oh, my gosh, I could get fired for that.'

'Would you care if you got fired?'

'Yes. I like this job. It's only a temporary contract but it's a delight to work in this place. Even in winter the bare bones of the garden will be inspiring. Did you know about the famous white garden? It was a radical planting in its time—only white flowers. Apparently it looks amazing dusted in snow. Truly white.'

Declan put his finger on her mouth to silence her. 'I'm sure that's fascinating stuff. But can it wait until later?' He stamped one foot, then the other. 'I'm freezing here and I'd rather talk about us than gardens.'

'Us?' Her breath caught in her throat.

'You. Me. Where you want to live. I can live anywhere, any country, for my work as long as there's electricity and internet. I don't want to live in the Bellevue Street house again—it had become a prison. I'm thinking of donating it to a heritage trust. Your professor in Melbourne is working on a proposal with me.'

'My...my professor?'

'Yes. With full recognition to you for having discovered the heritage garden.'

'You did that for me?'

'Yes,' he said simply.

She kissed him again. 'Thank you. That means so much.' There was no need to elaborate further. His actions proved his love for her and it was enough.

She didn't want to live in that house where Declan had been so unhappy either. Though she'd like him to retain control over the garden. It would be criminal for it to slide into neglect again or, worse, be ripped out.

'What about your television career?' he asked. 'Have you given up on that?'

'No way. The current presenter decided he wanted to do one more season before he bowed out so that gives me another few months before I'd have to start. The producer likes the idea of him introducing me to the viewers when the time comes.'

'So that means you going back to live in Australia?'

'Not yet. Maybe not permanently. But it's too good an opportunity to pass up.'

'I agree.'

'But I'm conflicted. I love it here,' she said wistfully. 'The ideal would be if I could somehow live between Australia and Europe for a few years at least.'

'That's entirely possible,' he said. 'First-class flights make the long flight bearable. Private jets even more so.'

'I wouldn't know about that,' she said with a rueful smile. 'It's cattle class all the way for me.'

'Not when you fly with me,' he said.

He silenced her gasp with a quick kiss. 'And if you want to live here, I've found a wonderful manor house nearby,' Declan said. 'The house is perfect but the garden is crying out for the Shelley touch to make it *your* garden.'

'Sounds promising,' she said, cautiously, not really certain of where he was going.

'It also has a stable and a few acres of pastures for a horse.'

'Sold!' she said. She drew her brows together and looked up at him. 'What did I just agree to, Declan?'

He cupped her face in his hands in the possessive way she loved. 'I hope you've agreed to be my wife,' he said.

'Your wife,' she said slowly. 'I... I like the idea.'

'Good,' he said. 'I'll take that for a yes.'

'Not so fast,' she said, taking a step back, her heart feeling like a parched plant that had just been watered. 'I want a proper proposal, please.'

He laughed. 'Why does that not surprise me?' He looked down at the mushy ground that surrounded them.

'I don't expect you to go down on bended knee or anything,' she said with a catch in her voice.

He took both her hands in his. 'Shelley, will you do me the honour of marrying me?' he asked very seriously.

She took a deep breath to steady her voice. 'I would love to be your wife. And...and the mother of your children. That is, if you want—'

He closed his eyes for a moment. 'Yes. I do,' he said as he opened them again. 'When...when the time is right for both of us to take that step.'

Shelley pulled him close and kissed him. She realised that might become another challenge. With past tragedy in mind, she could imagine how overprotective Declan would become if she were to fall pregnant. But they could face that challenge together when it came.

'I supposed you'd like a proper engagement ring too?' he murmured against her mouth.

'Well, yes,' she said. 'But I guess you mightn't have had time to buy one. I mean, what if I'd said no to your proposal? Not that I would have said no. I love you so much and couldn't imagine anything I'd like more than to be your wife.'

Declan smiled and her heart missed a beat at the love for

her she saw shining from his eyes. He pulled out a small box from the inner pocket of his overcoat.

'Oh…' was all she could manage to get out.

The ring was a huge sapphire flanked by two enormous diamonds. 'The colour of your blue dress, the one that isn't much dress at all,' he said. 'It suited you so well I thought a sapphire might too.' He slipped it onto the third finger of her left hand.

'It's perfect,' she breathed, looking down at her hand and admiring the way it caught the light. At the same time she caught sight of her watch. 'It's nearly time for me to finish. I'm sure they'll let me go a little earlier on the momentous occasion of my engagement.'

'I've already cleared it with the head gardener,' he said. 'You can come straight home with me.'

'Home?'

'I bought the manor house just on the off chance you'd like it,' he said.

'As billionaires do,' she said, laughing.

'You'll soon be the wife of a billionaire so you can do billionaire things too,' he said. 'The income from Estella will be all yours as well. One hundred per cent of it.'

Shelley pulled back from his embrace, looked up into his eyes. 'It's not about your money—you know that, don't you?' It was suddenly very important that he was aware of that. 'I love you, Declan. I'd love you even if we were going to live in the garden shed.'

'That's one more reason I adore you,' he said. 'We'll have a wonderful life together, Shelley.'

'I know,' she said, kissing him again.

* * * * *

MILLS & BOON®

The Rising Stars Collection!

1 BOOK FREE!

This fabulous four-book collection features 3-in-1 stories from some of our talented writers who are the stars of the future! Feel the temperature rise this summer with our ultra-sexy and powerful heroes. Don't miss this great offer—buy the collection today to get one book free!

Order yours at www.millsandboon.co.uk/risingstars

MILLS & BOON®

Cherish™

EXPERIENCE THE ULTIMATE RUSH OF FALLING IN LOVE

A sneak peek at next month's titles...

In stores from 21st August 2015:

- **A Wedding for the Greek Tycoon** – Rebecca Winters
  and **The Cowboy and the Lady** – Marie Ferrarella

- **Reunited by a Baby Secret** – Michelle Douglas
  and **An Officer and a Maverick** – Teresa Southwick

In stores from 4th September 2015:

- **Beauty & Her Billionaire Boss** – Barbara Wallace
  and **The Bachelor Takes a Bride** – Brenda Harlen

- **Newborn on Her Doorstep** – Ellie Darkins
  and **Destined to Be a Dad** – Christyne Butler

Available at WHSmith, Tesco, Asda, Eason, Amazon and Apple

Just can't wait?
Buy our books online a month before they hit the shops!
visit www.millsandboon.co.uk

These books are also available in eBook format!

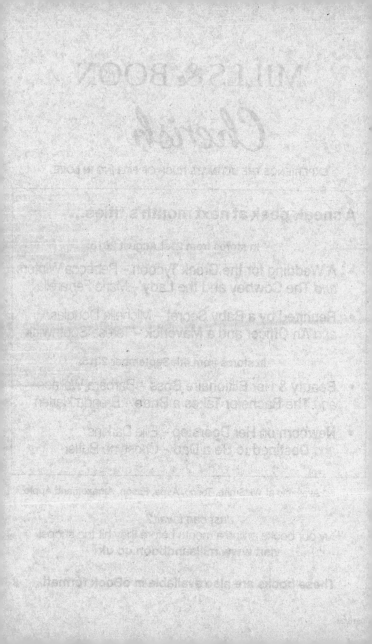

DO YOU TAKE THIS MAVERICK?

Since Levi Wyatt and Claire Strickland fell in love, life has been a fairytale – but the strain of work and a baby has brought them back to reality and driven them apart. Levi's sure they can survive anything...as long as he can convince Claire to stay.

HIRED BY THE BROODING BILLIONAIRE

Billionaire Declan Grant has been a recluse since his wife's death. But, when his garden needs taming, he reluctantly invites gardener Shelley Fairhill into his home. And, as he watches his garden come back to life, he feels his heart come back to life too...

Cherish Experience the ultimate rush of falling in love

£5.99

ISBN 978-0-263-25158-6

9 780263 251586

e book also available

MILLS & BOON

a MILLS & BOON book from

H HARLEQUIN (UK) LTD
www.millsandboon.co.uk

Join in

f facebook.com/ millsandboon

@millsandboon

millsandboon.co. cherish